PRAISE FOR

Fifty Words for Rain

"Novels like Asha Lemmie's debut allow me to experience the high of the endurance athlete—consumed by a far-flung odyssey, coming up only for a sip of water. . . . I inhaled *Fifty Words for Rain* in one day. I had no choice." —*The New York Times Book Review*

"Usually I take my time with books, but I found it very hard to step away from this story. Filled with mystery, music, sadness, and adventures, *Fifty Words for Rain* flies by—yet lingers long after. . . . Anyone who has ever lost a friend—or, more happily, found a family—will love this beautiful story." —Malala Yousafzai, Nobel Peace Prize–winning activist

"*Fifty Words for Rain* is a lovely, heartrending story about love and loss, prejudice and pain, and the sometimes dangerous, always durable ties that link a family together. This coming-of-age tale about a biracial girl in postwar Japan is an assured, confident debut by a talented new author." —Kristin Hannah, #1 *New York Times*–bestselling author of *The Nightingale*

"A hugely compelling debut about Noriko, a mixed-race girl growing up in Japan after WWII. Moving and honest and at times intense, Asha Lemmie takes us on an emotional journey that spans years, one which sheds light on Noriko's family traditions, prejudices, struggles, triumphs, and ultimate transformation. This is a well-researched and eye-opening tale, told with compassion that breathes through each page." —Abi Daré, *New York Times*–bestselling author of *The Girl with the Louding Voice*

"[An] epic, twisty debut . . . Sometimes bleak, sometimes hopeful, Lemmie's heartbreaking story of familial obligations packs an emotional wallop." —*Publishers Weekly*

"Lemmie's debut novel is a gripping historical tale that will transport readers through myriad emotions. . . . Lemmie intimately draws the readers into every aspect of Noriko's complex story, leading us through the decades and across the continents this adventure spans, bringing us to anger, tears, and small pockets of joy. A truly ambitious and remarkable debut." —*Booklist*

FIFTY WORDS FOR RAIN

A Novel

ASHA LEMMIE

DUTTON

DUTTON

An imprint of Penguin Random House LLC

penguinrandomhouse.com

Previously published as a Dutton hardcover in September 2020

First Dutton trade paperback printing: June 2021

LIBRARY OF CONGRESS CATALOGING-IN-PUBLICATION DATA
has been applied for.

Dutton trade paperback ISBN: 9781524746384

Printed in the United States of America
6th Printing

Book design by Katy Riegel

For Hannah, with love,
and for all the outcasts,
here's to tomorrow

CONTENTS

PRELUDE

Kyoto Prefecture, Japan
Summer 1948

The first real memory Nori had was pulling up to that house. For many years afterward, she would try to stretch the boundaries of her mind further, to what came before that day. Time and time again, she'd lie on her back in the stillness of the night and try to recall. Sometimes she'd catch a glimpse in her head of a tiny apartment with lurid yellow walls. But the image would disappear as quickly as it came, leaving no sense of satisfaction in its wake. And so if you asked her, Nori would say that her life had officially begun the day she laid eyes on the imposing estate that rested serenely between the crests of two green hills. It was a stunningly beautiful place—there was no denying it—and yet, despite this beauty, Nori felt her stomach clench and her gut churn at the sight of it. Her mother rarely took her anywhere, and somehow she knew that something was waiting for her there that she would not like.

The faded blue automobile skidded to a stop on the street across from the estate. It was in the traditional style, surrounded by high white walls. The first set of gates was open, allowing full view into the meticulously arranged courtyard beyond. But the inner gates to the house itself were sealed shut. There were words engraved at the top of the main gate, embossed in gold lettering for all to see. But Nori could not read them. She could read and write her name—*No-ri-ko*—but nothing else. In that moment, she wished she could read every word ever written, in every language from sea to sea. Not being able to read those letters frustrated her to an extent she didn't understand. She turned to her mother.

"Okaasan, what do those letters say?"

The woman seated beside her let out a stifled sigh of frustration. It was clear that she'd been a great beauty in her day. She was still gorgeous, but her young face was beginning to reflect the toll life had taken on her. Her dark, thick hair was bound behind her head in a braid that kept attempting to unravel. Her soft gray eyes were cast downwards. She would not meet her daughter's gaze.

"*Kamiza*," she answered at last. "It says *Kamiza*."

"But that's our name, isn't it?" Nori chirped, her curiosity immediately piqued.

Her mother let out a strangled giggle that made the hair on the back of Nori's neck stand up. The driver of the car, a man Nori had never seen before this morning, shot them a startled glance in the rearview mirror.

"Yes," she responded softly, eyes alight with a strange look that Nori's limited vocabulary did not have the means to name. "That is our family name. This is where my mother and father live, child. Your grandparents."

Nori felt her heartbeat quicken. Her mother had never before made any mention of relatives or family. Indeed, the two of them had drifted along in solitude so long it seemed strange to Nori that they could actually be anchored to a tangible place.

"Did you live here once, Okaasan?"

"Once," her mother said dryly. "Before you were born. A long time ago."

Nori scrunched her face up in a frown. "Why did you leave?"

"That's enough questions now, Noriko. Get your things. Come."

Nori obeyed, biting her lip to refrain from inquiring further. Her mother did not like questions. Every time Nori asked something, she was met with a disapproving glance. It was better not to ask. On the rare occasions Nori was able to please her mother, she was given a dry half smile in return. Sometimes, if she was especially good, her mother would reward her with some candy or a new ribbon. So far, in eight years of life, Nori had a collection of twelve ribbons, one for each time she'd been able to make her mother happy.

"It is good for a woman to learn silence," her mother always said. "If a woman knows nothing else, she should know how to be silent."

Nori stepped onto the pavement, checking to make sure she had all of her things. She had her little brown suitcase with the straps that were fraying apart and her purple silk ribbon tied around the handle. She had her blue satchel with the silver clasp that she had gotten for her last birthday. And that was all she had. Not that Nori thought she needed much more than that.

For the first time since she'd been roused at dawn that morning, Nori noticed that her mother was not carrying any bags.

The woman stood as if her pale pink satin slippers were rooted to the unnaturally white sidewalk. Her bright eyes were fixed on a spot Nori could not follow.

Nori took note of what her mother was wearing: a short-sleeved, baby blue knee-length dress. Tan stockings. Around her neck she wore a petite silver cross with a little diamond in the center. She had her hands clasped in front of her chest, so tightly that tiny blue veins had become visible beneath the delicate skin.

Nori reached out a hesitant hand to touch her mother's arm. "Okaasan . . ."

Her mother blinked rapidly and unclasped her hands, arms falling to swing limply at her sides. Her eyes, however, did not move from their perch.

"Noriko," she said, with such unusual affection saturating her tone that it left Nori in near disbelief, "I want you to make me a promise."

Nori blinked up at her mother, doing her best to look pretty and obedient and all that her mother would have her be. She would not spoil this moment with her clumsy tongue.

"Yes, Okaasan?"

"Promise me you will obey."

The request caught her off guard. Not because it was unlike something her mother would say, but because not once in her life had Nori ever disobeyed. It didn't seem like something that needed to be requested. Her confusion must have been evident because her mother turned and knelt down so that they were nearly eye level.

"Noriko," she said, with an urgency Nori had never heard before. "Promise me. Promise me that you will obey in all things. Do not question. Do not fight. Do not resist. Do not think if thinking will lead you somewhere you ought not to be. Only smile and do as you are told. Only your life is more important than your obedience. Only the air you breathe. Promise me this."

Nori thought to herself that this conversation was very odd. A thousand questions burned her tongue. She swallowed them back.

"Yes, Okaasan. *Yakusoku shimasu*. I promise."

Her mother let out a ragged sigh, caught somewhere between relief and despair.

"Now listen. You will go inside the gate, Nori. Your grandparents will ask you your name. What will you tell them?"

"Noriko, Okaasan. Noriko Kamiza."

"Yes. And they will ask you how old you are. And what will you tell them?"

"I'm eight, Okaasan."

"They will ask where I have gone. And you will tell them that I did not tell you. That you don't know. Do you understand?"

Nori felt her mouth begin to go dry. Her heart fluttered against her chest, like a little bird trying to escape a cage. "Okaasan, where are you going? Aren't you coming with me?"

Her mother did not reply. She stood up, reaching into her pocket and pulling out a thick yellow envelope.

"Take this," she urged, pressing it into Nori's sweaty palm. "Give it to them when they ask questions."

Nori's voice began to scale up in panic. "Okaasan, where are you going?"

Her mother looked away.

"Nori, hush. Do not cry. Stop crying this instant!"

She felt the tears that had begun to well recede inside her eye sockets with frightening speed. It seemed that they too were bound to obey.

"Noriko," her mother continued, tone softening to a whisper. "You are a good girl. Do as you are told and everything will be fine. Don't cry now. You have no reason to cry."

"Yes, Okaasan."

Her mother hesitated, searching for words for several long moments. Finally, she decided there were none and settled for patting her daughter twice on the top of the head.

"I'll watch you go. Go on. Get your things."

Noriko picked up her belongings and proceeded slowly towards the gate. It towered over her. Her steps grew smaller and smaller as she approached it.

Every few steps she'd peer over her shoulder to make sure that her mother was still watching. She was. Noriko swallowed.

When she finally reached the gate, she paused, unsure of how to proceed. It was open, and yet she was quite sure that she should not be entering. She waited for her mother to instruct her, but the woman remained on the sidewalk, watching in silence.

Step by step, Nori inched up the walkway. When she was halfway up, she paused, unable to continue any farther. She turned in desperation to her mother, who by now had made her way back to the car.

"Okaasan!" Nori whimpered, her previous calm leaving her in one terrifying moment. She wanted to run back to her mother, but something kept her pinned to the spot.

That something held her there, relentless and pitiless in the strength of its grasp. It did not let her move, nor breathe, nor cry out as she watched her mother give her one last, strangely bright gaze before getting back into the car and shutting the door behind her. She could not so much as blink as she watched the car speed down the street, around the corner, and out of sight.

Nori was not quite sure how long she stood transfixed. The sun was high in the sky when she finally resumed her slow march up the walkway through the courtyard. Still in a trance, she raised her tiny hand to knock lightly on the gates that obscured the house, leaving only its upper floors and looming roof visible. No one answered. She pushed, half hoping they would not open. They didn't, and they were far too heavy for her to make another attempt.

She sat. And she waited. For what, exactly, she was unsure.

A few moments later, the gates opened, moved by an invisible force. Two large men in suits emerged, peering down at her with disdain.

"Go away, little girl," the first one said. "No beggars."

"I'm not a beggar," Nori protested, finding her feet. "I'm Noriko."

They both stared at her blankly. Nori extended the envelope her mother had given her with a trembling hand.

"*Kamiza Noriko desu.*"

The two exchanged an indecipherable glance. Then, without another word, they disappeared back behind the gate.

Nori waited. Her head was spinning, but she forced herself to remain standing.

After another long moment, the first of the men returned.

He crooked his finger at her. "Come on."

He snatched up her belongings and marched ahead, leaving her to rush after him. The house was beautiful, more a palace than a house, but Nori's attention quickly focused on the figure standing in front of it.

An elderly woman, with her mother's eyes and streaks of silver in her neatly coiffed hair, stared down at her in utter disbelief.

Because there was nothing else to do, Nori did as she was told.

"*Konbanwa, Obaasama*. My name is Nori."

PART I

CHAPTER ONE

WATER SONG

Kyoto, Japan
Summer 1950

It came quickly, the pain. It arrived with startling fanfare. Nothing could stop it once it had set on its morbid path.

The pain came quickly. It was the going that took longer.

Nori almost welcomed the onset of the pain, knowing that it was the best of what was to come. First there was the tingling, like a little feather tapping out a jig on her skin. Then there was the slow burn. One by one, every nerve in her body began to scream until they were screeching in unison, forming a chorus of protest. Then there were the tears. Nori had learned in her younger years not to fight the tears, as it only made them worse.

The fight would lead to her gasping for air, sucking it in through her nose in ragged spurts and feeling her rib cage squeeze tight. Snot would dribble from her nose and mingle with her tears, forming a sickening brew that too often dripped into her open mouth.

It was better to accept the tears, with as much grace and dignity as could be mustered. They would fall silently down her cheeks, constant and cool like a babbling brook.

There was some self-respect in that, at least.

"We're done for today, Ojosama."

Nori forced her stinging eyes to focus on the speaker: a maid in her early thirties, with a round, jolly face and a warm smile.

"Thank you, Akiko-san."

The maid gently helped Nori rise from the porcelain bath-tub, offering an arm for the ten-year-old to lean on as she stood.

The sharp gust of air on her naked body made her let out a little cry, and her knees buckled. Akiko stopped her from falling and, with strength that was surprising for her petite size, bodily lifted Nori from the tub and into a waiting chair.

Nori began to rock slowly back and forth, willing the constant motion to steady her shaking core. After a few moments, the pain had subsided just enough so that she could manage opening her eyes. She watched as Akiko washed the mixture of warm water, bleach, and murky specks of almond-colored skin—her skin—down the drain.

"Is it working, do you think?" she inquired, resenting the eagerness that crept into her voice. "Akiko-san, do you think it's working?"

Akiko turned to look at the child who had been left to her care. Nori couldn't read the look on her face. But then Akiko offered up a tiny smile, and Nori was flooded with relief.

"Yes, little madam, I think so. Your grandmother will be pleased."

"Do you think I shall have a new dress?"

"Perhaps. If she gives me the money for fabric, I will make you a summer yukata. Your old one scarcely fits you anymore."

"I would like blue. It is a noble color, isn't it, Akiko-san?"

Akiko lowered her eyes and proceeded to re-dress Nori in a fresh cotton slip. "Blue would look very pretty on you, little madam."

"It is Obaasama's favorite color."

"Yes. Now, run along. I'll bring you your meal in an hour."

Nori forced her limbs to move, ignoring the dull thump of pain. They were working, she knew they were, the daily baths. Her grandmother had sent all the way to Tokyo for the finest magic bath soap that money could buy. Nori bore the pain willingly, as she knew in time that the results would be worth any sufferings. She would stay in the bath all day if Akiko would let her, but her skin was prone to burning and she was only allowed to stay in it for twenty minutes at a time. Her left leg had a mottled purple burn on it that she had to hide with extra-long skirts, but she did not mind so much because the skin around the burn was wonderfully fair and bright.

She wanted all of her skin to look like that.

She padded through the hall, careful not to make any noise because it was afternoon and her grandmother preferred to sleep in the afternoon. Especially in winter, when it was too cold to pay social visits and the sun set early.

She scurried towards the stairs to the attic, avoiding eye contact with the staff, who seemed to stare at her whenever she crossed their path. Even after two years living in this house, they were still clearly uneasy with her presence.

Akiko had assured her that it wasn't that they didn't like her; it was simply that they weren't used to having children around.

Either way, Nori was relieved to live in the attic, away from everything and everyone else. When she had come to stay here, her grandmother had instructed that the attic be cleaned out and converted into living quarters.

The attic was very spacious, and it was full of things, more things than Nori had ever had before. She had a bed, a dining table and three chairs, a bookshelf, a basket full of knitting and sewing materials, a little altar for her prayers, a stove for the winter months, and an armoire to keep her clothes in. She had a small little vanity with a stool that, according to Akiko, had once belonged to her mother. She still had her brown suitcase with the purple silk ribbon tied around the handle. She still had the pale blue satchel with the little silver clasp. She kept these two things in a far corner of the room so that she would always know where to find them at a moment's notice.

But her favorite thing, by far, was the half-moon-shaped window above her bed that overlooked the gardens. When she stood on the bed (which she was not supposed to do but she did anyway), she could see the fenced-in yard with its green grass and its overgrown, ancient peach trees. She could see the man-made pond with the koi fish swimming in it and splashing about. She could see the faint outline of neighboring rooftops. As far as Nori was concerned, she could see the entire world.

How many times had she spent all night with her head pressed against the cool, damp glass? Certainly very many, and she considered herself quite fortunate that she had never been caught. That would have been a guaranteed beating.

She had not been allowed to leave the house since the day she arrived. And it was not a terrible sacrifice, not really, because she had rarely been allowed to leave the apartment she'd shared with her mother either.

Still, there were rules, many rules, for living in this house.

The cardinal rule was simple: stay out of sight unless summoned. Remain in the attic. Make no sound. Food was brought to her at set intervals three times a day; Akiko would take her downstairs to the bathroom. During the midday trip, Nori would have her bath.

Three times a week, an old man with a hunched back and failing eyesight would come to her attic and teach her reading, writing, numbers, and history. This one did not feel like a rule—Nori liked lessons. In fact, she was quite gifted at them. She was always asking Saotome-sensei to bring her new books. Last week, he'd brought her a book in English called *Oliver Twist*. She could not read a single word of it, but she had resolved to learn. It was such a pretty book, leather-bound and glistening.

And so those were the rules. They weren't too much to ask, she didn't think. She didn't understand them, but then, she didn't try.

Don't think.

Nori crept onto her small four-poster bed and pressed her face into the coolness of her pillow. It distracted her from her skin's persistent tingling. The instinctual desire to escape from pain soon lulled her into a listless sleep.

She had the same dream as always.

She was chasing the blue car as it drove away, calling out for her mother, but could never catch it.

As long as she could remember, Nori's limbs had been prone to disobedience. They would begin to shake, randomly and uncontrollably, at the slightest hint of trouble. She would have to wrap her arms around her body and squeeze as tightly as she could in order for the trembling to subside.

And so when Akiko informed her that her grandmother would be paying her a visit today, Nori felt her body go weak. She slunk into one of her small wooden dining chairs, no longer trusting her legs to support her.

"Obaasama is coming?"

"Yes, little madam."

Her grandmother normally came once a month, sometimes twice, to inspect Nori's living conditions and personal growth.

It seemed that no matter what she did, her grandmother was never pleased. The old woman had impeccable standards and her keen gray eyes never missed a beat. It filled Nori with as much exhilaration as it did dread.

To please her grandmother was a feat that she longed to accomplish. In her mind, it was the most noble of quests.

Nori swept her eyes around her room, suddenly painfully aware of how messy things were. There was a corner of faint yellow bedclothes sticking out. There was a speck of dust on the kerosene lamp on the nightstand. The wood burning in the stove was popping and cracking, a sound that some would surely find irritating.

Wordlessly, the maid began to move about the room, tidying and putting things into their proper place. Akiko too was used to the demands of the lady of the house. She had been working here since she herself was a mere child.

Of course, that meant that Akiko had known Nori's mother. This was a curious dynamic between them: Nori always wanting to ask and Akiko always wanting to tell, but both too obedient to do either.

"What shall I wear?" Nori rasped, hating the sudden waver in her voice. "What do you think?"

Nori immediately began to rack her brains. She had a polka-dot navy blue dress, with short sleeves and a lace collar. She had a green kimono with a pale pink sash. She had a bright yellow yukata, which she could wear now that it was summer. And she had a dark purple kimono. That was all.

She began to gnaw gently on the skin inside her left cheek. "The black one," she said resolutely, answering her own question. Akiko went to the closet and laid it out on the bed.

Nori arrived at this conclusion relatively easily. In contrast to the dark hues of the garment, her skin would appear lighter. Akiko brought the kimono over and began to dress her, while her mind began to wander to other places.

She ran an unsteady hand through her hair. God, she hated her hair. It was thick and boisterous, stubbornly curly despite her daily efforts to tame it with a brush. It was also a peculiar shade of dark brown that Nori likened to the bark of an oak tree. She could not get it to fall straight and free around her shoulders, as her mother's and grandmother's did.

However, if she brushed the hair hard against her scalp, it would flatten enough that she could wind it into a long braid that she would tie neatly behind her head. It fell nearly to her waist, and she bound the end of it with a brightly colored ribbon. If she did it that way, it looked almost normal.

She was wearing the red ribbon today, one of her twelve. It was her favorite one, as she thought it brought out the brightness in her champagne-colored gaze. The one thing she did like about her face was her eyes—even her grandmother remarked once, in passing, that they were "quite interesting."

They were gently almond-shaped, just as they should be. At least there, she did not stand out so much.

Once Nori had been dressed, Akiko took her leave.

Nori made her way to the center of the room and stood, bone straight, waiting. She willed herself not to fidget. She folded her hands neatly in front of her chest, eyeing the skin with mild contempt. It was improving. Two years of the baths and she was starting to see a change. She estimated that in another two years it would be fair enough that she could leave the attic.

Unlike her grandmother, who visited occasionally, her grandfather did his absolute best to avoid her entirely, and besides, as the Emperor's advisor he was in Tokyo most of the time anyway. On those very rare occasions when they did cross paths, he looked at her with eyes as hard as coal. It always left her feeling cold. She sometimes asked Akiko about him. Her face would flatten and she'd say simply, "He is a very important man, a very powerful man." And then she would hurriedly change the subject.

Curious as she was, Nori was not fool enough to broach the subject with her grandmother. She remembered her mother's advice well, and though she still did not understand it much, it had proved to be quite useful. Of course, it did nothing to tell her where her mother was or when she was coming back. Nori tried not to think about these things.

The sound of footsteps alerted Nori to her grandmother's arrival. Rather than looking up, she lowered her eyes to the floor and dropped into a low bow.

The woman before her was silent for a moment. Then she sighed. "Noriko."

This was an indication that permission to rise had been granted. Nori straightened slowly, making sure to keep her eyes lowered respectfully.

The old woman walked briskly over to where Nori was standing and, in one deft motion, reached out and lifted her chin with a slender finger.

Nori looked at her grandmother's face. Traces of beauty were still present despite the marks of time. Fine wrinkles decorated the smooth skin, a shade of yellow so faint it was nearly eggshell white. Her grandmother's features were those of a classic belle: long neck, small hands, and tapered fingers. Dark hair, streaked with more white every passing year, that fell in a perfectly straight sheen well below the waist. Delicate nose and poignant, finely shaped eyes colored the striking shade of Kamiza gray-black that reminded Nori, with a none-too-gentle pang, of her mother.

And of course there was the swan-like elegance and grace that seemed to evade her so frustratingly, possessed by both generations that had come before. It was beautiful and maddening to behold.

"*Konnichiwa, Obaasama,*" Nori said, trying not to wither under the intensity of her grandmother's glare. "God grant you well-being and joy."

Yuko nodded, as if checking off a mental checklist. She backed away slightly, and Nori let out a barely audible sigh of relief. The old woman did a cursory sweep of the attic and then nodded once more.

Nori pulled out one of the chairs at her dining table in anticipation. But her grandmother made no move to sit.

"You have grown some, I think."

She nearly jumped out of her skin. This was a question she was not prepared for.

"A little, Obaasama."

"How old are you now?"

Nori bit her lip, willing her emotions to retreat back into their cavern, somewhere at the bottom of her stomach.

"Ten, Grandmother."

"Ten. Have you bled yet?"

Nori felt panic seize her. Bled? She was supposed to bleed?

"I . . . I am sorry. I do not understand."

Rather than reacting with disdain or fury, as Nori might expect, her grandmother only nodded yet again. These were all answers she expected.

"How are your studies?"

At this, Nori brightened instantly. For a moment, she forgot herself.

"Oh, they are wonderful. Saotome-sensei is a very good teacher. And he says I shall have more books when I can read a little better. I already have two new books and they are in English. He says that I have a natural facility for—"

Yuko turned a cold stare in Nori's direction, and it cut her off at the knees. She ceased speaking at once, tasting bile when she closed her mouth.

It is good for a woman to learn silence.

Nori lowered her head. She eyed the faded wooden floor beneath her feet, wishing she could become one with it. To her absolute horror, she felt the beginnings of tears stir behind her eyes. She blinked in rapid succession to push them back.

After what seemed like an eon of silence, her grandmother spoke.

"How much do you weigh?"

Nori knew the answer to this query at once, thank God. She was weighed every day before her bath.

"Thirty-nine pounds, Grandmother."

Her grandmother nodded again. "Your hair is growing out nicely. Your complexion is improved, slightly. I have sent for a new product. I expect it will arrive presently."

"Thank you, Grandmother."

"You could be pretty one day, Noriko. Quite pretty."

"Thank you."

Once, this statement would have filled Nori with joy, given her hope, given her a sense of a future outside of this attic. The future was something that racked her with constant anxiety. She had no knowledge of it or plan for it. And one day it would be there, staring her dead in the eye, and she would have nothing to say to it. So when her grandmother spoke like this, it should be cause for happiness.

But though the words still filled her with a sense of optimism, she now knew what followed this promise of tomorrow.

Wordlessly, her grandmother produced a wooden kitchen spoon from the folds of her sleeves. Despite the familiarity of this routine, Nori felt herself begin to shake almost to the point of convulsing. Once again, she had failed. She was one step further away from leaving this attic and joining the civilized world. She wasn't ready yet. She might never be ready.

Yuko licked her thin lips. "A girl must have discipline. You are learning, this is true. I hear reports on you from Akiko-san and your teacher. But you are still too impertinent. Too bold in your ways. Like your whore mother."

Nori clenched her hands around the wooden chair she was still holding on to. Without being prompted, she bent over.

Her grandmother continued. "You are good at your studies, but this is not so important. You lack poise and grace. I can hear your footsteps shaking the house, like a *zou*. We are royalty. We do not walk like rice farmers."

Without looking up, Nori sensed her grandmother move to where she stood bent over the chair.

"Discipline is essential. You must learn this."

She felt a hand pull up the back of her kimono and shift so that she stood exposed in nothing but a pair of thin cotton panties. She shut her eyes.

Her grandmother's voice went very low. "You are a cursed, wretched thing."

The first blow with the spoon landed with shocking swiftness. It was the sound, loud and sharp, that startled her more so than the pain. Nori's teeth came down on her bottom lip, and she felt the skin tear.

The second and third blows were harder than the first. There was no body fat on Nori's spritely frame to dull the force of the impact. As she always did, she began to count the blows. *Four. Five. Six.*

She felt a deep ache begin in her back, thumping away in a rhythm she swore she could hear. Her shoulder blades began to shake with the effort of staying upright. *Seven. Eight. Nine.*

It was hopeless now to fight the tears. She allowed them to come with as much pride as she could muster. But she drew the line at whimpering. Even if she had to chew a hole through her lip, she refused to utter a single sound. *Ten. Eleven. Twelve.*

Over the roaring in her ears, Nori could hear her grandmother begin to pant with the effort of such physical exertion. *Thirteen. Fourteen.*

That was enough, it seemed. For a moment, both of them stayed in their assumed positions. No one moved. The only sound was her grandmother's slow, ragged breathing.

Nori did not need to turn around to know what happened next. She was not sure if she was witnessing the events as they unfolded or simply seeing them in her mind's eye. Her grandmother slowly lowered her arm, taking care to readjust her clothing. Then there would come a look: stern, slightly apologetic. Perhaps there was even some pity there. But then the look would shift into polite indifference. Yuko's thought process had already moved on. It was not until Nori heard the creaking sound of her grandmother descending the steps that she allowed herself to stand up.

And now the third act of the play commenced.

The stitch in her side reacted violently to the change in position, and Nori twitched as if something had stung her. *Inhale. Exhale.*

She raised a hand to her face and wiped unceremoniously back and forth. In about an hour or so, Akiko would come up with a warm towel for her bottom. Until then, it was best to avoid sitting. The welts on her buttocks and upper thighs would disappear in a few days. Now that she was alone, the pain in her extremities made itself fully known. As if resentful at being left out of the mix, her stomach began to clench and release. But she kept her chin high and made no sound.

Nori didn't even know for whom she was performing at this point.

Sometimes she thought it was for the invisible eyes that she swore her grandmother had transplanted into the walls. Other times she thought it was for God. She had a theory that if God saw how brave she was, even when she was alone, He would grant her some kind of miracle.

Gingerly, she stepped out of her kimono so that she stood in nothing but her cotton slip. Though she knew she shouldn't, she left it on the floor. Akiko would see to it. As far as Nori knew, Akiko was not one to report back on all of her doings—for surely, if that were the case, Nori would receive a great many more beatings than she did.

She liked to believe that Akiko did not hate the task to which she had been assigned. Though it was insulting work to be assigned to tend the family's bastard child, at least it did not take much effort. Nori tried to make it easy on the poor woman, as much out of guilt as out of obedience.

She inched, so slowly that she began to feel comical, over to the prayer altar on the opposite side of the room. Though one of her assignments was to pray thrice daily, Nori did not mind. In fact, she rather liked it.

The altar was by far her favorite possession, though it was arguably not even hers. It was yet another cast-off possession of her mother's. It was nothing special—just a wooden table with a cloth of royal purple velvet spread across it. The edges of the cloth were trimmed with gold thread. An intricately crafted silver crucifix sat atop it, with two candles on either side. Nori struck a match and lit them both before kneeling on the small cushion she had placed on the floor.

They bathed her in comforting warmth and she allowed her eyes to drift shut.

Dear God,

I'm sorry for my impertinence. I will make sure to ask Saotome-sensei what "impertinence" means so that I can make sure not to do it again. I'm sorry for my hair. I'm sorry for my skin. I'm sorry for the trouble I cause others. I hope you are not too angry with me?

Please look after my mother. I am quite sure she must be very upset that she cannot pick me up just yet.

Please help me to be ready soon.

Amen,

Nori

As she often did when she had finished her prayers, Nori paused. Her favorite thing about God was that He was the one person she was allowed to ask questions. In fact, this privilege delighted her so much that she hardly even minded that nobody answered her.

The winter months drew to a close rather uneventfully. The days melded together seamlessly. Nori received two more visits from her grandmother in this time, resulting in twelve and sixteen blows, respectively. At one point, the family matriarch had remarked that out of concern for possible scarring, new methods of punishment might need to be implemented in the future.

As spring approached, Nori watched the world around her change. She watched the daylight linger on past its prime. She watched from her window as the flowers in the yard bloomed and became brighter. And though she was at first unsure, she began to notice changes in herself as well. Her chest, once as flat as a washboard, was starting to gain a minute amount of fullness. Her hips were broadening, if by a slight margin.

And her weight, constant at forty pounds or less for the past two years, was stubbornly creeping upwards. This alarmed her more than anything. She had asked Akiko to reduce her food portions, but the maid refused.

"You hardly eat anything as it is, Ojosama. You will get sick."

"I will get fat, is what I will get."

"Little madam, it is natural. You are becoming a woman. You are an early bloomer, it seems. When the time comes, your grandmother will explain what is happening to you. It is not my place."

It is not my place.

Akiko always said that when she didn't want to talk about things. Sometimes she would take pity and answer Nori's rare questions about why things were the way they were. But only in pieces. Then she would clam up, afraid she'd said too much, and Nori would be left to complete the puzzle herself.

She knew she was a bastard because of Akiko. That meant she could never be a Kamiza, not really, and that her grandmother needed another heir.

She'd concluded on her own that it could not be her mother because her mother was something called a whore.

But as many nights as Nori had spent on her knees praying for divine intervention in her life, Nori found herself resenting the changes that were now occurring.

It was horribly uncomfortable to feel time nudging her forward, tactlessly, in total disregard of whether she was prepared or not.

Her studies were progressing rapidly as well. She had nothing else. She read all night until her eyes burned because she had nothing else.

Saotome-sensei was incredulous. It seemed that no matter what new book he gave her, she was always finished in a day, two at most. And yet, when she told him this, he refused to believe her.

"It is not possible," he would say. "For a child your age. For a girl, at that."

"It is true, Sensei. I read it all."

At this, he would scrunch up his face so that his wrinkles would meld into one another.

"You did not read it properly."

Nori said nothing to this, only cast her eyes downwards into her lap.

Do not fight.

The topic was dropped and her sensei continued to drone on in a monotone. But Nori was no longer listening. "Song of Two

Poor Men" came to mind as her thoughts wandered to a distant place.

> *Yononaka wo*
> *Ushi to yasashi to omoe domo*
> *Tobitachi kanetsu*
> *Tori ni shi arane ba*

> I feel this life is
> Sorrowful and unbearable
> Though I cannot flee away
> Since I am not a bird

CHAPTER TWO

THE BOY WITH
THE VIOLIN

Kyoto, Japan
Winter 1951

One downcast morning at the end of January, her grand-mother arrived out of the blue and announced that Nori had a brother, and that he was coming to live with them.

She had a brother.

Nori blinked uncomprehendingly, her sewing needle still poised in the air. The cloth doll whose button eyes she was try-ing to fix lay forgotten in her lap.

"*Nandesutte?*" she queried dumbly, unable to devise any-thing cleverer. "What?"

Yuko scowled, clearly irate at having to repeat herself.

"I had not told you this before, but it is time you know. Your mother was married before her disgrace . . . before you were born. She had a son from that marriage. His father has just died, and so he is coming to stay with us. In fact, he should be arriv-ing presently."

Nori nodded, hoping that if she did so, her brain would some-how absorb the information being presented to her. Somehow the information about her mother and about the past, which she had so longed for, now seemed laughably irrelevant.

"He is coming today," she parroted. "To live here."

Her grandmother gave a stiff nod and continued, clearly displeased at being interrupted to begin with. "He is fifteen. I have had reports from his teachers and other family. They say the boy is exceptionally gifted. He will bring great honor to this family." She paused, waiting for Nori to react. When she got no such reaction, she let out a sigh of frustration. "Noriko, this is good news. We are all to be happy."

"Yes, Obaasama. I am very happy."

It was something she had never said before.

Her grandmother pinned her with a cold stare. For a happy woman, she appeared as mirthless as always. "He has been told of your . . . presence." The old woman made a sour face.

While her grandmother normally appeared quite indifferent to Nori's existence, though sometimes, paradoxically, perversely interested in it as well, she now seemed to have lost what little patience she'd once had. Nori could only assume that the impending arrival of this boy made the once tolerable shame of a bastard seem all the more heinous.

Her grandmother took a deep breath and continued.

"I have assured him that you will not bother him. If he chooses to acknowledge you, so be it. But you are to speak nothing to him unless you are spoken to. He is the heir to this house. You will show him deference and respect, beginning with silence. *Wakarimasu ka?* Do you understand?"

Normally, Nori would have nodded, or lowered her eyes, or done any number of things to show her willingness to obey, in the vain hope that these little gestures were somehow being seen by her mother, wherever she was.

But just as she was about to do this, something burst out of her. The word ripped through the seam of her closed lips.

"No!"

A dead hush enveloped the room. Nori looked around to find the person who had uttered that word. Surely it must have been someone else.

Nori looked at her grandmother, who appeared equally shocked. Those sharp eyes widened; that puckered mouth went slack. She too passed an inadvertent glance around the room to make sure there was not a ghost among them.

Nori tried to form her lips to retract her defiance, but instead more emerged. "I . . . What I mean is that I . . . I must speak to him. I have to speak to him. *Onegai shimasu, Obaasama.* Please."

This second time, Nori was not given the benefit of a delayed reaction. Her grandmother closed the distance between them in mere seconds. Nori heard the slap across the cheek more than she felt it. Her head snapped to one side, eyes losing their focus and seeing only white for a few seconds until they found a place again. The doll slipped onto the floor and Nori went with it.

Her grandmother lowered her hand, face betraying no traces of emotion. No anger. No nothing. She simply repeated her question, speaking slowly in a calm tone, as one would speak to the mentally deficient.

"Do you understand?"

In one crushing moment, the fear of God returned to Nori. The switch flipped back on. The world refocused. A little voice spoke from somewhere in the distance.

"Yes, Grandmother. Of course. As you say."

This response was met with a curt nod.

"Good. I will send for you when he arrives. Akiko-san has bought you something new to wear for the occasion."

It had been over six months since Nori had received a new article of clothing. She lived for receiving gifts: anything shiny, anything that she could tie into her hair or around her neck in a bow. They were by far the highlights of her existence. And yet she could find no joy in this news of a new dress. She could not even wonder what color it was.

Though she knew she should express gratitude, she could not bring herself to say the words.

She knelt there, perhaps for a minute, perhaps for an hour, as her grandmother went into further detail about the proper ways to behave.

"For God's sake, don't ask any ridiculous questions . . . None of that loud, uncouth walking . . . Don't slump . . . Eyes down and smile . . . You look like you've swallowed a lemon . . . Dignity . . . Respect . . . Grace . . . Decorum . . . Honor . . ."

Somehow, though she could barely hear the words over the thumping of her own heart, Nori managed to nod periodically. Despite the warm temperature of the attic, her skin was crawling with goose bumps.

Her mouth felt as if it were filled with sawdust.

It was only after her grandmother had turned and was beginning to walk away that Nori realized what she had forgotten. She took two tentative steps forward and reached out a shaky hand, unsure of what she was attempting to grasp.

"Ah . . . Obaasama!"

Her grandmother paused for a moment and turned her head,

the silky curtain of her hair rustling as she moved. The look on her face was thunderous.

"His name . . ." Nori stammered, blinking uncontrollably for some reason. "What is his name?"

"Akira."

And with that, she walked briskly away, clearly having spent more time on this exchange than she had ever intended to.

Nori was left standing there in silence. Her legs were shaking furiously as they so often did—but not from fear. Not from the unbearable anxiety that seemed to press on her every waking moment.

She was shaking for an entirely different reason. But she didn't know what it was. She didn't have a word for this feeling. Suddenly, her grandmother's stern decree that she must not speak to her brother uninvited seemed so meaningless. For the first time, Nori realized what an order truly was: a collection of words. Simply that.

Maybe this was what hope felt like. Real, tangible, hope.

She raised her index finger to her lips and traced them as she mouthed out the syllables to the name.

A-

Ki-

Ra . . .

"Akira"—bright, clear.

She let out a breath she hadn't even realized she'd been holding. A breath that seemed bigger than her whole body. And then she said the name again.

"Akira."

She could say that name every second of every day, so long as she lived, and never tire of the way it felt on her lips.

She didn't even realize that she was laughing until the sides of her jaw began to ache. She bit down on her finger to try and stifle it, but it was no use. The sound leaked out and echoed about in the high-ceilinged room. If it continued much longer and she was heard, things would go very badly with her in the near future. And yet she continued to laugh.

The dress was a stunning shade of lilac purple. It had puffed short sleeves and a collar that was trimmed with white lace. The hem, which fell just above her ankles, was trimmed with the same lace. She also received new white socks that she could pull up to her knees. She would pair the dress with her sky blue ribbon. She agonized over what to do with her hair. Today of all days, she needed it to be straight.

She ran the brush against her head savagely, pulling out entire tufts of her curly brown hair. The snarls fell to the floor. Akiko frowned at her.

"Maybe I should do that, little madam."

"I can do it."

When Nori was finished brushing, Akiko wove it neatly behind her head in two braids that she then coiled together to form a bun at the base of Nori's neck.

Nori inspected herself in the mirror. It would have to do. She had only so much to work with. It served no purpose to get upset over the things she could not change.

At least for the time being, she would accept it.

"Is he here yet?"

"Not since you last asked five minutes ago, my lady."

Nori bit her lip. It was growing dark outside. He should've been there by then. He should really have been there by then.

Where was he?

"Where does he come from, Akiko-san?"

"Tokyo, I think."

"That is where Grandmother sends for new things, right? The capital?"

"Yes."

"So he must be very grand, then."

Akiko laughed, though Nori was not sure what was funny.

"Not everyone from Tokyo is grand, little madam. But I am quite sure that your brother is. You come from a very great family."

"Grandfather works in the capital," she mumbled, more to herself than Akiko. "For the Emperor. It is why he is home so rarely."

"Yes," Akiko said, though she had told Nori this before. "Shall I get your dinner?"

"No, thank you."

It wouldn't do to have food in her teeth when Akira arrived. Already, she was apprehensive about speaking to a boy— something she had absolutely no experience with. She knew what boys looked like, of course. She had seen pictures in her books of many things, including great buildings across the sea. She had seen lakes, mountains, and ponds. She played little games with herself so that she would never forget to match the images with the words when it was finally her time to leave this place.

And surely this brother of hers had seen such things. She was determined not to seem ignorant when they spoke.

Nori gnawed on her lower lip. "Do you . . . do you think that he will like me?"

Akiko's face softened. She tucked a loose curl behind Nori's ear.

"I hope so, sweet girl."

This next question was even more dangerous. But Nori had to know.

"Do you think he knows where Mother is?"

The maid stiffened and glanced at the door. "Little madam . . ."

And that was all she needed to say. Their moment of familiarity was over. Akiko's duty to her grandmother always won in the end.

Still, Nori allowed herself to be confident.

Akira would speak to her, surely. He had no reason to hate her. She had done nothing to him; she had cost him nothing. She had cost her mother her rightful place—she saw that now—and she had cost her grandmother her honor. But she had done nothing to Akira.

Maybe this is it. The thought struck her suddenly. Maybe the arrival of this strange brother of hers, who was somehow older than she even though she had never heard of him, could be the test that her mother had set for her. Of course, he had to be. In Nori's experience, there was no such thing as a fortunate coincidence.

It was finally clear to her. All she had to do was pass one more test. She had to because then—*then*—her mother would come back to this place. And she would take the two of them away somewhere. And the three of them would live together somewhere with lots of tall grass and flowers, the big ones, like the kind that grew on the sides of mountain ranges. And there would be a pond there too, probably. Nori could wallow underneath the clear water until she felt the need to return to the surface. When she was done with that, she would lie in the sun. She would lie there for hours, until the palms of her hands and feet were bright red and tingling. And this brother, whoever he was, whatever he was, would lie there with her. And they would laugh at how silly it was that she had ever been afraid.

AKIKO

It is well past midnight when I finally lead the little madam down the attic stairs. As instructed, I hold on to her hand. It is painfully frail in my own; I can feel every bone. She descends the stairs with some trepidation, pulling at her dress as if she is afraid it will crease in the short distance from here to the foyer. Come to think of it, she has every reason to be cautious. She has not been allowed past the second-floor bathroom for over two years now. When we move past it, she lets out a soft wheezing sound. I think it is relief. Then again, it could be fear. She is a nervous child.

The girl does not say much, but she gives a lot away with her body. Often I find her staring into space, gnawing on a lip that is already swollen and bloody. I wonder if she feels it.

I cannot decide whether she is brilliant or a complete dullard. The other day I caught her reading a book in English—she was pointing to some pictures and sounding something out under her breath. She became skittish when she realized I was looking at her. I wonder if she is teaching herself—if she is capable of such a thing. Maybe she is. Maybe the traitor's blood flows in her veins and teaches her things that we cannot.

In all fairness, she is an easy charge. She never complains and rarely asks for anything. She is complacent with her "treatments," as I have been told to refer to them. She does cry, but she is careful not to make a fuss about it.

She is naturally curious—I can tell that much. Silence does not come easily to her. I see how she struggles with it. In this way, she is much like her mother. Lady Seiko never did take to the task of being a proper noble lady.

Nori-sama's mother fell to ruin because of willful disobedience. Lady Yuko says she was overindulged by us all, and that I am to make sure not to make the same mistake again.

But she's a sweet thing, really, and I find myself allowing too much.

Nori-sama tugs on my hand, as if to pull me from my daydreaming.

Even when her mouth is closed, her strange eyes are flashing like fireworks. I can see how much thought she puts into everything she does, even simple things that should require no such effort.

Again, I cannot decide if this is a sign of intelligence or stupidity. In any case, the child does have beautiful eyes, warm and light and full of brightness, a shade of amber that I have never seen before. They are the prettiest things about her by a mile, but they betray her every thought.

When we reach the main stairs, she freezes. Her free hand clenches the banister with a kind of desperation that I cannot comprehend. She surveys the surroundings below, alert and trembling. I suppose she is looking for her grandfather, Lord Kohei. But he is not here, and I am as relieved by that fact as she is.

The master is difficult. He has been known to strike the servants in fits of rage. He complains about the food and throws dishes he does not like in the faces of the cooks. I have even seen him strike his wife when they disagree, though he rarely dares. Yuko-sama's blood is far greater than that of her husband. It was her father's money that built this house and that earned her husband a place among the Emperor's advisors. She is a formidable woman; she is a Princess of the Blood, cousin to the Emperor. She runs this house with a firm, precise hand, and when there is anything that needs doing, we all know who ensures it gets done. Though she is just as demanding as her husband, everyone who works here respects her. She is a fair mistress. She is royal to the tips of her fingers, and one cannot help but bow to it.

I have allowed the child enough time to stand like a startled colt. I pull her forward and she comes, as I knew she would. She walks down the stairs on those unsure legs of hers, and I hold her firmly, afraid she will fall.

I lead her down the main hallway, and she is craning her neck behind her to take in as much as she can. She knows well that it may be a long time before she sees this part of the house again. She marvels silently at the rich surroundings, the fine rugs, the tapestries and the paintings.

She is trembling like a leaf as we approach the foyer. I can hear her mumbling something under her breath, a mantra of some sort. She sounds half mad. Maybe, after all these years in an attic, she is.

I have always wondered about her mental state, poor thing. And I have read that bastard children are of unstable constitution naturally. Not to mention the Negroes, who are said to be hopeless from birth, wild as lions.

We round the corner and can see him now, though he is not facing us: the slim frame of a young man staring absently out of the large window. She stops walking and stands perfectly still, like a woman transfixed by some merciless light.

As if touched by the sheer intensity emanating from the tiny creature beside me, the boy turns around.

I have done my duty for the moment.

I will leave them to their business.

Very few things would remain clear in her mind in the years to come. The passing years would force her memories of her time in her grandmother's house, like her memories of the time before, into a space too small to hold them, and they would meld together like watercolors on a page.

But the memory of this moment would remain, uncorrupted and undiminished.

He had a perfectly heart-shaped face with the same color eyes her mother had. His lashes were long, almost feminine. His lips had a slight fullness to them, and his skin was so pallid that his black hair came as a shock to the eye. And yet, of all his features, she loved his nose the most because it was exactly the same as hers. He wore a loose-fitting white button-down shirt with the top two buttons undone and a pair of black slacks. The way he stood indicated that he was used to being in front of people; the slight drop of his shoulders hinted at a casual indifference to his surroundings.

Nori looked away then, blinking rapidly as she focused her gaze on the floor. She could feel his eyes on her.

She wanted to become something else then, something more deserving of view. Under the intense scrutiny of that gaze, she suddenly felt nude, though the grip she had on the skirt of her dress assured her otherwise.

Because there was nothing else to do, nothing her mind could possibly conceive of to say that would be significant enough for this moment, she simply did as she was told.

She lowered herself into a stiff bow.

It seemed incredible to her that she had ever possessed the power of speech, so far removed was that ability from her grasp now. All she could do was wait: for seconds or years, depending on his preference.

"You're Noriko?"

She straightened up, but still, it took her a moment to fully realize she had been spoken to. This voice was unfamiliar, distinctly unfamiliar in her mental reserve of sounds. It was a quiet voice, soft but silky enough to indicate frequent use. She had nothing to compare it to, nothing to make the impact any easier on her senses. Her mind had no choice but to reluctantly absorb the foreign sound and, slowly but surely, give it a name: Akira's voice. Her brother's voice.

"Yes," she managed to respond, in a voice so clear that it actually startled her. "I am."

It seemed that at some point, her body had reached its maximum capacity for panic. As a result, it ceased to register. She felt herself go blissfully numb.

Akira's brow furrowed slightly, but he did not appear to be vexed. It seemed more like a habit than a reaction to anything she had done.

"They tell me that you're supposed to be my sister."

Nori could feel her nails cutting into her palms through the fabric of the dress. And still, she could muster no feeling because no feeling could ever be adequate for this.

"You look like her," Akira remarked casually. He took a step towards her before seemingly thinking better of it and halting. "Or at least, as much as you could."

"I don't remember," Nori managed. "I can't remember her face. I try, but I can't."

The boy in front of her looked as if he might say something but stopped short. He took two more steps towards her. Nori could feel him towering over her; he was at least a foot and a half taller than she was.

The ticking of the grandfather clock beside her seemed obscenely loud all of a sudden. It filled up her eardrums, selfishly hogging their attention.

"What year were you born?"

Nori let out a startled little hiccup. Akira waited patiently for a response, seemingly unperturbed by her stammering. It took her a moment to do the math, scaling backwards in time to find her origin.

"Nineteen forty," she finally concluded, flushing with pride at being able to figure it out. Her birthday was one of those things she didn't think about very often. She knew it was when the warm months came, but it didn't interest her much.

"Nineteen forty," Akira repeated bleakly. "Just before things got really bad. Makes sense."

Nori's mounting confusion must have been palpable because Akira shrugged his shoulders, a distinctly Western gesture. She knew because she had read it in one of her books about manners.

"Go figure. They haven't told you anything, have they? About what happened when you were born?"

Nori was completely unequipped for this line of questioning. She just looked at him, gaping helplessly and trying to rack her brains for an answer that would please him. Predictably, she came up with nothing.

"I'm sorry . . . I don't understand."

Akira shrugged again. Nori felt her heart attempt to vacate her chest and drop into her socks.

"I can read," she blurted out. The color began to rise in her cheeks. She had hoped to conceal her trademark knack for annoying those around her for just a little while longer.

Akira blinked at her. "What?"

"I can read," she repeated, like a total imbecile. She had already botched the thing completely; it seemed only logical to keep going. "I read books about Tokyo. I know that you used to live there. Kyoto is not very interesting in comparison, I'm afraid. But I don't really know because I've never been into the city. I've . . . never been anywhere, really, but you can find things to do, if you try. Did you know there is a summer festival coming up? Akiko-san . . . Akiko-san is one of the maids here, she is very nice . . . everyone who works here will be so happy you are here. Grandmother has always been sorry not having a boy in the house, she will be thrilled. But anyway, Akiko-san sometimes brings me the newspaper when everyone else is done with it. I know there was a war going on before I was born . . . when I was little. I know . . . that's part of the reason I look like I do. I have something to do with that war. But I'm a good girl, for the most part. Okaasan said so herself. When she comes back, maybe I can ask her about the rest. But it's good now because we're in the same place and she can get us both at the same time. Oh, and we have a pond in the backyard, with fish and everything. It really isn't so bad here, I mean. It's not so bad."

She finally brought herself to look up at him. He met her gaze calmly, his porcelain face impossible to read. There was a serenity about his expression that Nori could not fully grasp. His demeanor, his stature . . . all were things that would ordinarily have frightened her. But he didn't.

"You can read," he repeated after her. If she didn't know better, she would've said he sounded slightly amused.

Her skin burned so hot she wondered if he could feel it radiating off her. "Yes," she whispered.

She could sense that Akiko had reentered the room. The maid stood dutifully behind her, pressed against the door. To the untrained eye, it might have looked like Akiko was waiting on Nori's convenience. But Akiko never acted of her own volition. There was a greater hand behind it pulling the puppet strings and the message was clear.

It was time to go.

Nori resisted the urge to whimper. She had no way of knowing when she would be allowed to see Akira again. The knowledge that he was under the same roof but that she could no more access him than if he were on the far side of the moon seemed like a perverse practical joke.

She bowed once more, careful not to look at him as she rose up. She did not trust herself.

"*Oyasumi nasai.* Good night, Obocchama."

"Good night."

Nori swallowed the bile that had suddenly accumulated in her mouth. She turned around and walked back to where Akiko stood, taking the hand that was offered to her without question. Her caretaker offered up a mildly apologetic half smile.

Nori did not return it. She allowed herself to be led away.

"Oh, Noriko," Akira called after her, as if remembering some thought.

She turned at once to face him. Her eagerness must have looked downright cartoonish.

"Yes?"

"You don't need to call me young master. It's weird."

The wind deflated from Nori's sails so rapidly, it was a wonder she didn't crumple to the floor in a heap.

"*Hai.* What shall I call you, then?"

Akira's brow furrowed slightly, and once again, he shrugged. "Whatever you like."

Akiko tugged firmly on Nori's hand. There would be trouble for them both if they lingered here much longer.

She continued her march forward, up the first set of stairs, then the second, and finally the third. Akiko excused herself and Nori was left alone.

Her attic seemed so much smaller than it had before.

When she removed her new clothing and put it away, she did so briskly, without taking the time to admire the fine craftsmanship. It no longer interested her.

It seemed so deeply silly that she had ever cared about the new dresses her grandmother gave her from time to time. They were just objects—bolts of dyed fabric. They could never be enough to fill a life.

She reached behind her head and unbound her hair, tying the ribbon her mother had given her around her neck as she sometimes did. She did not like to have them too far from her. Knowing her luck, if she let them out of her sight, they would be gone when she woke up in the morning.

Nori scrambled onto her bed, standing up and pressing her face against the cool glass of the window. It was too dark to see outside, but her mind's eye had memorized the backyard so meticulously that she did not need her sight to see it. She trailed her pinkie finger in the condensation, scrawling the letters of her name as she had done hundreds of times before.

No-ri-ko.

She scrawled the letters over and over again, until she had all but run out of space. The repetition was her familiar lullaby. She felt her grip on consciousness beginning to slip and was instantly filled with relief.

Though it often eluded her, she liked sleep. It presented her with something that her waking moments perpetually denied her: freedom.

She lay down and slid underneath the warm covers. Just as she was about to drift off, a thought occurred to her. Tentatively, she traced a different name onto the misty glass, directly beneath her own: *Oniichan.* Elder brother.

CHAPTER THREE

HIKARI (LIGHT)

Kyoto, Japan
January 1951

Nori had once read in one of her science textbooks about the concept of gravitational pull. It had made little sense to her at the time, but she grasped the basic principle: the small revolves around the large. The earth revolves around the sun. And the moon revolves around the earth. It was part of the grand hierarchy of existence.

No matter how lonely, how frightened, how miserable she had ever been on any given day, it had never once crossed her mind to leave the attic unattended. Never. Her grandmother felt no need to lock the door, so absolute was her confidence that her charge would never dare to venture past it.

Nori's obedience lasted exactly six days after Akira's arrival. If it had not been for her extreme reluctance to disobey the parting words of her mother, it would have lasted half that long. As it was, an entire week was fairly impressive.

Even the most absolute obedience gave way to necessity

eventually. It was like giving a starving dog a command to stay and placing food on the other side of the room. The dog would eventually forget the command entirely.

Her mother had told her that the only thing more important than obedience was the air she breathed. But a new center of gravity had come to the house on the hill. And it had somehow managed to suck the air out of everything outside of a certain radius. One could only survive so long without returning to the center.

And the way Nori saw it, she was running out of air.

She spent those six days pacing back and forth, refusing to do anything but eat and bathe. Her books sat untouched on the shelf; her hair had gone wild and branched from her head like the leaves on a tree.

She ate only enough to keep the hunger pangs at bay. She replayed her meeting with Akira over and over again in her head, tweaking every little imperfection. Rehearsing conversation was a game she liked to play with herself.

Next time she saw Akira, it would be perfect. Next time, she would be prepared. Akira had to approve of her. That was the test her mother had laid for her. But that was not the reason she felt as if her very flesh were tearing from her bones in an attempt to get closer to him. She was not quite sure why she had formed such an instant attachment. Perhaps it had something to do with being related. Or perhaps it was because God was finally trying to tell her something.

She waited until Akiko brought her dinner on the sixth day to make her first move. This too had been carefully rehearsed.

"*Hamachi* tonight? Is it a special occasion?"

The maid shook her head. "I don't believe so, little madam. I think your grandmother is just in good spirits of late."

"I hope that my brother is adjusting well. Is he happy with everything?"

"I believe so, as much as he could be. It must be difficult for him."

Nori paused, for the first time remembering the unhappy reason he was here in the first place. She wished she could bring herself to feel more guilt than she did. It was unseemly to take pleasure in her brother's presence when she knew it was the death of his father that had brought him to her.

"How did he die?" she inquired as Akiko poured her a cup of warm milk. For the very first time, she was tempted to disclose how much she hated warm milk, but then thought better of it. She received a bemused look in answer to her question.

"You are talkative today."

"I wish to make his stay here as pleasant as possible. I just don't want to make any blunders, is all."

"Yasuei Todou was sick for a long time."

Nori hesitated, not wanting to push her luck. But it was rare that anyone answered her questions so willingly. She attempted to look focused on eating her dinner and tried to make her next statement sound as nonchalant as possible.

"Hopefully someone has given him a convenient room. He'll probably end up getting lost in this house."

Akiko chuckled, as this was a joke she often made herself.

"I believe he is near the staircase, little madam. I think your grandmother thought the same."

Nori made sure to keep her face perfectly composed lest it betray the gleeful little jig she was tapping out on the inside.

There were too many rooms on the second floor to search them all without being caught for sure. Now she had narrowed it down.

If one walked up the main staircase, there were two doors immediately on the right side of the hall and two immediately on the left. It had to be one of those four.

Akiko excused herself, and Nori ate the remainder of her meal in silence.

She then proceeded to tame the jungle on her head, dragging the comb through with such vigor that she thought it might break. It would not be the first time she'd broken a comb. She did her hair into two separate braids and tied the ends of them together with her lily-white ribbon. She did not wear her white ribbon often—she was always afraid it would get dirty. She saved it for the most special of occasions.

It matched the simple white nightgown she put on. She studied herself in the mirror. Surprisingly enough, she happened to think she looked quite decent.

When Akiko returned to collect the dishes, Nori made a great spectacle of pretending to have a headache. As she'd predicted, it was suggested that she take some aspirin and go to bed.

She spent the next several hours playing one of her favorite games with herself. She sat cross-legged on the bed waiting for evening to fade to dark, thinking of the stories that her mother used to tell her. One of her few memories of the time before was her mother telling her about a big black ship and how God had come to their family. The reason this memory was so distinct was because it was the only time her mother had ever mentioned being part of a family.

Nori did not know how much of the Bible she actually believed, though she knew that very thought to be sacrilege. But
she liked the stories. And she liked the constant access to conversation, albeit one-sided.

It occurred to her then that she had not spoken so much as
a single word to God since Akira's arrival. She sprang from
the bed and scrambled over to the corner where she said her
prayers. She could not risk lighting a candle. It was dark enough
now for her to proceed with her plan.

She struggled to think of an adequate apology for being so
remiss of late. Looking at poor, sad Jesus hung on the cross like
that made her guilt flare up instantly.

I'm sorry, God. You must be very angry with me. Please
forgive me. I am a wicked, wicked girl for being happy
that Oniichan is here because his father died. I did not
know the man, but if Mother liked him, I am certain that
he was very nice. I would very much like it if you could
bring Mother back, now that Akira-san and I are all together. I'm sorry for what I'm about to do. I know it is a
sin to disobey, so please forgive me that also. I will pray
more often. Thank you for listening.

Amen,
Noriko

When she had finished her prayer, Nori resolved herself to
the task at hand.

Somehow, she was going to find Akira and get him to talk to
her. She knew that her grandmother would defer to his wishes,
if only he asked. It was likely the boy had no idea how much

power he wielded. With a few simple words, he could change everything.

She took one last look at her surroundings before turning towards the stairs. Rather than lifting her feet, she chose to slide forward in her socks.

A floorboard creaked beneath her. She stopped at once.

No one needed to remind her of the consequences if she was caught sneaking about the house.

Unable to think of a better alternative, she dropped to her knees and began crawling on all fours. She felt ridiculous, but she noticed that the creaking noises stopped. She made her way down the stairs slowly, knowing full well that if she were to fall, it would wake the entire house.

She was able to get the door to the second floor open without much difficulty. She pressed herself against it until it opened. And here she faced her first challenge. Leave the door open, or close it and risk making a sound? After chewing her lip for a few moments, she decided to leave it open.

She took care to press herself as close to the wall as possible, crawling down the hallway like a toddler. These floorboards were sturdier and better kept, as her grandmother had the main floors of the house scrubbed and polished weekly. There was not a single speck of dust to be found, and the wood was in excellent condition; Nori could not help but notice that it shone like sunlit glass even in the darkness.

She didn't have much of a concrete plan for discovering which of the rooms she had narrowed it down to belonged to her brother. When she'd conceived the plan, she'd done so out of desperation. There had been less thought behind it and more need.

Had she not been so low to the ground, she might not have seen it: the faint light emanating from beneath the door closest to the railing.

Her breath hitched in her throat. Was it actually going to be this easy for her? But what if it wasn't him? But then, who else could it be? No, it had to be his room.

She inched forward, quicker now, acutely aware that she was in plain view of anyone viewing from the proper angle beneath her.

When she reached the door, she hesitated. After several moments of sitting in a stupor, she maneuvered into kneeling position and knocked twice on the door. She took great care to knock lightly, half hoping that she would not be heard and that it was not too late to renege on this fool plan of hers.

There was a stirring behind the door, and for a moment, Nori felt as if she might bolt in the opposite direction. The door opened, and Akira looked down at her in evident confusion. He was wearing dark red pajamas, and she was immediately racked with guilt, wondering if she had woken him.

Akira looked at her for a long moment. "Do you normally do things like this?"

Nori felt her cheeks blaze in the darkness. "I'm sorry. I . . ."

Akira let out a deep sigh and motioned for her to come inside the room. She scurried past him, and he shut the door behind her.

It was quite a nice room—very spacious, with large windows and an impressive king-sized bed with plum-colored drapes. Both bedside lamps were on. Piled atop the mahogany dresser were sheets of white paper with curvy black markings. There was a cardboard box filled with books next to it that looked to be half unpacked. And leaned up against the desk was a black case.

"What's that thing?" she blurted out before she could help herself.

Akira gave her a truly incredulous look that made her shrink back. "I play the violin," he said. "Noriko, what are you doing here?"

"Ah . . . I was just . . . I mean, I thought we could talk."

Akira crossed his arms. "Talk."

"Yes, talk. I mean . . . we do have the same mother." It sounded weak, even to her. She tugged on one of her braids.

"I really don't see what that has to do with you knocking on my door at three thirty in the morning."

Nori bit the inside of her left cheek in an attempt to steady herself. "I'm sorry. I didn't mean to wake you up."

Akira shrugged, a gesture that both fascinated her and served to make her blush.

"I wasn't sleeping. I was going over some sheet music."

Nori fidgeted, unsure what he was referring to. Akira pointed to the sheets of paper on the dresser.

"It's Bach."

She blinked at him. "What is that?"

"A composer. He lived a long time ago."

"Oh. Okay."

Akira locked eyes with her, and it took a conscious effort on her part not to turn away.

"You must've had a good reason for coming. What is it?"

"Obaasama likes you."

Sadly, she could not think of a way to state her purpose with more finesse. Her only hope was that Akira would somehow grow to find her ineptitude endearing.

The boy in front of her snorted harshly. "Well, yes, I suppose she does. She did insist that I come live with her."

Nori hesitated, not wanting to say too much but unable to help herself. The curiosity she had suppressed for years seemed to be leaking out of her very pores. "Did you not want to?"

Akira raised a dark eyebrow and looked at her as if she were a stray cat who'd wandered into his kitchen. "Did I want to come live in the middle of nowhere with a woman I've only met twice in my life?"

She could only stare back at him blankly, sure she was missing something but unsure what it was. Akira rubbed his eyes with the back of his hand.

"I forget you're only ten," he mumbled. "Apparently sarcasm is lost on you. I'm assuming you wanted to ask me something?"

Nori realized that it was now or never. There was no point mincing her words.

"I wanted to ask you if you would talk to her. She would listen to you. If you would . . . if you would please ask her if it would be okay for us to talk."

Now it was Akira's turn to stare blankly. "We are talking."

"Well, yes. Yes, we are. But I'm not . . . I'm not supposed to be here. She told me that I couldn't talk to you unless you talked to me first and . . . well . . . you didn't. And I'm not allowed to leave my room without permission."

Akira dropped his head into his hands. "Oh, hell."

The profane statement caught Nori off guard. She shrank back at once, sure that she had angered him. But he wasn't even looking at her. He was staring at a spot located past her head, brow creased in a tense frown. She managed to catch snippets of his grumblings every now and then. She caught the words "backwards" and "archaic." She didn't know what "archaic" meant, but she did pick up on the exasperation in his tone.

Nori did not dare speak. She waited in silence for him to address her.

After a brief pause, her patience was rewarded. He let out a deep sigh and gave her a tired look.

"Noriko," he said, "that isn't how the world works."

She cocked her head to one side, uncomprehending. "It's not?"

"No. You don't need her permission to talk to me."

"I know. I need yours."

"That's not . . . No. You're missing the point."

Nori felt herself beginning to panic. "I am?"

Akira did something then that she was completely unprepared for. He closed the distance between them in a few deft steps and rested his hand on her shoulder. She went stiff as a board for a split second before melting effortlessly into his touch. Right then and there, she decided that she loved him.

"You don't need permission to talk to me. That's stupid."

Nori was only half listening to what he was saying. She was preoccupied with the warm, liquid-like sensation that was overtaking her body.

"*Hai, Oniichan.*"

"And why on earth can't you leave your room? Are you being punished for something?"

She really didn't know why she was surprised. Of course her grandmother hadn't explained the rules to Akira—they didn't apply to him. And so when Nori went down the list of rules in as

dignified a manner as she could muster, she watched Akira's reaction carefully. She watched his facial expression shift from
bemusement to skepticism to pure incredulous disbelief.

"You're telling me that that old crone hasn't let you out of
this house in nearly three years? Not at all? Not so much as two
steps out the front door?"

Nori shook her head. She bit her lip as she watched him, trying to figure out what to say next.

"So is that why you came, then? To get me to do something
about it?"

She shook her head again. The more she thought about it, the
more she realized that this idea had been ill-fated from the
start. Whatever plan she might have once had was now gone.

"No, Oniichan. I just wanted to talk to you."

Akira's lips curled upwards. "Talk to me?"

"*Hai*."

"Well then. If you don't mind, I'd like to get some sleep."

Nori flushed a deep shade of mottled purple. She bowed
abruptly and stammered several apologies, all of which earned
her nothing but another smirk. She made her way to the door
and placed her hand on the knob.

"People call you Nori, don't they?"

She turned to look at him, taking a minute to process the
question. She didn't know what "people" he could possibly be
referring to. And she didn't know exactly what they called her,
but she was quite sure that she didn't want to know either.
Her grandmother had used the nickname once or twice, but
it seemed odd that she'd share this information with Akira.
Rather than try to figure it out, she decided to simply answer
the question.

"My . . . Our mother called me Nori."

Akira looked at her for a brief moment before waving a hand in dismissal.

"All right, well. I just wanted to know. Good night."

"Good night, Oniichan."

When her grandmother decided to show up unannounced two days later, in the wee hours of the morning, Nori was positive that her disobedience had been found out.

She didn't even bother to get upset. When she opened her eyes to the vision of the old woman standing before her in a blue yukata, she simply climbed out of bed and bowed low. For once, she was not shaking. There was no beating on earth that would make her regret what she had done.

Her grandmother's lips were pursed tight, and she took care not to look at Nori when she spoke. Her hands were coiled together like the knotted branches of a tree.

"It has come to my attention that a . . . child . . . of your age must be allowed a certain amount of exercise. Therefore, you will be allowed to roam the house from the hours of nine a.m. to five o'clock p.m. Akiko-san will supervise you at all times. Under no circumstance are you to touch anything without permission. Stay out of the way of the staff, they have no time for your nonsense. If you disturb things, I will discipline you. If you break anything, I will discipline you. If you attempt to leave this house, I will remove the skin from your bastard bones. Do you understand?"

Nori's head snapped up, and she looked at her grandmother in a dumb stupor. Despite the threats, despite the pure, unadulterated spite that was admittedly quite unusual for her stoic guardian, she only really heard one thing.

"I can go?"

Yuko's brow twitched. "Within the guidelines I have set for you. You will be informed in advance which days are acceptable for you to take your exercise."

Translation: the days when her grandfather was away at the capital. There were many things in this house that went over her head, but she was one hundred percent certain that he was not aware of this new development.

But that didn't matter so much. She tugged at one of her wiry curls, trying not to betray her budding sense of satisfaction. Just because she would tolerate a punishment, it didn't mean that she was going to encourage one.

"*Arigatou gozaimasu.*"

Her grandmother ignored the pleasantry. She turned and left as quickly as possible. Nori had to admire how quiet her grandmother managed to be, even when she was all but bolting from a room.

A few hours later, Akiko appeared. Nori all but tossed her book on the floor in her frenzy to get across the room.

"Are we going now?"

"Yes."

"Where will we go?" she demanded. If this newfound autonomy didn't take her to where Akira was, it was as worthless as tainted drinking water.

"Your brother is most likely in the kitchen, little madam."

Nori's mind tried to conjure up an image of the kitchen for reference and could not. She jutted out her bottom lip. It struck her that she had never been in there before, thus the reason she was drawing a blank. She had a vague memory of another kitchen, in the time before. Her mother hadn't really liked to cook. Most nights, she would bring food home. The noodles were always too salty and the rice was always dry. But she did remember that they would get ants in the kitchen every summer and her mother would spray them with a bottle of water and vinegar. The whole apartment would smell of vinegar for days.

The memories were coming back to her, one by one, as if to herald the arrival of another piece of the puzzle her mother had left her.

She started towards the stairs, and Akiko fell into step behind her. She didn't falter at the first set of stairs, or the second, or the third. She marched with the purpose of a soldier. All of her previous hesitation seemed to have evaporated into thin air.

She proceeded down the stairs as quickly as she could without dragging poor Akiko down completely. The bottoms of her feet became very sweaty all of a sudden in her socks. She paused at the landing, removed the socks, and offered them to Akiko. Akiko took them without a word and slipped them into her apron pocket.

Realizing that she, in fact, did not know where the kitchen was, Nori waited as patiently as she could for Akiko to lead the way. As the maid took her hand and led her down the long, winding hallways, Nori couldn't help but notice how nice the house smelled.

She spotted some flowers in a vase on a mahogany end table. They were a soft white with a small butter-yellow center, and they smelled of rain. She was possessed with a fierce urge to run them underneath her fingers.

It had been many years since she'd seen flowers this close up. She didn't remember what they felt like, if she'd ever known.

"Akiko-san, what are those?"

The maid looked behind her absently before they turned a corner. "Those? Those are *kiku no hana*. Chrysanthemums. They are the sigil of the imperial family, your cousins. Your grandmother always keeps them around the house."

"They're pretty. Are they very noble, then?"

"Yes, they are."

"And Grandmother is royal, isn't she, Akiko-san?"

"She is, little madam. She has royal blood in her. She is very proud of it."

Vaguely, Nori wondered if that meant she had royal blood in her too. But somehow she didn't think so. Somewhere along the way, it had been diluted out of her. Something had canceled it out, and that's why things were the way they were.

The kitchen was separated into two parts, one part counters and cooking appliances (she counted three ovens). There were two women standing there, chopping vegetables. They didn't look up at her when she walked in.

Then there was another part, a little off to the side, surrounded by large windows and a skylight above. The windows were hung with sheer curtains, long and billowing in the slight breeze. The sunlight flickered through them, and Nori could see the dust particles in the air. There was a round silver-rimmed glass table with more chrysanthemums in a vase resting in the center. There were plush silver-backed chairs with luscious white cushions around the table. Nori counted six.

And there, in the chair closest to the wall, was her brother.

He had his head buried in a book, long lashes casting the slightest hint of a shadow on his face. His dark hair was messy, as if hastily combed through once or twice, more to get the task out of the way than to actually tame it. He wore a plain short-sleeved button-down the color of the summer sky and white shorts. She let out a little gasp.

Akiko released her hand, bowed slightly, and whispered softly, "I'll be back soon. Be good."

Nori couldn't help herself. She made a clumsy, mad dash to where Akira sat and scrambled into the chair next to him. The women across the room shot her irritated glances as her chair screeched loudly across the floor.

Akira raised a dark eyebrow at her, shooting her a sidelong glance while still keeping his eyes on the book.

She waited for him to speak. To reveal his masterful tale of how he'd managed to convince their grandmother to extend the length of Nori's leash. She waited for him to tell her something. Ask her something. Anything.

But most of all, she wanted him to tell her why. Why he'd wasted even three sentences to help her. Why he was even allowing her in his presence. Why he, unlike the rest of the world, did not hate her for something that had happened before she was born. And then there was another part of her that was waiting to hear a harsh remark, a snide comment, or to feel the hiss of a slap against her cheek. There was a part of her that was waiting for this, this simple moment of contentment, to be snatched away from her.

She was waiting for God to send down something horrible, to remind her who she was and what her life was supposed to be. But there was nothing from God. And there was nothing from Akira.

Several moments passed in silence. Nori drew her knees up to her chest and waited.

Finally, after what seemed like a decade, Akira put down the book.

"Nori," he said, "aren't you bored?"

She stared at him blankly. Bored? What kind of ludicrous question was that? How could she possibly be bored?

"No, Oniichan."

Akira studied her for another moment, with those sharp gray eyes of his. It made her skin tingle. But the sensation was not entirely unpleasant.

"Your hair. Did you do it yourself?"

Nori perked up instantly. "Yes."

Akira noted her reaction with obvious amusement. He reached out a hand and fingered one of her braids lightly, brushing her ear as he did so. Something inside of her stretched and broke at his touch.

"It's nice."

Akira turned his eyes from her hair back to her face. His eyes went wide with something Nori couldn't interpret. She could only look at him, helpless. Helpless to move, helpless to speak. Faintly, she felt something touch her hand. But it felt like it was happening in a separate reality, in a place that was somehow irrevocably disconnected from this one.

"Nori . . . you're crying."

Akira's voice was gentle and unassuming. If anything, he sounded confused. His previous sarcastic edge was gone.

Her lips parted in an attempt to voice words, but nothing came. She looked down at her hand, resting on the table. There were indeed two drops of water there. But that was impossible. She had absolutely no reason to be crying. There was no pain.

Nori heard someone whimper softly, and to her horror, she realized it was her. She jerked a hand up to her face and swiped at the tears that had collected on her cheeks, wiping them away frantically. She tried to force out an apology, only to be met with a ragged sob. It was getting away from her. Everything was getting away from her, and it was cracked and broken and lying on the floor.

Oh, God.

Why? Why are you crying? Stop it. Stop it, stop it. Not in front of him. You're ruining it. You're . . .

Akira watched her sob in silence. She sat like that, curled in her chair, sobbing for no apparent reason for the next hour straight.

Every time she attempted to catch her breath or speak, the sobs threatened to strangle the life out of her lungs. She resorted to her old technique: relinquishing herself to the tears and letting them wash over her in waves until they were done. If the spectacle she was creating was attracting attention from the help, she didn't notice. Nor did she particularly care. She balled her fist into her mouth and bit down in an effort to stop the pathetic mewing sounds emitting from it. She tasted a mixture of bitter salt, from the blood and tears that had mingled together.

She wished someone would order her to stop. Because on her

own, left here to her own devices, she did not know if she would ever be able to. It felt as if a flood had broken free and now would not relent until it had sucked her down into its depths. She had nothing to hold on to as it tossed her about.

Finally, the racking gasps and sobs began to subside. She could feel that her face was hot and red. Her eyes burned with tears; her lashes felt sticky, and they clung to her face like spidery tendrils. She found it hard to keep her eyes open at all.

Wordlessly, Akira handed her a handkerchief that he drew from his pocket. She took it with shaking hands and wiped her cheeks, unable to look at him. It was over. Before it had even begun, she had destroyed any chance she might have had at making him respect her.

"Thank you, Oniichan."

Akira studied her with, as far as she could tell, perfect neutrality.

"Are you hungry?"

Nori looked at him in disbelief, sure that she had misheard.

"Hungry?" Her vocal cords thrummed in protest as she spoke. Her throat was completely raw.

"I'm starving, myself. I'm sure you like ice cream. All little girls like ice cream. Chocolate or vanilla?"

She looked him in the eyes, trying and failing to read them. He was simply Akira, with his usual serene expression and faintly curled lips.

"I've never had ice cream."

If Akira was surprised, he did not show it. He got up and turned his back to her, going to the icebox and rummaging around it. One of the servants stepped forward and offered to help him find what he was looking for. He waved her away.

Nori looked away from what he was doing, swollen eyes focusing on the book he'd left behind. It was a book of poetry. Forgetting herself, she reached forward and turned a page.

"It's Kazunomiya-sama. Have you read her work before?"

Nori retreated back into her position, not wanting to embarrass herself further. Akira took his seat beside her and placed a bowl of what looked like a creamy rice ball in front of her.

"No, Oniichan."

"It might be a little advanced for you, but you can read it if you like. I can help you with it. Here, eat."

Nori obeyed, placing a spoonful of the dessert in her mouth. It was creamy and sweet, sweeter than anything she'd ever tasted. The cold, while startling, soothed her aching throat. She finished the entire bowl within minutes. Akira handed her a napkin. Without looking at her, he pushed out his chair. It made no sound as it scraped across the floor.

"I'm going upstairs to read."

He got up and walked away without looking back at her, leaving the book open on the table. She hesitated for half a second, before tucking it under her arm and following.

CHAPTER FOUR

"AVE MARIA"

Kyoto, Japan
Winter/Spring 1951

They called her his shadow. She knew because she heard them whisper disparagingly behind their hands when she passed in the hall. Sometimes, when they were feeling less than kind, they called her his dog.

Nori didn't particularly mind. It was a nickname she had earned.

She was always behind him. Every day, he rose early and dined on a breakfast of rice, miso soup, fish, pickles, and eggs. He preferred coffee with a dash of milk, but sometimes he would have tea. He teased Nori about her habit of blowing bubbles in her juice. Once, he had allowed her a sip of his coffee. It was so bitter that she had spit it all over her dress. He'd laughed at her until she'd wanted to crawl into a dark hole and die.

Akira favored the warmth. At midday, when the sun was high, he liked to sit in the foyer, directly beneath the open windows. Though the servants had offered him a chair more than once, he would sit slumped against the wall with a cup of tea and a book or some sheet music. How anyone could drink tea in hot weather was beyond Nori.

She would sit across from him, hiding in the shade. The heat was too much for her. Periodically, Akiko would come to check on her, and she'd request some ice water. She'd pretend to read her books, but mostly, she watched him through her eyelashes. He didn't need to be doing anything. She just liked looking at him.

When Akira had finished whatever it was he was doing, it was usually late afternoon. For lunch, he often ate some fish and the pickled vegetables that Nori so despised. He smothered it all in so much wasabi that she wondered how he could even discern what it was that he was eating.

She had become addicted to ice cream and now gulped down at least three bowls of it daily.

Akira made her eat some real food before he'd let her have it, though. He also made her eat vegetables, much to her chagrin. But she felt that the ice cream was worth it.

When they had finished this late lunch, Akira would always retreat to the music room. Of all the rooms in the house, the existence of this room surprised Nori the most.

It seemed rather impossible that a woman like her grandmother would have an entire room dedicated to something that, until Akira's arrival, was never heard in the house.

Akira told her that the first time he'd discovered it, the door had been shut tight and the air was so thick he could hardly breathe. The instruments had been covered in a thick layer of dust—a decade's worth at least. He'd put in a request to have it cleaned, and by the next morning, the room was sparkling and pristine. It still smelled like lemon-scented cleansers.

The room was dominated by a baby grand piano, with glistening ivory keys and a sleek black finish. Bookshelves piled with scores lined the walls, and there was an empty shelf that was clearly designed to hold more instruments if the need arose. There were no windows, which made Nori very sad, as peeking out of the windows had become one of her favorite hobbies. The grounds around the house were manicured beautifully, and the patchwork of colors that came with spring made her heart ache.

But there was a very comfortable love seat in one corner that Nori could sit on while she watched Akira play.

And by God, did he play. Never in her life, or in her most euphoric and hope-filled dreams, had she heard a sound as beautiful as the music he brought into the world.

Despite her admittedly all-consuming adoration for Akira, she was aware that he was only human. In some vague sense, she recognized that.

He was human, and his violin was nothing more than an intricately crafted piece of wood with some strings attached. But the two of them together transcended mortality to become something divine. She knew it was blasphemy to have such thoughts, and she tried to atone for them in her prayers every night.

She would curl herself onto the couch and listen to him making paintings out of sound. And each piece was a different picture. In her mind's eye, she could see a garden full of trees with white leaves and a fountain with blush-pink petals floating in the clear water—that was a concerto. The volta: scarlet and plum-colored ribbons winding around each other, battling for dominance. A requiem . . . a lone horse walking down a dimly lit cobbled road, looking for a rider that had died long ago. From these dead foreigners whose names she was slowly growing accustomed to, Nori was learning what it was to live a thousand lifetimes of joy and sorrow without ever leaving this house.

Beethoven. Ravel. Mozart. Tchaikovsky. Names that she could hardly wrap her tongue around. She knew better than to interrupt Akira while he was practicing, but after, when he had exhausted himself and sunk onto the couch next to her with his eyes half closed, Nori would ask all the questions she could think of.

And he would answer. He didn't initiate conversation with her, nor did he encourage it. In fact, he probably said three unprovoked sentences to her from the time she joined him in the morning to the time she was escorted away at night. But he didn't discourage her, and he didn't ignore her when she spoke to him. Sometimes he would reach out and toy with her braids or fix her collar if it was standing up. Akira found her wiry curls interesting. He liked to wrap them around his finger and watch them snap back into place when he let go, a feat that his own straight hair could never accomplish. He was the only person who had ever liked her hair. Nori valued these rare moments, and she tucked them away in the most precious corner of her mind, right next to the memories of her mother.

One such evening, as Nori sat curled up on the sofa beside him, she queried hesitantly, "What was that song you played?" She was torn between her desire for interaction and her reluctance to break the tranquil calm that had settled over them.

Akira did not bother to open his eyes.

"Which song, little sister? I played at least fifteen."

Nori could not help but smile. Akira only called her "little sister" when he was happy.

"The last one. I liked it the best."

Akira paused for a moment, trying to remember. "Oh, that one." The lack of interest in his tone was palpable. "That's nothing. It's just a simple piece. All the pieces I played and that's the one you want to know about?"

Nori bit her lower lip. It was still raw from the gnawing she'd given it earlier, and it began to sting when her teeth came into contact with the open cut. "It was pretty," she mumbled. "Simple can be pretty."

At this, Akira snickered. She could see the corner of his lip curl upwards in a smirk. But when he spoke, his tone was soft. "You would say that, wouldn't you? It's actually no surprise you would like it. It's rather like a child's lullaby, isn't it?"

Nori said nothing, partly because she was sure he was making fun of her and partly because she didn't know what a lullaby was supposed to sound like and hated to look stupid in front of her worldly brother. Akira gestured for her to hand him the cup of tea he'd left sitting on the end table. She did so, waiting patiently for him to answer her question.

"It's Schubert, Nori. Franz Schubert. It's his 'Ave Maria.'"

Nori struggled to repeat after him, finding that the sound of the words eluded her mouth. Akira laughed at her again. She jutted her bottom lip out in a pout.

"Oniichan, will you teach me to play it?"

She had been working up the nerve to ask this question for a while now. Every time she watched Akira play, it captivated her soul. It felt like her very spirit was floating above her body, which sat dull and limp on the earth like an empty fossil. She wanted to be able to do that. To make people feel like that.

Akira removed his hand from across his face and straightened up slightly, meeting her eyes. "You're serious?"

"*Hai.*"

"Nori, the violin isn't a toy. It's an instrument. It takes years to learn."

"I can learn." She pouted, fully aware that her wheedling was not likely to get her anywhere with Akira's limited level of patience. "You learned."

"I have a natural facility for music, Nori. It's not something that everyone has. You can practice until your fingers are raw, but if you don't have talent, you'll never rise beyond a certain level. It's really just a giant waste of time. You find out, years after you've spent hours and hours training, that you'll never be anything but ordinary."

She felt her resolve weakening. It seemed unlikely that she possessed a natural talent of any kind. But she pressed on. "I would like to try."

Akira pinned her down with a cold stare. She looked back at him, eyes wide and quivering. But she held her gaze steady. Little by little, she was learning to minimize signs of flinching. Akira blinked. She took this as a sign that he had resigned himself to her request.

"If you really want to learn, I'll teach you. For a little while."

Nori perked up instantly, unable to resist the urge to throw herself on top of him. "Oh, thank you! Thank you, Oniichan!"

Gently but firmly, Akira carefully moved away from her. He looked only slightly irritated that she had touched him, which Nori counted as a personal victory.

"Fine, fine. Now, go on. Akiko-san should be expecting you."

"But, Onii—"

"Nori."

And she knew it was over then. When Akira said her name like that there was no point in arguing.

She rose from her seat and bowed slightly. *"Oyasumi nasai, Oniichan."*

"Good night, Nori."

Akiko was waiting just outside the door to the music room, as Nori had known she would be.

Nori answered the expected questions about her day with as much interest as she could feign. But her mind was already gone.

She ate her dinner quickly, anxious for Akiko to collect the dishes and retire for the night. She was struck with a sudden and intense desire to be alone. The thought of having another person around her made her skin itch. As much as she disliked solitude, she had grown so comfortable with it that prolonged exposure to other people made her uneasy.

Akira didn't count, of course, but Akira was Akira.

After she finished her meal, she delved into the book of poetry that Akira had lent her. He was right when he'd said it would be difficult for her. It was clearly an old, well-worn book— the pages were yellowing and curled upwards. The script was tiny and tightly packed so that the words blurred together on the page. The characters were complex, and many of them were entirely foreign to her. Akira had explained that the poems inside were several centuries old and that, over time, languages evolved. Though it was tempting to get frustrated and give up, she pressed on.

She read until her eyes hurt. Then she turned off the lights, lit her candles, and said her prayers before the altar. She asked

God to watch over Akira and her grandparents. She included her grandparents in her prayers by default. How genuine it was, she couldn't be certain.

And lastly, she prayed for her mother. She had no doubt that her mother would return, someday soon. She had to be patient. More importantly, she had to be deserving of her mother's renewed interest. Somehow, she had to make herself more appealing than whatever it was her mother had left her for.

There were some days when she thought she knew how to do that, even days when she fancied herself on the right track. But most of the time, she felt utterly lost. She clung to a tenuous standard, left to her in a conversation that she didn't understand. It was possible she didn't even remember it correctly. That, like so much else, it could have been twisted to a point where its true meaning was lost entirely.

But Nori didn't like to think about it like that. She preferred, as she did with most things in life, to simply have faith. It was considerably less complicated.

When she finally fell into bed, she was so tired that sleep came instantly. This night there was no faceless woman calling to her from a small blue car that sped up every time she got close to it, her bare feet covered in blisters from the hot asphalt.

It was a relief not to dream.

Akira was waiting for her in the music room the next morning, directly after breakfast, which he had been conspicuously absent from.

He wore a short-sleeved navy blue button-down shirt and

white shorts. He eyed her up and down when she entered, and she could not help but blush. She'd chosen her bright yellow yukata and her butter yellow ribbon. Rather than braiding her hair, she'd chosen to allow it to fall free. She wore the ribbon tied around her neck.

She bowed and greeted him, offering up a shy grin, hoping that he would notice all the care she'd taken to look pretty for him. He was clearly unimpressed.

"We'll be starting at nine o'clock in the morning from now on. If you're late, I'm leaving. Understood?"

Nori was caught off guard by such a blunt statement, but she nodded. She was learning to expect bluntness from Akira.

He gestured to a music stand, which he had lowered considerably so that it was around her eye level. She positioned herself in front of it, placing a tentative hand on the cool metal.

"You're slouching."

Nori arched her back and tucked her butt in, which earned her nothing but a clucking sound from Akira.

"Stand up straight. Relax your shoulders—no, *no*. Not like that, Noriko."

She felt two firm hands grip her lower back.

"If you stand locked up like this, you'll drop like a corpse on stage. Loosen up."

Nori did as she was told, melding into his touch. His skin was always so warm, almost uncomfortably so. But she did not even think of pulling away. "Stage?"

Though she couldn't see him standing behind her, she could almost hear her brother rolling his eyes.

"That's the objective, yes. Otherwise there's no point."

"Have you been onstage?"

He snorted. "Obviously."

Akira withdrew his touch and moved so that he was standing in front of her once more. "Are you ready?"

Nori nodded despite her sweating palms. If she could do this and do it correctly, it would build a bridge between her world and his . . . somehow.

Over the next several hours, he taught her about notes. Notes made music, like puzzle pieces make a puzzle. He taught her some scales, which she struggled to remember, but he wrote them down for her. He tasked her with practicing them before bed each night.

He showed her the strings of the violin and explained how each string represented a note and how, with the bow and the motions of the fingers on the neck, one could create variations to make all sorts of different sounds.

He explained how the violin was a very subtle instrument and how the slightest motion could alter the sound. "It's almost like a bird," he told her. "If you squeeze it too tightly, the sound will suffocate. But hold too loosely and it will slip away. Balance is the key."

Akira drilled her until her eyelids felt like lead and her stomach growls were audible. She could not suppress her yawns. He ignored them, pointing to a measure that she had been struggling with for hours. She'd only been allowed one bathroom break. Akira pointed at the passage on the sheet music yet again, as if this repetition would somehow make her any less oblivious to its meaning.

"Again."

"Oniichan . . ."

"Again."

"I don't know."

"It's simple. Use your brain."

Nori was beginning to regret asking for violin lessons. She began to chew on the inside of her left cheek, hoping that the mild pain would stimulate something in her head.

For God's sake, the one time Nori actually wanted Akiko to interrupt her time with Akira, and the woman was nowhere to be found.

"I don't know what it says, I'm sorry. I only recognize the middle C."

"There are four strings on the violin, Nori. At the beginner level, you'll be limited to about six notes per string. There are four standard hand positions . . . Nori, are you listening to me?"

"Yes, I am! I just . . . don't understand . . ."

Akira mumbled something and turned away for a moment. When he turned back, his eyes were kind. "It's not your fault. I wasn't made to teach. Never did have the patience."

He patted her firmly on the head. "Study those notes. I'll see if I can find you some introductory books. And you'll be needing a half-hand violin, mine is too big for you."

Despite not having the slightest clue what he was talking about, she made sure to nod and smile.

"Now, off with you. I need to practice my own pieces."

Nori bowed at the waist and headed towards the door, hesitating slightly as she placed her hand on the knob. She would be pushing her luck here, but she couldn't resist.

"Will you play me that song? The one from yesterday?"

Akira had already turned away from her and was fiddling with his violin case. He pulled out a waxy-looking block and inspected it thoroughly.

"I'll play it for you tomorrow."

Nori jutted out her bottom lip, disappointment coming like a sharp pain. She didn't want to argue, and just a few short weeks ago, the thought would never have entered her head. The cracks in her obedience were beginning to spread.

"Onii . . . forgive me but . . . I'd like to hear it now, if I could. It comforts me."

This much, at least, was entirely true.

Akira shot her a curt look from the side of his eye. She tried to keep herself from shuffling back and forth.

"Fine," he responded, with next to no enthusiasm. "I have no idea what you see in this piece. I've never liked it myself. But fine."

Nori sat where she had been standing, folding her legs underneath her and sitting up straight. She placed her hands in her lap and looked up at her brother dutifully, waiting for him to begin. He took the violin in his hands, and she closed her eyes, letting the sound wash over her like a soft tide. No, not over her—*through* her. So this was what it was like . . . a lullaby. When the song was done, she got up, bowed, and left the room without a word.

It seemed almost sacrilegious to spoil the silence that followed a perfect song.

The next few weeks followed in a similar manner. Right after breakfast, lessons would begin. The first two hours were spent learning to read music, the next two learning music history.

Then there would be a short break for lunch, though one could hardly call it a break, as they used their lunch period to listen to records. Then it was on to what Nori liked to call "the copycat game." Akira would play a simple melody and she was expected to copy it. The game was designed to hone her ear. They would do this until she managed to actually get one right (this normally took several hours, as Akira didn't bother making it easy for her). Not too long into their daily lessons, Akira presented her with a violin that fit her size, as her hands were significantly smaller than his. When she asked where he'd gotten it, he remarked shortly, "I bought it. You can do that, you know."

At the beginning of each week, she was assigned a piece to memorize and perfect. At the end of the week, she was supposed to perform it. She loathed this part. Her playing still sounded perilously close to the wailings of a dying animal. Akira sat there, sour-faced, through the entire performance. He never said anything. His pained expression was enough.

Though it seemed foolish in retrospect, she honestly hadn't expected learning the violin to be so hard. It seemed she had to think about a hundred things at once—her posture, her hand positioning, the pressure she applied with her fingers, her bow arm. She did not understand how her brain was required to fire in various directions yet remain whole. It only made the way that her brother's fingers flitted across the strings like nimble dancers all the more impressive to her.

One thing she had not been expecting was the pain. After running the same simple scale ten times, then fifty, then one hundred until she got it absolutely perfect, her delicate hands were covered in blisters. She could not help but pick at them, which caused them to split apart and bleed.

Akira ordered Akiko to bring a warm, damp cloth and some rubbing alcohol. He had Nori sit on the couch while he dipped the cloth in it. She whimpered when he pressed it against her hands.

He clucked his tongue at her. "Shush, now. They're just little cuts. In time, your skin will toughen and it won't hurt anymore."

"How long will that take, Oniichan?"

"It depends. You have frail skin, it seems. Hold still."

Nori did as she was told, though it took everything she had not to jerk her hands away. Her brother was certainly being liberal with the application of the alcohol. She hissed in pain, but Akira held her firmly in his grip.

"When I was your age, my teacher drilled me from dawn till dusk during the summers. My fingers used to bloody the strings and it didn't matter to him one bit. Trust me, I go easy on you because you're a child."

"You were a child once too, Onii."

Akira laughed. As usual, she hadn't intended to say something funny.

"Not really. Not like you."

He relinquished her hands. "There now, done. Go and have some sweets if you like. Then bed. You were yawning today."

As she lay in bed that night, she listened to the crickets chirping outside her window.

They almost sounded as if they were calling to her. Once again, she felt the deep yearning to be set loose in the outside world. The pangs in her chest caused her to push such thoughts from her mind. They only served to cause her pain. There was no benefit to dwelling on what she couldn't have.

When her mother returned, she could play outside as much as she liked. Akira didn't seem like the type who played tag or hide-and-seek but perhaps she could convince him. In one of her children's books, there were pictures of little boys and little girls chasing after a red ball. Perhaps, if she was very good in her lessons, Akira would agree to chase a red ball around with her.

Maybe.

As she sank into sleep, a memory struck her with painful clarity.

It was early winter, when the snow fell only in light flurries. The park near the apartment they rented was dormant. The fountain had a thin layer of ice coating it, and it glistened in the fading sunlight. The trees were bare and creaking in the wind. And a woman was walking through the midst of it, taking the shortcut home. Her slight frame was bent against the cold, and her long, graceful arms were laden with brown paper grocery bags. She wore a baby blue peacoat, beautiful but obviously worn past its wear. Her long silken hair blew freely in the winter wind, obscuring her face. She almost looked like a wraith, though a wraith of the benevolent kind.

Teetering along a few feet behind her was a child, no more than three or four, with warm honey skin and a wild mane of curls crudely crafted into a ponytail that was coming undone. Suddenly, the child let out a high-pitched squeak. She had noticed a swing set in the distance and was pointing at it in glee. She started towards it, only to be snatched backwards by the faceless woman.

"No time for games. We need to go home."

"But I want to play, Okaasan! I never get to play."

"Not now."

"But the park is empty, Okaasan. No one will see me. No one will know."

"Come along quietly and I'll give you a sweet. Come, now."

"But, Okaasan . . ."

"That's enough."

The child flung herself down and cried, with no regard for the cold ground beneath her. The woman before her said nothing, only waited for the tantrum to run its course. When it was done, the pair continued onwards, the cold wind freezing the child's tears to her face. The red ribbon in her brown mane was coming loose and was precariously close to flying away from her.

The child turned and gave the swings one last forlorn look before mother and child both were swallowed by darkness.

Nori's sleep that night was restless, and she woke abruptly—why, she did not know. It was early morning and still as death. Not even the birds were chirping. It didn't bode well, and immediately she wanted to call out for Akira.

She struggled to sit upright. Her limbs failed her, filled with a sudden, overwhelming weakness. She tried to scream but could not find a voice. Her body felt as if it were filled with water that could not be contained and was certain to begin seeping through her pores.

She was quite sure that she was going to die.

AKIKO

I am not particularly surprised to find the little madam still in bed when I enter her attic. It is only eight thirty and she is not a morning person. This brother of hers must tell me the secret to getting her out of bed without a bullhorn. Lately, she's been awake until three or four a.m. and up at seven sharp. She glows like a firefly despite the cuts on her hands and the sagging skin beneath her pretty eyes. I've never seen anyone so happy to receive such simple kindness.

One only needs to take a look around her room to see what she has been up to. There is sheet music strewn all across the table, along with two empty bowls. I suspect that her brother has been assisting her in smuggling ice cream up here. Yuko-sama does not like the little madam to eat sweets, for fear they will ruin her teeth and figure.

As for me, I think she is a child and should be allowed to eat as she pleases. But I am not Yuko Kamiza, cousin to His Imperial Majesty. I do not own half the land in Kyoto, with numerous estates scattered about the country. So what I think on the matter is truly irrelevant.

When Seiko-sama was a child, she was not allowed to have sweets either. And she grew up to be incredibly beautiful, with skin as clear as spring water and smooth as silk. So perhaps it is for the best.

I call out to the girl softly, to rouse her from her sleep. I know she would rather lose a limb than displease Akira-sama by being late to one of her lessons. Not that I have much to go on, but I am truly at a loss for why he is aiding her with her ridiculous notions. She is not very good. And even if she were, this little fancy of hers cannot possibly go anywhere. But then, she is still young. I suppose she hasn't realized yet that any attempt she might make to bond herself to Akira-sama is futile. Both of their destinies are written in stone, and they are as different as day and night. Maybe he is humoring her out of pity. Or maybe he's just bored. This isolated estate is a far cry from the bustling heart of Tokyo.

Of course, Akira-sama is exceptionally talented, which does not surprise me in the least. He is his mother's child.

The girl isn't responding. She needs to get up now if she has any hope of eating her breakfast before her lesson. I approach the bed with a resigned sigh.

Immediately, I know that something is wrong. Her face is drained of all color, save for an unnaturally bright flush on her closed eyelids. She has kicked herself out of the covers and is sprawled out. I can see her white nightgown sticking to her sweat. There is vomit crusted onto her pillow, and I know even before I touch her forehead that she is burning with fever. I feel my pulse flutter with fear and I surprise myself. Have I truly come to care for her so much?

I run to the garden, where I know I will find my mistress tending her prized flowers. Though we have several gardeners, she still insists on coming out every morning to personally inspect her yard. I wait for her to see me standing there. She rises, somehow managing to look dignified even though the skirt of her dark green kimono is covered in dirt and flecks of damp grass. She wipes a stray strand of hair from her eye as she addresses me.

"Yes?"

"Something is wrong with Ojosama, madam. I believe she is ill."

Yuko-sama purses her lips, a sign of her immense displeasure, likely as much by my referring to Nori as little madam as mentioning Nori at all. I know that she prefers to think about her granddaughter as little as possible. She was thrilled about Akira-sama, the legitimate male heir, coming to stay with us. She practically danced on her former son-in-law's grave with joy. I can tell she is irritated that he has chosen to spend so much time (or any time at all) with Nori-sama. I think she is afraid they'll contaminate each other. But she does not want to limit the boy. What she truly wants is his loyalty. The only Kamiza he has ever known was his mother, Seiko-sama, and well . . . I daresay that interaction didn't leave him with a burning sense of family pride. Yuko-sama is smart. In the coming years, she will need him. If he wants to amuse himself with his bastard sister, let him amuse himself with his bastard sister. It is a small price to pay to ensure the family legacy.

After a long pause, Yuko-sama relaxes her lips. "She is typically a healthy child, is she not?" she asks me, though she already knows the answer.

"Yes, Okugatasama." *Madam.*

"What is wrong with her?"

I hesitate. "She is hot to the touch. She is sleeping heavily, and I could not wake her."

My mistress lets out a frustrated sigh. It is clear that she was hoping to avoid involving an outside party. But she cannot ignore this. Kohei-sama, I'm sure, would love to use this as an excuse to get rid of the girl. But Yuko-sama is not like her husband. She holds no love for the child but, make no mistake, she is the only reason that Nori-sama wasn't taken to the dark woods and shot like a sick dog the minute she arrived on the doorstep.

I do hope she doesn't die. She is my charge. I am responsible for her well-being.

I admit, when the little madam first arrived, I didn't want to look after her. For the first few weeks I thought that I had been given an imbecile. I swear, all she did was sit on the floor all day and stare at the wall.

But now I do not mind her so much. It would be preferable if she didn't die.

I don't know what I will do if she dies.

Yuko-sama makes a discreet call from the study, and not an hour later, I open the door to greet a man, ancient and stooped. He smiles at me and I am tempted to cringe.

My lady greets him cordially, and he bows low to her, addressing her as Yuko-*hime*. She smiles at him and swats him lightly with her fan. Through this little gesture alone, it is obvious that they are familiar.

"Thank you for coming, Hiroki-san. Prompt as always."

He flashes her the same toothy grin he flashed me. He is missing several teeth.

"It is my pleasure. To be in your company, I would agree to treat the plague. Heaven forgive me, but I wish people in your house would take sick more often."

They exchange a few more pleasantries. He inquires about her husband's health and seems vaguely disappointed when she responds that he is fine. Then she leads him up to the attic.

I run to the kitchen to prepare a tea tray. I have been thumped over the head with that fan more than once for forgetting the tea.

Just as I am about to embark up the stairs with the tray, Akira-sama rounds the corner. I am so startled that I nearly drop everything in my hands. I never hear him coming—he manages to walk without making a sound. Though he is certainly polite, well-spoken, and charming, there is something about him that unnerves me.

He looks at me without smiling. "Akiko-san. *Ohayou gozaimasu.* Have you seen Noriko?"

Of course—he has no idea what is going on. Their little music lesson was supposed to begin some time ago.

"Ojosama is ill. Your esteemed grandmother has had to call a doctor. They—"

Before I can finish my sentence, he steps forward and takes the tray right out of my hands.

"I'll take it," he says. "Thanks."

And then he marches right up the stairs, just as prim and proper as the Emperor himself. He has this way of being rude while still maintaining the air of someone who was born and bred with manners. I wait a minute or two before following.

I find things much as I expected. Yuko-sama is sitting down at the table, fanning herself lightly and sipping at her tea. The young master is hovering beside the bed with his arms crossed. His face is difficult to read.

Hiroki-sensei is examining the girl. He touches her forehead and the sides of her throat, muttering to himself as he goes. He then reaches into his satchel and pulls out a wooden tongue depressor, which he jams rather roughly into her mouth. She does not move a single inch through all of this poking and prodding. When he opens her mouth, I hear the faintest hint of a groan. He touches the exposed skin on her collarbone, which I notice for the first time is raised and red.

When the good doctor has finished his examination, he makes a series of strange noises to signify that he is ready to speak.

Yuko-sama offers up a polite if slightly tense smile. Akira-sama's face is fixed in a scowl so tight that I have a hard time believing he's only fifteen. The boy is as frightening as his mother was when she was displeased. God help us all if we ever see a repeat of the day Seiko-sama found out that her music studies were at an end and she was to be married immediately. The day she came home from Paris to find a wedding gown already laid out on her bed.

"The child has the scarlet fever," the doctor announces, sounding a little too proud of himself for good taste. "I am certain of it."

Lady Yuko betrays no emotion, but I shoot her a covert glance anyway. Because I know, and she knows, that Noriko's mother got the fever when she was this age. It claimed part of the hearing in her left ear and nearly claimed her life.

But that was different. Seiko-sama was the only heir to the family name and titles. We couldn't allow her to die. She was our great hope for the future.

Of course, that was before.

I am broken out of my little reverie by the sound of bickering. It is Akira-sama, not quite yelling—but close—at his grandmother. The delicate blue veins in his forehead are standing up.

"What do you mean we can't afford it?"

Yuko-sama snaps her fan shut and meets his heated gaze with a level one. "I did not say that. I said that this expense is not in the budget."

The doctor has the decency to look uncomfortable. He has pressed himself against the bed, with one hand resting on the little madam's petrified body. As if a sleeping child will protect him from the cross fire.

Akira-sama lets out a rough bark of laughter. "Do you mean to tell me, Grandmother, that we have fallen so low that we can't stretch the budget for a few pills? Must I go begging in the street?"

"Not just medicine," peeps the doctor. "Antibiotics. They are a new development in the field of medicine and primarily reserved for soldiers. Especially now, with the occupation . . . they are expensive, as well as difficult to obtain. The Americans regulate—"

"I don't care," Akira-sama says curtly. "I have just heard you say that without them she could die."

The doctor bows his head. "Akira-sama . . . if I may . . . children have been surviving the fever for centuries without such things. There is a chance she'll recover if we just wait and see what happens. As I said, children have lived through this for ages."

"They've also been dying from it just as long. This isn't up for discussion. Go and get the medicine. I'll make sure you get your money."

My mistress rises from her seat, somehow managing to look intimidating even though Akira-sama towers over her. To my great surprise, she is actually smiling. If I didn't know better, I'd say that she finds Akira-sama's strong personality . . . amusing. I have never seen anyone defy Yuko-sama and receive a smile in return.

"Dearest grandson, there is no need. I will see it done."

She snaps her fingers at me. I know this is my cue to turn her wishes into action.

I don't really want to leave, but then I am not paid to want. I am not paid to think. I am paid to do. I serve the Kamiza family, but mostly I serve Lady Yuko. My family swore fealty to hers many years ago. We all have our calling in life. Mine is not glamorous, but it is mine and I will do it.

I serve the family. And somewhere along the way, I came to serve the little madam. She has a part to play in life also, and that much will be clear to her soon enough.

Let her have her Eden. Let her have a few more years of relative happiness. She deserves that much, I think.

The pain came quickly. It was the going that took longer.

Nori waded through the thick fog surrounding her, lifting her body limb by limb. Never had she felt such heaviness, as if a cinder block were tied to every one of her bones. Someone was touching her . . . head? Back? Hands? She didn't know. Her body felt like a singular blob. Something warm was pressed against her lips. A morsel of it touched her tongue, and somehow she recognized the taste: *okayu*, with just a hint of salt.

The spoon continued to press against her lips, and she accepted it, the instinct to swallow overpowering her confusion.

Hot. God, why was it so hot? It burned. She couldn't breathe. Every breath was a mercy, a gift from heaven that might not come again. The air in her lungs was too thick to be a relief. It had been so sudden, this feeling, this weakness so profound that she was sure she would melt into the mattress and fade away. No warning. Not even a cough.

She could hear people talking, vaguely. As if she were underwater and they were talking on the surface above her. She had no idea if it was day or night. Someone pressed something else against her lips. This time it was water. She welcomed it, hoping it would quench the oppressive heat in her bones.

Something else now, with the water . . . it was hard. It hurt her throat and she wanted to reject it, but someone was holding her mouth closed. They were saying something to her.

She was too weak to fight it. She swallowed and more water came to ease the pain as it went down. This cycle repeated itself, for how long she honestly didn't know. When she felt the spoon, she opened her mouth.

Sometimes she would feel something cool pressed against her forehead. She liked this. She attempted to muster a "thank you" but could not seem to form words.

Little by little, the fog lifted. She became more aware of what was happening. She could sit up in bed, propped against some pillows, if one of the shadowy figures helped her.

She knew now that the person holding the spoon was Akiko, and she recognized the shadowy figure lurking in the corner as Akira. He sat there in silence, reading one of his books. He was there when she woke up and there when she went to sleep. But she was still not strong enough to call his name.

More time passed. Be it days or weeks, she still wasn't quite sure.

When she grew a little stronger, she grasped Akiko's wrist

during a feeding session and asked for some ice cream. Her voice was raspy and weak from disuse. The maid looked stunned for a moment before breaking into a wide smile.

"Yes, little madam."

On her way out of the room, Akiko leaned down and whispered something in Akira's ear. The boy looked up from his book, and their eyes met from across the darkened room. And that's when Nori knew that she wasn't going to die.

CHAPTER FIVE

DELPHINIUM

Kyoto, Japan
Summer 1951

Summer began to draw to a close, and the mid-August days were both warm and breezy. Sometimes Akira would cancel a lesson or two to run some errands or go visit some friends in Tokyo. Nori sat by the door until he returned. There was always the fear that he wouldn't come back to her.

He placated her with trinkets from the city to keep her complaints to a minimum. He presented her with a stuffed rabbit when he returned from a weeklong venture into Tokyo for a violin competition. He refused to tell her whether or not he had won, but Nori did spy a shiny new trophy being carried up to his room.

"I saw it in a toy store window," he remarked dryly when he handed the toy to a squealing Nori. "It was the last one, so don't lose it because I don't think I'll be able to get you another one."

The stuffed bunny rabbit was exquisite, with snow-white fur and shiny, happy-looking black eyes made of half-moon-shaped buttons. Around its neck was a bright yellow ribbon tied in a bow. When Nori looked closely, she could see that there were tiny suns stitched into the silk.

She named the toy Agnes, after one of the characters in *Oliver Twist*. Thanks to Akira, who had grown up speaking English as a second language, she was about three-quarters of the way through. When she was still recovering from her illness, he would sit beside the bed and read it to her.

From that day forward, Agnes went everywhere with her. When Nori ate, Agnes went below the seat. When she was in her lessons, Agnes sat atop the piano. Her smile was stitched on—so even when Nori faltered and Akira winced in distaste, Agnes kept smiling.

During one such lesson, Nori joked that if Akira wanted her playing to improve, he should try beating her. She was expecting a laugh, but it did not come. The look he gave her was grave.

"Has she been hitting you?"

Nori was instantly uncomfortable. Stoic Akira she could deal with. Serious Akira was an entirely different beast.

"I mean . . . a little bit." This was a lie. The beatings had only gotten worse since she'd recovered.

Akira frowned and placed his tea on the end table. "Often?"

"Every . . . week or so. It's fine, really."

Akira would not relent. He pressed for details, and she was forced to tell him about the visits from her grandmother and the beatings that inevitably followed. She told him everything— the beatings, the special baths designed to chemically lighten her skin. He listened to her with a hard face.

"That's not going to be happening anymore," he said, shov-

ing her weekly assignment—four pieces of music to be memorized and performed—into her hands. "There's some Brahms in
here. He's new to you. His style will prove challenging, but I
expect you to learn it anyway. Understood?"

"I'll try, Oniichan."

"I didn't tell you to try, I told you to do it. Start practicing one
of the pieces from last week. I'll be back in a few minutes."

"Which one should I practice?"

Akira shrugged as he walked past her. It was clear that his
attention had already moved on. "Any of them, all of them. They
were all terrible, so you have a lot to work with."

And on that note, she was alone. She didn't waste energy
thinking about what Akira was going to do. He did what he
wanted to do when he wanted to do it, and the rest of the world
seemed to fall in line.

Truthfully, it had become painfully obvious that Akira could
have whatever he wanted. If he asked for the moon, her grandmother would probably find a way to bring it to him.

She needed him. Akira was the only legitimate heir. And her
dearest grandmother would saw off her own foot before she let
it be said that Yuko Kamiza was responsible for the demise of
the legacy—though, since Akira had explained to her that the
monarchy was dead in all but name, Nori didn't know what
good the legacy would do them now. The *kuge* nobility that the
Kamiza family had come from, the *kazoku* aristocracy of the
imperial court that her grandmother and mother and Akira had
been born into—both were gone. Everyone was to be equal now.
Cousins to the emperor or rice farmers, it made no difference in
the new Japan.

Akira told her that wasn't going over very well.

Why Akira explained things to her, why he cared what happened to her, was still a mystery to Nori.

She knew that her best hope was to be an amusement for him. Many years from now when they were both grown, he would be a very important person. Though the peerage and all hereditary titles had been officially dissolved after the war, many people still believed in the power of blood. Besides, the wealth and reputation of their family still carried a great deal of weight. Akira might no longer be called a prince or a duke, but he was still going to be treated like one.

And she would probably still be here, in the attic, watching the flowers bloom and die.

Nori shook her head to clear it. Such thoughts served no purpose other than to depress her.

She did not dwell too much on her mother, or her future, or the gaping, bottomless pit of emptiness that resided inside her chest where her heart should be. She had learned, in the years that she had spent here in utter isolation, not to think too much. Because if she did, she likely would have dashed her head against the ground until her brains spilled out to form a watercolor on the hardwood floor. And so Nori counted what she had and kept the rest at a distance, in a place where it could not destroy her.

When Akira returned, he gave her a gentle swat on the back to correct her posture but said nothing to her. She didn't ask where he'd gone or what had been said. But somehow she knew that no one would lay a hand on her again.

After a few more minutes, Akira sent her off. "Go play," he

said, motioning her towards the door. "I need to practice for nationals."

Nori was torn between disappointment and relief that she didn't have to flounder through pieces far too difficult for her anymore. "Can't I stay and watch, Oniichan?"

"No," he quipped smartly, without looking at her. "You get a ridiculous look on your face and it's distracting."

"But what am I supposed to do?"

"I don't know. What normal children do."

This meant absolutely nothing to her. "I don't know what that means."

"Then go stare at the wall for all I care, Nori. I can't entertain you all the time."

She bit back a retort and left the room. She spotted Akiko lingering not too far away.

"Done with your lessons already, little madam?"

"I got kicked out," she grumbled, knowing that she sounded petulant but too frustrated to care. "He has to practice for some stupid competition."

Akiko's upper lip curled upwards in a smile. "Your brother is the defending national champion for his age bracket. It is a matter of great pride for him."

"Pride, pride, pride," Nori grumbled. "That's all anyone ever talks about in this house."

"Pride is largely a male thing, Ojosama. You may never fully understand it."

"But Obaasama talks about it all the time too and she's not a man."

Akiko snorted. Her hand flew to cover her mouth and she

looked down, clearly restraining further laughter. "Your es-teemed grandmother is . . . not like most women, little madam."

Grudgingly, Nori made her way back up to her attic. She picked at her lunch, pushing away the milk Akiko offered her. She knew she was being difficult but no longer cared.

"I want something sweet. Have the cook make me a cake."

Akiko raised an eyebrow. "What kind of cake?"

"I want lemon cake. And I want whipped cream."

Akiko bowed and went out, leaving Nori to stew in silence. She paced around the attic in a huff before finally deciding to read a book. She plucked a book of poetry from her bookshelf and hunkered down to read by the window. She had been slack-ing on her reading lately.

The history book that Sensei had given her sat on the top of her bookshelf, collecting dust. When her lessons resumed in a few weeks, she would likely be in for a tongue-lashing. Saotome-sensei always went away all summer, but he expected her to keep up with her studies.

She sat there reading for several hours, and when her cake came, she picked at it for a moment before having it sent away.

She played with Agnes for a little while before growing bored with that also. She declined dinner and ignored Akiko's pro-test.

She fussed under her breath when Akiko told her to go to bed in that voice that meant *Don't argue or I'll tell your grandmother.* She had just pulled her nightgown over her head when she felt a presence behind her.

"Nori."

The way her brother said her name let her know that he was displeased with her. She turned to face him.

"Oniichan," she started, filling up with excitement the way she always did when he said her name. But the look he cut her told her that this was not a smiling occasion.

"I've heard that you're being a brat."

She didn't tell him that he'd heard this because it was entirely true. "I wasn't acting like a brat."

It was such a lie that she had a hard time keeping her face straight. But this was her pride at stake here. That damned Kamiza pride. Even a bastard could have some.

Akira rolled his gray eyes at her, glancing impatiently at his watch as if she were cutting into his meticulously planned schedule.

"Save it. Nori, I can't spend every waking moment with you. And even if I could, I wouldn't want to. What are you going to do when school starts?"

She felt her mouth go completely dry. *"Gakuen?* School?"

Akira rolled his eyes at her again, and Nori thought, somewhat bitterly, that it would serve him right if they got stuck in the back of his head. The dimly lit room accentuated his pale complexion all the more, and he glowed like Jesus before the sinners. His very presence shone a fluorescent light on all that she was not.

"Yes, school. I start in a few weeks. I've been putting it off as it is; my father's death has made a worthy excuse. I'm not exactly thrilled about the place the old woman picked out. But they have a world-class music teacher there. It was the deal for getting me to go. Anyway . . . I'm going to be gone all day. And you can't starve yourself when I'm gone."

"I want to go with you." Nori tried her best to sound like she was doing anything but pleading. Sadly, it wasn't very convincing. "Please? I'm good at my lessons. Really, I am. I could go with you. I wouldn't embarrass you, I promise."

His face darkened. "Nori, I'm in a different year than you. Besides, my school doesn't take people your age."

And the unspoken: *I wouldn't want you there anyway.*

"So? They have schools for girls my age. I know they do. Sensei used to teach at one. I can go to one of those."

Akira gave her a long, solemn look. "You know that's impossible."

Translation: *If you don't know that's impossible, you're a complete idiot.*

She dug her nails into her palms. "The school wouldn't care. They wouldn't and you know it. There are plenty of Americans—"

Akira raised an eyebrow. "Not in Kyoto, there aren't. And how did you find out about that?"

Nori looked at her feet. She was an idiot, there was little doubt about that, but even she could manage to find the simplest conclusion. Everyone hated the Americans. And everyone hated her. It made sense.

"I've been reading the newspaper. Akiko-san gives it to me sometimes even though she isn't supposed to. And I listen to the servants' gossip. I know that the Americans are here. They won the war, didn't they? That's why they're here. That's why . . ." She let her voice trail off into nothing.

She still didn't fully comprehend the war, but she knew enough to understand that her people felt threatened by these Americans. She had a secret fear that she had pushed away for years: she suspected that her father was an American. Where else had her skin come from? This skin that Akiko had called "colored" when Nori asked why she had to take the baths?

There were no colored people here. But in America, she'd read, there was every kind of person you could imagine. Every kind of skin, every race of people under the sun.

She had a deeper fear too, the very worst: that her father was a soldier for the other side. One of the men who had come into her family's homeland and attempted to destroy its people, its tradition, and its legacy for no reason at all; one of the people who took away the power of the monarchy, one of the people who unleashed fire that fell from the sky. It all made sense. The timing of it, the reason for all the shame: her existence was an embodiment of betrayal.

Akira closed the space between them and placed a firm hand on the top of her head. She looked up at him, quite determined not to cry. He had read her mind, as clearly as if her thoughts were letters sprawled across her forehead.

"You are not an American, Noriko," he whispered, slowly and clearly. "You are one of us."

Now it was Akira's turn to lie. She looked up at him, her bold gaze daring him to speak the truth. "My father wasn't one of us. He was an American, wasn't he? He was one of the people who hurt everyone?"

For the first time since Nori had known him, Akira looked truly unsure of himself. This conversation had gotten away from him, his control was gone, and it was obvious that he did not like it.

"Your father . . . didn't hurt anyone. From what I understand he was just a cook. He came before things . . . before."

"Before the war?"

"Nori, maybe this isn't—"

She balled her hands into fists and spoke the words she'd always been too afraid to say.

"Just tell me."

And there it was. The unleashing of the elephant in the room, the one that they had both been avoiding since the day Akira arrived on the Kamiza doorstep. Because the thing about the elephant was that it only existed if one acknowledged it did. In order to make it tangible, to give it power, one had to willingly step into the trap. Nori had been avoiding it. She'd been so overjoyed to have her Oniichan that she'd pushed all the rest aside. Because somehow she knew that once they had this conversation, things would never be the same.

But she could no longer cloak herself in ignorance and use it as her protection; whatever frail delusions she clung to were about to be freed from the shadows and cast into the unforgiving light, where they had no hope of surviving.

Akira looked immensely uncomfortable. He fidgeted with the sleeves of his burgundy button-down shirt. "This isn't my place to be telling you these things. Someone else should."

"And who is going to do that, Oniichan?" she demanded, seizing the hand he had on her shoulder and pressing her fingers into his palm. "Nobody. Nobody has ever told me anything. And part of me was grateful for that. But I'm not anymore. I want to know the truth. Tell me who I am."

Akira closed his eyes for a brief moment. When he opened them, he almost looked sad.

"Sit down, Nori."

The silence that followed filled the room like a noxious gas. Nori's mouth hung slack and gaping, her eyes rolled around like frantic marbles without a place to land. She was pulling at her hair so hard that it threatened to rip from her scalp.

Akira sat across the table from her, hands folded neatly in front of him. He looked at her with obvious concern. "Noriko . . . you must have known."

"I didn't," she whispered, not bothering to look at him. She didn't want to see the pity in his eyes. "I didn't know that my birth destroyed your family."

"Our mother and my father were never happy, Nori. They didn't hate each other, but happy? No. Mother didn't want to marry him. She didn't want to marry anyone, but she didn't have a choice."

"She broke her wedding vows," Nori whimpered, in a piteous little voice that she had thought was lost to her. "She betrayed your father. She betrayed God. She committed adultery. With an *American*."

Akira shrugged a shoulder. It was clear that if this had ever bothered him, he was over it now.

"She left when I was four. I don't really remember much about it, and she never told us where she was going. That's, I'm assuming, when she realized she was pregnant with you. Even before she left, she was never around. She hung around with strange people and stayed out all hours. I highly doubt your father was the first strange man she took to bed with her. Though, as far as I know, nobody ever saw her with anyone colored. That must have been a new curiosity."

If that was meant to make her feel better, it had a decidedly opposite effect. Her gut churned, and this time, it was more than just a feeling. She leaned over and retched, the acrid taste of bile causing her eyes to water.

Nori dragged her eyes from the floor and fixed them on her hands. They were shaking so badly that she couldn't stop them. Akira rose from his seat and moved around to where she was, tactfully avoiding the vomit. He offered her a glass of water, but she shook her head.

"I'm so sorry," she whispered, fat tears sliding down her cheeks. "Akira-san, I'm so sorry for what I am."

It seemed unlikely, as tasteless as her mother was, that she had ever bothered to apologize to Akira for abandoning him and bringing shame onto their entire family. So it fell on her to do it.

Once again, her brother shrugged at her. "Seiko made her own decisions. That's life. My father was a good man. He raised me well. In truth I was probably better off without her."

"But I—"

"It isn't your fault. So hush."

She wiped her eyes. "Where is she?"

It seemed strange that a question that had weighed on her for so long, that had consumed her and dictated in some strange way every single footstep she placed on the ground, could be so simply put: three little words. That was it.

Akira shrugged. "I don't know and I don't care. Nobody has seen or heard from her since the day she dropped you on this doorstep."

Nori could not bring herself to ask if he thought that their mother was dead. Instead, a very different question fell from her lips. "Do you hate her?"

Akira shut his eyes, and for a moment, he looked far older than his years.

"No," he said, running a hand through his messy hair. "I don't hate her. Do you?"

Nori's hand inadvertently found the forest green ribbon tied around her neck in a bow. She remembered the day she had gotten this, just as she remembered the day she had gotten the rest of them.

"No," she whispered, tears welling behind her eyes. But she stopped them there. They would not fall.

Not another tear would slide down her cheeks for the sake of Seiko Kamiza.

Akira's strangely warm hands lifted her from her seat. She went limp, and he cradled her in his arms like a fledgling baby bird incapable of moving on its own. They stood like that for a long moment. He had never held her close before.

Nori shut her eyes and listened to the sound of Akira's heart beating. Even his heartbeat was musical. His breathing was slow and steady, and it offered the cool reassurance that life would go on. When the moment had passed, Akira put her down.

"Go to sleep," he said. "And don't be late for lessons tomorrow. We're doing Schubert."

He left her standing there, and she watched him go, seeing the ghost of his outline in the darkness long after he had gone.

She did not sleep that night. She lay in bed, staring wide-eyed at the ceiling, suppressing tears with every inch of willpower she possessed. It proved to be quite a formidable amount. That invisible wall that separated her memories of the time before from the rest of her being was shattering piece by piece.

But she still couldn't see her mother's face: just a set of float-ing eyes.

And she realized now, finally, what that wall had been there for. It wasn't there to torment her, to keep her from remember-ing glorious days of bliss with a mother who loved her. It was there to protect her from a mother who didn't.

Smoke. Lots of smoke. The apartment always smelled like smoke and lye and vinegar.

Her mother cleaned, often, to cover the smell from the ciga-rettes. She would bring people back to the apartment some nights, on the days she wasn't gone all day. She'd put on her rouge and her red lipstick, and sometimes she'd let Nori help her. She'd spray herself with some peppermint perfume. A vase of tall purple flowers was never absent from her mother's van-ity. Nori remembered this, especially.

After the primping was done, there would be a knock on the door. Nori was told to stay in her room, and her mother would turn the key in the lock from the outside.

Her mother never struck her. Never struck her, never screamed at her, but she also never kissed her, never held her, never spoke tenderly. The woman was a paragon of neutrality. No hatred, no love.

Nori's body racked with silent sobs. She could stifle the tears and she could stifle the sound, but her chest heaved up and down with the force of a small hurricane, in total disregard to her will.

Her mother hadn't given her up so that Nori could improve herself. Leaving her wasn't designed to teach her a lesson or to make her "good."

It wasn't about Nori being perfect. It was about her being *gone*.

Without Nori, her mother could be free. She could be beautiful and free. No more shame, no more struggle. It was simple. Painfully, painfully simple.

All this time, she'd asked God for a gift. She hadn't realized that she'd been living in one all along. A sweet little bubble, filled with a combination of dreams, hope, and blatant stupidity. It wasn't a cage, as she had thought it was. It was a shield.

Her mother wasn't coming back for her. *She was never, ever coming back.*

And it was this realization that finally made the tears come.

CHAPTER SIX

AME (RAIN)

Kyoto, Japan
Summer 1951

Akira woke her at dawn the next morning and, without saying a word, dragged her down the stairs and then told her to wait in the living room. Nori watched in stunned silence as her brother disappeared into the study to "have a word with our dear grandmother."

Akiko was gaping at her, clearly unsure of whether she should even ask. She wiped her hands on her apron and frowned.

"Little madam . . ." she began.

"I don't know," Nori whispered, tugging on one of her curls. Unbrushed and unbound, it caught her finger in its tangles and refused to let go. She was still in her nightgown and shivered as a gust of air washed over her. "Go see what's happening."

Akiko nodded and started out of the room, but hesitated before turning the corner. She was supposed to be watching her charge. If anything should chance to be broken, they would both pay. Nori offered up a wry smile.

"Don't worry, Akiko-san. I won't go anywhere. Promise."

That was all the reassurance the maid needed, and she rounded the corner, leaving Nori alone. Nobody, not even her grandmother, seriously doubted her obedience. It was her one true skill.

The rugs beneath her bare feet were wonderfully plush and soft. They were probably obscenely expensive, and she carefully maneuvered herself off of them. Regardless of what Akira said, Nori knew that she was not impervious to beatings. Her grandmother was not a woman who could be told what to do, and she didn't intend to push her newfound luck.

She stood there, pressed against the wall, desperately trying not to touch anything. She still felt uncomfortable in the main house. Even when she had her clothes on, she felt naked.

Twenty minutes turned into an hour. With every passing moment, her anxiety mounted.

Nori had not the slightest clue what they were talking about now. But usually Akira's requests were greeted with a sigh, a flutter of the fan, and a calm "As you like, dear," or "If you must."

For the conversation to drag on for so long . . . what had her brother chosen to ask for this time? The prophet's head on a silver platter?

Finally, after what seemed like a thousand years, Akira reentered the room. The expression on his face told her that whatever he had wanted, he had won. He was looking at her with a twinkle in his eye that she had not seen before.

"Nori," he whispered, his voice queerly high-pitched. "Come with me."

She could ask why. She could ask where they were going. But she did none of those things.

Wordlessly, she held out her hand. Akira took it, and she realized that his palms were sweating. He guided her down the hallway and around the twists and turns of this seemingly endless house.

She'd only ever seen it from her window: the gardens. Now that she was standing behind a thin, sliding screen door, it struck her that she'd never seen it at eye level. She knew at once that the door before her led outside. Her mouth opened involuntarily. She could smell the air. It brushed across her skin like a gentle caress, so tender it nearly made her weep.

"I can't," she whispered. "This . . . this is the most important rule. I'm not allowed to leave. Someone will see me."

"Who will see you, Noriko?" Akira asked in earnest. "There isn't another house for miles. This entire property is gated off."

"But Grandmother says . . ."

"She's given her permission. All she asks is that I go with you, that you stay away from her roses, and not to go out when the sun is highest in the sky, for the sake of your complexion."

Somehow, Nori strongly doubted that her grandmother had used such docile language.

"I can't," she whispered again, digging her nails into her palms in the vain hope that it would somehow anchor her. Her head was beginning to spin. "I don't . . ."

"I see the way you look outside. It's pathetic. You look like a whipped puppy. And now you're saying you don't want to go?"

Nori bristled. He had no idea, this golden boy, how many nights she'd spent in silent desperation wishing for the open sky. She turned to face him.

"No, I'm saying I *can't* go. She will kill me, Oniichan. Obaa-sama would give you anything in the world, I know she would, but not this. If anyone finds out about me, the gossip will plague you and yours for the next hundred years. We'll never get rid of the stain. That's why I have to stay inside. That's why she bribes the servants with fine things. That's why she has told me countless times that to set one foot outside that door means death."

"And *I* am telling you," Akira growled back, lowering his face so that it was at eye level with her own, "that she needs me more than she needs the titles, or the money, or the estates. More than the servants or the cars or this archaic sense of pristine honor she holds on to. She needs me. She's far too old to have any more children, and Mother is likely dead in a ditch somewhere. She needs me here, she needs me alive, and she needs me to get a child on some dainty little flower of a noble girl from the capital. What she doesn't need is you. If she wanted you dead, *you'd be dead already*, you stupid girl."

Akira gripped her shoulders then, with such force that she wanted to cry out but could not. She was powerless to do anything but look at him with her mouth agape and quivering.

He wasn't just looking into her eyes anymore; he was looking into the core of her being. And he knew, and she knew, that he could see clear as day all the things that were missing there. She tried to protest but all she could manage was a whimper. It was ignored.

"Do you know what my father would have done if you'd been born under his roof? He would have pulled you out of our mother himself, taken you behind the shed, and bashed your skull against the rocks until it was as soft as a boiled egg. Or, if he were feeling kind, he'd have had you smothered. But you would not be alive and you would not be wearing silks, eating lemon cakes, and being catered to every second of the day. My father's family is not so great as this one, but they believe in the old ways. If there was ever a bastard child born, believe me, none of them lived long enough to be remembered. You have just turned eleven. Eleven years, you have lived, breathed, eaten, slept, and pissed in porcelain toilets. For God's sake, Nori, you were going to die from fever and they *saved your life*. So yes, they hate you. I don't deny it. They hate you. But that is absolutely no reason you can't go outside."

And with that, he released her. She stumbled backwards and instinctively placed a hand on her arm to finger the bruises that would be sure to form shortly.

Whatever had come over Akira, it was gone now. His expression was calm, almost bored. He was losing interest. But not just in this conversation: in her.

Panic surged through her and spurred her previously petrified feet to move. She closed the distance between herself and the door and pressed her palms against the thin paper and wood that separated her from the outside world.

She could hear birds chirping. It was late August, melding slowly into September. The days were not so hot as they were before, but Nori could feel pleasant warmth spreading through her fingertips. She had always thought that her mother would come back for her and lead her outside, with a smile and a "Let's go home." That had been her hope, her conviction, her constant prayer.

And she knew now that it wasn't going to happen. It wasn't that she didn't want to go outside, because she did. She really, really did. But to take this step, alone, was to acknowledge that the thing she had been so certain of was just a pipe dream. And it was one thing to know it. But to act on it, well . . .

She shut her eyes tight and pushed against the door. It slid to the side with ease, and all at once, the sunshine flooded in.

When she opened her eyes, it took them a long moment to adjust. She stumbled out onto the patio blind. The bricks were scalding and she let out a squeal of pain. Akira's hands pressed against her lower back and pushed her forward, though his touch was gentler than before.

Her feet weren't touching stone anymore. They were touching something cool and prickly, but soft. Nori's eyesight was starting to return, but her vision was still full of white and purple spots.

She dropped to her knees and spread out her hands, letting the blades of grass slide through the gaps between her fingers.

Oh.

She had forgotten the smell of grass.

AKIKO

I watch them from the doorway, half hidden in shadow. The boy has noticed me, I know he has, but he does not seem concerned by my presence. He sits on the stone bench beneath the old peach tree and observes, as I do. He watches her with absolute calm, his smooth, pretty face betraying nothing of what he might be thinking. He looks like a maiden posing for an oil painting.

She lay on her back in the grass with her dark curls billowed out beneath her, wide-eyed and unblinking, for at least an hour.

The sky is a pristine blue today, as clear and endless as the ocean. The clouds are thick, like spun cream, and float along like wayward ships in the breeze. I can understand her fascination with it. She has not seen the sky now in nearly three years. And to a child, it must seem like a lifetime longer than that. She is captivated.

But now it seems as if she cannot be held still. She is running from one place to the next, covering herself in dirt as she goes. Her white nightgown is not so white anymore, and I am in for a long night of scrubbing the stains out of it. She spent several minutes attempting to pet the fish in the pond and squealing in delight when her fingers touched their colorful scales, covering herself in water and bits of algae. That gown will never come clean and I will be the one who has to explain why she needs a new one. Wonderful. Oh, wait . . . she has moved. Where has she gone now?

Before I can form words to stop her, she is at the birch tree, attempting to climb it. What on earth has come over this child? That tree is a hundred feet high, and she is likely to break her neck.

Her brother gets to her before I can. He moves across the yard like a shot and grabs one of her ankles, yanking her down in one succinct motion. Though he attempts to catch her, he topples underneath her weight and they both fall to the ground in a heap.

Before he can get up, she is off again, this time headed for the peach tree.

"I want one," she hollers to no one in particular. *"Momo ga hoshi!"*

The boy is looking at her like he is starting to regret his decision to intervene on her behalf. And what a decision it was. Quite frankly, I am in shock that Yuko-sama agreed to it. If

Kohei-sama finds out, that girl will be in for a world of pain she cannot even comprehend.

Even Akira-sama is not safe from that man's rage. Seiko wasn't. Being the heir is no guarantee of safety from him.

But there is a general consensus in this house not to tell Kohei-sama anything that he doesn't need to know—and he is here so rarely that he never has time to notice anything anyway. He prefers the company of important men in Tokyo, and Yuko-sama prefers to have her rule unchallenged here in Kyoto. This is her native city, not his.

Akira-sama calls to his sister to stay clear of the rose garden. She is not paying attention to a word he's saying. She is attempting to pick one and nicks her finger on a thorn. But her joy is undiminished.

For the first time, seeing her run free and wild, I see her as a normal little girl. I am almost moved to tears at the realization that soon, very soon, this girl will be put back in her cage.

The sky begins to darken and I hear the distant rumble of thunder. If Noriko-sama hears it, she is unmoved by it. Akira-sama has taken shelter beneath the patio awning, just a few feet in front of me. He watches her with a look that can only be described as exasperation, but he makes no attempt to call her inside.

The heavens sound one final warning before the rain starts to fall, in thick sheets. *Harenochiame.* Rain after a perfect, clear sky.

The girl stands perfectly still, face upturned and arms stretched out wide as they'll go. Her thin clothing has gone completely see-through. She will catch her death. I can remain silent no longer and I call her name. I don't think she hears me.

She is twirling now, dancing to music that no one else can hear. The water pours down her face and into her open mouth. I cannot hear what she is saying over the roar of the rain, but I see her lips form the same word, over and over again: "*ame.*" *Ame*. Rain.

I look at Akira-sama's face from the corner of my eye. It is passive and blank, per usual. After what seems like an arbitrary amount of time to me, but a very deliberately planned interval to him, he calls her inside.

"Nori."

That is all he says. She drops the fistfuls of grass she had been holding in her tiny hands and makes her way to where her brother is standing.

She looks up at him, and never have I seen such an expression. It is one of pure and utter idolatry. It is too absolute to call it love. Love can be weakened by time or forgotten for the sake of another. Love can disappear, without a cause or an explanation, like a thief crept in and stole it in the night.

But what she wears on her face for him now cannot disappear and cannot die. He responds by patting her absently on the top of her soaking-wet head, like one might pet a puppy.

Poor thing. She has set her heart on something she cannot have.

The two of them run on parallel wavelengths that can never touch.

She, of course, has not realized this. But he has—I know it. He has lorded his genius over us too much for me to pretend that he is too dull to grasp this most obvious truth.

He is either a sadist or as foolish as she is. I cannot think which one would be worse.

Violin lessons were outside now.

They would sit on the bench beneath the peach tree, and the leaves would protect them from the harsh sun. Nori had discovered that her skin burned quite easily.

The scenic surroundings seemed to improve Akira's disposition. There was a little bridge over the pond and rows and rows of flowers, in countless colors that Nori had never seen before. Akira patiently explained to her the names of the trees, the tradition behind the water garden. He told her these trees were a thousand years old in some cases and that she must always honor the land, for her blood was in it and its blood was in her. Akira, who could never be called a spiritual person, seemed to hold a deep respect for anything that could be so constant, even if it was a tree.

Her missed notes and sloppy hand positioning seemed to irritate him less now.

She had gotten a little better. He had not said so, of course, but she knew that she had. As if to contradict her silent thoughts, Akira swatted her lightly on the back of the head. "Watch the trill."

"*Gomen, Oniichan.*"

She played it again.

Akira let out a deep sigh and gave her a withering look. "How is it when I give you a correction, you manage to play it even worse than you did before?"

"I can't play it any faster, Oniichan."

"Don't flatter yourself. You aren't even playing the notes right. Never mind fast. Look at the music."

Nori glanced down at the pieces of paper pinned to the music stand in front of her. Bit by bit, these strange markings were starting to mean something to her.

She saw what he had been talking about. Without waiting for him to give the command, she played it a third time, taking special care to pronounce each note. When she had finished, Akira shot her a rare half smile.

"That's enough," Akira said softly, gingerly removing the violin from her hands, with more care and gentleness than she'd known he was capable of. "We're done for today."

Nori was at once relieved and disappointed. "Can I stay for a minute and listen to you play?"

This was her favorite part of the day. If she stood on the bench, she was just tall enough to scramble into the lower branches of the tree. She could sit there quite comfortably, with her legs curled into her chest, and listen to her brother play. But he only allowed her to do it sometimes.

Akira cocked his head to one side, as if considering her request.

"If you be quiet. But I need to talk to you for a minute, Nori."

She frowned slightly.

"What is it?"

"I start school tomorrow."

Nori felt her stomach drop into her socks. She pulled one of her curls forward and began to chew on it, a new habit that she had developed. Akira found it disgusting and always swatted her hand when he caught her doing it. Her face must have looked as pitiful as she felt because Akira just clucked his tongue at her.

"We talked about this. I'll be gone most of the day, and when

I get home, I'll have homework. So I won't have much time for you. You understand?"

Nori bunched up fistfuls of her dress in her hands and looked down at her lap. "I understand."

"Practice your music."

"*Hai.*"

"If you behave, I may consider taking you to the festival next Sunday afternoon."

Nori looked up, scarcely believing her ears. "Eh? *Hontou ni?*"

He gave a curt nod, color rising to his cheeks. He slid his gaze away from her.

"Yes, really. I have to go into the city to run some errands anyway—don't make that *face*, Nori, gosh."

She immediately corrected her face, though she was not quite sure how it had managed to offend him.

"We should go back inside. It's going to rain. Violins and water don't mix."

She shrugged. "I like rain."

He laughed scornfully. "That's ridiculous. Nobody likes rain. Nobody ever says, 'I wish it weren't so sunny today.'"

She lowered her eyes. "You can't hear sunshine from the attic," she said quietly. "And it's always so quiet. In the summers, especially, with no lessons, and when Akiko-san doesn't come, it's . . . it's empty. Like there's nobody else but you in the whole world. But when it rained, I could always hear it on the roof, and then I remembered that I wasn't, you know . . ."

Alone.

Akira blinked. His face softened and he reached out to tuck a stray curl behind her ear.

"It rains a lot on this island," he told her. "So you'll be quite happy."

Nori smiled. "I know, Oniichan. I know about the rainy season, *tsuyu*, and I know what the poets say."

Akira frowned. "Poets? What are you on about?"

Nori looked away from the scrutiny in his gaze. "They say there's fifty words for rain. One for each and every kind you can imagine."

"Do they?" Akira asked, and he sounded almost amused. "Well . . . perhaps technically. But leave it to the poets to make a fuss over nothing. Rain is just rain."

She looked up to meet his eyes. "I don't think so, Oniichan."

Akira raised a dark eyebrow and considered her for a brief moment. "Well . . . who knows. Maybe you're right. Maybe I'm just too cynical to appreciate it."

Nori dared to contradict him once more. "I don't think that either, Oniichan."

He chucked her under the chin. "You give me too much credit. You always do. Now, off to bed."

"But . . ."

"Go, Nori."

Though she knew that he was growing irritated with her as it was, she could not help herself. Looking at him, sitting there bathed casually in the moonlight, was entirely too much for her heart to bear. She threw her arms around her brother's neck, burying her nose in his dark hair. He smelled like soap and lemons. And the wasabi he'd had for lunch. He always smelled like wasabi.

"*Arigatou*," she whispered, not sure if he could even hear her. "Thank you."

She had dark dreams that night and woke before the dawn, clutching at Agnes. Akiko came up a little while later with a glass of water and a small cookie.

The maid seemed unusually subdued. "Your grandmother is coming to see you in a moment. Hurry and eat."

Nori hopped out of the bed. "*Naze?*"

"I don't know why. Come here, let me dress you."

When her grandmother walked in, Nori started to bow but was waved aside.

"Don't worry," the older woman said absently, crossing her arms over her chest. "This will only take a moment."

She was wearing a dark blue kimono, with a white obi and sleeves down to the floor. Her hair was done up in a bun and dotted with white and blue nosegays. Her lips were painted red, and her gray eyes were lined with the faintest hint of charcoal.

For an older woman, she was still quite pretty.

"There are some people coming to see you today, Noriko," she said, in a surprisingly pleasant tone of voice. "Very important people. I've told them of your talents and they are eager to meet you."

Nori blinked in response. It was all she could do really. She thought, somewhere about now, that hell must be freezing over.

Her grandmother cracked a tiny smile at Nori's obvious confusion.

"I have had new kimonos made for you, as well as new dresses in the modern style. I have also commissioned some fans, shoes, and pieces of jewelry. I've also had some other things made for you that should accommodate your future growth nicely.

Akiko-san will be up shortly to prepare you. And I shall see you in the parlor soon. I have every confidence that you will represent our family well."

Nori watched her grandmother leave as quickly as she had come in stunned silence.

When Akiko arrived a few minutes later, carrying a large cardboard box, Nori was finally able to react.

"Are those for me?"

"Yes, little madam."

She scrambled over to the box, peering inside with a mixture of suspicion and joy. She could not help but let out a little squeal of delight as she began pulling things out.

Everything was lovely, but it was the kimonos that truly took her breath away. There were four of them, each more beautiful than the last. One was a shimmering gray, with a pattern of swirling clouds embroidered all along the fabric and a dark purple obi sash. The next was pale pink silk, with a pattern of butterflies on the train and sleeves. The third was sky blue with white and yellow flowers in a slanting pattern down the skirt, like a cascading waterfall.

But the fourth was her favorite. It was made of a simple cream-colored silk, with silver thread detailing the edges. The sleeves were bell-shaped and touched the floor. The obi was a gentle shade of peach, just like her favorite tree in the garden.

There were also fans and pearls—white, gray, black, and pink—but those hardly interested her either. While there was no doubt that they were beautiful—and very valuable—she was not accustomed to jewelry.

Akiko only allowed her a moment to fuss over her new possessions. The guests would be arriving shortly, and it would not do to be late.

"Who is coming, Akiko-san?" she asked. She did not dare speculate.

The maid looked down at her feet. "I don't know. But mind your manners. And come here, let me fix that hair."

Nori elected to wear the cream kimono, and she told Akiko to put her hair up in a bun like her grandmother's. It was then tied with her most precious white ribbon, which she did not like to wear often for fear it would get dirty. But if people were coming to see her, important people, then what else was she saving it for?

Akiko pulled out a tiny tube of red lipstick and brushed it across Nori's lips. "There you are, little madam."

Nori looked in the mirror. She looked considerably less awful than she normally did. "Are we going now?"

"Yes, my lady."

Akiko held out her hand, and Nori took it, taking comfort in the familiar rapport that had developed between them over the years.

They descended the stairs, and Nori could not help but recall how terrified she'd been at this very moment just a few brief months ago. So much had changed that she could still scarcely believe it.

Just before they rounded the corner, Akiko released her hand. Nori offered up a tiny smile. Akiko's dark eyes filled with something unreadable. For a moment, the maid hesitated, but only for a moment and then she was gone.

Nori saw the woman first. It was hard to miss her: she was absolutely beautiful. She was tall and shapely, with her ample bosom on full display in a kimono that had been modified to be especially revealing. Her face was painted white and her lips red. She looked like a porcelain doll.

It took her a little while longer to notice the man. He was sitting in the corner against the window, calmly sipping at his tea. He was wearing a dark gray three-piece suit and glasses. He was missing most of his hair, and what little he did have left was combed over to one side of his head, like a little cluster of grass on a barren sidewalk.

Her grandmother stood quietly in the opposite corner, face half hidden by her trademark fan.

Not knowing what else to do, Nori dropped into a bow, taking extra care to mind her posture.

The woman let out a chuckle, and Nori was surprised that such a feminine-looking person had such a low, brassy voice.

"You must be Noriko."

Nori straightened up and nodded. The woman was smiling at her, a brazen and unabashed smile that Nori was unaccustomed to. But she could not help but smile back.

"I'm Kiyomi," she said pleasantly. "It's very nice to finally meet you. Come closer, child. Let me look at you."

Nori did as she was told and, in the process, caught a whiff of Kiyomi's perfume. She smelled like cinnamon. Kiyomi looked Nori up and down, from her toes to the crown of her head. "Well, aren't you a pretty little thing. Very . . . exotic. Lovely eyes."

Nori had to suppress the intense urge to fidget. "Thank you very much, madam."

Kiyomi laughed again and ran a long finger with the nail painted bright red underneath Nori's chin. Years of conditioning taught her not to pull away. "How old are you again?"

"Eleven."

"Eleven," Kiyomi mumbled, shooting the man in the corner a sly glance. "Young. Malleable. But they can be troublesome at this age. Crying and whatnot."

"I assure you," her grandmother interjected, with her usual coolness, "she has been very well trained."

The man rose from his chair, and Nori noticed that he was very short, almost as short as she was. He had fat fingers with an abundance of hair growing on the knuckles, and she could not help but hope that he would refrain from touching her.

"She's pretty," he announced, to no one in particular. "Seems well-mannered enough. Halfway educated, I assume? Can she make tea? Read poetry?"

Her grandmother swatted her fan against her wrist, a telltale sign that she was irritated.

"You know very well that I would have nothing less, Syusuke. Are you interested, or are you going to continue to waste my time?"

Nori's breath caught in her throat. But the man did not seem bothered by her grandmother's behavior.

"Now, now, Yuko," he huffed, waving one of his fat little hands in the air. "No need to get snippy. She'll do nicely for my purposes. She should prove to be quite lucrative. A bit on the skinny side, though."

"She will bloom in time," Kiyomi interjected. "And I'll look after her until then."

She turned to Nori and flashed an infectious grin. It was spellbinding. "Are you truly obedient, Noriko?"

"Yes," she chirped, flushing with pride. Her years of training left her confident in this one thing. "Yes, I am."

"Yuko," the man puffed, pulling a handkerchief out of his pocket and wiping his sweaty face with it. "We've known each other a long time. And you've never agreed to deal with me until now. Your father was the proudest man I ever met, and he thought I was no better than the stuff he used to wipe his ass with. Why the step down from your pedestal?"

Her grandmother's face remained impassive. She seemed immune to this man's crudeness or, if not immune, very used to it.

"If you're quite finished. I want this settled as soon as possible."

"I'm leaving town tonight. Hurry up if you're going to do it."

Her grandmother's gray-black eyes flashed. "I realize that you're used to dealing with the small folk. But don't forget whose house you are in, Syusuke."

"If it's money—"

"I don't argue over money," her grandmother said briskly, snapping her fan shut. "It's vulgar. I'll resolve this with you later. But right now I want you both to leave the room." She turned her gaze to Nori. "I would speak with my granddaughter alone."

The man bowed low, and the woman shrugged as if it did not matter to her either way. When they had gone, her grandmother turned back to her. There was a long moment of silence that made Nori squirm.

"You did well, Noriko."

Nori blinked. Somehow, after waiting all these years for these simple words, they did not touch her now. "Thank you, Grandmother."

This earned her a wry smile. "What is it that you want, Noriko?"

What kind of question was this? She folded her hands together. "I don't want anything."

Her grandmother raised an eyebrow. "Everyone wants something. I've watched you for years, but I've never been able to figure out what you want. I'm not talking about what you wish for. I'm not talking about foolish whims. I'm asking you what your purpose is. What you're willing to devote your life to, what you are willing to die for."

Nori pinched the skin on the inside of her palm. This was a question that she had no answer for. She racked her brains but could come up with nothing but the truth. "I didn't think I was allowed to have one."

Her grandmother turned away from her and walked over to the desk, the train of her kimono sweeping behind her. She picked up a leather-bound book that looked to be very old.

"My purpose is clear," she said, her voice firm, her shoulders straight and proud. "It has always been clear. I was born with it. I will die with it. My purpose, my life's blood, is this family."

She beckoned Nori to come forward. Her gaze was bright with determination. "Do you know what this book is?"

Nori shook her head.

Her grandmother held the book up high. "This is the family tome. The name of every Kamiza for a thousand years is written in this book. My name, your mother's name. Akira-san's too. One day he will be called to take my place. It is my duty, my absolute duty, to see it so before I leave this world. Do you understand that, child?"

"Yes."

Their eyes met, and despite Nori's skepticism, there was

something incredibly moving about her grandmother's rapt conviction.

"Will you play your part, Noriko?"

Nori blinked. Something in her chest was squeezing and she could not speak.

Her grandmother nodded. "I have been wrong. I have been very wrong to hide you away in shame. You are your mother's daughter. You are my blood. And you too have a part to play. Your name will be written in this book. You will be remembered."

Something was roaring in her ears. "I will?"

"You will. But you must do your duty. When I die, which cannot be so far off now, your brother will take on my responsibilities. It is a heavy burden to bear." The old woman shook her head as if in wonderment that she had not collapsed beneath it. "Tell me something, girl."

Nori was tempted to say "Anything": anything for her name to be in that book, beside her brother's. "Yes?"

"What is most important to you in the world?"

This, at least, was a question she could answer. A flush crawled up her cheeks.

Her grandmother gave her a knowing smile. "It's Akira-san, isn't it?"

Her eyes welled with tears, and she ducked her head and wiped them away. "Yes."

"He will need your help. He needs it now, in fact. He needs you to do your duty so that he can do his. Only you can do it, Nori. Only you can protect him."

Her heart was thudding so hard she thought it was going to explode out of her chest. "I will. I would do anything. I won't fail you, Obaasama. I will be good."

"I'm so very glad to hear that, child," her grandmother whispered. She looked genuinely moved. "I truly am. As women, we do what we can. We do what we must."

She shot a glance at the door but quickly looked back at Nori again.

"We do things that we never thought we were capable of in order to protect what we love."

Nori was nodding now, trying to hold back the joyful tears. "I promise. I do promise."

The old woman smiled one last time before turning her back; as she turned, Nori caught sight of her clutching that old leather book to her heart.

The doors opened. The short, fat man stuck his head in. He was sweating even though the house was comfortably cool.

"Well?"

Her grandmother did not turn around. "Take her."

Nori looked from one to the other, her brow knitted in a frown even as her lips were still frozen in their smile.

He stomped into the room, and as he came near her, she caught the stench of tobacco. She backed away.

"Grandmother?" she whispered. She wanted to speak louder, but she couldn't. Her voice was all gone. "Grandmother?"

But her grandmother was not looking at her. Her head didn't even move to acknowledge that she had heard Nori speak.

Then there were arms around her waist and she was being dragged. The hem of her kimono caught under her scampering feet, and she pitched forward, clawing at nothing.

"Obaasama!" she shrieked, her voice coming back to her in a terrible rush. "I don't understand! Please! I don't understand!"

But the figure before her was frozen, a goddess of ice, immune to Nori's plea.

"Obaasama! Please!"

"Come on, girl! Mind me now!" the man huffed at her, panting with the effort of pulling her towards the open doors.

"Oniichan!" Nori cried, though she knew her brother was far away at school and could not hear her. "Akira!"

"He's gone," the man said simply.

There was a sharp pain at the back of her neck and then there was nothing.

PART II

CHAPTER SEVEN

EXILE

Fall 1951

AKIKO

The shout splits the air like a clap of thunder. "Where is she?"

My lady meets her grandson's eyes without flinching. "Akira-san, calm yourself."

I am cowering by the door of the study, a tea tray clattering in my hands. I have walked into a storm.

"Where?" he booms, and I find that I am surprised at his wrath.

Yuko-sama crosses her arms. "You're a highly intelligent boy, Akira-san. Surely you understand that this was necessary."

The veins in Akira-sama's forehead are bulging out, and his eyes are stormy. "What have you done with Nori?"

"She is no longer your concern. If you lack for company, I will find you some proper acquaintances."

Akira-sama is clearly stunned at her cool demeanor. "What is wrong with you?"

"The girl is fine," Lady Yuko says absently. "I assure you she won't be harmed."

"You're lying," he spits at her.

She sighs. "Dearest grandson, this conversation is at an end. It's time now to look to the future." She smiles broadly. "And what a bright future it will be."

He starts forward, and for half a heartbeat I think that he is going to strike her. I think she thinks so too. But then he shakes his head and turns on his heel to walk away, realizing that there is nothing more to be gained from this. Not today, at least. Maybe not ever.

I leave the tray on the table and scramble into the hallway after him.

He gives me a weary look. "Do you know where she is?"

I start to say no, but I choke on it. I really don't know where the little madam is. But I know I heard her scream. I know she is not safe. And I said nothing and let her go.

As if those clear eyes can see straight into the heart of my shame, Akira-sama tosses a last remark at me before he strides away. He sounds almost bewildered. "She trusted you."

I turn my gaze to the floor I polished just this morning. The light catches it, and it glints like thirty pieces of silver.

KIYOMI

There are fifty-two girls in the *hanamachi* right now, fifty-three including our newest addition.

And I oversee all of them. This may not sound like much,

but I was born on a straw floor in 1921, the youngest of four and the only girl. My father was a rice farmer, and my mother only had one good arm, so she could never get any work, even in the rich people's houses. We lived on a pathetic patch of land that was always wet and gray. That's all I really remember. Well, that and the hunger. There was never any food. The crop failed year after year, and my big brothers and I withered up too. When I was nine, my ribs were poking through my skin and you could trace my collarbone like a stencil.

I was so thin that the whorehouse my father sold me to almost didn't take me.

I glance at the pale girl kneeling in front of me in the darkened room, and I find myself wishing, not for the first time, that my sympathy had not all dried up many years ago.

At least she's not crying. Most of the girls who come to me are less than nothing, country girls with families who need meat more than another useless daughter. Some come willingly, knowing that they will have food in their bellies and a bed to sleep in, even if it is one they will have to share. Some are ugly and some are pretty. But all of them cry.

Not Noriko. Her back is straight, with her hands folded in her lap and her peculiar eyes fixed straight ahead. Even if she is coming apart at the seams, she will not show it to me. She has been raised in a hard school. Yuko, that old bitch, was telling the truth about that.

"Do you know why you are here?" I ask, as gently as I can. It's not my job to intimidate the girls. I was them once. They come to me with their grievances, and I do what I can, though it is next to nothing.

She doesn't say anything. Her little mouth is trembling. She has nice lips—already full though she is a girl of eleven, pleasantly soft—but there is a dimple in her chin. Perhaps some will find it endearing. For what we paid for her, she had better end up pretty. Her mother was a famous beauty. And even though nobody knows who her father is or what he looks like, save for his dark skin, I can't imagine Seiko Kamiza flinging her certain future away for anything remotely ordinary.

I tap my foot. "Noriko-chan, I intend to be kind to you. But you must do as you are told or it will go badly for you. You belong to us now."

I see something then, a hint of defiance, flash across her frightened face. She bunches her small hands into fists. "I don't."

"You do," I say patiently. This is not uncommon. It's a hard reality for any girl to realize that her family has traded her like cattle. Especially hard for a daughter of a noble house, even if she is nothing but a bastard. "Your grandmother sold you to us. You are ours to do with as we like."

Her eyes grow wet. "She wouldn't do that. This is a test."

I roll my eyes at her. She's an idiot, this girl. "No. She has sold you to us. She has relieved herself of an unwanted burden and added to her considerable fortune."

She looks up at me. "I'm her granddaughter," she says stoutly, though I know her courage has already failed her because I can see her hands shaking. "She said so herself. I am her flesh and blood."

"But she never wanted you," I say, and I make sure to put ice in my voice. "She never asked for you. She kept you locked away and now she has sold you to us. You will live here in the *okiya* with me and the other girls. And you will obey."

I can see her deflating, folding in on herself like a paper doll. "No."

"Your mother passed you off," I continue, and I catch the swift pang of agony that crosses her face. "Your grandmother has passed you off. They couldn't bear the shame of you. But here, we have no grand pretensions. We have no aspirations to be anything but accommodating to our patrons. We ask that you be clean, that you be pretty, that you be obedient and smiling. You can do that, can't you, sweet girl?"

I see the cogs turning in her head as she grasps at a defense. She won't find one.

"What are you going to do to me?" she whispers.

I show her a ready, charming smile. "Nothing. Not for many years yet. You're special, Noriko-chan. You won't be given cheaply. Your virtue is to be preserved and given only to one gentleman who is worthy of it." What I mean is, one who is willing to pay the highest price for it. Worthiness, really, has nothing to do with it, but it sounds better this way.

She emits a horrified squeak, and I am beginning to think that she has no idea what kind of business this house deals in. It appears that Yuko did not bother to educate her on the facts of life—or any facts, for that matter.

If I told her that this is sometimes a geisha house, sometimes a whorehouse, but always a house discreetly owned by her outwardly respectable grandfather, she would probably keel over dead and I'd have wasted all my money. I doubt the poor girl knows what the yakuza is or the foothold they've managed to gain since the war ended. I am certain she has no idea that it has anything to do with her. She has never worried her pretty little head about crime syndicates, or black markets, or where her family's money keeps coming from even though the government has turned off the tap.

But she certainly looks worried now. Poor little princess, thrown down in the gutter with the rest of us.

Clutching her stomach, Noriko bends forward so far that her forehead is pressed against the ground.

"Please. Let me go."

I don't know if she's talking to me, but I answer anyway. "There is nowhere for you to go. This is the only place for you now."

She doesn't say anything else. Her knees slide out from under her, and now she is lying on the floor, silent, broken in like a wild horse that is now tame to my will.

"Will you obey now?"

She raises her head just slightly, and I can see that her face is covered with tears. She chokes back a sob and nods at me.

Perhaps she is not so special after all.

There was an old shrine behind the main house, with bright red flowers blooming all around it like scarlet tears. Nori liked to think that they were weeping with her that holiness could exist alongside such bitter sin. She spent as much time as she could kneeling beside it, weaving flower crowns in her lap.

Kiyomi, as it turned out, had fewer rules than her grandmother. Nori was allowed outside, she could wander anywhere in the house except the guest rooms, and she could eat whenever she pleased because Kiyomi wanted her to fatten up. There were no maids here, though. All the girls had daily chores. When Nori asked Kiyomi what her task was, the woman smiled and told her not to concern herself with it. Nori was to spend her days reading poetry, learning the art of tea ceremonies and flower arrangements, and practicing the violin, whether she liked it or not.

"You can play the violin for our guests," Kiyomi explained with a wry smile. "I have to say, there's nobody else here who can play that kind of music. They lack your education."

Nori's sullen face was answer enough. Kiyomi sighed and flipped her long hair over one shoulder.

"You don't have a choice."

This task, at least, was rare. In the six weeks that she had been here, she had only been asked to play a handful of times. Every other Saturday night, twenty-odd men filed into the large hall that Kiyomi called the *hana no heya*: the room of flowers. It had tatami floors, silk cushions, and low tables with places set for tea, a set of sliding doors left open to reveal a blossoming water garden. The fountains made a musical sound as they splashed onto smooth rocks. There were freshly picked flowers on all of the tables, arranged into elaborate patterns to mimic origami. Nori tried to focus on all of this beauty. She tried not to look at the men.

In her mind, they had all been *oni*, ogres with twisted faces and curved talons. They had been horrible-looking, fat, deformed, covered in sores and fur, closer to beasts than men.

But they weren't. All of them were well-dressed, whether in loose summer yukatas or tailored suits, and some of them were even . . . handsome. The other girls, who had been avoiding Nori since the day she'd arrived, were hardly shy with them either. There was no screaming or crying. When Kiyomi clapped her hands, all of them filed in like a pack of peacocks desperate to preen. They all looked to be older than she. They had rouged faces and red lips, dressed up like a ghastly parody of true gei-sha. Though they played games and amused the men with their attempts to sing, Nori had learned what they did when they slipped out of the room holding a man by the hand.

A few of them exchanged coy smiles with some of the guests and went straight to their tables. Kiyomi explained to her at the start of the first evening that the best girls all had regulars. "Megumi got a gold bracelet from hers," she'd whispered into Nori's ear. "And he has promised her another." Nori's blank face had been met with a sour smile. "Of course, this means nothing to you, little princess. But most of us here never expected to know what gold feels like."

Nori stood in the corner, dressed in one of her beautiful new kimonos with her hair all done up and wearing more makeup than she'd ever worn in her life. She kept fidgeting, resisting the urge to wipe it off. She watched as Kiyomi flitted about the room, smiling brightly enough to dull the sun, laughing and chatting with the men like they were all old friends. Sometimes a group of girls would get up and dance to a record or Kiyomi would nod to Nori to play a tune.

The girls danced well. In their brightly colored kimonos they twirled about the room, filling it with giddy laughter. One of the younger girls could stand on one leg and extend the other to-wards the ceiling with a pretty pointed foot. When the dancing ended, the girls would gamble with the men, throwing dice and laughing. Even from her isolated place in the corner of the room, Nori noticed that the girls were always certain to let the men win.

The food was served mid-evening—heaping platters full of fresh-caught fish, sliced raw or served roasted in herbs and spices. There were piping hot soups of all kinds: beef, chicken, shrimp, and strange proteins that Nori had never eaten. And there was sake, lots and lots of sake, always poured by a girl into her gentleman's cup.

The room got louder then. Nori saw an older man with black hair and a gray beard slide his hand down the front of one girl's linen underclothes. She looked away. Akira would be so ashamed to see her in a place like this.

The room swirled, and she had to put a hand against the wall. Thinking of Akira was treacherous. It filled her with such a sense of hateful weakness that she could barely stand.

The evening wore on, pulling at her and making her limbs feel weighed down with sand. She forced herself to stand up straight, remembering her brutal lessons in maintaining a rigid posture at all times. She played until her arm grew sore and her neck grew stiff. Unless it was to look at her fingers, she tried not to open her eyes.

Little by little, the chatter grew quieter as more and more girls left the great hall, the men either leading or trailing behind them like eager bloodhounds. When the moon was at its highest point, everyone had gone. Kiyomi walked over to Nori and told her that she could leave.

"You did well tonight. You always play better than expected."

"*Arigatou.*"

Kiyomi nodded her approval. "You're very talented, you know. It's not really necessary, but it can't hurt. The right kind of man will appreciate it."

Nori resisted the urge to flinch. Anger boiled up in her belly, but she kept her voice sweet. "I'm glad you find it pleasing."

"I do. You're clever too. So I expect you to learn. You'll come to my room twice a week in the mornings, and I'll teach you what you need to know."

Nori wrinkled her nose. "I don't want to know anything you have to teach."

Kiyomi's dark eyes went cold, and she folded her arms over her half-exposed breasts.

"You're going to have to lose that arrogance," she said flatly. "It won't serve you here."

"I shouldn't be here," Nori whispered hotly, cheating her eyes sideways to avoid tearing up. "It's not right."

Kiyomi did not even dignify this with a response. She shrugged a slim shoulder at Nori's pointless lament. "This is the only place for you now. You can accept it with grace, or you can fight against it and destroy yourself in the process. In any case, I expect you to do as I say."

Nori bowed her head and said nothing.

The next morning, Kiyomi summoned Nori to her room.

It was surprisingly messy for a woman who was always so put together. Clothes were scattered on the floor, and at least a dozen cosmetics lay strewn across the vanity. Kiyomi was dressed in a simple red kimono. Her hair was down, her face was freshly scrubbed, and she looked . . . young. Almost inno-cent. Nori had never noticed before, but the woman in front of her had kind eyes.

"So," Kiyomi said, gesturing for Nori to join her at the card table. "How are you adjusting?"

Nori balked at her. "You can't mean that."

"But I do," the woman said, quite matter-of-factly. "Look, I don't expect you to love it here. But there's no reason this should be harder than it needs to be. I take it your room is com-fortable?"

"Yes," Nori said, her suspicion mounting. "It is. Thank you."

"Good."

The door opened, and one of the girls came in carrying a tea tray. She placed it down in front of them, and Kiyomi smiled and patted her hand.

"Thank you, Rinko."

The girl nodded and left as quickly as she'd come.

"Now," Kiyomi said. "Pour the tea, please."

Nori did. She was proud of the fact that her hands didn't shake.

This earned her an approving nod. "You move well. You have a natural grace."

Nori flushed. "I . . . I do?"

Kiyomi laughed. "Not used to compliments, I see. I wasn't either."

Nori fidgeted. "Why . . . why did you ask me to come here? For . . . for tea?"

This didn't seem like much of a lesson, though admittedly she was relieved. She'd been afraid she'd be expected to hear horrid stories or, worse, do . . . *those things*. Like the others.

The madam had clearly read her mind. "No one will touch you," she said simply. "Later, I will teach you some dances and songs. Flower arranging, tea ceremonies, and the like. But for today I just want to talk to you. You must become well versed in the art of conversation."

"I didn't know conversation was an art."

Kiyomi wagged a finger. "For a woman, everything is an art. I'll make sure you learn that soon enough."

Nori caught a glimpse of her reflection in her tea. The weight of all that had happened settled squarely on her shoulders.

She was driven to ill-advised honesty. "I don't think I want to be a woman," she whispered.

Kiyomi gave her a long look. For a moment, she looked as if she too could feel the invisible burden.

"Ah, my dear," she said, with a smile that did not reach her eyes. "Someone has to do it."

Nori did not sleep that night. The night air was sticky hot, though it was well into October. As far as Nori could tell, the heat decided to linger just to annoy her. Her room had no windows, and she rarely ventured outside, except for her required duties, the occasional meal, or to use the bathroom. The other girls all ate together at assigned mealtimes, but not Nori. When she wanted to eat, which was usually only once a day, she would wander down to the kitchen and tell the gruff men with tattooed arms what she wanted. They looked at her like she was a rat that had scurried into the cupboards to steal cheese, but they always gave her what she asked for. She usually ate in her room. It had a door that led directly to the outside area, where, far past the tables arranged for the guests, there was a little grove of trees that offered much-needed shade. Sometimes, if she was feeling up to it, she would eat out there or sit in the grass and knit. No one ever went back there, it seemed, and though it was nothing special to look at, it was a place she could feel slightly less caged.

The heat became too much. She threw off her nightgown and wrapped herself in nothing but a silk robe—one of her grandmother's parting gifts to her. The expensive fabric was cool against her skin. Not for the first time, she wondered why so much time and money had been put into her. Surely her grandmother could have just had her killed and been done with it. The only thing Nori could think of was that death was too quick. She had to be punished for the sins of her mother and father, for the sins of countrymen she had never known, for the sins of all the unwanted girls who had gone before her. Certainly, that was a great many people and it would take more than one lifetime to atone.

She put her hair on top of her head, winding her long plait and pinning it with three sturdy pins. It was nice to feel the air on her neck. She opened the sliding door that led to the patio and headed for the spot beneath the trees.

It was no cooler, but it was somehow still comforting. The quiet helped to numb her further. Nori had realized soon after her arrival here that that was the only way to survive. She pulled her knees up to her chest and let the grass slide between her outstretched fingers. She had neither energy nor faith left to pray, but in her most private moments, she whispered to no one that everything would turn out right.

This night, a voice answered.

"Who're you talking to?" the voice said.

Nori whirled around wildly, her eyes struggling to find the source of the sound. It was not a god or a savior. Rather, it was a chubby girl wearing an ugly pink robe. The girl smiled at her and stuck out her hand, which was covered in ink that didn't look entirely dry. Her smile revealed a large gap between her two front teeth.

"I'm Miyuki," she said. She had a strong country accent, so strong that Nori had to strain to understand her. "I've been watching you play in the great hall. It's real pretty."

Nori blinked. "I'm Noriko."

She reached out and shook the offered hand, which was, as she'd suspected, covered in wet ink.

"Oh, sorry," Miyuki said with a laugh. "I was writing. I don't write so good, though. Always make a mess. I bet you write really nice."

"I don't write much."

The strange girl plopped down beside her, uninvited, and wiped her dirty hands on the grass. "I was writing a letter to my sister."

Nori really looked at her then. Miyuki had tan skin and thin lips that looked like they'd been pulled too tight across a wide mouth. Her hair was thick and, at the moment, full of tangles. She was short, shorter even than Nori, and plumper by quite a lot. Despite this plumpness, she had no chest to speak of. All of her fat seemed to have settled in her arms and legs. Still, it was a comfortable kind of plumpness that hinted at warmth. And she had pretty eyes. Nori did not think that she could be much more than fourteen.

"Your sister?"

Miyuki smiled. "Yeah. She's only four, though, so she can't read 'em. But it makes me feel better sending her something. She's back in Osaka. She's in an orphanage right now, but that's just for a little bit, until I pay off my debt. Then I'm gonna go get her."

Nori bit her lip. "So your parents are . . ."

"Dead," said Miyuki without missing a beat. "Ma died right after Nanako—that's my sister—was born, and Dad got injured in the war. He never really recovered and died a few months after Ma did."

Instantly, Nori felt a bolt of guilt shoot through her. Her breath hitched. "I'm so sorry."

Miyuki scrunched up her mouth. "He wasn't the best."

"I'm still sorry."

Miyuki scooted around on the grass so that she was fully facing Nori.

"I heard," she said, lowering her voice, "that your grandmother was a princess. Is it true?"

Nori didn't like where this was going. "Yes, it's true."

The chubby girl beside her brightened. "So does that mean . . . does that mean you're a princess too?"

"No. The Americans stripped all the minor royals of our imperial status, so we're not allowed to use titles anymore. Besides, I'm just a bastard."

Miyuki's disappointment was obvious. "Oh."

"Sorry."

"Oh, no, that's all right," said Miyuki, perking right back up. "Still, what are you doing here?"

"This is where I was sent," Nori answered dryly. "This is where I am."

Miyuki nodded. Everyone in the *hanamachi*, it seemed, understood this much. No more questions needed to be asked.

"I went to the orphanage five years ago. Then I came here and I've been here for two years now. Gonna have to stay here for two more years, then I can go get Nanako."

Nori plucked a strand of grass from the ground. "You chose to come here?"

Miyuki's smile was pained. "Lots of the girls here did. It wasn't no worse than what we had before. Me, I could've stayed in the orphanage all right. They fed us and were nice most of the time. But Nanako's delicate. Always has been since she was an itty-bitty baby. So I decided I had to get her out. Needed money for that."

She took a deep breath as if to prove her conviction. "I'm gonna finish out my contract. I stay here for four years and then I get enough money to go get my sister. I can settle nearby, keep working. Raise her right." She laughed. "I'm gonna make sure she learns to write a lot better than me, that's for sure."

Nori didn't know what to say to this. Besides, this conversation was making her think of Akira. And that was absolutely forbidden. She would never see him again. She told herself this and swallowed down the agony of it. She would never see him again.

She stood up. "I should go to bed now."

Miyuki stood up also. "I didn't mean to bother you none."

Nori forced herself to smile. "You didn't bother me, Miyuki-san."

Miyuki smiled back, revealing her gap. "Oh, just Miyuki is fine. I should get back to trying to write this dumb letter anyway."

She turned and started off, shoving her hands in the pockets of her robe. Nori watched her cross the yard. Something caught in the back of her throat.

"*Ano . . . Miyuki-chan?*"

The other girl turned, her pretty hazel eyes wide-open. "Yes?"

"Did you . . . maybe want help writing that letter?"

Miyuki's grin widened. "*Eh, Hontoni?* You'd really help me?"

"Yes, well. I'm not really tired. So if you wanted help . . ."

Miyuki darted forward and seized Nori's wrists, yanking her forward before she had a chance to blink.

"Noriko-chan! That's great!"

"It's nothing—" But Nori didn't get a chance to finish her sentence.

"Can you write in English too?"

"What? *Sukoshi.* Just a little."

Miyuki barreled towards the house, dragging Nori with her. Nori was already wondering why she had offered to help. She had to get up early in the morning to help Kiyomi arrange flowers, and frankly, she thought it was a waste of time to write a letter to someone who couldn't read.

But she did not try to take back her hand.

Everything about their duties kept them apart, but they found ways to be together. Nori had lessons with Kiyomi in the morning, and in the evening she practiced her violin. During the afternoon, Kiyomi begrudgingly allowed her to take a few hours for reading. Nori was keeping up with her studies as much as she could. She'd been allowed a few books that Kiyomi had found lying around. Though Kiyomi scoffed and smacked her lips and went on at great length about how useless it was, she had provided Nori with some paper and pens. The only thing Kiyomi encouraged was Nori's interest in learning English, citing that it might prove useful one day.

Miyuki's life was very different. She woke up at dawn and went to help in the kitchens. In the afternoon she was sent to scrub the wide, wraparound wooden porch until it shone. Apparently, this was because Kiyomi deemed her too clumsy for dusting or other inside chores. This was an old house, and though it was well-kept, with new flooring and freshly painted walls, it needed constant care. There were private rooms for the guests, but those were not for daily use. The girls slept in the smaller rooms in the west wing of the house, which was not as well maintained. Miyuki shared a room with two others. "It's not so bad," Miyuki was quick to say. "Me and Nanako, at the orphanage, we shared a pallet. I have more space here than I'm used to."

Only at night did the tasks end and the two girls find time to be together, to share their secrets and fears. Nori didn't know if they were truly friends. She didn't know anything about friends outside of what she'd read in books. Besides, they never would have met if not for the misfortunes in their lives, and they had next to nothing in common except for bad luck.

Well . . . maybe it was more than that. And even if it wasn't, maybe that was enough.

They met in Nori's isolated room and huddled on the floor by the light of two candles. "Lights out" was one of the more lax rules, but it was still a rule. Nori always made sure to have a platter of treats ready for Miyuki. The older girl said that she was constantly hungry and Kiyomi never let her get enough to eat.

"She thinks I'm fat." Miyuki laughed, shoving some mochi into her mouth. "Of course, she's right. Ma always did say she didn't know how I managed to be so fat with so little food around."

Nori nodded. As usual, Miyuki was doing most of the talking. Neither of them seemed to mind it that way. She took a sip of her tea and then kept the cup between her hands, letting it warm her through. Some needlework lay forgotten at her side.

Miyuki scrunched up her nose. "Maybe I shouldn't eat so much. Get better clients. Richer. Get outta here faster."

Nori tried to be supportive, though talking about the real business that went on there still made her gut churn. "I'm sure eventually—"

"I'm not like you, Nori," Miyuki burst out suddenly, wiping her mouth with the back of her hand.

"What?"

"I'm not pretty." It was not a plea for sympathy or a question. It was just a fact.

Nori sighed and put her tea down. "I'm no expert on prettiness."

"But you're still pretty. And you're smart. You've been helping me with my writing and my reading, even though I'm not any good at it. You can read poetry; you can read English."

Nori crossed her arms. "I had lots of free time in the attic. I had nothing to do but read. And my English is dreadful. It's just . . . I like to try. And Akira-san . . . he was really brilliant, you know, and I wanted him to be . . ."

Proud.

"He sounds wonderful," Miyuki mused, propping her chin up on her hands.

He was.

"You can fix your reading," Nori said, changing the subject as she always did when it went this way. She found herself talking about Akira more than she should with Miyuki, but it was too painful. Her survival hinged on her ability to forget. "But you can't help that Atsuko and Mina have been the only thing anyone's interested in this month. There are not enough new clients, even with the economy doing so well, with our prices being what they are, and the regulars have had their favorites for years in some cases."

Miyuki grinned. "How do you know all this? Kiyomi-san doesn't hardly let you say 'boo' to the rest of us. You're always by yourself."

"Kiyomi mentions things during our lessons," she responded flatly. "She slips up, I think, and talks to me sometimes like we're . . ." She couldn't say "friends." She knew they weren't friends.

Miyuki looked around the well-appointed bedroom. Her eyes settled on a rope of pearls hastily thrown onto the vanity. "That's lucky."

Nori shut her eyes to quell her frustration. There was no point in getting mad at someone who had it far worse than she did. When she spoke, she made sure her voice was level. "I am a pig being fattened for slaughter, nothing more. My rarity, my foreignness, my cultivated isolation is what they will use to sell me like so much—" She broke off and did not finish.

Miyuki squirmed. "I didn't mean to upset you."

"You didn't," Nori assured her. "You didn't. I can't complain to you."

Miyuki showed that gap-toothed grin of hers. "It's okay. I wasn't getting anything out of it before. There were boys, but they never did what they promised me. At least it's better this way. I can get something out of it, for me and for Nanako." Suddenly her bright face crumpled. "You know, I can't think what else anyone would want me for. And I wouldn't mind doing this, but . . ." She faded off. She didn't want her sister exposed to this life, and Nori couldn't blame her.

Nori racked her brain for something supportive to say. This was not her area. "People would want you for something else. You learn fast. And I bet you're wonderful with children. You could be a teacher or . . ." She thought of Akiko briefly before shoving the memory back down. "There's lots of things you could do. I believe that."

Miyuki smiled sadly. "You *are* special, Nori. And not in the way they mean. I can tell, in a different kind of world, you could've been just about anything. But I'm not like that. I don't have much about me that's special. Looking after Nanako is just about the only thing I ever see myself doing right, and right now I can't even do that."

Nori reached forward and took Miyuki's hands in her own. Unlike her own, they were covered in calluses. "You'll get her back," Nori said, as if she had any power to make this happen. Nothing had given her any evidence that this was true either, but she found herself saying it. "You will. And that's special enough. Loving someone . . . that much . . ." Akira's wry smirk and stormy gray eyes appeared before her. She had to stop. Breathe. Start again.

"When you have that, you don't need anything else."

Miyuki blinked back tears. "I wish I could help you."

Nori smiled, though there were tears in her own eyes now. "It's okay."

They were both crying now.

"No, it's not," Miyuki whispered, finally admitting what they both knew but never acknowledged. She was not smiling anymore. She was making no attempts to qualify her pain.

Nori nodded. "I know."

CHAPTER EIGHT

TREE SONG

September 1953

KIYOMI

As usual, she is late. I take a moment to adjust myself in the mirror. The shadows under my eyes tell me that I am overworked, which is nothing new. The amount of concealer that I have to dab on to cover them up tells me that I'm losing my looks, and my resigned smile tells me that I'm getting old. I am thirty-two this year, older than I thought I would live to see. I pull down the front of my kimono a little. Nobody will notice the bags now. I glance at the door, but there is still no sign of my most troublesome asset. I go into the hallway and snap my fingers at her friend, Miyuki, who is chatting with an older girl. It's not warm inside, but Miyuki's face is glistening with sweat. I have told the kitchen to stop giving her treats, but they swear they aren't. At sixteen, she has not blossomed as I hoped she would. She is the least asked for of all my girls. Clearly, a poor investment for me, but there is no returning her now.

She turns to me and flushes. "Kiyomi-san?"

I cross my arms and look at her; we've been through this enough times for her to know what I want. She points outside. "She's out there."

I feel a great sigh leave my body, and the two girls hurry out of my way as I move past them and out onto the patio. It's high noon and the sun is blazing down. I cross the yard in swift strides, making my way to the pleasure grove that I worked so hard to make beautiful for the guests who come here to get away from their busy city lives, to spend a weekend in the countryside. It doesn't take me long to spot her, kneeling beside the little man-made pond, throwing bits of bread at the ducks.

She isn't even wearing a hat. "Ojosama," I snap, "how many times have I told you? Are you determined to ruin your complexion?"

She doesn't so much as look back at me. She breaks off the last chunk of bread she is holding and flings it towards the smallest duck in the pond. Only when she has watched him eat it before his brothers and sisters come charging forward to take it from him does she turn around.

"*Gomenasai*," she apologizes flatly, and it is wholly insincere. She stands up and brushes the grass off her pale pink dress.

I just give her a tired look. At thirteen, Noriko Kamiza is strikingly attractive, albeit not in a conventional way. She hasn't grown an inch—I suppose she will always be tiny—but her curves have filled out and she is shaped like a finely blown glass bottle. She keeps her necklines high, but there's no hiding that her bosom is already as large as mine. She's learned how to straighten her hair, and it falls in a thick, glossy sheen down to the small of her back. Rich amber-brown eyes that look champagne in sunlight, a button nose, and full lips that always seem to have a secret on them make it impossible not to look at her when she walks into a room.

But she's still difficult.

"You're late for your lesson."

"I know how to pour tea, Kiyomi-san. And dance, and arrange flowers, and flutter a paper fan. After two years you get the hang of it."

She has a point, but I don't show it. There's not much I can do with her, though, and I need to keep her busy. Nori is smart. Smart people with free time are dangerous. I point towards the house. "Go inside. Have you forgotten that Tanaki-san is coming to see you tomorrow?"

She tucks a strand of hair behind her ear. "I haven't forgotten. I just don't care."

I clench my fists. "You will be respectful to him," I warn, though he is a vile little lecher and I don't like him any more than she does. "He hasn't seen you since—"

"Since he dragged me out of my house," she finishes for me. She looks sleepy and bored. "I'll put on my show for him, Kiyomi-san. Don't worry. I won't shame you."

I relax a little. I've been working for Syusuke Tanaki for six years. He is, for lack of a more elegant term, a slaver. He deals in women, mostly, but he is not above selling poor little boys to sick old men. He works for Noriko's grandfather, who is the shadow king of a criminal empire that is only getting stronger. Tanaki spends his days acquiring girls—by bribing them, bribing their families, or just taking them as he finds them. Under the guise of running a travel agency, he ships them all over the world. The ones he doesn't, he sends to me. I like to think these are the lucky ones, and I try to make their lives as pleasant as possible. I don't expect anyone will ever call me a saint. But I have been on the receiving end; I have had a man's boot pressed to my cheek. I don't hit my girls, and I don't allow anyone under thirteen to touch a man. I don't deal in nine-year-olds, unlike the men who dealt with me.

Nori comes up to me and squeezes my hand. "I won't give him cause to hurt you, or me, or any of the other girls. I know what I have to do."

I am shocked by her perception. I have never told her I feared this. She smiles up at me with the smile I taught her, but her eyes are ever honest. She's afraid.

"Will he visit one of the girls?" she whispers carefully.

I don't bother lying. Of course she's heard the gossip. I have dealt with men like him all my life, men whose pleasure comes in forms that most women would never even speak of. Those who don't mind hurting us or, worse, enjoy it.

I hesitate before speaking. "I won't give him Miyuki."

She nods and goes into the house.

The next morning I tell Miyuki to stay out of sight for the rest of the day and assign her to help in the kitchen, which I know will only make her fatter, but it cannot be helped. I need Nori's best today, and I know I will have a better chance of getting it if she is not worried about her friend.

Once I am dressed and ready, I go to Noriko's room to make sure she looks presentable. She is wearing an elaborate gold kimono I got her last year, with red dragons embroidered all over it. Her hair is up in a bun. She looks quite pretty.

"Put some makeup on," I urge, though there isn't any real need for it; her honey-caramel skin is smooth as a pearl. "At least some lipstick."

She sighs. "I hate lipstick. It tastes awful."

"It's not for eating," I say crossly. "And it makes you look older."

She crosses to her vanity and does as I say, pulling out her lone tube of lipstick and brushing it over her lips. "It doesn't make a difference," she grumbles. "I still look horrible."

I sigh because she really believes this. Her abandonment has scarred her, her grandmother has brainwashed her, and she will always see something in the mirror that is not there.

"Hurry up. He doesn't like to wait."

She looks at me with blank eyes. "Has my grandmother ordered this?"

I stiffen. "Of course not, she has quite forgotten about you. This is to assess your progress."

"I have poured tea, I have arranged flowers, I have danced and played the violin," she goes down the list. "I have quite mastered the art of being useless wallpaper."

I cannot help but smirk at her sharp cynicism. "But you know nothing about men."

She shrugs. "I don't need to know anything about men. I just need to know how to listen."

She is wrong about this, but I don't tell her. "Come on."

She follows me down the hall and into the study, where Tanaki is already waiting for us. He is seated in a high-backed leather chair with Kaori, one of the new girls, perched uncomfortably on his lap. She's no innocent, I got her from a different brothel, but she's a pretty thing, and it turns my stomach to see his greasy hands on her.

"Kaori," I say sharply, "go get us something to drink."

She looks at me gratefully and jumps up, hurrying out the door. I doubt she'll be returning and I don't blame her.

Tanaki raises an eyebrow but does not reproach me. Nori stands a few inches behind me, hands clasped and head bowed.

"It's good to see you, Kiyomi," Tanaki says gruffly, standing up and crossing to the front of the desk. His eyes fall on my breasts, as they always do.

I force myself to smile. "It's lovely to see you, as always, Tanaki-san. I take it you had a pleasant journey?"

He snorts. "I swear the girls get uglier every year."

"They do seem to."

He laughs and mops at his sweaty face. "It's always a relief to come here and see some pretty ones." Finally, his eyes fall on Nori. I see his wet lips part.

"This is the Kamiza girl?"

I step back so he can see her better. "Yes. This is Noriko."

Tanaki comes towards her, but only I am close enough to see the anger snap alive in her downcast gaze.

"Not a word," I whisper as he nears us. "Not one word, Nori."

Tanaki takes Nori's chin in a viselike grip and forces her head up. She does not flinch. His eyes roam over her face and then up and down her body. He reaches a hand around and clenches her buttocks. I draw in a breath that he should be so brazen, but Nori doesn't react. Not even her eyelashes move.

Tanaki steps back and laughs. "Holy shit, Kiyomi. You are a miracle worker, aren't you?"

I smile, unable to hide my pleasure at his praise. "I do what I can. But she comes from good stock."

He looks at her again and speaks directly to her. "Your grandmother is a mean old bitch, but she was a beauty in her day—your mother too. I met her a few times, when she was about your age. Though she was petite. You—" He breaks off to laugh. "You've got some meat to you, girl. You'll make some man very happy, despite your skin."

I stare at the back of her head and hope she can feel it. She has to say something. He will not be satisfied with his taunting until she speaks.

She meets his gaze for a fraction of a second, and her eyes are as cold and blank as a doll's. "Thank you," she says softly. Then she looks away.

Tanaki seems satisfied. He rubs his hands together, and I know that in his head, he is already counting all the money he will make off of her. He turns to me.

"This is good. This is very good. I've arranged for some prospective buyers to come see her, and they won't be disappointed."

I do a double take, certain that I misheard him. I see Nori turn the color of ash.

I know that I am flushing with anger. "What? I haven't heard anything about this. I was not consulted."

He tries and fails to look apologetic. "I know, I know. But there wasn't time. I got a call last week, a friend of mine looking for a girl to take on his travels. He specified she must be younger than sixteen and pretty. Now, of course, to make things fair, I have to let everyone have a bite at the apple." He laughs. "End of next month, they'll all come here for a private viewing. I expect you'll have her ready?"

I just gawp at him for a moment before I can speak. "I thought we were all in agreement that she was to remain under my care—that is, under my supervision—until she is sixteen. She's just thirteen. It's not time yet. I'm afraid I can't approve this, Tanaki-san."

It was Yuko's express command that Nori not be touched until sixteen. But Tanaki doesn't care about that. If he has been offered a good price for her, he will take it.

I glance at Nori, who is shaking like a leaf. Her little legs look like they are about to give out.

Tanaki clears his throat. "My dear Kiyomi, the matter has already been decided. The gentleman will be here in one month's time. I believe he does some business in England, so you must be making sure she is learning English. Of course, you'll get your cut of the profits." He looks at his pocket watch. "It's nearly noon. I'm hungry. Have the girls bring me some food. And that girl from before . . . make sure she comes too."

Without waiting for my reply, he moves past me and goes out. Nori and I exchange a horrified glance.

Her eyes say, *Can you save me?*

I look away. And that tells her no. No, I can't.

We have a sulky few days. Whenever I go looking for her, she is elsewhere. I do try to speak to her in the little English that I know, but she acts like she doesn't understand.

I don't push the matter. I can't blame her for being upset. I'm upset. I had thought to keep her until she was sixteen, at the very least; I had thought to teach her more about men . . . about life. She is nowhere close to ready to leave me. And besides that, I quite enjoy her. She is educated, unlike most of the girls I have seen pass through here over the years. I can talk with her. Sometimes after her lessons she will linger and we'll have a cup of tea and she'll just tell me things she's learned from her books. It's not the worst way to pass an afternoon.

I make it a point not to get attached to my girls, especially to the ones whose ultimate destiny it is to be sold away from this place. But Nori is unconventional. So perhaps my feelings towards her have become unconventional too.

I find that I have trouble sleeping, as if my plush mattress is suddenly a bed of stone. I am too hot in the night, and I toss and turn, searching for a relief that won't come. I find that I am short with the men who come through here, brushing off their hands and refusing to stop and chat with them as I usually do. I avoid people as much as possible, and the strain of smiling, when I can avoid them no longer, weighs on me as it has not done in years. As the month ticks away and the date of Nori's sale approaches, I find that it only grows worse.

I know what this pain is. It is the resurgence of my conscience after long years of lying dormant, like a bitter seed trying to sprout through concrete. And it is agony.

I go into Nori's room a little past midnight when I can muster up the gall. I find her sitting on the floor, her basket of yarn beside her. She is knitting something, her fingers moving with practiced ease. I see that she is making a scarf for the coming winter months. She doesn't look up as I enter, but she doesn't seem surprised when I speak.

"I've come to check on you," I say.

She nods. "I figured as much. Will you sit?"

I shouldn't, but I do, pulling out the stool in front of her vanity and lowering myself into it. I feel weary. I was never meant to live this long.

"Don't you have enough scarves?" I ask.

She smiles a tiny smile. "It's not for me. It's for my brother."

I look at her as if she's gone mad. She knows better than this. In all her time here, I have never heard her mention him. I thought she had given him up. "Why on earth would you do a thing like that?"

"Because I'll be dead before very long," she says quietly. Her hands do not stop moving. "And I wanted to leave him something. This is all I could think of."

I go cold. "You're not going to die. Why would you die?"

For the first time, she looks at me. She looks eerily calm. "I won't be a slave, Kiyomi."

I hadn't known she would go this far. I never realized she had this kind of resolve. "Don't be ridiculous. Life is always better than death."

She laughs, but it is humorless. "You don't believe that."

I am grasping for words. "You don't know that he'll be a monster. He could be kind. He could even be handsome."

Nori stops her knitting. "Kiyomi," she says, very quietly, "there's no need to lie."

I just stare at her. I recognize the dead look in her eyes.

Bile rises in my throat.

She bends her head so that her eyes are shadowed by the veil of her hair. "I was hoping you could get the scarf to him. After I'm gone from here."

I look at her blankly. "You know that I cannot."

She nods. She expected this. "I'll leave it here, then. If you ever change your mind."

"I won't be changing it."

She pushes her hair back. A tear slides down her cheek, the first tear I have seen from her in two years. Something inside me rips in two.

"Yes. I know."

I wait outside the room where Tanaki is selling Noriko, commanding an auction for her virtue, tantalizing men old enough to be her father with the prospect of keeping such a prize at their side for as long as they desire. And when they don't desire her anymore? This is not spoken of. We aren't concerned with this part.

I can't watch. For the first time in a lifetime, I can't bring myself to watch. But I can hear. He is hardly quiet.

"This rare young blossom . . . just thirteen, so young, so fresh! She is untouched . . . of a fine form, gentlemen, a fine form . . . Who will be the first . . . Ah, thank you, Tono-sama, a very generous offer . . . Do we have another? Mutai-sama, not your type? That's all right, that's all right, we have other girls arriving within the month . . . Perhaps they'll be more to your taste. But back to the matter at hand . . . Don't be shy, gentlemen, don't be shy."

I know a few of the men inside the room. Some are worse than others. There's one, a young doctor with a terrible stutter and a clubfoot, who is not so awful. He always calls me Kiyomi-san, and he says "please" whenever he asks for anything. He would be kind to her. I don't even think he would bed her—he never touches any of the other girls. All he ever wants is company. He would be content to listen to her read poetry in her calming voice. I hope that for her. I hope so hard that I dig my nails into my palms until they are bright red.

Out of the corner of my eye, I see Miyuki trying and failing to be discreet. I gesture for her to come forward. She does so, and I can see that she is white as a sheet.

"It's happening now, isn't it?" she whispers. Her voice is hoarse. She has been crying.

I nod.

She wrings her hands together. "When will they take her?"

"Within the week. As soon as the payment is complete."

She draws in a breath. "Let me go with her."

I shut my eyes. I am far too tired to deal with this. "No."

"I'd go for free. I don't care."

"What about your sister?"

She deflates. Her big eyes well up with tears. "Please let her stay here. *Please*, Kiyomi-san."

I shake my head. "She is too valuable. I thought . . . I thought we'd have her for some years yet, but . . . it seems not."

Miyuki falls to her knees in front of me. She lays the side of her face against my feet. I look down at her, horrified.

"What the hell are you doing?"

She weeps into my socks. "You can't sell her."

"I have no choice."

"No!" she cries.

I try to wriggle free, but she is holding me like a desperate animal. I grab hold of her shoulders and push, but she is heavy as a slab of marble.

"What are you doing? What's come over you? Miyuki, stop it!"

She looks up at me and our eyes meet. I see the familiar look of a girl who has never known power, not even over her own life. "She's the only friend I have ever had."

"There's nothing I can do."

"You have a say—"

"I have nothing!" I say furiously to her, finally managing to throw her off. "I am a woman, just like you. I have only what I can charm out of others. I can't stop it. Don't you understand? I can do nothing. I have gained nothing—"

I break off. *I have gained nothing.* Since the days of my child-hood, when I ate grass to quell the hunger in my belly, what do I have? Since the days when I was a common whore to the days when I commanded a great price, what have I gained? Some nice clothes and the right to command other girls who have nothing, just as I did. I thought that I had risen in the world. But the truth is I had more respect for myself when I was a whore than I do right now.

I turn on my heel and start down the hall. I can hear Miyuki crying after me, but I don't turn around. I don't stop.

I swear to God, I have had my fill of the sound of girls crying.

It was the last night. Nori's room was full of packed boxes. In the morning, they would all be moved to somewhere else. She didn't know where. No one had told her and she had not asked.

She glanced at herself in a hand mirror. With the garish makeup all washed away, she didn't think she looked old enough for any of this. Thirteen, she thought, was awfully young to die. Miyuki's wailing broke into her thoughts. It had been going on for hours. Nori turned back around to face her friend.

"Miyuki," she said, as gently as she could, "it's all right."

Miyuki gasped. Her eyes were red and swollen. "It's not. How can you even say that?"

Nori smiled, and it was not forced. There was something strangely peaceful about knowing that soon she would return to the dust from which she came. Her life had meant nothing; her death would mean nothing. Her wandering destiny would come to a final, merciful end.

"What I say makes no difference to the way of things. But I would like to see you smiling, Miyuki-chan. I would like to remember you that way."

Miyuki wiped at her eyes with balled-up fists. "I can't bear it."

Nori knelt down and opened her arms. Miyuki crawled forward and, like a baby, laid her head in Nori's lap.

"You can. You'll get your sister back," Nori murmured, trying to sound soothing, just as she had the first night they'd met. "You'll get Nanako back."

"She'll have forgotten me," Miyuki cried bitterly. "She won't remember who I am."

Nori stroked the top of Miyuki's wild hair. "Of course she will. You are her family. Her only family. She loves you."

"What kind of life can I offer her?"

Nori lowered her voice, cautious even now that someone might be listening. "Under the floorboards in my closet is a pearl necklace. They're gray pearls, quite rare. Don't take them now— someone would notice—but when it's time for you to go get Nanako, take them with you. I hope they will help some."

Miyuki lifted her head and sniffled. "You have given me so much," she said. "And I have nothing to give you."

Nori looked away. "You have given me more than enough."

Miyuki wrapped her arms tight around Nori's neck. "I love you, Noriko Kamiza," she whispered fervently. "I won't forget you. Not ever."

Nori could not respond. If she admitted to herself what this was, she would have to admit what it was she was losing.

They stayed like that, holding each other on the floor, until the sun peeked over the clouds and filled the room with unwelcome light. Kiyomi entered. Nori let go.

Miyuki made a sound like a dying animal.

Kiyomi took Nori's hand and led her away.

They did not see each other again.

CHAPTER NINE

IMPASSE

Road to Tokyo
October 1953

They did not knock her out this time. Nori sat in the back seat of a black car with tinted windows. Kiyomi sat beside her. The driver was a man she didn't recognize. She thought he might be one of the men who guarded the premises. He had scars on his arms that looked like old knife cuts. She tried not to focus on him. She turned to peer out the window, at the orange and green countryside. When she rolled it down to feel the air on her face, Kiyomi did not scold her.

All she knew was that when they reached Tokyo, she would never again feel a chilly fall breeze make her cheeks numb. She would never again read or knit or play or bask in the sun. She would be a prisoner for a moment, and then, after that, she would be forever free. She let her hand hang out of the open window, and she faded in and out of sleep, dreaming of a clear blue lake with swans.

It was an odd thing, to be dying but in no pain.

The blade was cold against her inner thigh. She had stolen it from the kitchen when no one was looking. The staff had hardly noticed her these past few weeks; they had all looked through her as if she were already a ghost.

She had used three of her ribbons to bind the blade so it did not slice her. She had to wait for the perfect moment. Her ribbons had been her mother's only gifts to her. It seemed fitting they would be with her until the very end.

Only your life is more important than your obedience.

Only the air you breathe.

She pinched the skin on the inside of her palm. *I am sorry, Okaasan.*

This time, I choose.

Kiyomi glanced at her. "What are you thinking of?" she whispered, her voice low with suspicion and fear.

Nori smiled. It was a reflex, like a toy reacting when a knob was turned to wind it up.

"*Betsu ni,*" she said. "I am thinking of nothing at all."

Kiyomi reached out and touched her shoulder. "I know you have no love for me," she started.

"You have been a better guardian to me than most," Nori said dryly. It dawned on her how sad it was that it was absolutely true.

"So perhaps you will take my advice now."

Nori turned a blank face to her. "You seem distressed."

"And you don't!" the madam burst out. Even underneath her painted face, Nori could see the pallor. "The question is why you don't! You have said nothing since . . ."

Nori inclined her head but said nothing.

Kiyomi searched her face, her dark eyes trying desperately to seek out the truth, but she had done her job too well. Nori's face was a cool mask. There was nothing to be found.

"You haven't even asked me his name."

She did not even dignify that with a response. There were only two names that mattered here: master and slave. Kiyomi knew this. But she was clearly desperate to find something to say, anything, that would change what could not be undone.

Finally, Nori spoke. She could not explain it, but she felt an absurd kind of pity for the woman before her. Even though she had power and Nori had none, even though she would go on living in wealth and comfort while Nori would soon be cold in the ground . . . she found that she would not trade places.

"It is a long road to Tokyo. You should try to rest."

Then she turned her face back to the window, closed her eyes, and waited.

Her courage sat curled in her lap like a sleeping cat, waiting with her.

Soon.

The road was not so long after all. Perhaps they had not been on the edge of the earth, as she had thought. Perhaps their little world had existed right alongside this one.

Nori had never seen Tokyo before. She had heard stories, of course, stories of bright lights and busy people in modern clothes. She had been told of women who wore gel in their hair and painted their nails, of men who wore smart hats. This was a city full of neon signs, of scholars, of music and life. And somewhere, there was a toy store that had once sold their last silk stuffed rabbit to a beautiful boy who never combed his hair.

She did not allow herself to think his name. Even now, to think that name was to lose all of her strength and crumble into nothing.

She pressed her palm to the window and spread her fingers apart so that she could look out. Then she saw it, looming in the distance. The walled city in a city: Edo Castle, surrounded by moats on one side and a massive gate on the other. All designed to keep the rest of the world out.

"The palace," she whispered.

"Yes," Kiyomi said teasingly, pleased that she had finally gotten Nori to speak. "You must view it as your ancestral home."

She turned away from the window and looked straight ahead. "No. I do not."

"Well, that's not where we are going. Which you would know if you had asked me."

"I don't care."

"They are your cousins, you know."

"I am a bastard," she said stiffly. She folded her hands in her lap. "I have no family."

"You came from somewhere," Kiyomi pressed. "You did not spring up from clay."

Nori drew in a deep breath. "Why are you doing this?"

"I don't know—"

"Why are you doing this *now*?" Nori hissed. She could feel her pulse quickening.

Kiyomi folded her lips over her teeth and did not answer

right away. She glanced ahead. The driver had not spoken a single word, nor given any indication that he was listening.

Quickly, as if trying to do it before she changed her mind, Kiyomi pushed a button that brought up a black screen between the back seat and the front.

This was as alone as they were going to get.

"I was wrong," she whispered. She seized Nori's hands in her own and spun her around so that they were facing each other. "And now you must listen to me."

"Stop it."

"Noriko!"

"It's not your concern anymore. I don't belong to you now. Why do you care?"

"Death isn't what I wanted for you. None of this is what I wanted for you."

"What we want doesn't matter. You have taught me this."

Kiyomi's expression was pained. There were tears behind her eyes. "My God, Nori. You have to live. You have to survive. You . . . you just have to survive. I cannot save you from this. I cannot give you hope, for it would be a lie. But you must *live*."

"This isn't your concern," Nori repeated through cold lips. Her calm was slipping away from her, as it always seemed to. "It's not as if you'll have to give a refund."

"But think!" Kiyomi burst out, and finally, the tears fell. They fell down her rouged cheeks and pooled at her collarbone. "Think what kind of woman you could be."

Nori had never, for one solitary second, thought of what kind of woman she could be.

"You . . . you told me to resign myself."

"And now I am telling you to fight."

Nori shook her head. "I can't fight anymore."

Kiyomi started to say something but broke off. Nori felt it too.

The car was slowing down. They kept their eyes locked on each other, breathless, saying so much with no words.

Nori squeezed Kiyomi's hand. The sound of the engine winked out.

"I'm sorry," Kiyomi whispered. "For all of it. I am sorry."

Nori hesitated. She could hear that the driver had gotten out and was coming around to open her door. She had only seconds. She could not think what to say to this woman. Here they were, madam and whore, raised pauper and fallen princess, master and servant. But in this moment, they felt like none of those things. They were simply two women with their heads bowed against the wind. Nori decided that if it did not make them friends, it made them something.

"I'll miss you, Kiyomi-san."

It was absurd. But it was also true.

Her door opened. Without being asked, Nori got out of the car and blinked into the autumn sunlight. She knew where they were. Every child in Japan knew about this place.

Chiyoda-ku was the royal ward of Tokyo. All the government buildings, embassies, and monuments were here. And so were the richest, most powerful people in the country.

The house before her was not a palace, but it was close.

Nori found herself standing in an enclosed estate, with high walls of whitewashed stone. The house before her was old and grand, low and sprawling, with a tiled roof the color of red clay. There was a family crest she did not recognize emblazoned onto the gate behind her.

It looked old, but cared for. The only things neglected were the plants. There were some sad-looking plum trees, with leaves the same color as the roof, that had clearly seen better days.

Kiyomi came up to stand behind her. Nori knew she had to walk forward, into a house that did not welcome her, with people who would not love her.

She had been here before. She knew what to do.

And so she walked. The hem of her best kimono dragged behind her, stirring up the fallen leaves. Her hair was parted in the middle and allowed to fall free to signify her virgin state. Her skin was flushed and her heart was beating fast as a sparrow's, but she was not afraid.

She walked up the wooden steps and through the sliding door to the antechamber, which a maid on the other side opened without a word.

She stopped to remove her shoes and then continued on, until a woman appeared before her, dressed in a kimono of sky blue silk.

"*Douzo agatte kudasai*," she said. "Welcome."

Nori bowed.

The woman did not even look at her. "Thank you for the prompt delivery. You may leave her things outside, someone will come and get them."

Kiyomi hesitated. She could not speak freely now. She had a part to play, the same one she had played dozens of times before.

Nori turned to face her. Just for a moment, with her face hidden from the stranger with the veil of her hair, she allowed herself to smile.

"*Arigatou*. For all you have taught me."

Kiyomi bowed low. "Goodbye, little princess."

Nori felt a twist in her gut. For a moment, she wanted to

reach out and cling to Kiyomi, the way she had never clung to her mother, to her grandmother.

The words bubbled up in her throat.

Don't go.

Don't leave me.

Don't leave me, again.

Not again.

Please.

But she could not speak. Her lips closed on the words and she turned away. In a moment, Kiyomi had gone.

And, as she had been at the beginning, Nori was alone.

She was led to a large room with tatami floors. All other furniture had been removed, save for a lone silk pillow in the center.

"Wait here," the woman said shortly.

Nori lowered herself onto the pillow with her knees folded underneath her. She knew how she was supposed to sit. Her mother had taught her when she was three. It was one of the few things Seiko had bothered with.

She waited until she heard the *fusama*-style doors slide shut.

Nori did not know how much time she had left. A few minutes, maybe. She imagined that her new owner was sitting behind a desk somewhere. Maybe he would have a drink or two before coming down to see her.

If she did not gather up her courage now, she never would.

So she had a few minutes. Six.

Five.

She didn't know exactly—but she knew that it was not enough.

She pressed her hands against her face. For the first time, she let herself feel the full injustice of everything that had brought her to this.

She wasn't even fourteen years old and she had never had a day to herself, not one day that had not been dictated to her by someone else. She had never seen the summer festival, or made snow angels with other children in the winter. She had never been kissed, or acknowledged, or loved as in her storybooks.

Well . . .

Maybe, in a way, she had been loved. She held tight to that, clinging to that warm little feeling. She wrapped herself in every happy memory she could find.

This was her armor.

The smell of her mother's peppermint perfume. The sound of Akiko's laugh, with the snort at the end. Kiyomi's wry smile. The feel of Miyuki's clammy fingers intertwined with hers.

The rain on her face. The first time she'd heard the violin.

And Oniichan.

Akira.

Nori did it in one deft motion. The pain was sharp and deep along her thigh. Even though she should have expected it, it knocked the wind out of her. The knife fell from her hand, and instinctively she placed her palm on the cut. It wasn't going to be deep enough. She knew, somehow, that she'd missed the artery her books had told her about.

She couldn't even die right.

She fell backwards, hitting the floor hard but without feeling it. With her hair spread out and her arms opened wide, she could almost pretend that she was back in the garden in Kyoto.

Gomen, Oniichan.

I wanted . . . to see you . . .

Her head began to feel very heavy. The pain in her leg was almost gone. She thought she could hear the crack of a door. Someone screamed, but it felt very far away.

It did not touch her. She knew there was nothing they could do to stop it now. Was that . . . footsteps? Two sets, one behind the other.

And then someone was leaning over her, touching her, cradling her in strong arms.

Someone was shouting.

"Nori!"

She smelled lemons and wasabi.

"Nori! Wake up. Wake up! I found you. I finally found you, so you don't get to die. Do you hear me? You can't die. Please, no, no, no, no, no."

She squinted. She could barely see anymore, but she thought she felt something on her face. Something wet.

You smell like Akira, she thought. *I missed . . . that . . .*

The roaring in her ears was deafening now.

Okaasan.

I'm sorry.

There was a bright white light and then there was nothing.

CHAPTER TEN

SONATA

Tokyo, Japan
October 1953

For a single day she lay floating. This was the in-between.

It was different from a dream. She could see nothing, but it felt different from being blind. There was no hunger or pain, no fear or sadness, no angels or demons here to greet her.

There was only the white.

And then, bit by bit, there was the sound.

At first it was distant, like someone shouting across an immense void. She latched on to that sound. She wrapped herself around it and let it pull her up from underneath the white. It grew louder and louder until she could hear it as surely as if someone had their lips pressed against her ear.

And then she could see the tiniest flicker of color.

She felt herself floating upwards, from the very depths of nothing to just beneath the waves.

And when she finally reached for one gasping breath, she was able to catch it.

And when she opened her eyes, there, right there, was the sun.

He was kneeling beside her pallet, with his dark head bowed and his hands laid over her heart.

"Oniichan."

His head jerked up. His gray eyes widened as he met her gaze. She noticed the dark circles under his eyes, the greasy film on his skin, and she wondered how long he had been there.

"Noriko," he said, and his voice cracked. "My God. My God, finally."

She pushed herself up onto her elbows, ignoring the way it made her head spin. "Is it really you?"

Akira leaned forward and kissed her on the side of her face, right onto one of the deep dimples in her cheeks. The gesture was foreign, like so many of his mannerisms picked up from his time in Europe as a child. But to Nori it felt foreign for another reason.

He had never been so affectionate with her before.

"You have been in and out all day," he whispered. "Your leg . . . we managed to stop the bleeding, but then you spiked a terrible fever. I thought . . . for a moment, I thought . . ."

The leg. She had completely forgotten about the leg. She slipped her hand beneath the blanket, and sure enough, her left leg was wrapped in heavy bandages.

"We had to suture it shut," Akira told her. He looked queasy, though it was hard to tell in the darkened room. "You may have a limp. We can't be sure. But there will be a scar."

She just looked at him. She hardly cared about the leg, a limp, or a scar; she just wanted to look at him.

Akira smirked as if he knew this already.

"I found you," he said, with a quiet but deep sense of satisfaction. "It took me two years, but I found you and I made a plan to get you back."

She nodded. It seemed impossible to her that she was alive. She could not process that she was here, well, and reunited with the brother she had tried so hard to force herself to forget.

She did not want to feel anything, in case this was all just the devil's last joke before he threw her into hell.

Akira went on. "Once I realized you were . . . you were in one of those places, I had one of my father's old servants pose as a buyer to find you out."

Nori's heart began to beat faster. It hurt, almost as if it was out of practice.

"I had him arrange for you to be delivered here. This was my uncle's house, but now that he is dead, it's part of my inheritance. I knew I could get you here. Grandmother will realize what's happened soon, but I will protect you. I swear it."

Nori forced herself to sit up. She pitched forward so that she was in his arms, with her head nestled in the crook of his neck.

"I'm so sorry," she moaned. The tears began to fall heavy and free. Her whole body ached, but she was not crying for the pain. Like two ships passing in the night, they had almost missed each other. She had almost let him go. "I didn't know what else to do."

Akira patted the top of her head. "Hush. It's my fault. They sent you to that horrible place because of me. I couldn't stop it. I tried . . . I tried everything, but they threatened to hurt you if I didn't . . . if I didn't stop meddling and do my duty to the *family.*"

His voice was filled with a poisonous spite. "They told me you were somewhere safe but that I could never see you again. They told me to forget you. To go on with my schooling and my music like nothing had happened. Grandmother said she would buy me whatever I liked, Grandfather told me that he would get me a princess to marry."

Nori lifted her face up and pulled back so she could look him in the eyes. He had grown. His face had lost what little baby fat he'd had, and his cheekbones were sharply defined. Even with him kneeling, she could tell that he was taller. And there was something else too. The shine had been taken off him. He was a lucky boy no longer.

From birth, Akira had been divinely favored. That's what her grandmother had always told her and Nori had come to believe it herself. He had floated through life effortlessly, assured of a warm welcome everywhere he went. He had rarely known disappointment, scarcely known pain, never known what it was to be overlooked. And so he had the confidence, or, in truth, the arrogance, of someone who knew that nothing could ever go wrong for him.

But now that confidence had been badly shaken. His certainty was gone, and whatever had been left of his innocence was gone with it.

When she realized this, she had to ball up her fist and bite down on it to hold back a scream.

"You should have forgotten me like they told you," she whispered brokenly. "I have ruined you."

Akira tugged sharply on one of her curls. "Hush."

"But—"

"I said shut up."

She bowed her head against his will. Akira shifted his weight and glanced over his shoulder.

"I should fetch the doctor. It's the middle of the night, but I've had him staying in one of the guest rooms."

She did not want him to leave. She seized hold of his sleeves.

"They won't let us get away with this," she said, her foggy brain slowly starting to fit the pieces together. "This is to declare war against our own grandparents. They will come after us."

Akira nodded. Of course, he knew this. He had known when he started that there was no turning back.

"We won't be safe," Nori breathed. She could feel her chest tightening. "We've humiliated them now, we've tainted their honor and they won't let that go. Not ever."

Akira nodded again. His face was grave, but he did not try to soothe her with lies. Whether she wanted it or not, he always told her the truth.

Nori went perfectly still as the full reality of the situation dawned on her. Confining her had not worked. Banishing her had not worked.

She sucked in a little breath.

"They're going to kill me."

Akira pressed his forehead against hers, and she could feel the determination radiating off of him.

"They're going to try."

Akira never left her side for more than a few moments. When the doctor came to see her, her brother retreated to the corner, but he kept his gaze on them the entire time.

After the doctor signed off on her, giving her some pills to take for the pain and strict instructions to avoid putting undue stress on her leg, a maid came with some food. A few moments later, another maid came with some water for Nori to wash and a fresh change of clothes. When the woman left, Akira turned to face the corner so she could try to wash the smell of blood off her. She brushed out her hair as best she could and winced as she pulled a clean cotton slip over her body. She did not look at the bandages. With a little cough, she let Akira know that he could turn back around.

She didn't want to eat, but Akira's expression made it clear she had no choice.

She picked at her rice with her chopsticks. "What happens now?"

It was nearly morning. Nori could hear the world starting to wake up.

Akira rubbed his eyes. "They'll find us soon. They have spies everywhere, they're little better than high-born criminals."

Nori pushed the rice aside.

"No, *tabete*. Eat."

"Should we leave Japan?" she asked.

Akira shrugged. "That's impossible. They'll be watching the ports. And there's no paper trail on you, no documents for customs. Legally, you don't exist."

She bit her lip. "You could go without me."

His face soured. "If you're going to be stupid, kindly shut up. I have enough to think about."

She wrinkled her nose. Perhaps he hadn't changed that much.

"I'm not a child anymore. I could manage without you."

He flicked his wrist. "Nori, I didn't go through all of this to find you for you to speak of leaving. You cost me a small fortune."

She snorted. "Rather too much."

He looked at her, and she could see the dark shadows under his eyes. "I'll have to find a way to deal with our grandmother.

She's a vile old bitch, but she's not stupid. She knows she has to win me over if she wants her precious name to live on."

"I won't have you selling your soul to her on my account," Nori blazed. She started to stand up, but the pain in her leg was still too much. "It's not right."

Akira sighed as if to say that he was disappointed that, after thirteen years and a life hard enough to break her, she was still a fool.

"It's the only way forward for us."

Nori racked her brains for a rebuttal. "Can't we stay here?"

"I have no doubt that her spies already know we're here. Or if they don't, they will very soon. There's only one person here loyal to me. Otherwise these aren't my servants, I didn't grow up with them. I can trust them only as far as I can pay them, and she can pay them more."

"Well, can't we go somewhere else, then? Can't we live in the country and hide?"

Akira looked at her blankly. "And do what? Raise pigs like peasants? Farm rice?"

She let out a frustrated cry. "You can't just let her win!"

He narrowed his eyes at her. "Winning means staying alive. Staying somewhere safe and warm, where we are kept and fed. That's what winning is. Our victory will be in outliving them. We will dance to their tune now, but they are old and soon—in five years or ten—they will be dead and we can dance to whatever tune we play."

"But—"

"I've thought about this. You don't think I want to go to Europe? I've wanted to go there for years, to study music . . . I had planned to in a few years anyway, I'd hoped . . ." He looked away, and she could see that he had harbored hopes of his own, hopes that had been dashed by the reality of being saddled with her. He shrugged them away. "Anyway, this is the only way. Without my inheritance, we have nothing."

She bowed her head beneath his relentless logic. "I hate her."

Akira came over and sat beside her, wrapping one long arm around her frail shoulders.

"I know. I don't have a choice," he said wearily. "I'm sorry. I can't keep you safe from her if I don't offer her something. I swear to you, we'll never go back to Kyoto as long she lives. But . . . I don't have a choice."

Nori clenched her fists. She hated this bed. She hated this room. She hated how powerless she was, how powerless she always was, and the weight of it was excruciating. She could do nothing. Again.

"What are you going to give her?"

There was only one answer. There was only one thing that was worth more than gold to Yuko and Kohei Kamiza. Only one thing that was worth more than the slight to their pride, more than their burning hatred for their bastard granddaughter.

Akira shut his eyes. "Me," he said simply.

Nori felt a powerful urge to vomit. "You're making a deal with the devil."

"Actually," Akira said wryly, "the devil might give me better terms."

She heaved a racking sigh and reached out her arms to him. Wordlessly, he lifted her, scooping her up as if she weighed nothing. He got to his feet, and she let her legs dangle, uselessly, clinging to him like she would die if he let her go.

"I had really hoped you'd grow out of the crying."

She tried to laugh, but all she got was another sob. "I can't lose you again."

He flushed, the color pinking up his pale cheeks. Even now, he was uncomfortable with deep displays of emotion or proclamations of loyalty. That was simply not Akira's way.

"I'll carry you outside so you can sit in the sun. So stop crying."

She reached for her determination, buried somewhere deep beneath her impotent rage and her fear. It was much easier for her to find the courage to die than for her to find the courage to live under her grandmother's vengeful shadow. It stretched across Japan like a dark, glossy mourning veil. Somewhere in this country, her mother was hiding too, safe in the knowledge that she had sacrificed her children for freedom from this poisonous name. Miyuki was sleeping in a cold room without enough to eat. Kiyomi was coming to terms with the destruction of her soul. And now Akira was steeling himself to fight her battle.

She knew, without a single shadow of doubt, that she was cursed, as her grandmother had always told her: a cursed bastard, born under a hateful star.

CHAPTER ELEVEN

FEAR NO EVIL

Tokyo, Japan
November 1953

Unbelievably, the days leading up to Akira's planned meeting with their grandparents, skillfully arranged by letter and set to take place in the great dining room, were perfectly calm.

The clocks did not stop. The sun did not refuse to rise. Everything trudged slowly on.

Akira was in and out of the house, running between this estate and his childhood home just a few blocks away. He always took two servants with him and went in broad daylight, but Nori was sick with fear every time he passed through the electronic gate.

Nori had been strictly forbidden to leave the property for now, which made her smile. This, at least, was not new.

She spent most of her time wandering around the house, trying to stay out of the servants' way. They were not unkind to her. They called her Ojosama or "madam."

But it was clear that she made them uncomfortable. From what Akira had told her, their former master, his uncle, would be turning in his grave to know that she was in his house, eating at his table, being served and honored.

She retreated, as she always did, to the garden. It wasn't in the best shape—the trees needed pruning, and the flowers needed weeding. There was moss atop the water in the fountain, and the bushes were overrun with animals and droppings.

It was clear nobody went back there anymore.

Still, there were some ancient trees that she liked to sit under. Sometimes she would have a book of poetry or ancient myths, other times a language book as she tried to improve the English that her brother spoke so well. She hated to be behind him. She was always trying to keep up. She wanted to be useful to him so badly that she could taste the desire in her mouth.

Other times she would practice her violin. It wasn't so difficult for her anymore; even Akira had begrudgingly admitted that she shared some—*some*—of his natural talent. She could play some of his favorite pieces now, and when he was home, he would lean on the other side of the wide oak tree and listen to her.

He never praised her—this was asking for too much—but the tender way that he stroked her hair when she was done made her heart soar.

Today, Akira was out, starting the process to obtain forged documents for Nori; it was the easiest way since she had no birth certificate. With papers, she could pretend she was a person. Just in case negotiations went sour and they had to flee after all.

He'd taken a picture of her for the documents, and so for the very first time, she'd found herself smiling shyly into the lens of a black metal box.

Nori was feeling unusually cheerful. Akira had told her to

stop moping and she was doing her best, trying to keep busy. She was in the garden making flower crowns when the woman in blue, who had greeted her when she first arrived, came out to check on her.

She always wore the same color kimono. Nori could only assume that she was in charge of the rest of the staff.

She bowed her head. "My lady. It's time for your pills."

Nori frowned. Ever since her "accident"—that's what they were calling it now—she'd been forced to take pills to prevent infection. They tasted like chalk.

"No, thank you."

The woman inclined her head. She was pretty and looked to be around twenty or twenty-one. "I'm afraid that the master was quite insistent. Please come inside and take them."

"Oh, is Oniichan home?"

"No, he's out. But he entrusted me with this task."

Nori jutted out her bottom lip. "Did he say anything else?"

"He says bedtime is at ten. And to eat all of your dinner, not just the rice."

She shoved down her irritation. "When is he coming back?"

"Morning, I think. He's at our old estate."

Nori frowned. "'Our'?"

The woman said nothing. Nori looked at her as if seeing her for the first time.

"Who are you?"

She ducked her head. "My name is Ayame. I served in your . . . in Akira-sama's father's household. Since I was a child. When he decided to reestablish a household here, he asked me to run it."

Nori had to resist the urge to let all her questions spill out of her mouth at once. "How long have you known my brother, then?"

Ayame went very still. "From the day he was born."

Nori stood up and brushed the grass off her dress. "I'll take those pills. But I would speak with you again, Ayame-san."

She bowed and left. She could avoid the questions now, but Nori knew, and she knew, that this was not over.

Akira came home early the next morning. Nori ran to greet him, still in her nightgown. Her leg smarted, but she could walk just fine. No sign of a limp.

She bowed and he patted her gently on top of the head.

"You need a haircut," he remarked.

She smiled. "What did you bring me?"

He handed her a package wrapped with bright yellow paper. "Some normal clothes. A few dresses, some sweaters and skirts. You can't walk around Tokyo dressed like a woman from last century."

She gasped. "And did you get me very fashionable things from the store windows?"

He rolled his eyes at her. "I got you what I got you. But anyway, you can open it if you want."

Nori was already starting to unwrap the package. At the very top, she could see a short-sleeved, collared dress the color of toffee.

Akira's cheeks were pink. "Do you like it?"

She looked up at him. "Very much, Oniichan. Thank you."

He looked satisfied. "Well, good. Go and change, then. We're going out."

She froze, sure that she had misheard him. A shiver went down her entire body, from the crown of her head to the tips of her toes.

"Out . . . where?"

Akira crossed his arms. He hadn't even taken off his leather jacket. "Into town."

She gaped at him. "But that's one of the rules."

His gaze softened. "Aren't I your guardian now?"

"Oh, yes."

"It's not my rule. I thought this was what you wanted."

"It is!" She gasped. Her eyes were starting to burn. "It's . . . Yes. But you said it wasn't safe."

"Obaasama won't do anything before the arranged meeting. It's a matter of honor."

"But . . ."

Akira saw straight to the heart of the matter, as he always did. "You're afraid."

She could not deny it. "I just thought you wouldn't want to be seen with me."

Akira clucked his tongue. "Don't insult me."

Nori had to admit that he had never treated her as an outsider. He found plenty of faults with her, to be sure, but it was always for what she did. Not who she was. Still, it was a serious thing he was suggesting—no one outside the family or the *hanamachi* knew about her.

Akira's suggestion was to fly in the face of a thousand years of tradition.

"There will be a terrible scandal," she whispered. "Grandmother will be very angry."

"Good. With any luck she'll have a stroke and we can move to Paris."

"How can you be so sure it will be okay?"

Akira gave her that look he gave her when he expected her to figure something out.

"Can't you just explain it for once?" she asked irritably. "You're too clever for me."

"Do you know why she has been able to do whatever she wants to you?" he asked, clearly hoping that he could lead her to water and she would be smart enough to drink.

"Because she's rich. And noble."

"Besides that."

Nori racked her brain. "Because . . . because I'm a bastard."

Akira's stormy eyes were wide. "And?"

"And . . ." She broke off. "And because . . ."

Akira sighed. Clearly he had lost patience with her. "Because you're a secret."

She looked at him blankly. She had always thought that being a secret was the only reason she was allowed to live in the first place.

Akira continued. "Ah, think, Nori. Come on. You have no birth certificate; Mother probably had you at home. You've never been enrolled in school. Legally, you don't exist. And if the law doesn't know who you are, it can't protect you."

Realization finally dawned on her. She covered her mouth with a shaking hand.

"If people knew about me . . ."

"If people knew about you, if you had legal documents . . ."

"I would be safe," she said, and it sounded like a miracle.

Akira allowed himself a bright grin. "It would help. She couldn't just make you vanish. People would gossip. People would know that she had done something to you, and she couldn't bear it. She is desperate not to be seen as a criminal, she is desperate not to have the nobility know of her dirty dealings."

"And the law?" she whispered. She could almost feel her grandmother's wrinkled hand on her shoulder, clawing her backwards, away from any glimmer of hope.

"The law is mostly useless," Akira confessed. "Everyone is in the pay of someone. But they would at least have to admit that they knew you were here, that you were real."

I could be real?

She hesitated. "But if people knew . . . honor would demand my death, according to the old way."

Akira snorted. "Honor gives that right to the family of the cuckolded husband. Which, in this case, would be me."

She met his eyes. "I suppose that ship has sailed."

He tapped her lightly on the nose. *"Aho."*

"Do you really think this could work?"

"I'm going to try," he said earnestly. "Tomorrow I'm going straight to the courthouse. I've been trying to get an appointment for weeks. I've already called a lawyer. I wanted to do this before, in Kyoto, but Grandmother has eyes everywhere in that city. The forged papers are still being made just in case, but I'm really going to try, Nori."

She pressed her face into his chest. "Don't put yourself in danger for me," she mumbled.

"I suppose that ship has sailed," he teased her. "Now, go and get dressed."

She could hear her heartbeat blaring like a trumpet in her ears.

"*Hai, Oniichan.*"

AKIRA

I walk out into the crisp autumn weather and I think, *My God, I love this city.*

Tokyo is mine and I am hers. I am certain of this, as I am certain of most things.

But I am never sure of her.

Nori trails behind me, wearing a dress of deep navy blue and her hair in two pigtails, each tied with a different color ribbon. She is chewing on her lip, and it's already starting to swell.

"*Dame,*" I tell her. "You're going to make yourself bleed."

She stops immediately and winds her hand into the crook of my arm. Instinctively, I pull away. I am not used to being touched. My father was a good man, wise but stern. I never saw him laugh. He was sick for years and tried to hide it from me. I noticed, of course, but I didn't know how bad it was. I didn't know that he had a cancer eating away at his insides like termites in dry rot.

One day I came home from school and they told me he was dead. I moved to Kyoto the day after we buried him.

My mother was different, but she was gone before my fifth birthday.

I remember she played the piano beautifully. She practiced all the time and used to sit me beside her on the bench. When I started playing the violin at two, we'd play together and she would always humor me and tell me that I was her muse.

She smelled of peppermint tea, her favorite. And later, when she started smoking, she wore peppermint perfume so Father wouldn't know.

She was all laughs and smiles and warm kisses. She would come wake me at five a.m. so that we could play games in the garden. She tried to build castles out of snow in nothing but her nightgown. She was famously beautiful, famously graceful, but she could be as giddy as a little girl. When I found out about the affairs, later, it was hardly news. She needed amusement; she needed to know that she was adored. My father gave her neither of those things.

She cried a lot too. Sometimes she locked us both in the music room and cried for hours.

"Little bird," she would whisper into my hair. "My poor little bird."

I remember the day she left. She came to my room and kissed me. She said that she was going into town to run some errands.

And then she was gone.

My father and grandparents sent a search party after her, but I knew, even at four years old, that she was never coming back.

Sometimes I look at Nori and it is all I can do not to flinch. The resemblance is becoming more striking as she grows. I find myself watching her, waiting for the first cracks to show. I have forgiven her for what she tried to do. And I can understand it.

But I'll never trust her again.

"Oniichan," she pipes up, in that high, clear squeak she calls a voice. "Where are we going?"

I think that she is my responsibility now and she will be asking me that for the rest of my life.

"Just there," I say, pointing to a crowded area fenced off with white rope. There are several market stalls and booths, with food, toys, and jewelry. Half the district has come out, bringing their rowdy children with them. "There's an autumn festival. I thought you would like it."

Her little face lights up. She stands up on her tiptoes. "You promised to take me to a festival years ago. I thought you'd forgotten."

At last, she moves me to a smile. She is teaching me her easy joy. I am someone who is not easily satisfied, a consummate perfectionist, but Nori is delighted with everything.

"We're early now, but there will be performing mid-afternoon—drummers and dancers, all kinds of things—and when it gets dark, there will be paper lanterns. You make a wish on one and then you let it go."

She wraps her little arms around my waist. This time I let her.

"*Arigatou*," she whispers.

I nod. "Do you want to go and play?"

She has forgotten her fear, it seems. Her eyes are bright.

"Are there games?"

"Oh, yes. Bobbing for apples and . . ." I trail off. I really don't know. I never played games after Mother left.

It doesn't matter that I don't know. She is off like a shot. I have to laugh as she bounds towards the festival grounds. The bright autumn leaves form a canopy over everything and the sunlight filters down through their colors so that all of us are bathed in orange light.

I am determined to give her this day.

She flits from booth to booth, and when she finds something that she wants, she looks at me with the slightest hint of a pout and I hand her some money. Eventually, I just give up and give her my wallet.

She buys a large sack to keep her trinkets in, and before I know it she has collected two teddy bears, a box of candied apples, and some jewelry made of seashells from the coast.

I was afraid that someone might say something unkind to her or question her skin, but my fears are baseless.

This is a lighthearted event, and no one is looking for a reason to be unhappy. The war years were hard—not for me, of course, and not for any of the other rich people in the country, but for the common people, they were very hard years indeed, and now everyone just wants to be carefree. Tokyo is coming to life again. Her people have always been decades ahead of the rest of the country. Perhaps my sister will be happy here.

Besides, she is not without a kind of appeal. Her joy is catching, and before long she is playing tag with a group of boys. Someone puts a crown made of leaves in her hair.

She is pretty. I'm going to have to watch her. Pretty and trusting is a poor combination. At thirteen, she is still very much a child, with a child's desperate desire to be loved.

"Oniichan," she calls out to me, "I'm hungry."

I buy her some *takoyaki*, and she leans her head against my arm as she eats it. We watch the dancers swirling around in their elaborate costumes and she hops up and down in time to the music.

"Do they do this every season?" she asks me.

"Yes."

Her eyes fill up with quick tears, but she is off again before I have a chance to say anything about them. I spot her throwing some rings around glass bottles.

Unbelievably, I do it. I manage to tolerate an entire day of something that I have no interest in whatsoever. Nori is teaching me patience I never knew I could possess. It's like a well that I am constantly digging.

When the sun has set and the stars are starting to wink down at us, she finds me again. She is holding her paper lantern and her hands are wet with ink because she has tried to scribble in kanji, using a brush in the old way. She has a smudge of ink on the side of her mouth, and there are leaves sticking out of her hair.

"I could have done that," I chide her. "Look at you, you're a mess."

"I can do it myself." Her voice drops an octave, the way it always does when she is serious about something.

I frown at her illegible scribble. "I can't even read that."

She shoves it into my face so that I can see clearly. "It says *kibou.*" Hope.

My lecture dies on my tongue. I told her to make a wish, and that is what she has done. She is determined to help me, to help us, and this is all she can do. She wanted to do something herself.

I look into her honest eyes, and I know that she is a rare creature, this little half sister of mine.

"Very well, then."

She beams. "Do you think God will understand? Even though I drew it wrong?"

I don't want to crush her spirits, but I can't lie. I have never believed in anything but my own talent, death, and the ability of people to fall far short of expectations.

"I don't believe in anything. You know that."

She smiles as if she knows a secret that I don't. I can never keep track of her mercurial faith. One moment, she is devout; the next, she swears that she has outgrown it. I think she just needs someone to complain to.

I can't say I blame her.

"So who are we wishing to?" she presses. "Where does the lantern go?"

I am driven to honesty. "I think it goes as far as it goes, Nori."

She presses the lantern into my hands. "That's okay. We'll let it go together."

After a moment, I let it go. She is a second behind me. It floats upwards, a glowing little ghost among hundreds of others, before disappearing into the night.

She tucks her hand into mine and sighs deeply, as if a great weight has been lifted from her tiny shoulders. Mine are still heavy. I lack her faith. In truth, I have very little in common with her at all.

I am still coming to understand, every day, what it is that makes her feel like mine.

The day of the meeting finally dawned. If Nori believed in omens, she would say that the thunderstorm raging outside last night was a sign that it was all over for them.

As it was, Akira had assured her that it meant nothing. He was confident of their success.

"She needs me," he insisted. She wondered which one of them he was trying to reassure.

He had drawn up a list of demands that he would not let her see. Nori assumed that he didn't want her to be disappointed if they didn't get all of them.

She had asked to be present for the meeting and was turned down flat. She was to stay in her room, with the door bolted shut.

Akira spent the afternoon pacing in the garden, rehearsing his speech. She watched him from the porch but did not approach him. She had dressed in her finest, with her pearls wrapped around her neck like a heavy chain. Somehow, this made her feel better.

Akira had not bothered, and was wearing a simple button-down and black pants. But then, he had less to compensate for.

She could wear a crown of solid gold and he could wear a dirty sheet, and it wouldn't change the way that the world viewed either of them.

Akira breezed back into the house, his anxiety seemingly spent.

"Can I get you anything?" she offered.

He looked at her with a raised eyebrow. "Like?"

"Coffee?"

"Do you even know how to make coffee?"

She bristled. "I've seen Ayame-san do it."

"And if I want coffee, I'll ask her. That's what we have staff for."

Nori rolled her eyes. Not for the first time, she wondered if he was as willing to part with his status in life as he claimed. She doubted that he had ever cooked a meal for himself, or even thought about how to wash his own clothes. That was servant's work, and what's more, it was woman's work.

Not that she had either, but she was prepared to learn. She liked to be useful, and she had no pride to speak of.

"Can you keep paying them out of your inheritance?" she asked nervously. "If Obaasama doesn't give you the allowance you want?"

Akira shrugged. "For a while, at least. My father was not so rich as others, but he left me everything, and I received it last year. Mother came with a dowry worth a fortune, but I can't touch it until I turn twenty."

She shifted from foot to foot. "I could take up some duties around the house," she suggested. "We don't need quite so many staff. I could cook and clean."

He offered up a small smile. "Really? Shall I send you down to the fish market with the rest of the housewives? Will you mend my clothes? Are we thrifty now?"

She flushed. "I don't mind."

He laughed at her, and though it stung, she liked to see the light spring to his eyes.

Now was as good a time as any to broach the subject again.

"I want to be with you today," she said, barreling on before she lost her nerve. "I want to sit next to you."

Akira's face darkened. He did not miss a beat. "No."

"But—"

"No."

"Oniichan!"

"*Zettai ni*. Absolutely not."

"I'm old enough to speak for myself," she protested. "I could help you."

"You'll ruin everything," Akira said crossly. "I don't have time for this. They'll be here in an hour, go to your room."

Her body moved to obey before she could stop it, her muscle memory absolute. But she stopped herself, digging her heels in. She remembered the first time she'd seen him, in a house like this, in a room like this, surrounded by old heirlooms that seemed to radiate disdain towards her presence. She had decided then and there that she would follow him anywhere.

But she wanted to walk beside him now. Not behind him. Not anymore.

"No."

Akira looked at her incredulously. No one told him no.

"I said—"

"And I said no, Oniichan."

She doubted if Akira had been interrupted in seventeen years. He looked bewildered, as if he had been presented with some strange new language that he could not decipher.

"Noriko," he started, his voice low with anger. "I'm not going to ask you again."

She winced but did not fall back. "Are you going to beat me if I disobey? Like Obaasama? Or drag me by the hair like the man she sold me to?"

He looked away from her. She had caught him on the raw, and she pressed her advantage.

"I'm going to be grown up like you one day. I need to learn these things. I need to learn how to negotiate, how to get people who don't like me to give me my way."

Akira hesitated. "It's . . . not time for that yet."

"We don't know that."

He gave her a weary look. "It's easier for me if you aren't there."

For the first time, she saw the vulnerability on his face. He was motherless, like her. He was fatherless, like her. He was the golden child, and she was the cursed child, but they were both caught in the same web.

"I'm your sister," she said awkwardly. Her words failed her; she had never been a great speaker like him. She spread her palms open in a gesture of surrender. "I'm . . ."

He sighed and looked her in the eyes for a long moment, searching them for something. Then he took off, starting towards the kitchen, before changing course and darting towards the stairs.

She trailed after him, wondering if she should accept her defeat or pester him further. He paced back and forth, whirling on her as if he were going to yell and then biting it back. She had never seen him so unsure.

Then.

"Ayame-san," he barked.

She appeared out of thin air. "Obocchama?"

Akira didn't look at Nori.

"See that there is a place set at the table for my sister."

Ayame nodded and left as quickly as she'd come.

Nori's eyes widened and Akira turned to face her.

"No crying. No speaking. No moving. You keep your face as still as a corpse, do you hear me?"

"I promise," she said quickly. "I do promise."

"We're soldiers today. Do you understand?"

She nodded. For him, she could be brave. His face softened.

"If you get scared, think of some music," he told her. "Think of it and you will feel safe."

The dining room table was set for afternoon tea. The porcelain china was in perfect condition and the silver was freshly polished. Someone had designed a beautiful arrangement made of white chrysanthemums and a red flower that Nori could not name and placed it in the corner of the room.

Akira's chair had been placed at the head of the table, with another great chair set across from him. There was a smaller chair set a little behind each of the larger ones.

Nori liked the idea that she would be able to hide a little. Her bravado had vanished. Akira was still as a stone, his tea untouched in front of him. Nori kept her hands folded tightly in her lap. She was once again conscious of her skin, which was now tan from spending so much time basking in the sun, and her hair, which had been straightened for the day but was already starting to frizz again.

She decided not to focus on that. She focused on the back of Akira's neck. His hair curled a little at the nape, just as hers did. He smelled like clean linen today.

The doors slid open, and Ayame announced that the guests had arrived.

Yuko came in first. She was wearing a purple kimono with a gold obi, with a matching gold fan tucked in her obi.

Nori's hands and feet went completely numb. She kept her face perfectly still.

Next came her grandfather, a man who she had before only seen in passing. Now, from beneath the veil of her hair, she looked at him fully for the first time.

Kohei Kamiza was as large as an ox. He seemed to fill up the entire room just by stepping into it. He had dark eyes as hard as diamonds, gray hair, and a beard that was still black.

Even beneath his flowing robes, there was a solidity that hinted at strength.

She felt his eyes on her like a physical pain, and she nipped the inside of her cheek with her teeth to stop herself from crying out.

Yuko took in her surroundings with a cool glance. She waited a moment, but Akira did not rise to greet her. Akira hadn't moved at all.

She nodded, as if making a note.

Then she sat in the smaller chair, allowing her husband to take the larger one. But the way her slim body was angled forward left no mistake as to who was in control of this conversation.

For a long moment, no one spoke. Nori was sure that everyone could hear her heart beating frantically inside her chest.

Then Yuko smiled. "Honorable grandson. I have missed you."

She gestured for the servant standing in the corner to pour her some tea.

"I'm happy to see that you are well," she continued, and anyone who didn't know her would think that this was nothing more than a friendly social call.

Akira inclined his head. "Grandmother."

He nodded to their grandfather, who nodded in return.

"Now," Akira said smoothly. "Shall we talk some business?"

Kohei stirred in his seat, and when he spoke, he had a voice like a low rumble of thunder.

"Listen, boy. This has gone far enough. You are coming home with us. Today."

Akira didn't falter. "I will not."

Yuko fluttered her fan. "Now, now, *anata*. Akira-san has made it clear that he wishes to remain in Tokyo. I think we can allow this for a few years. He is a young man. He should be allowed a certain degree of freedom."

Nori's hands began to shake. She tucked them into her sleeves and out of sight.

"I understand," she went on, "that you think we have acted unfairly as far as the girl is concerned. You have gone to great lengths to acquire her—indeed, you have shown remarkable cleverness. I clearly underestimated you."

Akira's brow knitted in a frown. "You don't think you acted unfairly?" he asked, his voice cold. "Even now?"

Yuko waved her hand. "I did what had to be done. Indeed, it is because of my soft heart that the matter is still not resolved. I should have been more careful."

Nori could feel her temper boiling over. She had not expected an apology, but to know that the only thing her grandmother regretted was not sending her far enough away was galling.

Her grandmother turned to face Nori, those pensive eyes appraising her in one glance. It was clear from her small smirk that she had found nothing of value. Again.

"You are a kind boy, Akira-san," she said. "But this really is such a waste."

Akira bristled. "I don't require your approval. Just your word that you will leave us alone."

Yuko narrowed her eyes. "So this is really it, then? You are determined to go down this path?"

Akira crossed his arms. "If you came here to change my mind, I am afraid you've wasted a trip."

Nori could not restrain a grin. It did not go unnoticed by Grandfather, who shot her a look so ruthlessly cold that it froze on her face.

Her grandmother sighed. "Very well, then. You may stay here, in Tokyo. But you must return to Kyoto during the summers, starting after your twentieth birthday, for your education. You have much to learn."

Akira tapped his fingers against the wooden table. "Twenty-fifth birthday."

Yuko didn't miss a beat. "Twenty-first."

Akira hesitated. "Fine," he said reluctantly. "Twenty-first. And just July and August."

"And you must marry," Yuko insisted. She dropped a spoonful of sugar into her tea. "As soon as I can find a suitable bride."

Akira's upper lip curled. This was clearly his least favorite part of the agreement.

"Might I ask you not to pick an eyesore?" he asked dryly.

"Of course. She must be pretty and well-mannered. Halfway intelligent, enough to read with the children—but I don't want a scholar. I won't have a woman getting above herself."

"Fine. But I won't marry for years yet."

Yuko tapped her chin. "I was married at your age. Your mother—" She broke off. "It would have been better if she had married young instead of going off to Paris. She was corrupted. She learned immodest ways. The French are notorious. But that too was my weakness."

Akira did not react. "I will marry at twenty-five. No sooner. And she'll stay here with me, in Tokyo."

Nori could not imagine her brother married. Akira was entirely uninterested in anything but his music.

Yuko accepted this stipulation without a fight. "And of course, the girl must go. No well-bred girl will agree to share a house with a bastard."

Nori's breath hitched in her throat, and she peeked out from behind Akira's shoulder. For just a moment, she forgot her orders and she started to speak, but Akira was one step ahead of her.

"Nori stays," he said simply.

Yuko snapped her fan shut. "I will pay for her to have an estate of her own, somewhere abroad. She will have servants to look after her. I understand now that you feel responsible for her—wrongly, of course—but I understand it. Your mother failed you terribly; she has passed you her burden. But now I can lift it from you. You want her to be safe. I can provide this. You need not be troubled by her any further."

Akira did not even pretend to entertain this suggestion.

"Nori stays," he said again.

"For the next few years—"

"For as long as she likes. She stays."

Nori bowed her head. This was all beyond her deserving. She could do nothing but marvel at it.

Her grandmother let out a hiss. "This is most unreasonable of you. She is such a nothing that you should not consider her at all."

Nori flinched. She felt a part of herself sink inwards.

Later, I will learn to play something new. A sonata. I will learn all by myself to surprise Oniichan. Mozart, or Liszt. Anything but Beethoven.

Akira bit back his irritation. "I'm not interested in your opinion, Grandmother. Now, let's discuss the allowance I asked for. Something reasonable should suit."

Yuko at last fell silent. Her face was drained of all color.

"Akira-san," she managed, after a long moment of silence, "this will be the ruin of everything. You are too young to understand. I beg you. Listen to me now. You have no mother, no father. You have no one to guide you but me. You must listen to me, as your grandmother. I am the only one left who can set you on your path. This is your destiny."

Nori recognized the look on her face: it was the rapt conviction she wore the last time they had seen each other. It was wholly captivating. It was the look of a prophet who was sure of their purpose, sure of their connection to the divine.

Akira was immune to it.

"I've spoken to a lawyer about Nori," he said softly. It was as if he knew that he was delivering a mortal blow and he wanted to do it gently. "I'm going to get her papers in order so that she can go to school. She's staying with me. And that's all there is to it."

Yuko gasped, as if someone had pierced her through the heart. She doubled over, placed her head in her hands, and was still.

Absurdly, Nori felt sorry for her.

Her grandfather stood up. The veins in his forehead looked fit to burst.

"I won't have this," he roared. "The bastard should have been shot like a dog the day she was dropped on our doorstep. I won't have her ruining you, boy. I won't have you forgetting who you are, what you were born to do. I won't have it!"

Akira winced but did not tremble. "I take it the allowance is off the table."

Kohei's face was brick red. "Damn you!"

Akira spread his palms. His eyes were bright. "I will never forget who I am. When I am head of the family, I will change it. I will change the Kamiza way; I will bring this family into the modern era. Give it life. Give it humanity. I can promise you that, Grandfather."

Yuko had regained her composure. She placed a hand on her husband's arm to steady him and turned a sharp gaze to Nori.

"What about you, girl?" she snapped. "You must have some ambition. I can give you land, money. If you will just go away and leave this family in peace, I will see to it that you are taken care of. I was wrong to punish you, I see that now—I will reward you instead."

What is it that you want?

She had been asked this question once before.

Nori stood up before she could stop herself. Her body moved, all on its own, guided by some deep force inside herself that she had no control over. She draped her arms around Akira's neck and curled his collar into her fist. She grabbed hold of him as if he were a hunting dog that was wholly hers.

"I will stay with Akira-san, if Akira-san will have me," she said, in a clear voice. "And there is nothing you can do to change my mind."

Yuko gasped. "You will be the death of him," she said simply. "And the ruin of this family. You will destroy us all."

Nori squared her shoulders. "I am sorry you think so."

Her grandfather slowly turned so that he was looking

directly at her. She met his eyes and did not falter, though it was like being glared at by a block of stone.

"You," he growled. "You are *nothing*."

Akira started to stand, but she kept a tight hold on him. She swallowed down her fear and dug in her heels.

"I am your granddaughter," she challenged, and though her voice wavered, she pressed on. "I have always been your grand-daughter, I will always be your granddaughter. I am your family. You cannot erase me. Even if you kill me, I existed. I was here. And Akira-san has chosen me."

A stunned hush fell over the room. No one moved. Yuko's jaw was hanging open, her precious decorum utterly forgotten.

And then.

There was a brutal weight on top of her and the sound of glass breaking. Ayame screamed, and there was a great clamor of running and a loud thump as something came crashing down.

But all Nori could see were the eyes: black as obsidian against a backdrop of white, with red veins branching out like bloody rivers.

They were an inch above her own and she felt them pulling her in, drowning her. She could hear a high, thin whistling.

She couldn't breathe. It was like being crushed beneath a mountain. There was no breath and there was no hope of breath; it was impossible.

She could see fiery red spots dancing at the edges of her vision. Then, fingers tearing at the face above her, but they were shrugged away.

It took her another moment to realize that there were hands wrapped around her neck.

She fought, her small legs kicking against the air, her fists beating helplessly against a chest that felt as if it were made of steel. It was pointless. She knew that, but she fought anyway.

I don't want to die here!

It was different from before. She was not resigned. She would not submit herself to the knowledge that her life had been worthless and her death would be worthless too. She didn't know what she had to look forward to, or if she had anything to look forward to at all. But she wanted to find out.

Not yet. Mada mada. *I can't . . . leave . . . yet . . .*

Her brain felt like a light that was struggling to stay on, flicking off, then back on, but growing weaker every time. Even still, Kiyomi's words bubbled to the surface.

Think what kind of woman you could be.

The hands tightened. The spots were gone now, and she could see nothing but blackness.

And then, in a single moment of clarity, she heard it: Akira's voice. A sharp crack, like thunder, and then the mountain howled like a baited bear and let her go.

The first breath was like inhaling a box of needles. Tears emerged at the corners of her eyes, and then someone was holding her head, leaning down to whisper in her ear.

"Nori!"

She couldn't speak. Her throat had all but caved in. She clawed blindly for Akira, and he pulled her head into his lap, seizing hold of both her hands.

"It's all right," he soothed her, his voice frantic. "It's all right, Nori."

Ayame's voice again: "Oh, my God . . . Obocchama, he's bleeding. He's really bleeding."

Akira's voice was flinty. "I don't care. Get him out of here. Get them both out of here, now."

Yuko now: "Kohei! I told you not to let her bait you! I warned you what she was like, the filthy creature—she is her mother's child."

Akira raised his voice. "GET THEM OUT!"

Nori tried to sit up, but the ringing in her ears was too much and she fell back. For the next several moments, she heard and saw nothing.

When her vision returned, she saw that the table had been knocked over. Pieces of broken porcelain and shattered glass lay all around her.

And a few feet away, a candelabra stained with blood.

Akira's face hovered in front of hers. "It's okay, Nori," he hummed, and she did not know which one of them he was trying to convince. "They're gone now. They're gone."

She still could not speak. She looked into his eyes, searching, reaching out with her soul and hoping that he could hear her question.

He leaned down and kissed her forehead.

"Yes," he whispered, and she knew that he had heard her, as clearly as if she'd spoken directly in his ear. "We've made our point. For now, Nori, we have won."

CHAPTER TWELVE

THE ONLY THING
IMMORTAL

Tokyo, Japan
December 1953

It was several weeks before she could speak normally again. She knitted herself a scarf to hide the unsightly bruising on her neck and chest, but there was nothing to be done about the ruptured blood vessels in her eyes. She became dizzy if she stood up too quickly, and there was a splitting pain on the left side of her head. She tried to conceal her pain, but Akira's gaze was all-seeing.

He could barely look at her. Though he came to her room every morning to check on her, he found excuses to be away from her for the rest of the day. She accepted this with as good a grace as she could muster.

She had nearly gotten herself killed twice in the span of a month. She supposed he was allowed to be bitter.

Akira drew up a list of servants to let go. Without the allowance, they had to cut down on expenses if they wanted to make Akira's modest inheritance last for the next two years. It was a hard day when he turned a half dozen men and women away, including the cook.

"I can cook," Akira had declared pompously.

Of course, he never even attempted to boil water. Nori took over the duty of cooking their meals without a word.

She was allowed to go to the market, but only if Ayame went with her. She blushed to feel eyes on her, but no one was ever unkind. She haggled over fish and filled her cloth sack with seasonal fruits. She had convinced Akira to get her a few cookbooks, and she liked to spend hours in the kitchen, obsessing over the perfect balance of spices or just the right texture for pastry crust.

Cooking, it turned out, quieted her mind. She very much enjoyed it.

Akira had announced his plans to complete his last year of school in the New Year, back at his old school in Tokyo. The school was under the patronage of his late father and would allow him almost anything. Besides, everyone knew Akira was a *tensai*—a genius. No one wanted to stand in his way.

For now, Akira busied himself with his music, spending hours poring over new pieces in his bedroom. Though he refused to let her inside, she sat outside the door to listen to him play.

She had a feeling that he knew she was out there.

Nori waited as long as she could. But on the morning of Christmas Eve, she tapped on Akira's door.

"Ayame-san?" he called out.

"It's me."

She could almost hear him rolling his eyes. Then, after a beat: "Fine."

She went in. There was music everywhere; he had literally plastered the walls with pages ripped from scores. He had written all over them in his neat, curly script. Her eyes were drawn to a blank score, with just a few notes written in. But the notes were written in Akira's own hand.

"Are you composing something?" she asked.

Akira flushed. "It's nothing. It's just started."

She smiled at him. "*Otanjoubi omedetou gozaimasu, Nii-san.* Happy birthday."

He snorted. "I had hoped you'd forgotten."

"I know you don't like birthdays."

"Quite."

Nori shuffled her feet. "I won't bother you too much. I have a present for you."

Akira leaned back against his pillows. "I told you not to get me anything."

She pulled the package out of her long bell sleeve. "I made this."

She handed it to him, and Akira inspected it, in that infuriating way he inspected everything, as if he was already preparing himself to be disappointed.

Realizing that she was not going to go away until he opened it, he sighed and peeled back the wrapping paper.

Inside was a handkerchief made of ivory silk, with little treble clefs embroidered in the corners in gold thread. In the bottom right corner she had sewn the kanji for his name.

Akira looked up at her. "How many tries did it take you before you ended up with this?"

She concealed her hands, which were covered in tiny needle pricks. "Not many."

Akira smirked at her. "A dozen?"

She cheated her gaze to the side. "A bit more, actually."

He laughed. "Well, I did tell you not to go through the trouble."

She nipped the inside of her lip. "I know you did."

He gestured to the score in his lap. "Well, as you can see, I'm busy."

"It's your birthday," she protested. "We really should celebrate."

Akira shrugged. "I was born. Now I'm one year older. What is there to celebrate?"

She was, not for the first time, amazed at his cynicism. "Life?"

He shrugged as if there were not much to celebrate about that either.

"I have work to do."

She hesitated. This was the part where she was supposed to leave.

"I think you are angry with me," she ventured. "Are you?"

Akira *tsked*. "No."

"If this is about what happened with Grandfather—"

"That wasn't your fault," Akira snapped. "It was mine. You never should have been in that room. I knew your presence would inflame him beyond reason. That's why I planned it the way I did."

"I insisted on being there," she said sulkily. "I taunted him. It was my fault."

"I knew you couldn't be trusted," Akira said. "I knew better. But I listened to your childish wheedling instead of my own judgment. I won't make that mistake again."

She stepped forward. "Oniichan . . ."

He held up a hand to stop her from coming closer. "From now on, I expect you to do what I tell you. There will be no more negotiation."

"But that's—"

"I'm not going to argue with you. Just do as you are told."

She looked at him, and his silence, in the face of her anguish, said all that needed to be said.

"Happy birthday," she mumbled again and went out.

Nori tried to speak to him again the next day, but he brushed by her without a word. She could feel a cold wind blow as he passed. She let it be, and for the next month, she saw very little of him. Soon Akira would return to school for his last year. Though she did not look forward to him being away during the days, it was better than him actively ignoring her.

At eighteen, he was only part adult. It was not until twenty that he would reach full majority. She comforted herself with the thought that it would be several more years before he would be expected to return to Kyoto. But she knew that he would never be content to sit by the fire and knit, as she was. He was ambitious and restless, and sooner or later, the tides would carry him away.

She found things to do, as she always did. In the mornings she helped Ayame with laundry. They hand-washed the delicate silks in large basins full of soapy water scented with rose petals. Then they would hang them on the line and watch them blow in the breeze. They didn't say much to each other. But Nori didn't think that Ayame disliked her. So that was something.

She spent her afternoons reading. This house had a great library, full of all kinds of books. She asked Ayame to pick out some that girls her age might be reading in school. It seemed like, for now at least, the issue of her education had been dropped. It was likely that after the incident in the dining room, Akira had decided it was best not to push the issue. Her existence was not the closely guarded secret it once was, but they didn't flaunt it either. He'd finally gotten her papers through the black market, not the courts, but he'd assured her this would suffice if they were needed.

Her evenings were reserved for music. Sometimes the few remaining servants would gather around and listen to her play. Afterwards, there was a contented silence that enveloped the room like a warm blanket.

The nights were the worst. She avoided sleep like it was a deadly plague. She walked the house aimlessly, trying to keep her eyes from drifting shut.

The nightmares she'd had as a little girl had returned. But they had grown, just as she had. And they were bigger than she was now. She couldn't fight them. She would wake up gasping for air, sure that there were hands around her throat. And then she would cry and cry until she retched all over the floor.

Tonight, she was determined to stay awake.

"No sleeping," she mumbled, pinching the cold skin on her inner elbow. "No sleeping."

It was nearly morning. The sun was just starting to peek over the clouds, casting a blush-colored hue across the tops of the trees. From her perch in the oak tree, Nori could see it perfectly. It was cold today, but she barely felt it. She rubbed the side of her face against the rough bark. It had been two days since she'd last slept. She felt herself losing control, of her body and her thoughts, but she didn't see a choice. She'd resorted to drinking coffee, as bad as it tasted, but it didn't help much.

She hoisted herself up an extra branch, swinging her body to make it easier to carry her weight. Her leg began to pulsate, and she winced, but deep down, she was grateful for the pain.

She had learned to carve out a place inside herself, somewhere between sleeping and waking. She could float there, for hours sometimes, in a white plane where nothing touched her.

It took her a few minutes to realize that Akira was calling her. She perked up immediately, poking her head out from between the leaves to smile at him.

"Oniichan. Good morning."

He did not return her smile. His look was disapproving. He was still in his red silk pajamas and his hair looked like it was in desperate need of a wash.

"I checked your room and didn't find you."

"I wanted to be outside."

He frowned at her. "It's cold. You should be wearing a coat if you're going to be outside. And since when do you climb so high?"

She felt her stomach drop. Now she was sure that she didn't want to come down.

"I can manage."

"Not with your leg. I want you to get down."

She jutted out her bottom lip. "I'm fine."

She saw the quick flash of irritation cross his face. "Nori."

She climbed down without another word, landing on her feet with a hard thud. "Why were you looking for me, anyway?" she asked crossly. "You've been locked in your room for days."

"I wanted to see if you'd like a violin lesson," he snapped. "Ayame-san has told me you've been practicing every day. I thought it might be nice to spend some time together, as we did before in Kyoto."

She was too tired to hide her petulance. "Nothing is the way it was before."

Akira looked like he wanted to yell but thought better of it. He reached out to brush his palm against the side of her cheek. "Your face is all scratched up. You're bleeding."

She winced. "It doesn't hurt."

He lowered his eyes. "You're always hurt," he said softly. "I see it. And I can do nothing."

Instantly, she felt that pull, the one she'd felt since she first laid eyes on him. She went to him and nuzzled her face into his chest.

"It's not your fault. Nothing is your fault, Oniichan."

He sighed as if he did not believe her. "I have to tell you that you can't go to school. I know I promised. I'm sorry. I've made some inquiries, it's just not safe."

She accepted this latest disappointment with the ghost of a nod. "But I'll have a tutor?"

Akira smirked. "Actually, I was planning on doing it myself in the evenings. If you'll allow it."

This was a double-edged sword. On the one hand, any time she got to spend with Akira was a blessing. On the other, he was notoriously impatient. She could clearly see a future of having books flung at her head.

She giggled. "And what will you teach me?"

She expected him to smile, but the look on his face was grave. "Practical matters. How to handle money, how to read a map. English, for that will certainly be the language of the world in a few years."

Nori hesitated. "I thought we could do more poetry?"

"We can do that too. But it's important that you learn these things. Don't worry about it now. What would you like to do today?"

She felt a chill go down her spine. Akira was wearing a forced smile.

"Why are you being nice to me?"

He snorted. "Do I need a reason?"

"You're always nice when something bad is about to happen," she accused. "*Itsumo*. Every time. What are you going to tell me now? Is somebody dead?"

Akira rolled his eyes. "Name one person either of us knows whose death could be anything but good."

"So what then?"

Days without sleep had made her vulnerable, and she could feel the tears threatening to fall. Her emotions were like a frayed cable about to short-circuit.

Akira shuffled his feet. "I have to go away for a little while."

She dug her nails into her palms. "What? Why?"

"I've been invited to go play in Paris. At a competition."

She bristled. "By who?"

"It doesn't matter who."

"So you don't have to go away. You're not being drafted into a war. You're leaving of your own free will."

Akira shrugged. "You'll be fine. Ayame-san will look after you."

"I don't *need* her to look after me. You shouldn't be leaving at all."

He cut his eyes at her. "It's not as if I vowed to spend every second at your side. I have my own wants, you know. My own life. You aren't the center of the universe, Nori."

She felt her temper flare. "So that's it? Now that I'm safe, now that you can be sure that I'm not going to be raped, or murdered—at least this week—you're going off to Europe? You're done with me now?"

The color rose to Akira's cheeks, and he took two steps back. "You're behaving like a child. I'm not leaving forever. I'm coming back."

No, he's not, the dark voice inside her mind whispered.

Her stomach dropped, but she knew that she could do nothing to change his mind. And it brought her no joy to see him so unhappy, so crippled by the weight of his responsibilities.

"Fine," she managed. "Fine, go. Have a nice trip. Make sure you win."

Akira did not look pacified by her submission. "You will be fine."

"I'm sure of it," she lied. Her hands started to shake, and she tucked them out of sight.

He looked doubtful. "It's just for a little while."

He can't breathe. He can't breathe here anymore. Because of me.

There was no reason that both of them had to drown. She would not pull him down with her. Her misery flourished in isolation; it always had. It didn't want company. Especially not Akira's.

She pinched the skin on her palm to steel herself for what she was about to say.

"I want you to go."

Akira looked like he desperately wanted to believe her but didn't. "Really?"

"Yes," she continued. Her legs began to shake now. "I think it will be good for you to get out of Japan for a while. Just make sure you bring me a new dress."

At last, he relented. The lines faded from his face, and he looked like a happy boy once more. She made sure to etch that image into her mind. She was going to need it.

"I'll bring you whatever you want," he promised. "Anything."

Nori bowed her head. "Just come back."

Akira nodded and went inside the house. Nori climbed back into her tree and stayed there until the sun had vanished back behind the clouds.

The night Akira left, she had the first dream. The oldest one that she could remember. And it was always the same.

She was chasing the blue car. Her mother was leaning out of the window, faceless, with her dark hair billowing around her head.

Nori.

She ran. The asphalt was hot and her feet were bare. But she ran and ran after that car until there were blisters on her feet.

Nori.

I'm here, Okaasan! I'm here!

But the car never slowed down. So Nori ran faster and faster, as fast as she could, until she was gasping for air like a dying fish.

Okaasan, I'm here!

She would never catch the car. When she would get very close, so close her fingers would graze the bumper, it would speed up and wink out of sight. The dream never changed, not one iota.

Silly girl, her grandmother's voice would say. *Have you forgotten who you are?*

Nori woke up in her bed. Ayame was seated in the corner.

Wordlessly, she got up and handed Nori a damp rag.

"Do you want something to drink?"

Nori shook her head. She knew better than to try to speak. They locked eyes, and in that gaze was the only question worth asking.

Ayame bowed her head. "You've been asleep for hours."

Nori waited.

"Your brother is gone."

Nori nodded. Waited.

Ayame hesitated. "When you are up . . . if you like . . . we can talk about your mother."

Nori found a tiny voice. *"Hai."*

Ayame hesitated. "He'll come back, you know."

Against it all, against the dull ache inside her chest, Nori smiled. She'd been raised to be fearful. But underneath that, like buds pushing through the cracks in concrete, she could see a sliver of something largely foreign: hope. Hope for a future not written in stone, dictated by the circumstances of birth.

Akira was in Paris, basking in his talent and ambition, not in Kyoto, reading ancient tomes with her grandmother.

And she . . . she was *alive*. Miraculously, unbelievably alive.

"I know."

You see, Okaasan, she thought. *You have two disobedient children. And in failing you, maybe we will manage to be happy.*

PART III

CHAPTER THIRTEEN

TRAITOR'S REQUIEM

Tokyo, Japan
February 1954

On a chilly February morning, Ayame handed her the box. They were sitting in the study among the belongings that Akira had brought over from his childhood home. He hadn't saved much. He was never one for sentiment.

"Is he really going to sell the old house?" Nori asked. She was feeling a little stronger than usual today. Her body was adjusting to going long periods of time without sleep. But the dark circles around her eyes made her look like a raccoon.

"He might, little madam. The money would go far. But he may not be allowed to. The house is a family heirloom of sorts."

"Well, why don't we live there, then?" She had wondered about this for a while, but knew better than to ask her brother.

Ayame fidgeted. "The old master . . . Obocchama's father was a proud man. I don't think he would have . . ."

Nori nodded. Of course. The half-breed daughter of his adulterous wife living in his house would probably send Yasuei

Todou flying out of his grave. It would be the ultimate disrespect for Akira to bring her there.

Ayame looked guilty. "That's not the only thing. It was not a happy home. Obocchama . . . I think he wants to be rid of that place for his own reasons."

Nori's curiosity was piqued, but she knew not to press her luck. There was nothing she could do either way. She weighed the box in her hands. She recognized the feel of the contents and her heart sank.

"These are books. Why have you given me books? You said when I was feeling better you would tell me about my mother."

Ayame raised an eyebrow. Like Akira, she was often short on words. But her face was far more telling.

"Just look."

Nori did as she was bid. Inside, there were several leather-bound volumes. She counted half a dozen.

"What are these?" she whispered, but deep inside, she already knew.

"Diaries," Ayame said. "Your mother's diaries. She always kept them, since she was a girl. These are just the ones we found. After she disappeared, she sent one final diary back to my mother, and it later passed to me. She asked that we save it for Obocchama and give it to him when he was old enough to understand. She wanted him to have it."

Nori's blood whooshed into her head, every drop of it, all at once.

"I don't remember her keeping diaries."

"What do you remember?"

She ran her fingers over the cover of the first diary, hoping that she would feel some kind of spark. But nothing happened.

"I don't remember anything," she confessed, and she was surprised at how much shame she felt. She was hardly a little girl anymore, and her memories had still not returned to her.

Ayame leaned forward. "Obocchama already knows about them. He won't read them. He asked me to keep them for him."

The idea that Nori could ever be privy to something that Akira was not seemed entirely implausible to her.

"He . . . Does he know about this?"

Ayame's face fell. "No. And if he knew . . ."

"I won't tell him," she swore. She hesitated. "But you love my brother. You've been loyal to his family your entire life. Why are you doing this for me?"

The older girl looked away. "I loved your mother too," she said simply. "And I think you have a right to know who she was."

Nori allowed herself a wry smile. "And do you think I will love her? When I'm finished?"

Ayame shrugged a slim shoulder. "I cannot say, my lady."

"Have you . . . have you read them?"

"No, my lady. It is not my place."

"Do you . . . do you have pictures too?"

"Yes, many. Would you like to see them?"

A part of her wanted to say yes. But she knew it was the wrong part.

"No. Not yet. Maybe tomorrow."

Ayame nodded. They both knew it wouldn't be tomorrow.

"I'll leave you alone, then. Before your brother gets back from Paris, everything will have to be put back in its place."

Nori made a small sound to indicate that she'd heard. She wasn't really listening anymore. She opened the cover of the first diary and saw a date written, scrawled in a shaky hand.

August 1st, 1930

She snapped the diary shut. Her knees began to shake. It was several moments before she could bring herself to open it again.

Today is my birthday. I think that I'm a very lucky girl to have my birthday here in Paris, and not at home under Mama's watchful eye. She would have me in a room full of very old men. How very boring that would be.

But instead I received this lovely journal from Madame Anne, and now I can write all about my travels. I will write about my studies and the concerts I will play.

I did not want to take the piano, but as it turns out, I am very good at it. This is good because Mama says that I am an idiot. It's nice to be good at something. And look where it has brought me! I am studying here in Paris, and all of those other girls are stuck in Kyoto being engaged to gray old men. I don't want to marry, as it sounds ever so horrible according to Mama's descriptions of wifely duty, but I do want to fall in love. I want to feel what the poets feel. I want to know what it's like to turn someone's world.

And maybe I will.

And maybe I will. Everyone in Paris says I am very pretty, of course. This happens everywhere I go.

Mama was a famous beauty, so it is nice that I'm not ugly. She'd never forgive me. But she never forgives me for anything anyway.

I wasn't her boy.

Oh, they are calling me for dinner. I will write more later,

though I know I am only writing to myself and nobody will
read this. It is much more fun this way.

Nori did not know this woman at all. This was not the mother
she remembered in tortured fragments. This was a silly girl,
just turned eighteen years old, full of hope for the future.

She had none of Nori's racking insecurity, none of Akira's se-
riousness, none of their grandmother's fervent devotion to the
Kamiza name.

This Seiko was a stranger.

Yet just five years from this diary entry, she would be a wife
and mother. Eight years after this, she would be a fugitive with
a bastard girl in her belly.

Nori wondered where she herself would be in ten years,
when Akira had a wife and child. Perhaps back in the attic. Perhaps nowhere at all.

He will be home in two weeks. She wrapped herself up in the
thought of it.

That was enough of the diary for today. She would try again
tomorrow.

It was three more days before Nori found herself perched high
on a tree branch with the diary spread open in her lap.

September 15th, 1930

I've received a letter from home today. Mama asks after my
health and my virtue. Unfortunately, both are still intact. If I

die here, I will die romantically. I could contract the artist's disease and perish at the peak of my beauty. Maybe they'd write poems about me.

And I'd never have to go back to Japan.

I have met a gentleman, but he speaks of marriage so I will have to keep looking.

I will never marry. I would rather have a noose around my neck, it is over more quickly.

Maestro Ravel played for me today, I could die. He is such a brilliant man. I would love him if he were not so very old.

He says that I am a rare talent. He is composing again, and the whole city is holding its breath waiting to hear. Or at least I am.

I cannot think what else to say, in spite of how much has happened this week alone. I've been having pains in my hands. One of the other students says it is nothing but a woman's weakness. He says I strain myself studying with great masters and should attend to less difficult things.

A woman's weakness. He is no different from the men back home. I pay even less attention to him than I do to them.

I'm sure he would like it if I quit. He doesn't want the competition.

September 30th, 1930

I have found him at last. He is tall, very tall, with eyes as blue as sapphires. He has hair like spun gold. I think he is the handsomest man I have ever seen. Just like a prince from a story.

He plays the violin, which I have never given much thought to.

He is rich, from an old French family. He had three brothers, but two died in the Great War so now he is left with only one. He favors strawberries, as I do, and he doesn't like tea.

We have spent three whole nights together but have not passed beyond kissing.

No words of love yet. How long is it meant to take?

I thought I was in love once before. But it was nothing but a pale shadow of the true thing. And anyway, he was only a servant and he is gone now. Sent back to his family.

At least, that's what Mama told me as she was beating me into convulsions.

Mama always says I will ruin myself and our name. But I don't live for her, or her name.

I will have what I desire. I will always find a way.

October 12th, 1930

I love him.

I truly do love him. And he has promised that he loves me back. It is true this time, I know it.

I really can't bear to go back to Japan now. Kyoto even less, with Mama standing firmly rooted in the last century. She lives in perpetual atonement and would have me do the same. She would have me married and locked safely away from the world like a princess in a tower.

Mama was married at seventeen. She had given birth to three dead sons at my age. She thinks there is a curse on us, I know she does. Her brothers all died too. That is why when Papa married her, it was he who took her name.

There is only Mama and I left now. And Mama is nearing the end of her fertile years. My family looks at me like starving wolves desperate for a piece of flesh.

They care nothing for love, or for my happiness. They want to breed me like a horse.

Mama says that I must do my duty regardless of what is in my heart.

But I think I would die before I live as she has done.

October 31st, 1930

Today I am a woman.

This truly is the city of love. I am a creature of love.

I will stay here and be happy.

"Ojosama!"

Nori looked up. She was seated on the snowy ground with the diary held up to her face.

As much as she was trying not to, she quite liked the image of her mother that was emerging before her. She was enjoying her time spent lost in a past that she had been forbidden to know of.

This Seiko was passionate and defiant, silly but clever. This was a woman with a desperate need to walk her own path.

This was the bundle of beautiful contradictions that Akira

sometimes hinted at that inspired devotion in everyone who met her, from Akiko to Ayame.

But Nori still did not understand how her heart could have grown so cold that she left both of her children behind.

And today, clearly, was not the day that would be figured out.

Ayame's face was bright. It could mean only one thing.

"Akira-sama's home," Nori gasped. He was a day early. She scrambled to her feet and thrust the diary into Ayame's open arms. "Put this back in its place. I'll come back for it later."

"Yes, little madam. But—"

Nori gathered up her skirt around her knees and bolted inside the house. She had felt Akira's absence like a physical pain, a dull thud that never waned.

She heard voices in the dining room and threw open the doors, all dignity forgotten.

"Oniichan!"

Akira was there, just as she'd expected. He looked tired but content, with the hint of laugh lines around his mouth. He greeted her with a warm smile, but there was something in it that warned her not to speak.

He was not alone. Two strangers stood beside him.

The boy looked to be about Akira's age but stood a few inches taller. He was white but tan, with the brightest blue eyes she had ever seen. His hair was . . .

Like spun gold.

She blinked at him, as one might blink after staring too long at a bright light.

Her eyes moved to the girl. She was a blur of red, from her high-heeled shoes to her lipstick. She had skin the color of cream, gray eyes with flecks of gold, and silver-blonde hair.

She was the most beautiful person Nori had ever seen.

"Sister," Akira said, "as you can see, we have guests."

Nori flushed with shame. Here she was, with the snow still melting in her uncombed hair and the dirt still on her knees. She had never seen white people before.

Akira repeated it in English. She grasped for the words he had taught her.

"Welcome," she managed.

Akira nodded. Apparently that was all he required of her.

"This is William Stafford," he continued, gesturing to the boy. "And this is his cousin Alice Stafford."

The girl smiled at her.

William laughed. "She's just as you said. Little kitten."

Nori bowed her head.

"They will be staying with us for a while. I take it you will be a gracious host."

"*Hai, Oniichan.*"

"Speak English whenever you can."

"Yes."

Akira sighed. "Good. Ayame-san!"

Ayame appeared like the morning mist, without a sound. "Yes?"

Of course she spoke English.

"Please see our guests to the spare bedrooms. We've all had a long trip."

"Of course. Please, follow me."

The foreigners followed Ayame out, with only the girl pausing to cast one last curious glance over her shoulder.

Once their footsteps could be heard on the stairs, Nori turned to face her brother. She did not have the energy to yell. And she knew better than to try and undo what had already been done.

"Why?"

Akira slid his gaze to the side. He looked uncomfortable.

"Will is my friend," he said. "I met him at the competition. He's a brilliant pianist. He's from London and can't go back for a while, so I made an offer for him to stay here with us. He understands things, I don't have to explain—"

"And the girl?" Nori whispered, trying and failing to keep the suspicion from her voice. "What is she to you?"

"She's his cousin. She's sixteen."

"I asked what she was to *you*."

"She's a child," Akira scoffed. "And a fool. Don't insult me."

"She's beautiful."

Akira wrinkled his nose. "I don't favor blondes. Where is this coming from?"

She was a little mollified. "It's just . . . Paris is the city of love. I thought you might have . . ."

"Don't be ridiculous. Who told you that?"

Mother.

"Nobody. I'm sorry."

Akira gestured for her to come closer, and she did. As he placed his hand on the top of her head, she felt the ache inside her vanish.

"I won't be traveling again for the rest of the year," he promised her. "I have to finish school. So it's not as if I'm leaving you alone with them. And I think you will like them. It will be nice for you to have a girl around, won't it?"

Nori nibbled her lower lip. "Maybe." She didn't see what a

European girl who looked like she belonged on a movie screen would want to do with her. "I will be gracious to them."

"We will fill the house with music," he said gently, tweaking one of her curls. He smirked. "And I will be considerably less grumpy."

"If it makes you happy, I am happy."

He kissed her forehead. "You look a fright. Go clean up for dinner."

"Did you bring me a new dress?"

"I brought you two. Now, go on."

Thank you for coming back.

She bowed her head and did as she was told.

Just as Akira had promised, the foreigners were pleasant company, though she really only saw them at meals.

The girl, Alice, had finally learned to take her shoes off in the house, and she walked around shamelessly barefoot, no socks in sight, her brightly painted toes on display. She wasn't in the house much during the day.

Will was more subtle. He was constantly at Akira's side, and even though Nori felt a twinge of jealousy, she had to admit that they made a well-matched pair. They spoke too rapidly for her to understand at times, but there was always laughter between them. They spent most of the day barricaded in the music room.

And Nori spent most of her day just outside with her ear pressed against the door, listening.

It really was miraculous.

Akira seemed happy. In fact, she had never seen him like this. His youth had returned to him; he was the boy he was never allowed to be.

Though she went to his room every evening before bed so he could read aloud to her, she never stayed long. Tonight, he read her a chapter of *The Tale of Genji* before closing the book and letting out a deep sigh.

"Forgive me. I'm tired."

"That's all right."

She had finished the book on her own already, days ago, but she would not tell him that.

"You've been well? Ayame-san says you've been having night-mares."

"They've passed," she assured him, and it was only half a lie. They had eased greatly since his return, and since the faceless wraith had been replaced by the love-struck girl who kept a diary full of dreams.

"How's your leg?"

"It's fine. The scar is less noticeable than you'd think."

"Good. I know I've been busy. But I'll take you somewhere soon."

This was quickly becoming a common farce. He would promise, to appease a guilty conscience, and she was sure in the moment he said it, it was wholly true. But then the moment would pass and she would be forgotten.

She inclined her head in reply and was rewarded with a sharp laugh.

"You have become quite docile, haven't you?"

Outwardly, perhaps. The less that was expected of her, the more she could get away with. It had taken her a long time to learn this. Meekness was not weakness. And boldness was not strength.

"I don't want to fight with you."

He looked suspicious. "You've given me no grief over our guests."

She shrugged. "I see no point. They are far from their country, their home. I would not see them thrown out onto the street."

"I know it's more cooking for you."

"Ayame-san helps."

Akira nodded. "She is kind to you?"

"She is, Oniichan."

"Well, the help will not be needed soon," he told her. "We have the funds now to hire back the servants we lost. Or, better yet, some new ones. People I can trust."

She frowned. "I thought we were poor?"

Akira laughed. "We are frugal, not poor. And anyway, Will is paying us for our hospitality."

"I thought they were poor."

"The furthest thing from it. They come from a very old, very rich family."

She crossed her arms. "So why are they here? Surely there are hotels for such very rich people."

"It's not a matter of money. They are . . ." He paused. "Actually, they are rather like us, Nori. That's why I invited them to stay here."

"I don't understand."

Akira slid the book back onto the shelf. "It's not my story to tell."

She felt her frustration bubble up inside her chest. He was always dancing three steps ahead of her.

"If you say so."

"You could try talking to them, you know. They don't bite."

"You know I have no experience with regular people."

Akira chuckled. "And you won't get any from these two. But it's a start. You might surprise yourself. Alice is not so much older than you, you might like her."

She shifted from foot to foot. "I thought you said she was a fool."

"Precisely why you might like her." His smile told her that there was no sting in his words. "Now, off to bed."

She went without a word.

But not to bed.

She slipped down the stairs, through the kitchen, and out to the patio.

The night sky was etched with stars, each one placed so meticulously that she was sure God had taken special notice. She started to reach for the basket she kept her sewing in, only to find that she was not alone.

Will was seated in one of the wicker chairs, smoking a cigarette. His eyes met hers, and she froze like a deer caught in a hunter's gaze.

"My apologies," he said with a wide grin. "I did not mean to startle you."

She allowed herself to look at him up close for the first time. He was obnoxiously attractive. Right now, this only served to irritate her.

"You did not."

He looked her up and down, but she didn't notice anything indecent about it.

"How old are you?"

"Fourteen," she lied. *In summer.* But even her lie sounded too young, too childish in front of someone like this.

He smirked as if he knew she was lying. Akira had probably told him her true age. She felt like a fool.

"But not in school."

Nori wanted to fidget but made herself resist. "I don't go to school. Oniichan says it is better this way."

"Oniichan?"

"Akira."

He scanned her face and she held steady. When he looked at her, she felt tiny pinpricks all over her body. The sensation was not entirely unpleasant.

"And do you always do what Akira tells you?"

There was no inflection in his voice for her to read. And he had not dropped his playful smile.

"Sometimes."

He stood up and gestured to his empty seat. "Well then, Noriko. Don't let me interrupt your disobedience."

He breezed past her, and she could smell smoke and something sharper beneath it.

"Don't—" she started, and she regretted it before the word had fully left her mouth.

Will raised a blond eyebrow. "What?"

She flushed hot. "Don't call me that. Nobody calls me that. Call me Nori."

He shrugged as if it did not matter to him either way. "Well then, little Nori. Good night."

Once he had gone, she stumbled into the chair he had left empty for her. Her heart was thudding in her ears and she felt strangely warm. Her knees were knocking together.

This felt like fear. But different. This was more dangerous. And less.

What's happening to me?

Nori was careful not to be alone with him again. But from that night on, they danced around each other like characters in a masquerade. Never touching, but drawing ever closer.

At breakfast, his hand grazed hers when she passed him the sugar. Their eyes met, for just a moment, and when he looked away, she felt shamelessly caressed.

He was nineteen, just a year older than Akira but a lifetime older than she. He had traveled all over the world playing the piano. He spoke English, French, and German and he collected artwork. Nori could tell that he was no stranger to the company of women. He radiated a magnetic confidence that managed to draw her in against her will.

When Will and Akira would lounge in the sitting room and drink in the evenings, discussing politics or art or any number of things that Nori knew nothing about, she would slip into the room and sit in the corner.

Neither of them acknowledged her, but they also didn't make her leave, so she counted it as a victory. When Akira was distracted, Will's eyes would fall on her lips.

After Akira went to bed, Nori would climb up into her tree and try to count all the stars. Sometimes she would hear music coming from the house and she would know that Will had thrown open the windows of the music room so that she could hear him play.

She knew it was for her, as sure as if her name was written on the notes.

No one else knew she was not asleep.

But Will did. He had seen what everyone else around her had missed, and he stayed up in the nights with her. He didn't say a word about it, but the sound of his piano let her know that she was not alone.

And that in itself was a gesture as intimate as a kiss. And maybe, just maybe, this feeling was a bit like love.

She'd never been looked at the way he looked at her. No one had ever drawn closer when she spoke, hanging on every syllable.

And certainly nobody like him.

One night she left her tree and went into the music room to find him perched before the piano. She stood there, trembling. It took all she had not to bolt from the room.

He turned to face her, his blue eyes calm as a frozen lake.

Nori felt her cheeks blaze. "You . . . watch me."

He didn't falter. "Of course I watch you. You're beautiful."

"I'm not," she said, quick as a shot.

"Not like the girls back home," Will amended. "Not even like the girls here. But you are to me."

She felt herself soften at the praise. But it was not enough.

"Is that . . . the only reason?"

Will raised his sandy eyebrows. "Why are you here, Nori?"

She didn't have an answer. Or at least not one she wanted to admit.

"I shouldn't be here," she whispered.

"But you are," he pointed out. "Because you're lonely. And curious. And a tiny bit afraid of me, but more afraid of what will happen if Akira notices. Because you watch me back."

He saw through her like glass.

Nori looked down at her feet. "I'm . . . I'm here for the music. That's all."

Without saying a word, he got up and kissed her full on the mouth.

She let him. And the next night, she kissed him back.

For months it went on like this, until the frost melted away and the sunlight lingered on well into the evening.

She'd play the violin for him sometimes, and he'd tease that music must run in the blood. He always did most of the talking.

They met only in the nights. Come the dawn, she'd slip back to her room like a phantom, sometimes unsure if she could trust her own memory.

If anyone else noticed, nothing was ever said.

Akira was true to his word and spent more time at home. On the weekends, he would sometimes accompany her on her errands to the tailor for fabrics or to the docks for fish.

He taught her more English, though she was now nearly fluent, and sometimes Alice would join their lessons to pick up bits and pieces of Japanese or throw in a suggestion. She appeared to have grown bored with her endless shopping. She had taken to wearing yukatas around the house, though she always tied the sash wrong. Nori didn't have the heart to tell her.

Nori began to serve the dishes of summer at their evening meals. Fish soups served chilled and brightened with fresh herbs, grilled *unagi* and *somen* noodles that she made from scratch. Will picked up the use of chopsticks with ease, but Alice continued to struggle.

The boys never said anything, but one day, as they were eating ramen, Nori decided to speak up.

"You can use a fork, Alice."

Alice looked up from her bowl. Her pale cheeks were flushed. The front of her dress was splashed with stains. "Oh, could I?"

Nori nodded. Kiyomi had taught her to use a fork.

"We should have a few in the kitchen. I can get one."

"Have a servant fetch one," Akira said lazily. He was reading a book under the table and only half trying to conceal it. As promised, he'd hired back a gardener and two maids. He'd wanted to hire a cook too, but Nori's protests convinced him otherwise.

"She doesn't need one," Will objected. He snapped up a long strand of noodles on his chopsticks as if to further emphasize the ease of it. "She needs to learn to do things. Besides, it's rude."

Nori raised an eyebrow. This was the side of him that she did not like. He had all of Akira's arrogance.

"It's not rude."

Akira looked like he was going to say something, but Nori's irate glance silenced him. He shrugged.

Will smirked. "She doesn't need a champion. It's just a fork."

"Every night she sits here, and every night half her food is left on the plate. It's just a fork indeed. I'm tired of watching you two ignore it."

Will's blue eyes went cold. "My dear—"

"Don't," she snapped. "I'm the one who cooks. It's my right to be offended if my food doesn't get eaten."

Alice was red as a tomato. She looked down, and her silvery hair came forward to cover her face.

Will looked to Akira for support but received none.

Will conceded with a smile, but something about his demeanor shifted. He waved a hand.

"If she's going to use a fork, she can go eat in the kitchen. I'm not going to encourage her failings, heaven knows she doesn't need my help with that."

Without a word, Alice picked up her bowl and went into the kitchen.

Disgust washed over Nori like a wave. Akira was lost in his book again, and Will was gesturing for a servant to bring more wine. Neither of them seemed bothered. But then neither of them knew what it felt like to be overlooked.

It was in the small things. And then, one day, without even realizing it, you looked in the mirror and you were small too.

Nori picked up her bowl.

"Oh, will you sit down," Will snapped.

Finally, Akira spoke. "Will," he said, "let her be."

She went into the kitchen and found Alice standing at the sink and looking confused. She was taller than Nori by a foot, with the long legs of the women in the magazines. She looked older than her sixteen years.

But right now, with her makeup scrubbed away, Nori saw vulnerability for the first time.

"You can just leave that."

Alice turned to face her. "I'm sorry. I couldn't find the trash."

"It's all right."

Already this small exchange was more than they'd shared in five months under the same roof. Will had a way of sucking up all the air in the room.

Alice hesitated. "Why . . . why did you help me?"

Nori decided on the simplest answer. "Why not?"

Alice flushed, and quick tears sprang to her gray eyes. "I thought you didn't like me. That you looked down on me."

Nori could only stare in stunned silence. She'd never heard something so absurd. After a beat: "Why?"

Alice shrugged. "I assume they've told you why we left London."

Nori shook her head. "I asked Akira-san once. But he said it wasn't his story to tell. And I've never asked Will."

Alice laughed, and it was spellbinding. "It's not his story to tell either, though that's certainly never stopped him. It's mine."

Their eyes met from across the room, and a mutual understanding surged between them like a low current.

"You wear your yukatas wrong," Nori said shyly. "I can teach you the right way. If you like."

The smile she received in return was all the answer she needed.

ALICE

She keeps her promises. That's more than I can say for . . . well, anyone.

Nori's small hands move deftly as she dresses me in the silk robes of this little island. She shows me step by step the correct way to do it. When she's finished, she sits me at her vanity. She takes her ivory comb and parts my hair down the middle.

"I'm going to tie it up into two pieces first," she tells me. "This is how the proper ladies wear their hair in summer."

Her touch is so gentle that it makes me want to weep.

I must admit that I judged her rather harshly at first. She is funny-looking, without doubt, with no fashion sense to speak of. Her hair is a tragedy. She doesn't read magazines or watch television; she has no interests outside of her books and needle-work. She doesn't wear makeup—at all, doesn't even paint her nails!—and the only music she listens to is that ancient classical nonsense that Will plays.

Truthfully, she is dreadfully boring. If she were not so odd-looking, I might mistake her for wallpaper.

If we were back home in London, I would never even look at her.

But this is not London. This is not my home. I am a stranger in her country, a guest in her house, and she has shown me kindness. Even before the other night. I have seen her in the kitchen, practicing Western dishes so that Will and I may feel more at home. She makes sure that the servants bring tea to our rooms in the morning. Though she has done it quietly, she has set upon the impossible task of trying to make everyone happy.

"Did your mother teach you this?" I ask her, eager to know more about her. She is always so quiet, and though she smiles often, there is a lingering sadness about her.

Her hands don't miss a beat, but I see the swift flash of agony cross her face. She composes herself quickly, but I catch it.

"My mother is gone," she says simply. "Someone else taught me this."

I reach up to catch her hand in mine. "When did she die?"

Nori twists the two sections of my hair together and binds them with a pin. "She's not dead. Just gone."

I cannot fathom this. I am stupid—everyone in my family has always assured me of this—but still. I decide to try a differ-ent tack.

"My mother died when I was seven. I have two older sisters, Anne and Jane, and they raised me along with my father. So I know what it is like not to have a mother to look after you."

Nori smiles as if she finds my comment very quaint indeed.

"I am glad you had your siblings. That must have been a comfort."

I wrinkle my nose. Some comfort. Jane is a hateful cow, and Anne is just generally unpleasant. I don't love either of my sisters. I don't even like them.

"Well, you have Akira. You seem close."

This is not quite true. Her fervent devotion to him seems painfully one-sided. She is always hovering at the edges of his vision, hoping he will look at her. From what I can see, he rarely does.

She places one of her decorative flower pins in my hair. "There, done. You look radiant."

I smile appreciatively at my reflection. I do know that I am very beautiful. I don't think this is vain—everyone tells me I am—and besides, it is the only thing I have going for me, so it's just as well.

I have no money, for Will controls the purse strings. He gives me an allowance, but it's only to keep me out of his way. I have no name, for my father has stripped me of it.

For now, at least.

"You have such lovely hair," she says longingly. She plucks at one of her curls. "So silky and straight. I wish . . ." Her voice trails off into nothing.

Now I feel guilty for thinking she looked odd.

"Nonsense," I say. "You have the prettiest eyes. Your skin is perfect and I'd kill for your figure."

She flushes. "You don't have to flatter me."

I gesture for us to switch places, and she takes my seat on the velvet cushion. I must say, now that I think on it, she's not the worst case I've seen.

"What do you want to look like?" I ask her.

Her eyelashes flutter. "I don't know. More like you."

I look at her honest face and am deeply moved. There's something about her that lets me know I can trust her.

The same simplicity that made me look down on her is the reason I know she won't hurt me. And the same things that drew me to my old friends, my old love, are the reasons that I have their knives buried in my back.

"You never asked me why I came here."

She inclines her head. "Alice."

I feel sick all of a sudden. "Yes?"

"Why are you here?"

I tell her before I lose my nerve.

"I didn't have a choice. My father sent me away for bringing shame on our family. I fell in love with a stable boy, it's so cliché, really, it's . . . I thought he loved me too but . . . he betrayed me, he sold the story to the newspaper, so I . . . I . . . Nobody writes to me, nobody. I was sent along with William on his travels, but he hates me, he has hated me since we were children. He treats me like—"

I break off and feel the hot tears pouring down my face. I can see myself clearly in the mirror looking like a fool.

"I have been abandoned by everyone I thought I could trust. I can't go home. I don't know when I'll be forgiven, if I'll ever be forgiven. Even in Paris there were too many people from our circle, so we couldn't stay there either. So now I have nobody."

The truth of this washes over me and I say it again, in the vain hope that I might finally feel clean.

"I have nobody."

A hush falls over the room. Nori's face doesn't change. She turns to face me and takes both of my hands in hers. Her touch is like salve on a burn.

"I have something to tell you."

I stifle a sob. "What is it?"

She gives me a wry smile. "You should sit. It's a long story."

Tokyo, Japan
July 1954

Nori turned fourteen in a haze of blue light.

The summer festival was bustling with people, and she held tight to Akira so that she would not lose him. He had bought her a deep blue kimono embroidered with golden butterflies and tied with a gold sash. She'd spent hours straightening her hair, and she'd sewn together a flower crown she'd made from scraps of silk.

Akira noticed neither of these things, but Nori did not mind.

Alice was home with a chill, and Nori missed her dearly. The two of them had become inseparable. Akira gave his tacit approval, but William was not handling it well. He couldn't stand to be eclipsed. He had no patience for anything, and worse, he had no empathy. She had thought he was like Akira: that underneath the initial coldness there would be a deep well of kindness.

But she was not sure anymore.

He had become so unpleasant towards her lately—never in front of Akira, of course—that it had become second nature to avoid him. Their nighttime meetings were gradually fading away to nothing.

Thankfully, he had chosen not to come.

Nori did not have to share her brother with anyone, and that was just the way she liked it.

Akira cast her a suspicious glance. "You're awfully quiet today."

He was carrying a pack full of things he'd bought for her on his back. It was already fit to burst. He was carrying three yakitori skewers wrapped in paper in his free hand.

She stuck her tongue out. "I'm not plotting anything, Oniichan. I'm just happy to spend time with you."

Akira's face softened and he smiled. "I am sorry I've been so busy. Composing is difficult. And I'm just a few exams away from finishing school. I just want to get things right."

"You do everything right," she assured him. "I am sure this will be no different."

He kissed her knuckles. "Ever the optimist, aren't you, little one?"

She beamed. Akira's mood had been sunny for weeks now. He always had a kind word or a fleeting touch; sometimes he even gave her little pieces of candy or bows for her hair.

"Not so little," she protested playfully. "Catching up to you every day."

He laughed. "Not quite."

She pressed her palm against his heart. "It's time to make my wish. Will you get me a lantern?"

He raised an eyebrow. "Do you still believe in that kind of thing?"

"*Hai.*"

She expected a reprimand, but he just sighed and went off to do as she asked.

A group of boys ran past her and knocked her off-balance. She took two steps back, trying not to fall, and felt a hand grasp her elbow. Her right ankle rolled and she felt something twist. She turned to face a short man wearing a large pair of glasses.

"Ah . . . *arigatou.* I didn't mean to."

He showed her a gap-toothed smile. "You're welcome, *chibi hime.* It's no trouble at all."

Little princess.

She frowned. "You . . . you know who I am?"

He bowed very low. "Only in passing. I am Hiromoto. I own the antique shop on the other side of Chiba. I used to see your noble brother's father from time to time. You would have no way of knowing a poor man like me."

At once she felt her guilt flare up. "I'm sorry, I . . . I didn't . . ."

"No, no, no need. I won't keep you. But if you ever have a free afternoon, I would be honored if you would stop by my shop." He smiled at her again. "I think you will be impressed. I have a large collection of rare and beautiful things."

She inclined her head. He swept her another bow and disappeared back into the crowd.

She felt Akira tap her lightly on the top of her head. "*Aho.* Why are you standing in the middle of the road?"

"*Gomen, Oniichan.* I didn't notice."

He handed her a blue paper lantern with a lit candle already inside. "Are you ever going to tell me what you wish for?"

Nori was indignant. "No!"

He laughed at her. "Well, get on with it. We should get home before it gets too late."

She squeezed her eyes shut and let the lantern float upwards until it was lost among all the others and there was no way of telling them apart.

Dear God,

    Please don't change anything. This is just fine.

Ai,
Nori

She opened her eyes and yawned.

"Home?" Akira asked.

She nodded.

"Well then, you walk ahead. You should know the way."

Nori hesitated. "I twisted my ankle."

Akira frowned. "How?"

"I tripped. Back there."

He rolled his eyes.

"Come on. I'll carry you."

She tried not to look eager but obviously failed.

Akira shifted his pack to the front to make room for her on his back. "It's just for today. *Ne?*"

"Mm-hm."

"I mean it, Nori. It's ridiculous."

"I know, Nii-san."

He crouched down, and she hopped onto his back, wrapping her arms and legs around him like a koala clinging to a sturdy branch.

They walked all the way home like that, and she let herself drift into a half sleep, basking in the smell of his bath soap and the smoky aroma of barbecued meats from the festival.

They went in through the back gate, through the garden. He laid her underneath her favorite tree, and she realized that he had never stopped watching her. He still knew her better than anyone. The rift that had been growing between them had all but mended, without a single word needing to be said.

He handed her a lollipop. "Don't stay out here too long."

Nori smiled up at him. "Strawberry?"

"Of course. *Oyasumi.*"

"Good night."

She watched him slide open the wooden screen door. The light hit him and his shadow fell over her. Then the door shut and he was gone.

Nori finished her candy and watched the stars. She liked to imagine that if she could climb to the very top of the old tree, she would be able to grab hold of them and stitch them together.

What a fine cloak that would be.

She laid her face against the tree. It wouldn't hurt to close her eyes for just a little bit. She would go to sleep in a while, but out here, with her face towards the sky, she felt so gloriously free.

She did not hear the footsteps. By the time her eyes opened, there was already a body on top of hers. She could smell smoke.

Even before her eyes adjusted, she knew it was Will.

"Oh, Will," she sighed. "You scared me."

He rubbed his nose against her hair. "Do I frighten you, little kitten?"

She felt a flash of irritation. "Not so little anymore. Get off."

He ignored her protests and kissed her. She allowed it for a moment before pulling away.

"You're drunk," she said, not bothering to hide her distaste. "You taste like sake."

He kissed her again, deeper this time. She could feel his hips grinding against hers. She tried and failed to wriggle free. She had never allowed him more than the occasional furtive grope over her dress. She wrestled her mouth away from him so that his kisses fell on her cheek.

"Will, that's enough."

"You're always saying 'not so little,'" he hissed. "But you're still afraid. Just like a child."

"I'm not a child!" she protested.

"Then do you feel for me no longer?" he asked, and he sounded genuinely hurt. It was rare for him to be genuine about anything.

She hesitated. She could not deny that he inspired something in her that could only be called affection. But he was turning out to be more than she could handle.

His cruelty towards Alice and his love of mind games hinted at something that frightened her.

"I don't know, Will," she whispered. "I don't think . . . we should keep doing this."

His face was half hidden by shadow, but there was no mistaking the rage on it. "So you're taking her side, then?"

"I'm not taking anyone's side. Alice is my friend—"

He growled. "And what am I?"

She recoiled now. "Will, you're hurting me. *Hanashite.* Let me go."

"I saw you first."

"Will, this has nothing to do with—"

He bit her shoulder so hard that she cried out. "You aren't going to take the word of that stupid slut," he whispered. "You aren't. Not after all I've done for you."

She felt the tears forming at the corners of her eyes and tried to hold them back. This was William. He was a wealthy gentleman. He was her brother's best friend. He was Alice's cousin.

And he had been something to her too. He had been kind. He wouldn't hurt her.

"William," she said, and she was proud, so proud, that her voice did not waver. "You know that I care for you. Truly. We can talk about this in the morning. I promise."

His grip on her wrists loosened. Her breath hitched.

"It's okay, Will," she soothed. "It's all right. I just need to go to bed now. I promised Akira, *ne*? Please just—"

It was exactly the wrong thing to say. His grip tightened again, and this time, it was like steel.

He lowered his face onto hers, and all she could see were those blue eyes, blazing with cold fire. Her voice left her. She felt herself turn to stone.

"'Akira, Akira,'" he mocked her, with his mouth pressed against her ear. "That's all you can ever say. Do you have a brain inside your head, little girl? Do you have a single thought of your own?"

Speak. You have to speak.

Will's fingers moved swiftly. He had beautiful hands. Perfect piano fingers. Perfect.

"Time to grow up, kitten."

Her eyes would not close. All she could see was the blue.

Blue, like sapphires. Blue, like the car in my dreams. Blue, blue, blue.

Vaguely, she felt the fabric of her kimono as it slid up her thighs and across her belly. She heard the jingle of a belt buckle as it came undone. She heard an owl cry out.

And then there was red.

The pain was sharp. It knocked the wind out of her, and all she could manage was a low whimper. Her muscles contracted, protesting this new invasion, but still her eyes would not close.

Speak.

She could feel a solitary tear pooling at the base of her neck.

Speak.

"Now you're a woman," he whispered, his breath coming faster and faster. "And now you are mine."

CHAPTER FOURTEEN

NIGHT SONG

Tokyo, Japan
July 1956

Sixteen now," Akira mused. He held up his glass, and Ayame refilled it. "That was fast."

Not so fast, Nori thought. The sunlight was pouring down on her, but her skin still felt cold. The locket Akira had given her this morning was cool against her neck. It was white gold, with a treble clef engraved on the front of it. When he'd handed it to her, she'd thanked him politely, like a grown-up. Then she'd cried in her room for half an hour.

Now they were sitting on the patio having an early dinner in her honor. Akira had hired a real chef for the occasion. Alice was wearing her new red yukata, tied properly now. She was seated beside Nori and squeezed her friend's hand underneath the table.

There were no secrets between them anymore. They spent their days together, and often they had the house to themselves.

Akira had finished secondary school with honors and was now an official member of the Tokyo Philharmonic, the youngest member at only twenty years old. He was relegated to third chair first violin, but he did not seem bothered. In his mind, this was only a stepping-stone to far greater things. Nori was desperately grateful that he had chosen a local posting and did everything she could to make Japan appealing to him. Namely, she tried not to annoy him very much.

Yuko had started to make overtures, routinely sending gifts of money and cards imploring Akira to return to Kyoto. He gave the money to Nori and burned the cards unopened.

He had their mother's inheritance now. He would never need money again.

Will was constantly traveling and was sometimes away for weeks or even months. A pity he was here today. He'd cut short a stay in Brussels to attend. For her benefit entirely, he claimed.

Nori had her doubts.

Without his disapproving gaze, Alice had flourished, and Nori could clearly see the passionate, flighty girl she had once been. She had been careful to avoid any hint of scandal, not that anyone was likely to notice in this far-flung corner of the world. She had never bothered to learn Japanese, but Nori was happy to translate for her on their frequent shopping trips.

Nori slept in Alice's bed a few nights a week, and they would stay up late reading through Seiko's old diaries.

Akira turned to speak to Ayame, and Alice sneezed.

In that instant, Will's eyes met hers.

No secrets.

Except for last night. Except for what happened two years ago and now happened nearly every month. Except for the way she tortured herself daily, agonizing over the insane mix of feelings that fought for dominance inside her.

Nori excused herself from the table and retreated to the

bathroom off the kitchen. She caught a glimpse of her reflection and winced.

There was nothing visibly wrong with her. In fact, she looked rather well today. There was no sign of her sleepless nights.

She went to great lengths to conceal the truth from Akira. She didn't want him to see.

But she could not help but be somewhat hurt that he had not.

The door opened and Will slipped inside. Without saying a word, he handed her his glass of plum wine.

"Thank you."

He chuckled. "You could have chosen a better place to hide."

She shrugged. There was no hiding. She was Alice's friend, Will's possession, and Akira's ever-doting sister. She often felt that she was the only thing holding the entire ridiculous charade together. This makeshift family of exiles would collapse into nothing without her.

She downed the wine in one gulp. It burned the back of her throat, but the anxious knot in her belly began to loosen.

Will smirked. "Happy birthday, my love."

She closed her eyes. Not for the first time, she felt an unworthy surge of affection for him. So much so that she tolerated his three a.m. visits to her bedroom in silence. But still, she had never been able to shake the feeling that something was deeply wrong. It was like a chill that never left her.

"You look tired," he said, his voice tinged with sympathy.

"I am tired."

He frowned and, without asking, moved to lift up the hem of her dress. She knew that he was eyeing the bright purple bruises on her skin.

"I told you to stop pinching yourself."

Nori shrugged again. "And I told you I'd try."

Will *tsked*. "I'm telling Akira. I warned you twice."

She felt a ripple of irritation. Nori met his gaze full on. "Since we are in the business of telling secrets, perhaps I should speak to him too."

He did not falter. "Akira adores me," he said smugly. "He would never hear a word against me, kitten. You know that."

Nori hesitated. "He . . . I . . . me too."

Will's eyes went dark. "Are you sure of that?"

The words died on her tongue, and she tasted ash. She *was* sure. But then he looked at her, far more confident than she could ever be, and she was laid bare. Like mercury, he slipped through the cracks of her certainty and found the poison seed of doubt.

He smiled at her, and his eyes lit up again. It was like a switch flipped on and off with him, all the time. It made her dizzy.

He took her hands and kissed them. "Don't fret, little love. Don't fret. I would never betray your secrets." He played his trump card. "I love you, remember?"

She folded in on herself. She simply had no more fight left. It was so much easier to believe it.

"You do?"

"Of course I do," he soothed. "That is why you must trust me. Only me. Always."

It was another week before Nori could get a moment to herself. Will had left for a piano competition in Prague, and Alice was occupied writing desperate letters to London begging for forgiveness. Now that she was eighteen, she needed to return to London and court marriage prospects. Otherwise she would have no future at all.

Akira was home, for once, but he was locked in his room. All he said was that he was composing something. He would not say what, but whatever it was, it was consuming him. The trays of food she made for him were sent back uneaten.

Nori settled onto her new favorite tree branch. It was much higher than her old perch. Nobody could come up here after her.

The house had gone to sleep and now she was free. She opened the diary. It was the last one in the box, and as much as she loved Alice, she needed to read this one alone.

She had followed her mother through four years in Paris, caught up in a torrid love affair with a man who was never named. She had witnessed Seiko's defiance, her refusal to return to Japan even after she was cut off. She had felt a jolt of pain when Seiko's lover had turned out to be false, having been secretly engaged to another woman all along.

And now, as her mother ran out of money, ran out of friends, and ran out of hope, Nori could finally see the start of the transformation into the woman who'd birthed two children and abandoned them both.

It was time to finish the story.

December 15th, 1934

He won't see me. He won't even answer my letters, and anyway, I have no more money for postage. I have no more money for food. Mama will send me nothing else. Someone has told her what I have done—I don't know who, she has her spies everywhere—and now she is insisting that I come home. She says that I am an old maid at twenty-two and that if I tarry much longer no one will want me. She says I am used goods and I must come home.

I will not.

They tell me he is married now. I refuse to believe it. He wouldn't do it. He wouldn't do it. His wicked mother may be able to keep him from me, but he would never marry another woman. He was engaged to her, I know this now, but he never loved her. How can he have loved her if he never mentioned her to me? In four years?

He promised me he'd love me forever.

It cannot be. Life is different here. Love is different here. For the first time, I can see how marriage can be a marvel, a safe haven in a dangerous world. It is not a meat market, or a sentence to a slow death.

A marriage of true souls is just below the angels. And he taught me this, he believes this too. I know he does.

So I know that he will not marry her just to please his mother. The landlords say they will have me thrown out onto the street if I do not pay soon.

They will not.

The world will be as I say it is. I am Seiko Kamiza, the only heir to my house and ancient name. I am blessed. I am favored by God.

He would never forsake me this way. He would not.

January 1st, 1935

He has married her. They tell me she is already pregnant.

My letters were all sent back unopened. His mother has left a message with my landlords. She says that if I try to see him, she will have the police throw me in jail before sending me back to my filthy heathen island.

Mama has sent me a one-way boat ticket back to Kyoto. It leaves next week.

I can't go. I can't be caged again. I swear I will die.

I will throw myself into the pond and drown. Then they will all be very sorry they treated me so horribly.

My love, my false, lying love, will find my body and think, "See. Look what I have done."

Papa will be sorry that he never loved me for being a girl.

And Mama will be sorry for nothing because she thinks her will is God's will and so she can never be wrong.

And I will not be sorry either for I will be dead and past my pain. Good riddance.

January 10th, 1935

I can see the ocean from my cabin. I can think of nothing but drowning. I imagine it would hurt for a while. But then the pain would stop forever.

I heard of a girl who hung herself but I would not like the marks on my neck, so I cannot do this.

I have lost. Mama has won, as she always does.

I have buried my girlhood in Paris. I return to Japan as a woman, with all the bitterness that comes with it.

I have no place outside of my name. I thought I could carve one, I truly did, and for a moment I thought . . . but . . . that woman laughed at my hopes and called me a savage. I loved her son, I would have died for him, but all she saw was a foreign whore.

That's what I am to Europe. A curiosity at best, something to be fawned over like a newborn. But beneath that, they deem me inferior. I could never have married one of their men. I could never have had his children.

I am a fool.

Mama warned me. I wouldn't hear it. But I hear it now.

The worst part is that it wasn't she who broke me. I broke myself.

I don't think I will ever be happy again.

February 1st, 1935

I am to be married. His name is Yasuei Todou. He is thirty-three and apparently still unmarried because he has no money to speak of, so none of the other noble girls will have him, and he is too proud to settle for someone newly made.

This is good for me, as he is in no position to turn down a cousin to royalty. Mama will give him a fortune to marry me.

Enough to overlook any whispers that he is getting a sec-ondhand bride.

Still, he has an old name and a manor house in Tokyo. The rumor is that his father was a drunk and a gambler and they have nothing left but the house and the name.

Mama says he has good prospects and will be sure to rise. Whatever that means. She will pull her strings, same as always.

She has given me a miniature photograph of him. He is certainly serious-looking. He is not handsome but he is not ugly, so I suppose it could be worse.

I do wonder what he is like. I've never met him. But then I'll find out soon enough.

We're getting married tomorrow.

There was a wedding dress already laid out on my bed the day I arrived home.

I have no choice. As it turns out, I never had a choice at all.

February 12th, 1935

My husband has just left my room. I can still smell his sweat on me.

He is mercifully quick about it. There's that, at least. It took him a full week after the wedding to manage the deed. He hates me, I think, though he is too proper to say so to my face.

I have all the time in the world to write, he gives me noth-ing to do. I am not allowed to have friends over. If I had any friends in Tokyo, I imagine this would distress me. There are barely any books and I have no allowance yet, so I cannot buy more.

There is not even a piano here. I have asked for a music room.

He says he will consider it if I give him a son.

I doubt he will get any living sons from me. My grandmother could not manage it. My mother could not manage it. And they were penitent, desperately penitent to a foreign God. They did everything in their power to lift the curse on our boys.

I have lived all my life as a sinner.

I will probably give him a three-headed girl. And then I won't get my music room.

March 28th, 1935

I have missed my course.

I pray for a dead child.

It would be a mercy. Poor girl. Poor, damned girl.

September 8th, 1935

It's been a long time since I have had the strength to write.

The baby will come in December or January. They say I am past my dangerous months and that a healthy child is sure to be born. I feel so tired all the time that I would lay no bets on it.

Mama has sent me an endless amount of teas and tonics to drink. She says she has had a priest and a shrine maiden bless them, that they will give me a healthy son.

One of them smelled like blood. I wonder how many peasants she had sacrificed to make it.

Luckily, my husband thinks she is mad and forbids her from sending me anything else. His mood has improved considerably and I am allowed a small allowance now. He is having a library put in for me.

He doesn't read. All he does is smoke and play chess by himself.

The doctor says from the way I am carrying that it's a boy. I am sure my mother threatened to have his family skinned alive if he said otherwise, though, so I do not allow myself to be hopeful.

I will never allow myself to be hopeful again.

"Little madam!"

Nori jumped and almost slipped from her perch. She dug her heels in and stuck her head out from between the leaves. Ayame was looking up at her.

"I've been calling you, my lady."

Unseen, Nori slipped the diary down the front of her blouse.

"I'm sorry. I didn't hear."

Ayame frowned. "You're up too high. Your brother would not like it."

Nori swung down, expertly navigating the grooves in the

wood where she could fit her feet. She spent half her life in this
tree; she trusted it more than anything. Except Akira.

Once her feet hit the ground, she gave Ayame her best smile.

"But we won't tell him, will we?"

Ayame sighed. "My lady . . . I wish you would not take such
risks."

When did you grow to care for me so much?

"I'll be careful," she promised. "What did you need, Ayame-
san?"

The servant shuffled her feet. "Obocchama has asked to
see you."

Nori blinked. "What? Why?"

"He didn't say. He won't say."

She sighed. Akira never sent for her; he simply showed up.
For him to send Ayame did not bode well. "Why do you look so
terrified?"

Ayame's face was pale. "He's in a mood, I'm afraid."

She felt her stomach turn over. Akira had said three words to
her all month. He hadn't even bothered to take her to the festival for her sixteenth birthday; she'd gone alone.

Something was clearly bothering him, but Nori had been too
afraid to ask what. Apparently she was about to find out.

"Where is he?"

"He's in the study, my lady."

Nori handed Ayame the diary and headed off without another word. There was no point delaying a storm. If she had to
face one, she would face it head-on.

She took off her shoes and took the shortcut through the now
unused room that had once been used to house the family shrine.

Even now, she could see the spot where she'd nearly died. The servants had replaced the mats, but beneath that, the floorboards were discolored. The bleach had removed the stain from her blood, but it had left its mark. If she really tried, she could smell the sharp scent of her fear. She could still feel that raw desperation buried somewhere just beneath the surface.

It seemed like so long ago now that she'd had no one.

But it wasn't. She would never forget any of it; every person she'd ever met was seared into her skin like a brand.

Sometimes she looked in the mirror and thought it was nothing short of a miracle that she still drew breath.

She tapped lightly on the door to the study and heard the sound of the violin break off. She recognized the song. It was Schubert's "Ave Maria," one of the first things he'd ever played for her. He'd often told her he didn't favor it.

"Come in," he said.

She went inside, closed the door, and waited. Akira looked her up and down in that infuriating way he always did. His nose wrinkled.

"Why do you always look like you've been living in the woods?"

She had no rebuttal. She was covered in dirt and leaves, with scuffs on her arms and bruises on her knees. Her blouse had a wine stain on the front. Her hair was a lost cause; she would need to have Alice see to it later.

"*Gomen.*"

"And you stink."

She winced. "I'm sorry."

Akira crossed his arms. "We need to talk."

Nori felt the pit of her stomach fall out. Her knees began to buckle.

"About?"

He took a deep breath. If she didn't know better, she'd say he was gathering his courage.

"I have to go away."

She sighed with relief so strong she could almost weep with it. "Oh, God. You scared me. Just that, then. Where are you going this time?"

Akira did not meet her gaze. "Vienna."

"Austria?"

"Yes."

"For how long?"

This was the core question. He never left her for more than two months, three at the most. He'd taken only four trips in the last two years. She had been dreading this moment, but she was prepared.

Akira still did not look at her. "Nine months. Maybe more."

She folded like a paper doll. Only his quick reaction stopped her from falling to the floor.

"Nori—"

"*No.*"

"But it's—"

"No."

"Sit down," he urged, gripping her elbow. "Sit down before you fall and crack your head open."

The world was spinning. She felt the blood rush to her temples. "You can't go."

"Nori, just listen."

She dropped to the floor, and her grip on his collar meant that he was pulled down with her and forced to look into her pale, horrified face.

"You can't leave me alone with him," she whispered, too low for him to hear.

"What?"

Why don't you see me?

"You can't fucking leave for nine months!"

He gasped. "Where did you learn that word?"

She pushed him with all her meager strength, and he fell back.

The strings that had held up for so long, as she was passed from one puppet master to another, had finally snapped.

"I lived in a whorehouse, Oniichan, I know how to swear," she blazed. "I know many things, though you give me credit for nothing."

He stared at her blankly. She had never seen him at a loss for words. But it did not last. His face darkened.

"You don't know anything," he hissed at her. "I have received an invitation from the foremost concert violinist in Europe. He wants to train me, Nori. He wants to take me as his pupil. This is the pinnacle of my ambitions, this is beyond them. I have to go."

She clenched her fists. "What about me?"

Akira was incredulous. She had never raised her voice to him before. "Nori—"

"What about me, damn it?" she cried.

Her brother got to his feet and brushed himself off, as if that would remove the lint and everything else that was beneath him from his presence.

"What about you?" he said coldly. "You have servants to look after your every want. No one beats you here, no man will lay a hand on you. You are fed, you are clothed in the finest silks, you have a playmate in the form of that stupid girl. I have remained in this miserable country day in and day out for you. In a few years I'm going to marry some spoiled bitch just to keep our grandfather from skinning you alive and wearing your flesh as a shirt. I'm going to give up my music, my traveling, my dreams of touring Europe forever. I'm going to take up the reins of this cursed family of ours and try to make a world where bastard children are not murdered in their sleep. And now I want something for myself—nine months—and you rage like a child."

Her eyes filled with angry tears. "That's not fair."

"It is exactly fair," he corrected her. "You're a child. And a fool. And I'm not your father, for God knows he could never be bothered with you."

She felt a swift pang of agony. She found her feet and held out her hands, as if she could stop what must inevitably come next.

Akira's eyes were harder than she'd ever seen them. There was no tenderness in them, none at all. His well of patience had finally run dry.

"And of course, we know that I'm not Mother," he scoffed. "Seeing as you ran her off already."

A hush fell over the room. Even the clocks stopped their ticking.

She went perfectly still. Akira's eyes widened; his mouth opened like a fish gasping for air. He took a half step towards her.

Nori picked up the glass vase on the table beside her. She looked at it, looked at him. He blinked.

And then she threw the vase squarely at his head.

He dodged but barely. It shattered on the wall behind him.

She laughed.

"Have you lost your mind?" he whispered. He put a hand to his temple where the vase had grazed him.

Nori contemplated this for a moment. "Maybe," she said, bending down to pick up one of the whiskey glasses that Akira kept stacked neatly on a shelf near the door. "As far as I'm concerned, I am long overdue."

She threw the glass. Akira yelped and ducked behind the couch.

"*NORI!*"

She picked up another glass. This one was heavier than the first—it must have been part of the expensive crystal collection that Akira had inherited from his father.

"Stop it!" Akira cried. "Not that one! For God's sake, Nori, it's an heirloom."

She shrugged and felt her blouse slip off her shoulder. She had lost so much weight that almost nothing fit her anymore.

"Mother left because she was terrified," she said. "And miserable. And because she had a song to sing, and our grandmother and your father jammed it right back down her throat until she was suffocating on it. She couldn't breathe. She could never *breathe* . . ."

She should have been unnerved by the way her voice sounded, but she couldn't feel anything anymore. She wasn't even angry. Just numb.

"And that wasn't me," she continued. She could feel the emotions she'd ignored for so long spilling over. "That wasn't my fault. Everyone has always blamed me, but it's not my fault . . . and now you . . . you too, Oniichan . . ."

Akira's eyes were fixed on her.

She felt her fist close on the glass. Vaguely, she heard it shatter, felt the shards dig into her palm. A warm rush told her she was bleeding, and it felt like freedom, like that terrible, wonderful moment when she'd thought that she was forever past her pain.

"You were all I had," she whispered.

Is this what it comes down to in the end, Mother? Do we all end up alone? Dancing figurines in a music box, moving, but never going anywhere at all?

Her brother's face changed. He was pale and shivering, but once his eyes fell on her blood, his strength appeared to return to him.

"Ayame," he croaked. He tried again with a stronger voice. "Ayame!"

Nori looked down at her hand. There were three large shards of glass sticking out of her palm and two smaller ones between her thumb and forefinger. The cuts weren't particularly deep, but it looked bad.

But it didn't hurt. Her emotion spent, she sank to the floor.

She sensed a flurry of movement at the door, some rushed words. Akira said something to Ayame twice before she finally left.

Nori wrapped her hand in her blouse.

Akira knelt in front of her with the medicine kit at his side. His hands were shaking as he tried to open the tin lid.

"Give me your hand."

She didn't move.

Akira reached for her. "Nori, give me your hand."

Her head was throbbing. She didn't have the energy to fight him anymore. She did as she was told.

Akira's face was a funny green color. He picked up a pair of tweezers and started to pull the largest shard out of her palm.

Nori winced but did not cry out. She watched with a kind of macabre fascination.

Akira cursed under his breath. "Look what you've done. What's wrong with you, Nori?"

She looked away. "Nothing. I'm sorry."

He touched the side of her face, and against her will, she met his gaze. Something inside of her stretched and broke at his touch.

"Are you okay?"

She felt tears starting to fall. "It doesn't hurt."

"That isn't what I asked you."

She choked on a tiny sob. "Oniichan . . ."

Akira hesitated. "I know you think I don't see you," he whispered. "But it isn't true. I just don't know what to say to you. I have never been able to protect you the way I wanted. And I'm not . . . I was never meant to take care of anyone. I'm not built for it."

Nori shook her head. "You have done more than enough."

He sighed. "You know, when they told me about you, I wanted to hate you. It would have been so much easier for me to hate you. I never understood why Mother left, and then they told me about you and it made sense. I blamed my father for years, but then he died and I had no one to hold my anger. No one to put it on. And then they moved me to Kyoto and I found you."

She bowed her head.

"But then I saw you and you looked . . . so much like her. And you were such a frail little thing, I just couldn't do it."

He plucked the next shard of glass from her palm, so quickly that she didn't have time to cry out.

"You're a lot like her too, you know," he continued.

Nori didn't dare breathe. Akira never talked about their mother this much.

He met her eyes. "You terrify me, Nori."

She nipped her lower lip. "But . . . how?"

Akira's eyes were shining with unshed tears. "I don't think she ever had a happy day in her life. She was beautiful and she smiled often, but she always seemed sad. She used to sit me at the piano beside her, you know, and she'd play . . . she played remarkably well. And then when she'd finish, she would smile for just a moment and it was . . ." His voice cracked. "It was the only time it was real."

His cleared his throat. "She adored me," he confessed. "And I tried . . . I tried to make her happy. I started playing the violin to make her happy. And . . . then one day, she kissed me on the forehead, told me I was her world. And then she was just gone. And my father would never talk about her. For the next eleven years, I never knew . . ."

Nori felt a tear slide down her cheek. But there was still no pain her hand.

"I'm sorry," she mumbled.

Akira shook his head. "Before I met you, I was certain of everything. I was completely self-absorbed, there was no one I cared about, so nothing could ever hurt me. And I convinced myself that I was happy."

"And you weren't?"

He smiled at her. "I was safe. I was convinced of my own worth and that was all I needed."

He wrapped her hand, layer by layer, in thick white bandages. Then he pressed it to his heart.

"You taught me another way."

She looked at him, speechless. "I've never taught you anything."

He smiled again, and this time, it pierced her heart like an arrow.

"You have, Nori. And if it comes down to a choice, between our family or my music or anything else . . . I will always choose you."

Her whole body erupted in chills. She drew back her hand.

"Because I'm your responsibility? Or because I'm your half sister?"

Akira tapped her lightly on the bridge of her nose. "Because you are you."

For a long time, neither of them spoke. Then Akira stood up.

"I told Ayame-san to get the doctor. That hand might need stitches," he said quietly, as if he too was reluctant to break the silence. "I should go check on that."

She looked up at him. "You should go to Vienna," she said simply.

He shook his head. "I can't."

"I want you to go," she said, and miraculously, it rang true. "I think you should go and make beautiful music, and see beautiful buildings, and be happy. And when you are finished, come back. Take your lessons from our grandmother, marry a girl, do your duty."

Akira looked grave. "You know everything will change when I become head of the family. Everything will be different."

She smoothed down her skirt. "Everything is always different, Oniichan. Just come back to me."

He nodded and went out.

Nori was alone but felt it no longer. The warmth in her belly radiated outwards, until she was sure that she glowed like a firefly in the dark.

December 24th, 1935

I have done it. God works in mysterious ways for I have given my family what it needs above all else: a boy.

He is a beautiful creature and the doctor says he is perfectly healthy. My husband is overjoyed, Mama is on her way from Kyoto to see him. She will throw the largest party the city has ever seen.

All I want to do is rest. They place my boy on my chest and I watch him sleep.

He has a head full of dark hair and the most wonderful eyes, my family's shade of gray-black. His tiny hands have pink fingernails and he has big feet. I think he will be tall.

He looks as if he were hand-carved just for me.

Mama wants to name him after her father, and my husband wants to name him after his. They want to saddle him from the cradle with the ghosts of dead men. As if his burden is not heavy enough.

But I will name him myself. He is their miracle, their heir, but he is my son.

And I will name him Akira.

The tap on Nori's bedroom door pulled her from the pages. Carefully, she slipped the diary beneath the pillow. She took a deep breath. She had been waiting for this.

The cracks were sealed shut now.

Without waiting for an answer, Will slipped inside. He was still dressed.

"I knew you'd still be awake," he said smugly.

She met his gaze. "I think you should leave."

He laughed at her. "That's cute. Move over. We don't have to do anything tonight, I just want to be near you."

She held out her bandaged hand. Her nightgown slipped off her shoulder, and she felt his eyes on her.

"Please leave, William."

He frowned and crossed his arms. "What are you on about?"

She took another deep breath. "I think I understand you now. It took me long enough, but I think right now I see you for what you are."

He scoffed at her. "Really? And what do you see, kitten?"

Nori inclined her head. "You shine so brightly it blinded me at first. Truly, you do. When I first saw you, I thought you were golden."

Will's lips peeled back from his teeth. "And now?"

She stood up. "And now I see that you are like enamel. You shine on the outside, but on the inside, there is nothing. I actually feel sorry for you. For I may be a half-breed and a bastard girl, but I am not so sad that I need to steal other people's light to fill the hole in myself. You . . . you have everything and you still have nothing."

Will looked as if he'd been struck. He stood there, teetering back and forth. Then he moved towards her.

"Stop it."

He froze. "You . . . you're confused. You know that I love you, little Nori."

"I know that you are jealous of my brother," she said levelly. "And your cousin. Because I love them both. And I could never love you. Even when I didn't know why, I knew it was wrong."

"You don't know the first thing about love," he hissed at her.

"No," she confessed. "But I may one day. You never will because you are capable of loving only yourself. And I feel sorry for you."

"I'll be damned if I accept pity from you," he seethed. He moved forward in three steps and caught her in his arms. "Who has filled your head with this poison? Was it that whore Alice?"

"I have made up my own mind."

"Impossible," he taunted. "You have no mind of your own, that is why you are so delightful."

She looked into his cold blue eyes without flinching. It amazed her how she could have ever been afraid of him, ever thought that she loved him, ever thought that he was anything like Akira.

"I don't know what love is," she told him. "But I know it is not this."

He squeezed her shoulders. "I'm sorry if you think I hurt you. I never meant to."

She offered up a small, sad smile. "I think you mean that. I really do."

"Then—"

Nori pushed him away from her. "You're leaving."

Will flushed. "We'll talk again in the morning."

"You misunderstand. You're leaving Japan. You're going back to London and you are taking Alice with you. You are going to tell everyone that she's been a model citizen and that she'd make a fine wife. That's what you're going to do. And you're going to do it by the end of the month."

He gaped at her. "And why on earth would I do that?"

Nori gestured towards the door. "Because I think your affection for my brother is genuine. And I would spare him from knowing the truth, ever. But you have to go. You have the world at your feet now with your music, you don't need to be here. And you have to give Alice another chance to have a life."

"I will not!" he raged. "I don't take orders from you. You have no power here. You have no power anywhere. You exist only because of the pity of your betters. Nobody would believe a word from your mouth."

"Akira-san would," she said quietly. She held tight to her dignity and did not waver. "Alice would too. And perhaps the London papers. They seem to love a story."

He cut his eyes at her. "Nobody would listen to you."

"Maybe not," she reasoned. "But they can't stop me from speaking. And I can't prevent what will happen to you if my brother ever finds out the truth. Or did he not tell you about our family?"

The color drained from his cheeks. He had the look of a cor-

nered wolf on his face, finally outsmarted by the sheep. She realized how easy it must have been for him to manipulate her
insecurities. She wore them on her sleeve, and he was nothing
if not perceptive.

"I don't want to leave you," he rasped. "I . . ."

She shook her head. "I am sorry, Will. You . . . you were . . ."
She hesitated. Even now, she didn't hate him. "Thank you for
everything you have taught me. I hope you find peace."

He swallowed. "Don't make me go back there," he whimpered. "They're all . . . None of them are anything like you."

She smiled. "That's hardly a tragedy."

He gave her the most stricken look. "It's more of one than
you will ever know."

The tragedy was that had he not been so richly indulged, so
ensured of his own superiority from birth, he might not have
turned out this way at all. But there was no way to know.

Nori held out her hand. "Goodbye, Will."

"We have . . . we have some more time . . ."

"After tonight you will never speak to me again. You won't
try to catch me alone. This is the end of our game, William."

He looked struck to the heart. "I don't want it to end."

"I know," she said gently. "But this is what I need. So
goodbye."

He hesitated. He looked as if he wanted nothing more than
to seize back control, as if he was wondering if he could get her
to change her mind. Apparently the look on her face told him
there was no hope.

"I really did want—" He broke off. "Oh, Nori."

She said nothing. There was nothing else to say.

She watched him go, and when the door shut, she felt a small pang of sadness. But so much larger than that was the sense of soaring freedom.

She remembered, from so long ago, her favorite poem.

> I feel this life is
> Sorrowful and unbearable
> Though I cannot flee away
> Since I am not a bird

Nori crossed to the window and threw it open. The moon was half hidden by clouds, but it was still there.

Maybe I can be a bird.

Tokyo, Japan
October 1956

It was a chilly October morning by the time the Stafford cousins were finally ready to leave. After much pleading, and a begrudging endorsement from Will, Alice was at long last permitted to return home.

Nori and Akira saw them to the docks where the ocean liner was waiting to take them back to the West.

Alice cried buckets as she clung to Nori. Her makeup had already sloughed off.

"I wish you could come with me," she sobbed.

"I'll write to you every week," Nori promised, stroking her friend's silver-blonde hair. "And you must tell me all about the wonderful parties you go to and the pretty dresses you will wear. And when your father arranges your marriage to a handsome gentleman, I will want to know all about it."

Alice wiped her face with her sleeve. "I love you so, my sweet girl."

Nori smiled and kissed both her cheeks. "And I you."

Will and Akira's parting was considerably more restrained. They shook hands and mumbled some things at each other. In all likelihood they would see each other again, perhaps sooner than Nori would have liked.

"I'll see you around, then," Akira said. He failed to hide the disappointment from his voice, and Nori shoved down her guilt for parting them.

Will nodded. "Finish that composition of yours. It's going to be brilliant."

"And yours. I think you should take out some of those fermatas. You know I hate them."

Will smirked. Someone from the boat hollered at them to get on or get left behind.

His eyes fell on Nori.

"Goodbye, then," he said stiffly.

She inclined her head. "Safe travels, Mr. Stafford."

He winced. If he'd expected her to have a change of heart at the last moment, he was destined to be disappointed.

She turned to Alice. "Don't let them break you," she said simply.

Alice smiled that dazzling smile of hers. "Not this time."

They boarded the boat. Akira draped his arm across Nori's shoulder, and they watched it get farther and farther away until it winked off into the gray twilight.

"Are you going to miss them?" Nori asked shyly.

Akira sighed. "A little. But I always knew they'd have to go back to where they belong."

She felt the guilt wash over her. "Well, you have Vienna to look forward to. You leave in just two weeks."

He smiled and his eyes lit up. "I am excited," he confessed. "And I've already told the servants to get everything in order for you. You won't want for anything, I promise."

She suppressed a giggle. She had been managing the house for years now. Akira didn't even know where to find the salt shaker.

"*Hai, Oniichan.*"

"Do you want to go straight back? I have a few hours. We could go into town."

"That sounds nice."

He suddenly frowned. "I wish you wouldn't go out without a coat. You're going to get sick."

She wiggled her nose at him. "You worry too much. I am practically indestructible, Oniichan."

He took off his coat and draped it around her shoulders. "Wear it."

"Oniichan! You'll be cold."

He shrugged. "I'm fine. Let's go."

She folded her arm into the crook of his elbow and let him lead the way. They never really came to this part of the city; they rarely left the safe enclave of wealthy citizens. The festivals were held closer to where they lived, while still offering a neutral meeting place for everyone.

This part of the city was different. It was full of ordinary people.

As they wound their way through the crowds, Nori watched

the messenger boys go by on their bikes and the children walking their dogs. They wound their way through the crowd of people. She let herself drift off into a comfortable waking dream, retaining only enough consciousness to keep her feet moving.

She could smell cooking meats and fish fresh from the ocean. She could hear mothers shouting after their children and men playing dice. There were a few white people too, mingling about with no one giving them a second glance.

Even Nori seemed to blend in seamlessly. Perhaps Japan was more than her grandmother's Kyoto. Perhaps it was like a tapestry of many colors and she could find somewhere to fit after all.

Akira halted, and Nori snapped out of her trance.

She found herself staring at a short, balding man who was drenched in sweat even though it was cool outside. He was wearing an ugly tweed suit and glasses that were too big for his face. He was looking up at Akira in awe.

He bowed low and nearly dropped the stack of scrolls he was carrying.

"Akira-sama," he stammered. "It's such an honor. Such an honor."

Akira frowned and started to move past him, but Nori pinched his hand. Akira didn't like being fawned over, but it happened fairly often.

He shot her a swift look that said, *Fine, I'll humor him*.

"*Konnichiwa*. I'm sorry, have we met?"

The man laughed. "Oh, you wouldn't remember an old fool like me. You were just a child. Your honored mother brought you to my shop years and years ago. You used to like to play with the golden dragons I keep by the register. And she—God bless her—she had a fondness for my silk fans."

Akira blinked. "Oh. You're the antique-seller. Hiromoto-san, isn't it?"

"Yes!" he burst. "Oh, why, yes, you do remember. What an honor. What an honor. It is so wonderful to see you again after all of these years. And so tall!"

Akira flushed. "Yes, well. Thank you."

Hiromoto turned to Nori and bowed. "And what a pleasure to see you again, *chibi hime*."

The memory came back to her in a flash. Though she had done her best to forget that night, it was etched onto her like a tattoo.

"Oh . . . the festival. I bumped into you."

He laughed. "Indeed, indeed you did."

Akira glanced at his watch. "Well, if you will excuse us, Hiromoto-san, we really do have to be going."

He cleared his throat. "Actually, if you would do me the honor, I have a proposition for you. I've heard about your music, of course, such a talent you are. Such a credit to this fine city."

Akira nodded. "Yes, well. Thank you."

"I am having a small event on Christmas Eve, you see," he said. He pulled a handkerchief from his pocket and dabbed at his sweaty forehead. "Nothing too special. But there will be some important people there. Politicians and such. And I would be so honored if you would play. Your mother—God bless her—she played the piano at an event of mine. She moved the audience to tears. This was right before . . ." He coughed. The official story put out by the family was that Seiko had died, but almost everyone knew she'd run away.

"Anyway. I was hoping you would play at my event? I would pay, of course."

Akira tried and failed to look remorseful. "I am afraid that won't be possible. I have a prior engagement and will be away for some time."

Hiromoto's face fell. "Ah. I see. I understand, of course, I do. I just thought it would be nice to honor the memory of your mother." He turned to Nori. "I hope you will attend? The more, the merrier."

She waited for Akira to apologize on her behalf. He'd come up with some excuse, surely.

Akira hesitated. He looked vaguely sentimental, which was rare.

"Well, in that case . . . my sister could play in my stead."

Nori looked at him, dumbstruck. She was sure she'd misheard.

Hiromoto beamed, revealing the rotten teeth towards the back of his mouth. "Ah! Could she? Why, that would be wonderful, just marvelous. I didn't realize you had a pupil."

Nori's cheeks burned. "He doesn't."

"I do," Akira corrected her. "I trained her myself. She is quite competent. And she has no shortage of free time."

Nori shot him an irritated glance, which he tactfully ignored.

"She'd be happy to take my place."

Hiromoto dropped his scrolls to the ground and seized both of her hands. "Would you? Oh, would you, madam?"

She gaped at him. "I . . ."

But she knew there was only one answer, between his pleading puppy dog eyes and Akira's stern gaze.

"I will," she said weakly.

He bowed to her. "Perfect. Just perfect."

The party was to be on the twenty-fourth of December, Akira's twenty-first birthday. Neither of them spoke of it, but both of them felt the weight of it. When the summer months came, Akira would have to go back to Kyoto.

It was time for him to honor his end of the bargain. The bargain he'd made for her sake.

She had no words for the pain of it; it was like swallowing broken glass. Nori would have given anything for the power to stop it, for the power to change things. For any power at all.

Akira tapped his baton against the music stand. "Nori. Pay attention. We have one more day to get these pieces right."

She rolled her eyes. Akira was leaving for Vienna tomorrow, but right now, all he cared about was making sure that she didn't embarrass him.

Which would've been a lot easier if she had been allowed to choose all her own pieces. Hiromoto had chosen Mendelssohn's Violin Concerto in E Minor, op. 64. He'd hired a small chamber orchestra to accompany her, and she was to play the solo. She'd only have a few hours before the event to practice with them. The thought made her want to vomit. Now, in addition to having never played in front of an audience before, she had to play with an orchestra. Her complaints had been met with a whap on the nose. Akira was hearing none of it.

There would be a pianist there too, to accompany her for her second piece. She'd played a handful of pieces with Will. It was the only time she'd felt . . . safe around him.

Akira had chosen the second piece: Vitali's Chaconne in G Minor. She'd heard him play it many times with Will. It always reminded her of a dark love song. It was a beautiful piece, but it seemed . . . haunted.

And so Nori had been left to choose only one piece. She'd chosen Schubert's "Ave Maria" without a second thought.

It was the Vitali piece that threatened to break her.

Akira winced. "Sharp. Play that passage again."

Nori did.

"Do you know what 'sharp' means?" he snapped. "And ease off the bow. For God's sake, you know better."

She swallowed a lump of air. "Why did you pick *this* one? It's not meant to be played alone, anyway; the arrangement has a part for piano. I should be practicing with a pianist."

He ignored her question. "I have my reasons."

"But, Oniichan . . ."

"Hush."

He stood up and made his way behind the piano.

He sat down at the bench.

"What are you doing?" she asked.

He gestured for her to start playing. She did.

And then he did. And it was note perfect.

She nearly dropped her bow. "*N-naze?* Since when can you play the piano?!"

He didn't stop playing. "I've always been able to play the piano, Nori."

She stared at him like a fool with her jaw hanging slack. "W-what?"

"Mother taught me," he said simply. "I had piano in the mornings and violin in the evenings for years. Not to mention with Will here, I could hardly be outdone."

She started to feel faint. "You never played in front of me!"

He shrugged. "I wasn't ready to share it with you."

Nori felt her palms start to sweat. "And now you are?"

He offered her a small smile. "I suppose I am."

"Is it possible for you to be bad at something?" she said irritably. "And here I thought I was catching up."

He smirked. "Maybe next year."

She felt a new passion seize her. She wiped her hands on her dress. "The pianist they have there will be good, I'm sure."

"Certainly. I am just a poor stand-in so you can learn the piece."

Nori tilted her bow. "From the top, then."

They played well into the early hours of the morning. It was like being transported to another realm, where they needed neither food nor rest. The sunlight began to pour in, and still, neither of them stopped.

When Ayame came in to tell them it was time for Akira to go, Nori finally put down her violin.

Wordlessly, she went to sit beside him on the bench. The spell they'd cast was broken.

Her eyes filled with tears. This was the beginning of the end of life as they knew it.

He leaned down and grazed his lips across the dimple in her left cheek.

"I know you can do it. I taught you myself all of these years, you must have learned something."

She nodded. "*Hai, Oniichan.*"

"Behave."

"Yes."

"And watch your trills. You are always sloppy on your trills."

"Oh, Oniichan, can't you stay? At least until after the concert. Please don't make me do it alone."

He sighed. "I'm sorry, Nori. Not this time."

She buried her face in his chest.

Please, God. Bring him back to me.

November passed uneventfully. There were no letters from Akira.

Nori did her best not to be disappointed.

She put her mother's final diary aside, for now. There was no time for it, and if she was being honest, she was afraid. Eventually, it was bound to get to the part about her. About her father. And Nori didn't know if she really wanted to know these things after all.

She spent her days practicing incessantly. She was quite sure that the servants all hated her, but she couldn't be bothered to care.

Her nights were spent knitting a series of scarves for Akira. Vienna was bound to be cold. Once they were perfect, she'd mail them all off at once.

She had the address of his hotel written on a scrap of paper that she kept in her violin case.

She slept fitfully or not at all. Her anxiety gnawed at her like fleas. She had tiny red marks all over her arms and legs from pinching herself.

She sat by the fire and watched the windows mist over with frost. She had never really liked the snow, but this year for whatever reason she felt differently about it. It was beautiful.

Bundled up in her coat and scarf, she walked outside in the garden every night. It was a far cry from the neglected ruin it had been when she first arrived. Akira had seen it restored to glory, and though he never said it was a gift for her, she knew that it was.

Tokyo, Japan
December 24th, 1956

They sent a car for her a little after seven o'clock in the morning. The event was at Hiromoto's country estate about an hour outside of the city. So much for being a poor man. According to Ayame, he'd recently come into a great deal of money from some trade ventures abroad. These events were his way of sucking up to the city's elite, of trying to get his grubby, lowborn feet in the door.

Nori thought he was an odd little man, but she rather liked him.

He insisted on sending his own driver to fetch her. Nori curled up in the back seat and watched the city slowly fade away outside her window. The world was blanketed in a thick layer of snow.

She thought about rolling down the window and feeling the cold on her face, but she decided against it. She didn't want the driver to scold her.

Nori drummed her fingers against her lap. She'd memorized all the pieces down to that last fermata.

She understood what Akira was trying to do by making her do this. Really, she did.

But she still didn't want to.

Akira had spent his life trying to be extraordinary in his own right. He would never be able to comprehend what it was to want to be in the background.

When they pulled up in front of the manor, the driver got out and opened her door.

"Madam."

She thanked him, picked up her violin case, and went inside.

This house appeared to be newly built, on an empty plot of land surrounded by nothing but trees and bordering the edge of a man-made lake.

Nori wondered why anyone would build a house in the middle of the woods and then laughed at herself for wondering. It was exactly the type of thing she would do.

She was immediately led into the foyer, which appeared to take up most of the house. It had marble floors that looked new and floor-to-ceiling glass windows. The caterers were already setting up long tables with gaudy gold tablecloths. There was a raised platform in the corner with a grand piano and fifteen chairs.

The other musicians were already set up, with the exception of the pianist. They were all men who looked to be at least twice her age. There was no sign of Hiromoto.

A maid came up to her to take her purse and her garment bag.

"I'll put these in the closet. I'll fetch them for you when it's time. You can join the others, if you please, miss."

Nori crept up to the others, half hiding behind her case.

"I . . . um . . . *shitsurei shimasu . . .*"

The conductor turned to face her. He was the youngest one in the bunch, with a bright smile and a head full of long, dark hair.

"Ah, here's our soloist. Welcome."

Nori nodded. "Thank you for having me."

He gestured to a podium that was set up a little behind his.

"It was suggested that you have one too," he explained. "Being as you're so short."

She flushed. "Thank you."

"We should get started. We'll do the Mendelssohn first, then you'll do your Schubert, and we're done. You and the pianist will finish with the . . . What is it?"

"Vitali. Chaconne."

He raised an eyebrow. "I must say, that's not an easy piece."

Nori blinked.

"No, it's really not."

"Let's begin."

Akira had warned her about following the conductor's baton. It wasn't as difficult as she'd feared.

But the blending with the other instruments, well, that was . . .

They spent three hours on the Mendelssohn alone. It was two before they made it to the middle of the piece.

Nori could feel eyes burning into her back. Clearly, these were all professionals wondering whose daft relative she was to be playing here in the first place.

"All right," the conductor said after a while. "We'll take a rest. Why don't you run through the Schubert? You're playing it alone, right?"

Nori nodded and bit her lip so hard she could taste blood. "I'm . . . There won't be many people here, right?"

He gave her a puzzled look. "Not too many. Only two hundred or so."

She nearly fainted. "Oh, well, then. Only. All right."

He gestured for her to begin.

This, at least, she could do. This song was burned deep into her muscle memory, and she went through it without a hitch. The whispering behind her told her that she had managed to redeem herself.

A little.

The conductor nodded at her. "Well done. You're clearly a soloist."

Nori had to restrain a snort. "I have more practice playing alone. But . . . where is the pianist?"

He frowned. "I haven't seen him. I'll go and see. We only have a few hours left."

He put down his baton and disappeared into the next room.

"That's his sister, isn't it?" someone behind her whispered. "Funny-looking thing."

"Half sister," someone corrected him. "And don't say that too loudly. Her family is . . ."

The conductor stalked back in with a scowl on his face. "He's delayed," he snapped. "Wonderful. Because there's not enough that could go wrong tonight."

Nori swallowed. "What do we do?"

"We keep practicing the concerto. It's all we can do." His face softened. "You play very well. Your brother would be proud."

"You know Akira-san?"

The man laughed. "Indeed, I do. We used to go to the same conservatory. He called me a few days ago. He let me know not to expect you to be as good as he is."

She choked down a snort. "Well, he's right."

The man smiled. "He's a once-in-a-generation genius. A *ten-sai*, you know? There's no competing with people like that."

You don't need to tell me this.

"You do, however," he went on, "have something that he does not."

She looked up, startled. "What?"

He winked. "Best let him tell you. Now, shall we try it again? From the top?"

And she did try, with more confidence this time. She let the others lift her up like a swelling tide. She was the soloist, yes, and she had to soar above them—but not too far. It was a delicate dance of cat and mouse.

Nori closed her eyes and tried to feel what she'd felt when she'd first heard Akira play. It was foreign and familiar, extraordinary yet simple, and even though it sent chills down her spine, it was always, always warm.

After three more hours, a maid came out to tell them the guests would be arriving within the hour and they all needed to get dressed.

Everyone else seemed to know where to go, and they drifted off, leaving Nori standing there alone.

"If you please, miss," the maid said. "There's a room for you to change in upstairs. I've laid your dress out."

Nori nodded and followed her up the winding staircase. The upstairs floor had walls that were only half painted. Clearly, nobody ever really came up here. This house was more for entertaining than living in.

Nori put on her shimmering white gown, doing her very best not to rip the delicate fabric. It was too long for her, having originally belonged to Alice, and she had to be careful not to trip. She released her hair from the bun she'd wound it into and let it pool over her left shoulder, pinning the right side of it down with a long ivory clip.

She brushed a hint of lipstick across her lips and squinted into the mirror.

It could be worse, she thought bleakly.

She could hear the front door opening and closing repeatedly downstairs along with the sounds of laughter, the kind of pretentious laughter that belonged to people with too much money and too much free time.

She sat on the edge of the bed and sighed. There was no point in praying for strength.

There was a tap on the door.

"Just a moment."

It opened anyway.

And it was Akira.

He was dressed in his concert suit, with a red rose pinned to his lapel and his hair slicked back with pomade.

He raised an eyebrow at her shocked face.

"Ah, come now, Nori. You didn't really think I'd let you embarrass me."

She flung herself into his arms. "Oniichan!"

"I thought I'd surprise you," he said warmly. "Aren't you always complaining that I'm too serious?"

"But . . . but you're in Vienna!"

"I flew back. I nearly didn't make it. I just got in a few hours ago and I can't stay long. I'm going back in three days."

She looked up at him, and she was hard-pressed not to weep tears of joy. "Oh, thank God. You can play in my place now."

He chuckled. "Not a chance. I will be your pianist for the evening, sister. But the rest is up to you."

She dug her nails into his wrists. "Oh, please don't make me do this. You would do a much better job."

He snorted. "Well, naturally. But I want you to do it."

"But I'm nobody!" she burst out. Her sleep-deprived brain was struggling to keep up with all that was happening, and she could not help but wish herself back to her own bedroom, curled up with a mug of hot tea.

He tapped her on the nose. "You're not nobody."

She glared at him, unconvinced.

"Look," he said. "You know I never do anything without cause. So you're going to have to trust me."

Nori held back her tears. There was no time for them. The relief of having Akira by her side again outweighed everything else. If she was to go down in flames, at least he'd be there to . . . well, at least he'd be there.

She took hold of his hand and squeezed it tight.

"Happy birthday."

He shrugged. "No ceremony."

"I have questions," she teased him. "Many questions. This is most unlike you, Oniichan."

He smirked. "Maybe later. Now, let's go."

Don't look at them.

It was the only way. After searching the crowd for Hiromoto and not being able to find him amidst the throng of people in black suits, she had given up and was now staring firmly at the floor.

Akira was sitting at the piano, after being warmly embraced by the conductor and half the players in the orchestra.

It was obvious that he belonged here and she did not. But here she was.

Someone she didn't recognize came up to the stage and said a few words, thanked the guests on behalf of Hiromoto for attending tonight. He introduced tonight's soloist as Miss Noriko Kamiza, and she could hear the crowd erupt in murmurs.

Nori had never wanted to be somewhere else so badly. And that was saying quite a bit.

The gown was itchy. Her hands were sweaty. She should've worn her hair differently. The strings on her violin were strung too tightly.

Akira's gaze was the only thing holding her steady.

He believes in you.

She took a deep breath and did not release it until the conductor nodded at her that it was time to begin.

Now.

Off she flew. With the first bravura of ascending notes, she claimed the piece as her own.

Perfect.

She could almost feel Akira's hands on hers, guiding her. Over the sound of the orchestra, she could hear his voice in her head.

Good. Not too fast, now. Slow down for this part . . . it's like a caress. It's sensual almost.

Just like that.

Now, higher. Don't go sharp.

Faster. Faster. Faster.

She was breathless. Her face was hot, but her hands were steady. She would not be humiliated. Not today.

The orchestra slipped away from her, and she hastened to catch them. The sound of the flute pierced her to the heart.

Is this what it feels like?

Is this what Akira always feels like?

To be in the middle of such a sound?

She opened her eyes. There was a different sound now, entirely unfamiliar.

It was applause. Thunderous applause.

Nori swayed. It did not stop for a full three minutes.

Her chest heaved up and down.

"Encore! Bravo!" someone shouted.

"Yes, more!"

Akira looked at her out of the corner of his eye. It was traditional to take a small reprieve between pieces.

Nori was already out of breath, but she nodded that she was ready to continue. This next one was her song.

The "Ave Maria" went perfectly as, deep down, she had always known it would. It was an extension of herself and therefore impossible to forget.

She heard someone crying.

And then the roaring began again. This crowd was insatiable, apparently.

She felt Akira's hand on her shoulder as he leaned down to whisper in her ear. "If you need a break . . ."

"No."

"It's been nearly an hour. You look a little faint."

"I want to finish this."

If she stopped now, she would never be able to start again. The adrenaline was the only thing propping her up.

Unseen by the rest of the crowd, he lightly kissed the back of her head.

"Faith," he whispered.

He went back to the piano. The murmuring from the crowd ceased. Nori could swear that some celestial being had actually frozen them.

Akira let the first note fall. Then the second. Then the third. Each lower and more ominous than the next.

She felt something shatter in her.

And then, without even thinking, she answered the call.

She was not behind him; she was not ahead of him. Her sound was entwined with his; they were two halves of a whole.

A tear slid down her cheek.

All of her fear, all of her pain, all of her hatred flowed out of her and into the sound.

The difficulty was forgotten; the audience was forgotten.

There were only two people here.

Faster and faster it went, until they were dancing in a delirious red haze.

And then, as the song slowed for the final time, a message clear as day:

The end.

She folded like a paper doll and covered her eyes. Her violin clattered to the floor.

She didn't hear the applause.

All she felt was Akira taking her hand and whisking her

through the hall, out the front door, and into the cold winter night.

She felt the air on her face and gasped.

"You're fine," he said simply. "Now, now."

She continued to breathe in short, desperate spurts.

"I did it," she wheezed.

Akira sat down, right there in the snow so that she could rest her face against his chest.

"You did," and there was a quiet but powerful sense of satisfaction in his voice.

"Was it good?"

Akira snorted. "Sloppy on the trills. As usual."

She knew better than to get upset. "But the rest?"

Akira was silent for a long moment. "I am . . . glad I came back."

Nori tucked these words into her box of sacred things.

"I'll get our belongings," Akira said. "Pay our respects to Hiromoto. Unless you want to stay for the party and revel in your triumph?"

She shook her head.

"Let's go home."

The driver was the same man as before. He smiled at Nori as he opened her door. He gave Akira one brief, baffled glance before averting his gaze. Akira had taken a taxi straight from the airport and had only a small suitcase with him.

The night was perfectly still under a black, starless sky. There were no other cars on this winding back road.

Akira leaned against the window with his eyes half closed. Nori blew on her window and traced the characters of her name with her pinkie finger.

No-

Ri-

Ko . . .

Once that had been all she could spell.

She nudged Akira with her foot.

"Akira-san."

He turned to face her. *"Nani?"*

"Do you think I could come with you, to Vienna? And we could play again? Together?"

She expected him to scoff or roll his eyes, but the look he gave her was clear and honest.

"You're not ready for that yet."

Nori bowed her head.

Akira lifted up her chin with two fingers and tugged on one of her curls. "But maybe next year."

Nori started to smile but never got the chance.

Everything happened in an instant.

The car veered to the left so sharply that it knocked her back. Her skull hit the window. She thought, vaguely, that the trees were getting awfully close.

Akira's face was frozen. She saw him mouth her name.

Nori.

Then the loudest sound she'd ever heard. His body came flying forwards. The last thing she felt was his arms closing around her.

Because in the next moment, she could feel nothing.

She knew the ground she was lying on must be cold, she

knew that the flames around her must be hot, but she could feel neither.

She saw the driver twenty feet away. He was only a speck. His head was cracked open like an egg. She never knew people had so much blood inside them.

The light from the flames caught the shattered glass that lay all around her, covered in a layer of freshly fallen snow.

Her eyes found the large, jagged piece sticking straight out of her chest.

It blazed like a comet fallen from the sky.

CHAPTER FIFTEEN

AURORA

I think I have gone deaf. And blind. And dumb.

Every day, all day, people come in and out of the room. They sit by the bed and ask me questions, but I can't hear a single word. If I try to sleep, they wake me up and ask me more questions.

I think something very bad has happened. I have this deep sense, even here in this floating plane, that there is a huge piece of me missing. I need to find it. I need to find whatever that thing is.

But first, I really need to remember my name.

Noriko.

There, I have it. I am not sure how many days it took me to figure this out. Someone has covered the window with paper, so I have to rely on my ears to tell me what o'clock it is.

Someone came today—or was it yesterday?—that I thought I

recognized, but then I lost it. It slipped away from me like rain off a wing.

They rub an ointment on my chest that smells like sulfur. It stings and I cry out, but I can't hear that either.

I can do nothing but cry.

They let me out of the room.

If I walk between two of them and lean a little, I can move around the hallway.

I think now that I know this place. It is not a strange prison, as I first thought.

This is . . . familiar to me. I feel a tiny spark of affection, of hope, but I cannot remember why.

I take hold of one woman's sleeve and look into her pale, tearstained face.

"Something's wrong," I tell her.

It is the first time I have tried to speak, and my voice is feeble and useless. But I think she understands. I still can't hear, but I can read her lips.

"Nori . . ."

The other woman cuts her off. "Don't tell her. She won't re-member. You're just torturing her."

"She has a right—"

"Remember last time? It's pointless. And it's cruel."

I feel a deep pang in my chest, like someone is ripping me in two from the inside out.

I wake up many hours later. The pain is gone.

But I still cannot stop crying.

There is someone I must find.

I am Noriko, Noriko Kamiza, and I have a mother who is gone, and a father who I have never known, and a friend with silver hair who is across the sea.

And I have something else.

I have the warmth of the sun and the weight of it too.

Why can't I remember?

It all descended on her in one moment of startling clarity. It was powerful enough to jolt her from her sleep.

Nori stood up. Every limb in her body was screaming, and she was half naked, stripped from the waist up, but she did not care. She wrapped the blanket around herself and walked.

She had the most surreal feeling, like none of this was really happening at all.

She made her way down the hall, stopped at the third door to the right. Knocked.

There was no reply.

She opened the door.

Akira's room was just as he left it. The bed was made; the binders and binders of sheet music were stacked neatly on the desk. The many scarves she'd knitted him were hanging on a hook next to the mirror.

And there, sitting on the bed, was a figure half cloaked in darkness.

She crept forward, ignoring the fact that it felt like walking through flames.

The figure looked up.

"Ayame," Nori whispered.

Ayame said nothing. Her pallor was deathly; her hair was greasy. Her blue dress looked dirty.

And she was crying.

Nori felt a deep wave move through her. Something told her to leave, to go back to her room and go back to sleep. To sink back into the delirium.

Because this was unspeakable. Impossible.

Nori shut her eyes. "Where is he?"

Ayame let out a broken sob. "I'm not . . . I'm not supposed to . . ."

For a brief moment, Nori allowed herself blind, stupid hope.

"Is he in Vienna?" she asked, in a squeaky little voice that sounded pathetic even to her.

Ayame stared at her, wide-eyed and white-faced, saying nothing.

"I know he was going to Vienna," Nori pressed on. "But then he was going to come back."

Her voice broke and she tried to take a breath, but the pain in her chest was so great that it nearly knocked her over.

"He was going to come back," she breathed. "He promised he'd come back."

Ayame rose from the bed. "He did come back," she said softly. "For your concert. Don't you remember?"

"I . . ."

The world turning upside down. Broken glass.

Fire.

"I . . ."

Ayame took another step towards her, and Nori found herself holding out her hands as if she could keep the truth at bay.

"Don't," she raged weakly. "Don't say it."

But Ayame did not stop. "He did come back. You were on the way home. But it was dark and . . . it was snowing. The car—"

"I said *DON'T!*"

"The car went off the road."

Nori tried to run away, but she tripped over the hem of her blanket and fell to the floor. She bowed her head and put her hands up, pleading.

"Please don't," she whispered. "Please."

"It slid down the embankment, into the woods. You hit the trees."

Finally, Nori looked up. Her eyes were dry. And though she was kneeling, her shoulders were squared.

She took in this moment, this room, down to the last speck of dust floating in the air. She let it all absorb into her very bones. She forced herself to remember, with exacting clarity, the moment before. She held it tightly in her hands, like a wriggling little bird.

And then she let it go.

"Where is Akira-san?" Nori asked.

And in the smallest voice, Ayame answered her.

Nori's mouth opened.

She remembered now.

Lying there, on that frozen ground, there had been someone beside her, just a few feet away.

Akira.

His body had been curled up, almost as if he were sleeping. His hair was slightly tousled, just as it always was.

And his face . . . his face . . . was *gone.*

Nori doubled over.

And then she screamed.

They give me something to make me sleep.

But I don't sleep, though it is all I want to do.

I lie awake and I stare at the ceiling and I think over and over again: Let me die.

Please, God.

Just let me die.

I do not die.

Though I lie here all day, every day, and turn my face to the wall and wait for death, nothing happens.

I see Akira's faceless body, just like my mother appeared to me all those years in my dreams, and I have to retch into the bowl beside my bed.

I drink a little water to appease Ayame, who looks close to death herself, but I eat nothing.

The doctor comes to check my wounds, and I feel a ridiculous, unworthy rage when I see him.

I hate him like a scorpion.

Where was he when he was needed? Where was he to help the one worth saving?

I tell him to let me die and he says he cannot, that he is a doctor, and anyway, I don't deserve to die.

Yes, I do.

I have always deserved to die. But I refused.

And now I have killed him.

Ayame says that I must get up.

She says that I cannot stay in this bed forever. She has bathed and put on a new, starched dress. She is restored.

He has only been dead for three weeks.

I hear sounds outside my door, of people moving and speaking, of cooking and cleaning and life.

But the sun has gone away.

Don't they know? Don't they know that the sun has gone away and everything is finished?

So I cannot get up.

I will never get up.

AYAME

Tokyo, Japan
March 1st, 1957

The messenger arrives at the crack of dawn on a miserable day. The fog is so thick that I can scarcely see out the window. It poured all night, a wretched *hisame*: cold rain, the kind that seeps into the air, and seeps into the house, and seeps into your bones. You can't get warm no matter what you do.

I have been waiting for this since it happened. I divide my time between sitting vigil in her room and sleeping by the front door with a knife beneath my pillow.

I wrap a shawl around my shoulders and meet him at the front gate. I won't allow him to take even a single step past it.

He bows his head and hands me the letter. It is marked with the seal of the Kamiza family: a white chrysanthemum with a purple center.

"Please be advised, Ayame-san, that this will be her first and only warning."

I want to be angry, but I cannot. I cannot seem to feel anything anymore.

I have known Akira-sama since the day he was born. I used to hold him, when I was just five years old, and sing him to sleep. I watched him change from a loving, happy little boy into a secretive child who rarely spoke.

When he left for Kyoto, I thought it was over. I even went to work for another great family.

And then he came to find me. He was standing right in front of me, smiling at me, just like a miracle. He asked me to run his household; he said he would trust no one else.

And all of these years, I have watched over him. As my mother watched after his father.

Every day I brought him his coffee, and every day he would look up at me, smile softly, and say, "Thank you, Ayame-san. You always take such good care of me."

And every day I pretended that I wasn't desperately, passionately, impossibly in love with him. Because I am a servant. And he is . . . he was . . .

I cannot fathom a world without him.

I clutch the letter in my cold hands.

"That woman can't come here," I say in a furious whisper. "It is out of the question."

He smiles thinly at me. "Do make sure she reads it. My lady will be expecting a reply soon."

I am shaking. "How soon?"

"Three days."

He bows again, turns around, and disappears back into the fog.

I go back into the house.

It takes me too long to find the strength to go upstairs. I know what's waiting for me there. And I don't want to face it.

I finally will myself to move, and it amazes me how heavy my limbs have become. I have aged a hundred years in weeks.

I don't knock. I open the door and I find her there, as I knew I would.

She is lying in bed with her face turned up to the ceiling, completely unblinking. Her hair is matted with sweat; it will probably have to be cut.

But the worst is her skin. Her skin, which was once the most peculiar shade of almond brown, is now as gray as ash.

She is turning into a dead woman right before my eyes and there is nothing I can do.

"Nori," I whisper.

She doesn't stir. I don't even know if she hears me. She has not spoken a single word since I told her of her brother's death.

I go to sit at the stool by her bedside and am repulsed by the smell of her. She smells of death, of decay.

"Nori," I say again, more forcefully this time, "there is a letter for you."

Her cracked lips part. She mouths *no* and then turns on her side so that she is facing the wall.

I see red sores on her back.

When the police found her and took her to the hospital, it was I who went to fetch her and bring her back here. Once they pulled the glass out, the doctor said she would live and recover fully, but that she would have a terrible scar.

I almost laughed in his face.

I never got to see Akira-sama. He was already in the morgue. And anyway, he had no face. They told me he had no face.

I had to get Nori out of that place before her grandmother arrived. I had to do it, for Akira-sama.

"There is a letter from your grandmother."

Nori-sama cranes her neck over to squint at me. "What?" she breathes, and her voice is that of an old, broken woman.

"Your grandmother sent a messenger with a letter for you."

For the first time in days, she sits up. She has to grab hold of me to steady herself, but she reaches out her skeletal arm and takes the letter from my hand.

She removes the seal and opens the envelope, pulls out the letter. I see her eyes scan the page, once, twice, three times.

Her face betrays no emotion; her eyes are as blank as a doll's.

She hands me the letter and turns her face back to the wall.

I find that my hands are shaking as I try to read it. The morning light streaming through the covered window is gray and dull, but I can still make out what it says.

February 28th, 1957

Noriko,

You will be glad to know that you have achieved your ambition. Your brother is dead. The future of our house is dead. My legacy, which I have worked so hard to protect, will end with my death.

Perhaps now you will believe me when I tell you that you are cursed, you are wretched, you are a child of the devil.

They will have told you that his beautiful face was ripped in two. He died on a cold road in the middle of the night, alone.

He was twenty-one for all of a day.

We, his family, your grandfather and I, have buried him with great honor in Kyoto, his ancestral city.

You have until the end of the first week of March to leave Japan and never return.

This courtesy is out of respect for my grandson, for God knows you deserve none.

You have killed your brother. You have destroyed your mother and your father too.

I will tell you now that he was a common farmhand from a common little state called Virginia, in America. His name was James Ferrier. He died in 1941, shortly after you were born.

I tell you this so that you are very sure that you have no one and nothing. You have no name, for I strip it from you. And you have no family, for you have ruined them all.

Leave Japan. See if you can find some wretched corner of the world that will have you.

Though for my part, I doubt it.

The Honorable Lady Yuko Kamiza

I press a hand to my mouth to stop myself from crying out.

What an evil woman.

"Nori," I gasp, taking hold of her thin shoulders and forcing her to look at me. "You have to go."

She blinks.

"Nori, they will kill you! This is no idle threat, they have no incentive anymore, there is nothing to hold them back!"

She tilts her head. "Good."

I am dumbstruck. "What?"

She shrugs. "I deserve to die. Let her."

I slap her across the face. I do it without even thinking. All of my grief, all of my rage at a random, cruel universe, comes pouring out.

"How dare you. How dare you say such a thing, you stupid girl. Obocchama risked everything for you, to give you a life, to give you a chance at a future worth having."

Her cheeks flush. "Yes," she spits, "and now he is dead."

"And that was not your fault. It was an accident. It was an act of God."

Her eyes well with tears. The mask cracks.

"What kind of God would allow this?" she sobs.

I cannot answer her. I don't know.

I hold her to my chest, this frail little thing, and hold her as she cries.

"You have to live," I tell her, my voice shaking with fervor.

"You have to get yourself out of the country, somewhere safe. Go to your friend Alice in England. Leave Japan, leave all of this behind. Start a new life."

She shakes her head. "I don't *want* to live at all."

I shake her, hard, and her head snaps back and forth.

"It doesn't matter what you want. Don't you dare insult Obocchama's memory by allowing yourself to die. Now, get up."

She hesitates.

"GET UP!"

I all but yank her out of the bed. She stumbles around the room on shaky legs. She looks like a doe learning to walk.

She collapses against the wall, and for a long time, she does not speak.

"Will you come with me?" she asks in a tiny voice.

Poor, sweet girl. I wish I could. I have never known any other kind of life, never even dreamed of one.

My place is here. The rest of the household will be dissolved; the estate will go into limbo until it is determined which relative it will pass to next . . . but I will remain here as caretaker.

With Akira-sama's ghost. Perhaps he will see me now, as he never saw me in life. I am the only one left.

My face gives Nori-sama my answer.

She tries to smile, but her face spasms—clearly she has forgotten how.

"Well then," she says quietly, "you had best pack my things."

I am flooded with relief. I close my eyes to hold back the tears.

I will keep her safe for you, Obocchama. I know she was your most precious thing.

As you were mine.

The day she left Japan, the sky cried.

Shinotsukuame. Relentless rain. Rain that would never stop.

But she knew the tears were not for her.

She took with her these things: twelve dresses, two kimonos, the ribbons her mother had given her, six blouses and six skirts, all of her pearls. Her mother's last diary, which she had not yet finished, and a miniature photograph that Ayame gave her.

It was a picture of Akira right before he came to Kyoto. He was unsmiling, staring straight at the camera. But there was a light in his eyes.

She took his violin. She took all the money from the safe, a small fortune, enough to take her far away. She took the forged papers and passport he'd had made for her, just in case.

And lastly, she took the locket Akira had given her for her sixteenth birthday.

Everything else was hers no longer. She was no longer Noriko Kamiza, the bastard girl.

She was no one at all now.

It was a terrifying prospect: to be free.

She stood in the rain, with her hair matted to the sides of her face, waiting for the boat to start boarding.

Ayame was speaking to the captain. Nori saw money being exchanged. Probably a bribe, to make sure that she was well looked after on the long journey.

Nori looked up at the sky. A wild desperation seized her, a crack in the absolute emptiness she'd felt for days now.

One last time, she pleaded with God. *Bring him back to me.*

Take me instead. Please. I beg you. Let it be a dream, a horrible dream, and tell me I'm going to wake up.

Tell me life is not so random, so cruel, as this.

He was good, which is better than nice, and he was honest, which is better than kind.

Tell me you didn't let him die.

Bring Akira back to me.

Please.

The thunder rolled, and Nori was positive, for the first time in her life, that God had heard her.

The answer was no.

Ayame came and took her by the shoulders, guiding her out of the rain and underneath the awning covering the ramp.

"It's time to go now," she whispered brokenly, "my sweet girl."

Nori wanted to feel sadness at leaving Ayame. But she could not. The sun was gone; she couldn't be sad about anything else.

"Thank you for everything you have done for me," she said, and she meant it. "I'm sorry it ended this way."

"It's not your fault, my lady."

Nori managed a small smile. "You don't have to call me that anymore. It's just Nori."

Ayame kissed her on both of her cold cheeks.

"You remember who you are," she whispered.

They shared one last long embrace. Deep in her frozen heart, Nori knew that they would never see each other again.

She climbed the ramp onto the boat.

Instead of going down into her first-class cabin, where there was a warm bed waiting for her, she went to the side of the railing and looked over it.

The ocean seemed never-ending. But somehow, somewhere, it did end.

Perhaps it was the same with her grief.

Though she could not see it.

She turned around to look at the country of her birth, the country she had wanted so desperately to love her, growing farther and farther away.

"Goodbye," she whispered.

Akira's image came to her.

Goodbye, Oniichan.

The wind rustled, and she strained to hear his voice, as she had always been able to do even when he was far away. When she was deaf to God, when she was deaf to hope, his voice had always been there.

But not now. Now there was nothing.

Akira was gone.

PART IV

CHAPTER SIXTEEN

SKIN

Paris, France
March 1964

The cobblestones were slippery. She hadn't bet on that. Her plan had been perfect; there was no exit that she had not scouted, no route that she had not mapped out. She knew exactly what the last piece was, and she'd planned to slip out during the final six measures, before the lights came up.

No one would ever know she had been here tonight.

But she had not planned on the cellist collapsing in the middle of the Rachmaninoff. She had not planned on him grasping at his starched collar and falling against the screaming woman beside him.

She had not planned on the panic, on the lights coming on in the hall, on the pianist rising to scour the crowd in search of help.

And even then, things might have been saved. She tried to stay seated, with her head bowed. There were a thousand people here, she was wearing a black gown, there was no reason for her to be spotted.

Until the person beside her sprang up, saying that he was a doctor, and please could she move to let him through?

Then, as she stood, as the sapphire blue eyes of the pianist met hers, she knew that her plan was ashes scattered to the wind.

And she ran.

She had a head start, but he was faster. And she was in heels.

She made it out of the hall, made it out of the front doors, managed to tumble down the stairs and onto the wet cobblestones. She went down, hard, but managed to scramble back up and into a nearby cab. Mercifully, it had been right there, dropping off an elderly couple.

If it hadn't been, he would have caught her.

She could see his face in the rearview mirror, calling out the name that had once been hers.

Nori!

She had no answer for him.

She had no answers for herself.

You fool. You never should have gone.

Nori looked at her reflection in her teacup. The tea was good here. That was one of the things she liked about this little room that she rented from a kindly French widow.

The other thing she liked was the privacy.

She knew she wouldn't be found, but it didn't matter. She couldn't stay here. The bubble had been popped.

For the past seven years, she had moved from place to place, never staying anywhere for too long. Vienna first, then Rome, then Malta. She'd spent a few months in Switzerland before coming to Paris. She'd been here close to a year now.

Chasing ghosts.

So many people she'd lost had loved this city of lights.

She'd hoped coming here would bring her some peace. Maybe she'd even feel compelled to stay, to build a fledgling life here.

At first, she hadn't wanted to settle anywhere. She'd been content to go to the most beautiful cities in Europe, sit in the warm sunlight, and listen to the street musicians play.

It's what he would have done on his days off.

She had become like a migratory bird, flocking from one place to another, never any thought but what to eat, where to sleep, and where to fly next.

But now she was tired. Very, very tired. And at twenty-three, she was a girl no longer.

He would have expected more from her.

Nori pushed her teacup aside. Thoughts like these were dangerous. She'd had to take special care over the years not to fall too deeply down that rabbit hole. She'd never make it out.

Time for a walk.

She wrapped a shawl around her shoulders and descended the narrow spiral staircase. As she always did, she stopped to pet her landlady's one-eyed orange tabby cat before walking out the door.

She liked cats. As far as she could tell, they made better companions than most people. Marriage, children . . . those weren't for people like her, nor was she suited to either of them. But she'd like to have a cat one day.

It was a picturesque day. Not too hot, not too cold. The sun was half hidden behind creamy clouds, and there was a breeze that carried the scent of the baker's bread from down the street.

Nori walked along the road, expertly avoiding the reckless bicycle drivers, until she came to a small bridge overlooking the Seine.

She wondered if her mother had walked here.

Perhaps Seiko had looked out at this water and watched the bold pigeons swoop in to steal the pastries from the hands of unsuspecting children. Perhaps she'd listened to the whirring sound the ferries made as they passed below.

Probably not.

Nori tightened her shawl. She had two dozen of these, in every color. She'd knitted them over the years to keep her hands busy and to occupy the sleepless nights. She'd also become halfway decent at a random assortment of things—gardening, jam making, upholstery, painting. She was always in the market for new hobbies.

Anything to quiet the voice in her head that whispered *your fault* over and over again.

But now she had enough shawls. She had enough shawls, and scarves, and quilts, and sweaters. She'd had enough rented rooms and cottages. She wanted something else now, but that was a dangerous thing.

There was no question of returning to Japan. There was no question of a joyous homecoming, because there was no such thing as home.

She'd been a ship blown from its mooring since the day he died.

A kingfisher swooped down from a branch beside her, pulling her back to where she stood.

It was probably time to leave. She had better pack. She could not delude herself into thinking that Will would have the grace to pretend he hadn't seen her. He'd tell everyone who cared, which was exactly . . . one person.

It hit her like a bolt of thunder from this clear sky.

There was no somewhere for her. But maybe there was a *someone*.

Nori had never allowed herself to entertain this notion. Ayame had written a letter to London, a lifetime ago, but that had been the last of it.

Alice would be in her mid-twenties now, probably married, probably in the place she'd been born to. Maybe she'd forgotten. Or maybe she hadn't forgotten and Nori was the last person she wanted to see.

Maybe it was too late. It was almost certainly too late.

But as Nori lay in bed that night, the embers would not flicker out.

She felt it burning in her belly, spreading out to her fingertips, to the crown of her head, to the soles of her feet.

She remembered this feeling.

Wild. Fickle. Treacherous.

Hope.

ALICE

Kensington & Chelsea
London, England
April 1964

In the moment of waking, I am happy.

I slip out of bed, careful not to wake my husband. There's no fear of that. George sleeps like a dead man after a few drinks, and last night, he had more than a few.

I go inside the adjoining master bath without turning on the light, and I look at my face in the mirror.

I still have my looks. I am comforted by this, at least. My skin is flawless, my gray eyes are bright, and my hair is thick and shiny, still that rare shade of silver blonde that has me so renowned.

My figure is intact, even after two children. I still have the ability to make men walk into walls when I pass by.

But the older I get, the more I realize how empty this is.

I am married to the Duke of Norfolk's only son. When my father-in-law dies, which can't be very long from now, for he is ancient if he is a day, I will be the premier duchess in all of England.

It is the best marriage I could have possibly hoped for. As fortune would have it, when I turned up, George was in need of a wife and my past was delightfully forgotten.

He has never asked me about my time in "finishing school," and I have never asked him how much money my father gave him to marry me.

We have two girls: Charlotte, who is five, and Matilda, who is two.

Charlotte takes after her father. She is brawny, brown-haired, brown-eyed, and clever. But God forgive me for thinking it, she will never win any beauty pageants. They will write no poems about her looks.

Matilda is my little doll; she looks like me, and actually, I think she will be a greater beauty than I ever was. My husband adores them both, and though he has no passion for me, he is respectful and kind.

But we still need a boy. Such is the world.

I am still young, amen, with at least a decade of fertile years ahead of me. But I have a secret fear.

I dress in a hurry and go down to the kitchen, where a maid is already serving my breakfast. I always eat breakfast alone.

While my husband sleeps, while my children are upstairs in their nursery, I can be the selfish woman I was always meant to be for a few short moments in the day.

The light pours in from the bay windows I had installed last spring.

It is April again.

She was supposed to come to me in April. I was expecting her, there was a letter sent ahead by the maid, but she never arrived.

She did not come the next year either, or the year after that.

And so here I am, seven Aprils later, and still waiting for the girl I loved like a sister.

She is probably dead. As much as it pains me, I can see my sweet, melancholy girl tying stones around her waist and walking into the ocean.

She adored her brother, with a fervor I did not understand until I had my own children. If anything happened to them, I think my heart would seize in my chest. I would simply cease to be.

I feel the tears coming and I push them back. I miss her. Even after all these years, even though I am exactly where I need to be, in the place I was born to be, I still miss her.

She had the softest touch and this deceptive fragility—I thought she needed protecting, but it was she, all along, who protected me.

She told me once that she was born under a mercurial star.

It has taken me all of these long years to believe her.

The commotion on the stairs tells me that the children are up. Charlotte comes flying down the steps in her new blue dress, and the nanny comes down behind her with Matilda still groggy in her arms.

I hug them both close to me, and I breathe in the scent of their innocence and their joy.

My husband finds me in our garden. I never used to favor the gardens, but now I do. Yet another gift she gave me.

He sits on the bench beside me, and I try not to be irritated by the sight of him. He is a good man, to do him justice, but he is terribly plain and boring, *so* boring. I am confident I've met more interesting silverware.

"Any word from the doctor?"

The hope in his voice is like a child's.

I turn to him and try to smile. "Yes. I am expecting after all."

He turns the color of a strawberry and then kisses me on the lips, as clumsy as always.

I endure our lovemaking with the patience of a saint, part of my duty as his wife. I don't expect to ever feel the rush of passion again; I don't expect to be feverish with desire the way that I was long ago, with that beautiful, beautiful traitor.

But the last few sessions I have tolerated have done their work. I am fourteen weeks now.

"I was thinking of going shopping today. I'll take the girls."

He shakes his head as if to clear it. "Of course, of course. Take however much money you need."

He's a good man. Not for the first time, I wish that were enough for me.

I load the girls into the pram and off we go. I want to keep my mind off of the child growing in my belly. I am full of fear, and I don't want my fear to poison him—or at least, I am hoping it to be a him.

I have a secret. I have a sin. And all these years, I have evaded punishment for it. But it is always there, beneath the glittering surface of my charmed life.

I buy two stuffed bears for the girls and stop for lunch at a little café that has just been opened by an Indian fellow.

London is changing. We have all kinds here now. I quite enjoy it. I have always been mystified by how one person can judge another based solely on the color of their skin.

There are so many better things to judge others on. Really.

After lunch I buy the girls spiced peanuts and take them to the park to play.

I hope that they will stay close as they grow up. I never loved my sisters and they never loved me. I found my true sister on the other side of the world.

I wait until dark to take the children home. They are both exhausted, and I pass them off to their nanny and sink into an armchair to rest.

"Bess," I say, "bring me some tea, will you please?"

My maid appears from the other room and her face is flushed.

"Your cousin is here, my lady."

I push myself up and stare at her blankly. "What?"

"Your cousin Lord Stafford is here."

"You mean William?"

"Yes, my lady."

I am so angry I could spit. Who does he think he is to come calling on me at this hour? The years have done nothing to erase the tension between us. I cannot forgive him for the way he lorded his authority over me when I was at my lowest point. We see each other only when required.

"Send him away," I say pompously, and I feel a twinge of pleasure.

Will pushes past her and barges into the room. "Bit late for that."

I jump to my feet. "You've got some nerve."

He smirks. He is handsome as ever, with all of his arrogance and devilish charm.

"I am sorry, dear cousin, but I have news that can't wait."

I feel my eyebrows shoot up into my hairline. "What?"

"I think I saw her."

The world beneath my feet rocks. I sink back into my chair, speechless.

Every other year or so he will torment me with a sighting. But it's never her and I am always left feeling as if someone has burned a hole in me.

"Don't start," I say wearily.

"I swear I saw her in Paris," he protests. "I am sure this time, I've sent someone to look into it."

"Enough already," I mumble. "Just enough."

Will has been consumed with finding her ever since word of Akira's death reached us. It was, to this day, the only time I have ever seen him cry.

I can't bear even to try. I know her better than he does, though he would never accept it. I know if she wanted to be found, we would have found her.

I have never told him about the letter.

"But I am certain—" he starts up.

"You were certain in Rome," I snap. "And in Vienna, where you were sure she'd go chasing a ghost. You have been certain in every city your music has taken you to, and she is *never* there. Because she is *gone*, and I am so sick of your ridiculous quest to soothe your ego, to rescue her and make her fall in love with you at long last. Let it go."

He turns a mottled shade of purple. "You have no idea what you're talking about."

"I know exactly what I'm talking about. This has never been about her, and it's certainly not about me. It's about you being unable to accept that you've lost."

He rips off his suit jacket. "Oh, shut up, Alice."

I gesture towards the door. "Good night, William. I look forward to your next delusion."

Actually, I don't. These conversations take away chunks of me. He storms out grumbling, and when I hear the front door shut, I put a hand to my mouth.

"Bess," I whisper.

She is at my side in an instant. "Madam?"

"Take me upstairs. I need to rest. I'm tired. I'm very, very tired."

I sleep for hours. In the morning, I take a long hot bath and try to release the weariness in my bones.

I hate April. It truly is the cruelest month.

I wrap myself up in a towel and sit on the side of the tub for an hour before I have the strength to dress.

The girls are playing outside with Bess, and George is— somewhere. Lunch club, maybe. I can never keep track.

I peer out from one of the many windows. The clouds are dark and thick, threatening rain. How original.

I walk down the stairs and only make it halfway down before I curl up on the landing.

I don't know how I'm going to make it through the next five months.

The doorbell rings.

I sigh and wait for one of the servants to get it. It's probably my sister Jane come to raid my closet, as if I have anything that will fit her.

Nobody comes. I look around irritably, wondering what I pay these people for.

The doorbell rings again.

I haul myself up and go slowly down each step.

The doorbell rings for a third time.

I make my way to the door, and a strange feeling comes over me. I am here, but I am not here. I am in the past, in the future, in a place I cannot even name.

Somehow, I know.

I open the door and there she is.

She is exactly the same. Her face is still round, with a deep dimple in each cheek. Her hair is black as a raven's wing and as curly as ever. She has cut it short so that it falls just below her chin.

She doesn't look twenty-three—she appears both too young and too old. She doesn't look noble, for she is dressed in nothing but a simple blue dress.

But she is *alive*.

Nori smiles shyly at me. "I'm sorry," she says simply.

I hear a roaring in my ears and then all the lights wink out.

I wake up in my bed.

Nori is sitting on the edge beside me, looking guilty.

I blink at her. "Bess," I rasp, and she is there at once.

"My lady?"

"Leave us now. And don't let anyone in the room until I say."

She nods and goes out.

Nori fidgets. "I see you have a very grand life, my dear. Just like we used to talk about."

I gape at her. "You . . . you're here."

She smiles and nods. "I am."

I feel a deep pulse of rage. "Where have you been?"

She looks away. Clearly, she was expecting this. "It's complicated."

"You could have written me," I say furiously. "You just dropped off the face of the earth for seven bloody years. I thought you were dead. You let me think you were dead."

She bows her head. "I'm sorry. If you want me to leave . . ."

I snatch her hand and hold it tight.

"Nonsense, I'm never letting you out of my sight again."

She laughs. "Oh, Alice. I have missed you."

"And did they tell you I have children?" I blurt out. "Two girls. Charlotte and Matilda."

"I saw them," she says warmly. "They are beautiful, my dear. I cannot wait to meet them properly."

"I'm expecting now too," I say, and I find that I am shy about it.

She kisses my flushed cheeks. "How wonderful."

I fix my eyes on her. She has grown into her looks. She's a lovely girl, even with the corners of her mouth turned down. She looks so sad.

"And what about you, Nori?"

She hesitates. "It's really not that interesting of a story."

"I want to hear it anyway," I insist.

Nori goes very still.

And then she tells me. She tells me, and I can see at once how lonely she has been, and how much she believes that she deserved it. My anger vanishes.

She has been martyring herself all this time. That she is here now means she is ready to stop.

"Why didn't you come to me in the beginning?" I wail. "I would've taken care of you. We would have been like sisters!"

The color drains from her face. "I didn't want to be near you. Or, rather, I didn't want you to be near me. I was no good for anyone, Alice. I was convinced that I was . . ."

I look into her eyes. "What?"

She nips her lower lip. "Nothing. It doesn't matter. I'm here now."

I am not satisfied by this, but I know better than to press her. She is like a frightened filly; if I push her too hard, she will bolt. All I need to do is look at the way she holds herself to know that she is a hairsbreadth away from shattering.

I'll try again tomorrow when she has gathered her strength. I know she will. She just needs time.

I sit up and wrap my arms around her. We cling to each other like frightened children.

"You will move your things in today," I tell her. "You will stay here with me. You will be an aunt to my girls and god-mother to my boy when he comes. That is how it will be, Nori."

She makes that little sound she always made when she was trying not to cry. "It's not safe," she says.

I have no idea what she's talking about. All I know is that I need her desperately, I have always needed her, and now I have her back.

I was never supposed to meet her.

But I would not change a single thing.

"Safe be damned. You're staying."

Nori pulls back to look at me. She gives me a tiny smile, and at least for the moment, her eyes are clear.

"I'm staying."

She settles in remarkably well, as I knew that she would. The last seven years have not been wasted on her—she has grown into a sophisticated, cultured young woman, with a woman's painfully acquired knowledge that there is more, always more, that can be put on our shoulders. And that we cannot show it.

My husband adores her. She talks to him about her travels, and they play chess together sometimes in the evenings. She is able to cook his favorite roast duck, and he tells me that she can stay as long as she likes.

The girls both fall easily under her spell, as I knew they would. They demand that she watch them play, and she puts on puppet shows for them and reads them to sleep.

She is gracious to the staff, and they all go out of their way to do little things for her.

So all in all, her introduction to my household has been a great success. But I cannot help but want her all to myself. I even hire a music teacher for the girls, just to give them something to do during the day so that I can be alone with her.

I take her all around the city—well, the good parts of the city—and buy her every pretty thing I can think of. I so enjoy dressing her up; she is still my little doll.

I notice the stares, of course. I am sure she notices them too, but she never flinches. Sometimes she will turn and nod gently, and the offender will blush and scurry away.

We both know it won't be long until my cousin realizes that he was right, and that he really did see her in Paris. We don't discuss it. We just know.

Now that I have children, I can read her so much better, for she communicates much like a child. She doesn't say much, but her eyes and the slight motions in her body tell me what she is feeling.

I don't ask, but I know that she is afraid. She carries her fear with her like a second shadow.

I slide my hand in hers as we sit on my favorite park bench and watch the orange sun dip below the clouds. Today I helped her put in the paperwork for her to stay in London for good. I feel a warm sensation in my belly, and I drape my other hand over it, feeling the hard curve. I know that my son is happy too.

"We really must make a formal introduction for you."

She laughs. "Don't be silly."

"I am quite serious," I tell her. "The vultures won't dissipate until they've had their fill of gossip. Half the city knows you are living with me; the rumors grow more ridiculous every day. Wouldn't it be better to be in control of the narrative? Get a grip on things?"

She sighs. "I don't care what they say about me."

"They stare," I point out, and she snorts.

"Yes, I've noticed. They must think I'm terribly ugly."

I roll my eyes because she really believes this. I swear, I don't know what they told her in that attic, but it lives in the very marrow of her bones.

But then, I am also to blame. I've always been shallow. I've always happily fed into a hierarchy based on looks. It was the only way I thought I could win anything. But now I see how it cuts. And I am ashamed of myself.

"We can throw a party," I prompt. "Something small. Intimate."

Nori withdraws her hand. "I'd rather not."

"My dear, it's really quite normal. All young women of marrying age have a debutante ball."

She turns to look at me, slowly. I see her smile twitch.

"Alice," she says gently, "I'm no lady. And there's no need for this. I am content to live quietly with you and your children."

But that's just the problem. I am not content, and I feel an inexplicable sense of irritation with her. She doesn't understand that it's always better to be the center of attention on your own terms. For God knows they will talk about you anyway. I know this, and I know it's true because I've learned that I'm not nearly as stupid as everyone has always tried to make me believe.

And since she is in my house, they will talk about me as well. I have already heard that Mary Lambert, my tennis partner, has been hinting that Nori and I are secret lovers. That I am hiding her out of spiteful jealousy and forbidden lust.

How ridiculous.

I turn to her and squeeze her hand.

"Won't you please?"

Her brow knits, but I can tell by the tilt of her mouth that I have won.

"But it will be small?" she peeps.

"Oh, quite. And we'll do it at my country house. It will be lovely."

She folds. "As you wish."

Windsor, England
June 1964

Small. Intimate.

Small . . . intimate.

Meaning two hundred people all packed into the grand ball-room of Alice's country estate, a few miles away from Windsor Castle.

But the chatter around Nori was nothing more than white noise.

This was the way she had survived.

She retreated to a place, deep inside herself, where nothing could touch her. The years had stretched on, one cold winter into the next, and she floated along as best she could. It was all she could do to keep her head above water.

But she had made a promise. To Ayame. And to Akira.

Even now, to think the name nearly took her out at the knees.

Loneliness and exhaustion had finally got the best of her, driving her into the arms of the closest thing she had to family. But just now, she was wishing she'd stayed in the rented cottages and hotel rooms, the cabins on the sea voyages she took with no specific destination in mind.

She was a wanderer, and she was meant to be alone.

It was who she was, who she had always been destined to be. To deny that was disastrous.

But for the first time since her sun had set all those years ago, she was truly torn. She wanted, so desperately, to believe that she had been punished enough.

There was a flutter of motion above the surface. Someone was talking to her.

It was a large woman wearing a sparkling pink gown, long white gloves, and too much jewelry for good taste. She had Alice's delicate features, but they were all but lost in the wide, white moon face.

Jane. Age: thirty-one. Alice's sister, whom she hates. But not as much as the other one.

"And are you enjoying your time in London, Miss Noriko?"

"Oh," she said. "Yes, thank you. Alice is so gracious for having me."

Jane squinted. "And how did you meet my dear little sister again?"

This lie had already been repeated half a dozen times.

"We met in finishing school," she parroted. "It was great fun."

Jane nodded. She of course knew that Alice had never been to finishing school. But she let the comment pass.

"And what about you? What brings you here now?"

Nori smoothed out the skirt of her lavender gown. It was the simplest thing she'd been able to find in Alice's closet.

"Just on my travels," she said simply.

Jane nodded vigorously. "I see, I see, and will you go back to China soon? Or will you be staying?"

Nori felt a ripple of irritation.

"Japan, actually. I've never been to China."

Jane waved a hand as if it really made no difference whether it was one savage Eastern country or the other.

"Yes, yes. And you're planning on staying here?"

"Alice has asked that I do, yes."

Jane stretched her thin lips over her teeth in a pained smile.

"I *see*. And you have no family of your own? Nothing to speak of? No money? You're just going to live with my sister and eat her food, then?"

Nori flushed.

"And I see that's her gown as well," Jane continued. Her blue eyes were sharp. "Though in fairness you fill it out much better.

But still, Miss Noriko, I do wonder what you hope to gain from all of this."

Nori felt something she had not felt in a long time. It was just a spark, but it was there: pride.

"My family is kin to the royal house of my country," she said quietly. "And as a result I have a great deal of money."

This was still partially true. She still had most of the money she'd inherited. A combination of frugal living and the occasional odd job knitting sweaters or embroidering curtains meant that she was still a wealthy woman in her own right.

Jane raised an overplucked eyebrow. "I see, I see. But you're not married?"

"No."

"And are you on the market, then?" Jane spit, her polite facade finally dropped. "Is that your plan? To trick my sister into getting you a rich Englishman to marry?"

Nori blinked at her. "Why would I be remotely interested in that?"

"Because that's what your kind always wants," Jane snapped. "Grasping social climbers. New money, or old money with no name attached. D'you suppose we're all as stupid as she is? You come here, with your exotic charms—"

"I have no interest in any men."

"So you are unnatural, then? The rumors are true?"

"What? No, I—"

"It's obvious that you're half-caste," she said, lowering her voice to a chilling whisper. "At *best*. You're not fooling anyone, with that horrible Negro hair of yours. I see you for what you are. I know you're not some pretty little Eastern blossom. You're a *weed*."

And with that, she stalked off into the crowd.

Nori stood there, with the champagne glass shaking in her hand.

Jane had found, with perfect precision, the weak spot in her armor.

She put the glass down and left the room.

By this point in the evening, she was hoping everyone would be too drunk to notice that the guest of honor was gone.

She slipped through the corridor and down the back stairs. There was only one place she could go to put her fractured pieces back together.

The air was sticky and humid, but Nori didn't care. She walked out into the English-style garden and hid behind a hedge manicured to look like a cherub.

There was an old willow tree in front of her. She wondered if it was possible to climb it in a designer gown.

It would take some concentration to erase this new memory. But she knew she could do it. And then she would slip back beneath the surface, into the place where the lights danced above but never touched her.

She caught a flurry of motion out of the corner of her eye. Before she could even blink, William had pulled her into his arms.

"I knew it was you," he whispered into her hair. "I *knew* you'd come back to me eventually."

She sighed. She'd known it was only a matter of time before she'd have to face him.

"William. How did you get in?" she asked quietly. "Alice went through a great deal of trouble to keep your name off the list."

William pulled back to look into her face, and his sapphire eyes were sparkling with triumph.

"I bribed a servant to let me into the back gardens. I knew you'd come."

Nori sighed again. Somehow, it was not jarring to see William again. It was as if she'd seen him only yesterday.

"Am I so predictable?"

William grinned widely, but then it faded. He looked down.

"I was deeply sorry to hear about Akira."

"I know," she said, and it was true.

"But you survived."

Nori turned her face away. "In a manner of speaking."

William hesitated for the first time. "Are you . . . are you all right?"

She nodded. "Your cousin Jane . . ."

His face darkened. "What did she say to you?"

She waved a hand. "It doesn't matter."

He took her hand and guided her over to the willow tree. "And has it been very difficult for you?"

She stared at him. He turned scarlet, realizing too late what a stupid question this was.

"I'm sorry. I shouldn't have . . . I mean . . . You're even more beautiful, Nori. You look so well. I just wondered if you . . . if you've suffered all these years. Or if you've managed to find some level of peace."

She shrugged. "A bit of both."

He lifted her chin so that she was forced to look into his eyes. His touch was familiar and, this time, nonthreatening. He wasn't the giant he'd once been to her.

"I won't hurt you," he whispered. "If you allow me . . . I will keep you safe. I loved Akira like a brother. I loved you too, even if I was—" He broke off. "You were right about me. I was jealous, I was fatally jealous. I wanted your light. I wanted your adoration, I wanted you and I didn't know how else to . . . I'm sorry, Nori."

Against all odds, she felt a rising sympathy for him—the only person who had known Akira as she had, regardless of what else he was.

"There's no need for this," she told him gently. "It's okay."

"So it can be just as it was," he demanded. "But better."

She shook her head, a sad smile tugging at her lips. "It can never be as it was, William. I'm not the same girl."

He lifted her up and spun her around.

"I'll fix you. I love you."

She felt the tears come. They were rare now, and they came from a place inside her she thought had already died long ago.

"Oh, William. You can't."

He kissed her tearstained cheeks, then her nose, then her lips. The last one set her teeth on edge.

"Watch me."

"Will, stop."

"Marry me. Be mine."

And there it was.

She felt, as if it were fresh, the pain of a night in another garden, a world away, a lifetime ago. She pulled away.

"I can't," she whispered.

"Nonsense," he scoffed. "Of course you can. I don't care what anyone says, my family can all be damned. And we know Alice will support us—once she gets over the shock."

"That's not why."

He drew back to look at her. "Then why, little love?"

"I . . ."

"Don't you care for me?"

She closed her eyes. "I did. Once. But, Will, I already told you before—"

"Hush. We just need to get accustomed to each other again. So marry me."

"I will never marry," she said quietly. "I will never have children."

He accepted this without a fight. "Fine, then. Convention be damned as well. Just stay with me."

Nori took a deep breath. "Will. I don't want you. I don't want to see you. I don't want to keep opening this wound. Please leave me alone."

Will staggered backwards. "I don't understand."

"I'm asking you nicely. If you don't, I'll tell Alice the truth."

He glowered at her. "Tell her what? That you threw yourself at me? Shamelessly sneaking into the music room at night to see me? That you paraded yourself in front of me like those whores in your brothel?"

She didn't shrink before his anger.

"I was an innocent," she said, very low. "And I wanted someone like you—someone like I thought you were—to love me. And you twisted it. You can't twist it now. I'm not weak anymore."

He rolled his eyes at her. "Don't be so dramatic."

"Don't belittle me," she hissed at him. "The scales fell from my eyes long ago."

He switched tactics. She could see it now—the very moment that he decided to be charming.

"Ah, love. Let's not fight."

"We aren't fighting," she said clearly. "You're leaving."

His eyes went cold, though he was still smiling. "Why did you come to see me, then? In Paris? If you wanted nothing from me?"

She hesitated, and he pounced.

"Just give me a chance to make you happy," he insisted. "Can't you do that? For old times' sake, for him, can't you do that? He would have wanted you to be happy."

He took her hands and pulled her close. "Nori?"

"I want to be happy," she managed. Her heart was pounding.

"So stay with me."

She shook her head. "Will, there's nothing you can say to change my mind. This isn't a negotiation, or a game you can find a way to win. This is no."

He looked dumbfounded. He took a step towards her, and she took a step back.

"Nori?" he said again, in that pitiful way that let her know that beneath it all, there was a spoiled child who couldn't bear to be refused. "Nori?"

She drew herself up to her full height. "Goodbye, Will."

He didn't say anything. He just lowered his head and walked away.

Bath, England
August 1964

Alice's belly was curved like a fat cauldron as she neared full term. Nori helped her friend as much as she could now, as Alice was tired most of the time. She spent most of the day sleeping.

The summer estate in Bath was large and beautiful, having

been mostly unchanged since the sixteenth century. It sat on a large patch of land bordering a clear lake.

Nori felt more at home here than she did in bustling London.

Escaping the city had been a good decision for them all. George had been unable to come but sent little gifts and tokens for his wife and daughters every week.

Nori loved to take the girls on boat rides, and often they would dock in a quiet, shady spot and have a picnic. She had come to care for them both as if they were her own, and as she very much doubted she'd ever have any children, they were especially dear to her.

It was just the four of them now, and a few select members of the staff—Bess, Alice's favorite lady in waiting; Maud, the nanny; and Noah Rowe, the new music teacher. The girls were quite attached to him, and Charlotte, who was nearly six, swore she wouldn't go if he couldn't come too.

Though she tried to stay away, sometimes Nori would sit in on the music lessons.

Charlotte was learning to play the piano, and Matilda would shake a small tambourine and giggle.

They sang too, learning songs about queens and kings, fairies and heroes.

Noah was a bright, smiling youth of nineteen with a mass of curly black hair and dazzling pale blue eyes, as wide and dreamy as the summer sky. He was from a place called Cornwall, and his accent was far less refined than Alice's. But he spoke clearly and his voice was warm.

Nori had liked him on sight.

But she kept her distance.

She could feel his eyes on her, sometimes at first, but now it was constant. Every time she entered a room, his head would snap up and he'd pin his gaze on her and turn the color of a tomato.

Alice noticed, of course, being terribly bored in this country setting and ravenous for a hint of scandal or gossip.

The two of them lay sprawled out on a blanket in the garden. A Beatles song was playing on the radio. A little ways away, Noah was chasing the girls through the trees as they screamed and laughed.

"He's a sweet one, isn't he?" Alice said lazily. She hadn't even bothered to change out of her nightdress today.

Nori closed her eyes and spread her palms up to face the sun. "Yes, he is."

"And do you think he is very handsome?"

"Oh, Alice, don't start."

"Well, he *is*," she pressed cheekily. "Though he has no name to speak of and certainly no money, for I pay him next to nothing."

"He is little more than a child."

Alice snorted. "You're twenty-four, not ninety. How can you call him a child?"

"He knows nothing of the world."

Alice raised an eyebrow. "I'm guessing from the way he looks at you that he's seen more than you have in some departments."

"*Alice.*"

"Well, it's true!" she protested. "I don't know how you manage it, it's like you have ice water in your veins. All of these handsome men looking at you and you stand like a statue. I have never once seen you look back."

"I'm not interested."

"And there was no one in your travels? Not one?"

Nori sighed. "No, Alice."

"How do you manage? I'm married, so I have no choice. But you are free to sample many delights and you turn your nose up at them all."

"Why do you have to be so primitive?" Nori grumbled. "It's hardly ladylike."

Alice leaned up on her elbows. The rest of her was so thin and her belly was so big that she looked like she was constantly about to topple over.

"That is a term invented by men who wanted the freedom to have their hypocrisy go unchecked," she said smartly. "And there's nothing wrong with desire. It's human. And I feel sorry for you that you've never known it."

"I'm not made of stone," Nori said wearily. "And I'm not blind. Of course he is very handsome. And he's kind and funny and . . ." She felt warmth creep into her voice against her will. "And honest. I think he's very much himself."

Alice squealed and seized Nori's hands.

"You *do* like him. I knew it!"

"It doesn't matter," she said levelly, "as there isn't any point."

Alice's gray eyes were knowing. "Oh, my dear girl. You can't shut yourself away from love forever. For you are love embodied and it will never stop trying to find you."

Despite her better judgment, Nori found herself hovering outside of the door to the music room that evening. She could hear the sound of rudimentary piano playing.

Charlotte was laughing.

Nori went in without knocking. Just as she'd suspected, Noah was sitting on the bench beside Charlotte. The little girl's face lit up when she saw who it was.

"Auntie Nori, look," she exclaimed. "I can play 'Twinkle, Twinkle'!"

Nori beamed at her. That incoherent key bashing could in no way be called Mozart.

"That's lovely."

"And Noah says he will teach me Butthoven."

Nori bit back a laugh. "I'm sure he will."

Noah's eyes met hers, and they exchanged a rueful glance.

"Charlotte," Nori said, without looking away, "I think it's time for bed."

The girl frowned. "Must I?"

"Yes. Mummy went to bed hours ago and you should too."

Charlotte sighed, but got up to do as she was bid. She was levelheaded and well-behaved, traits Nori assumed she must have gotten from her father.

Nori bent down to kiss her on both cheeks. "Good night, sweet girl."

After Charlotte had gone, Nori was acutely aware of her proximity to Noah. She had never been alone with him before.

He smiled shyly at her. "Do you . . . maybe want to sit?"

Part of her did. "No, thank you. I should be going."

"I'm teaching Charlotte Mozart's twelve variations," he said.

"Yes, I know."

She turned to leave. She didn't want to be rude, but she knew better than to start down this road.

"You're a musician, aren't you?"

Nori froze in her tracks. She turned back around to look into his bright face. "What?"

Noah grinned. "You aren't new to any of this. I can tell. And you don't just look at the music I give the girls, you read it. I hear you humming the melody."

She shrugged, flushing. "I dabbled. Years ago."

"Lady Alice says—"

Alice. Of course she couldn't stop herself from meddling.

"I really have to go," she said, because this conversation only led one place. And she wasn't going to talk about her brother with this boy. Not ever.

She left before he'd had a chance to drop his smile.

Nori woke in the night to the sound of a bloodcurdling scream. It was like a banshee.

She shot up and threw a robe over her nakedness. She ran down the hall to Alice's bedroom, but Charlotte had gotten there first.

She was clutching her stuffed animal to her chest and her eyes were the size of dinner plates. With a horrible sinking feeling, Nori realized that Alice hadn't been the one who had screamed.

It was Charlotte.

And when Nori saw why, a scream rose in her own throat and froze there in horror.

Alice was on the floor, half tangled in the sheets. It was clear that she had tried to stand but had become caught and fallen.

Her white nightgown was stained, terribly stained, with bloody water. And there, lying in the mess of sheets, was something . . . solid.

Nori snatched up Charlotte and shoved the little girl's face into her chest. But it was too late. She had already seen.

"Bess!" Nori cried. "Noah! Someone, please! Help, please!"

Alice raised her head off the floor. Her skin was green. There were tears streaming down her lovely face.

"It's too late," she whispered. "It's too late. He's already gone."

Nobody knew why. The doctor said that it was rare this late, but that it happened, and there were no answers.

"He never breathed," he said, as if that was supposed to bring comfort.

Alice was a ghost, pale and silent. She slept in Nori's bed because she couldn't bear to be in her own room. She stayed there all day, for weeks, until the October leaves started to fall.

Nori knew the bleak, endless despair that she was caught in. There were no words.

All she could do was sit by the bed and wait for Alice to be ready.

George came as soon as the news reached him, but ultimately, there was nothing he could say. They buried the half-formed body of Alice's son in the garden, underneath an ancient oak tree, in a small ceremony presided over by a local priest. Alice refused to attend.

George took the girls back to London with him afterwards,

leaving Alice in the care of Bess and Nori. Charlotte had worn the same shell-shocked look on her face since that night, and Matilda's screaming for her mother could be heard even as the car pulled away.

Surprisingly, Noah had refused to leave.

"I'll stay with Lady Alice," he said simply. "And with you."

Nori did not have the energy to ask what use a music teacher, and a second-rate one at that, would be in a situation like this. It was all she could do to keep her beloved friend from starving to death.

Bess brought hot water and soap to the side of the bed every day, and sometimes between the two of them they could coax Alice to sit up so that they could wash her and change her into a fresh nightgown.

Nori cooked all of Alice's favorite dishes in a vain attempt to get her to eat more than a few bites.

Noah was mostly useless, but he'd stand in the doorway and sing in a low, clear voice. Absurdly, Nori felt better having him here, though she'd never admit it.

Bess pulled her aside one morning. "She can't go on like this," she said simply. "It's been months."

Nori hesitated. "We can't force her."

Bess blinked at her. She was a tan, sturdy girl with freckles and wild strawberry-blonde hair.

"I can't, certainly," Bess corrected her. "But begging your pardon, miss, she listens to you."

Nori felt the pit of her stomach fall out. She groaned. She had been here before, on the other side of the door. Mired in darkness. Now it was her turn to pull someone back to the light.

"I'll tell her to get up," she said.

Bess nodded and gestured to the closed bedroom door. "I'll leave you to it, then."

Nori took a deep breath and opened the door to the bedroom. The shutters were drawn, and it was so dark that she almost stumbled.

She crept to the bed slowly.

"Alice," she whispered.

There was no response. The figure in the bed did not even stir.

"Alice," she tried again, more forcefully this time.

Still nothing.

Nori knelt down so that the two of them were at eye level. "Alice," she said, "it's time to get up now."

Alice's lips moved, but she did not speak.

Nori tried again. "We have to go back to London. The summer is over. You have duties. Your husband has called, again, to say that the girls are asking for you. It's time to go home."

Alice's face was full of hatred. "Go," she hissed, with quiet fury.

"I can't go," Nori said gently. "I'm so very sorry. But today is the last day of this, my dear. You have to get up."

Alice looked into her eyes. "Go away, Nori. Everything was fine before you came here. Just go away."

Nori ignored the twinge of agony she felt. It was not the first time she had thought this herself, but there was no time now for self-pity.

"It makes no difference now," she said evenly. "Horrible things happen and we will never know why. You must bear the injustice of it, you must swallow it down like a bitter pill and carry on. You must get up."

"I demand to know why!" Alice shrieked. She bolted up. "Why take him?" she raged. "I want to know why, damn it. I want to know *why*."

"God's will," Nori said, and it cost her a great deal to say it.

Alice folded over and sobbed. "It's my fault," she moaned. "It's my fault. I have a sin, I have a horrible sin. I was sixteen. In Paris, I . . . I was so afraid. I was so afraid, Nori. They never would've let me come home if they'd found out I'd gotten pregnant. It would've been the end of me. And I had nobody. I was alone."

Nori took in this latest revelation without blinking. "That's not a sin. And even if it were, it is between you and Him. He wouldn't punish anyone else."

It was so eerie to say these words out loud. She wondered who she was really speaking to.

Alice let out a heartrending cry. "I'm supposed to be past my troubles."

"You *are*, Alice. You have recovered from everything that's happened. And you are so young, and you have the girls already. You will have other babies. I promise you."

Nori held out her hands. After a moment, Alice took them, and the two women rose to their feet.

Alice swallowed down an endless stream of tears. "But I wanted *this* baby."

Nori didn't say anything. There was nothing to say.

The next morning, they left for London.

CHAPTER SEVENTEEN

BUT HOME IS NOWHERE

London, England
December 1964

B y winter the mood had lightened. Alice was restored to her usual good cheer and had thrown herself wholeheartedly into planning for the holiday season. Nori knew it was a front, but she of all people knew how necessary it was to have distractions. She let it be.

Nori withdrew as much as she could. There was no question at all of her attending any more parties.

Besides, she was preoccupied. Avoiding Noah was growing increasingly difficult. His gazes grew longer and more heated. She began finding little gifts of silk or paper flowers in her room. There were poems and candies, ribbons and tiny painted figurines.

She ignored them all. But she knew that eventually she would have to face him.

He caught her on the back stairs one morning before breakfast.

"Do move," she said, politely enough. "I'm expected."

"Have you gotten my gifts?"

Nori cheated her gaze to the side. "I have."

"And? They don't please you?" he asked, in a tone so earnest that it made her heart ache.

"It's not that. They're very pretty."

"I read a book about origami," he said, his cheeks rosy. "And I thought you would like it. I hoped it would remind you of home."

My God. You poor, sweet fool.

"Mr. Rowe, it is not appropriate for you to be sending me gifts."

The boy before her shifted awkwardly, and she was reminded of just how young he was. She wondered if she was the first girl he'd ever set his heart on.

"I know I'm beneath your station," he mumbled. "And I don't mean to offend. It's just I . . . I think you're beautiful."

She felt a warm tingle in her spine.

"You're not beneath me," she said clearly. "No one is beneath me. Trust me. But I am a foreigner, and much older than you."

Noah smiled and revealed perfectly white, straight teeth.

"Hardly. Barely five years."

She shook her head. "You are a charming young man. I am sure that there are many lovely English girls that would love to receive gifts from you."

He frowned at her. "But I don't want to get them gifts. I got them for you."

Nori hesitated. She could twist herself in knots all day trying not to hurt him. But she needed to put an end to this.

"I can't give you what you want, Noah."

He took a step closer to her, and she caught the scent of warm cedar and freshly cut grass.

"And what do you think I want?"

"I imagine you want what all men want."

He paused.

"Is that what you think of me?" he asked, and if she didn't know better, she would have said he sounded disappointed . . . but in her, not in himself.

Instantly, she was awash with guilt. "I didn't mean—"

"You wouldn't think that if you knew me."

"But I don't know you! And you don't know me! We've barely spoken!"

Noah scratched his chin. "Well, that is true."

"So now you see," she said hopefully, "why this must come to an end."

He grinned at her. "Ten minutes."

She blinked. "What?"

"Ten minutes. Spend ten minutes with me every evening for the next month. And then if you want me to leave you be, I will."

She had all the power here. One word to Alice and he would be sent packing straight back to Cornwall.

"Why should I say yes?"

"You're asking the wrong question. Why should you say no? What are you afraid of?"

She was immediately on the defensive. "I'm not afraid."

Noah clapped his hands. "Good. So I'll see you tonight."

"B-but . . ."

"The library. Nobody ever goes in there. Say, ten o'clock?"

She stared at him, at a loss for words. He took that as an assent, winked at her, and walked away.

You stupid girl.

Look what you've done.

He was right about the library. Though it was clean, it still looked brand-new. It was not a lived-in room.

Like most things in Alice's house, it was probably just for show.

Noah was seated in a plush high-backed armchair, with his hands folded across his lap. Though he had the face of a boy, she could see the ripple of his muscles underneath his shirt. He was sure with his hands, and she did not doubt that he was used to an honest day's work.

He smiled at her. "You came."

She sat across from him and crossed her ankles. "Ten minutes."

He nodded. "Best get started, then. Where were you born?"

Nori shifted slightly. "I don't know."

He frowned, and she was immediately irritated that he'd managed to touch, with such a simple question, on how utterly dysfunctional her life had always been.

"How do you not know?" he asked softly, and his voice was free of judgment.

"My mother had me at home. There's no record of it. We lived in an apartment . . . for a while. But I didn't ask her. And then she left, and I was raised by my grandmother in Kyoto."

Noah nodded. "I've heard gossip, of course. That you're . . . that you're, well . . ."

"A bastard," Nori said clearly. "Yes. I am."

Noah flushed. "I didn't mean to offend you."

"And you haven't. It's what I am."

He looked unconvinced but decided to let it go. "And did you like Kyoto?"

She looked at her hands. "I didn't see much of it from the attic."

He looked at her, dumbstruck. "What? They kept you in the attic?"

"They did."

"They can't do that!" he burst. "You can't keep a child in the attic."

She laughed. "They can and they did."

He went very pale. "But why? Surely you weren't the only bastard in Japan."

She showed him her arms. His eyes fell on the smooth skin, tanned to a coconut brown from all her time in the sun.

"Because of this," she said simply.

"Your skin?"

"Yes."

Noah looked at her with wide blue eyes. "But there's nothing wrong with it."

She wrapped her arms around herself. "My grandmother thought differently. She deemed it a mark of inferiority, a sign to the world that I had foreign, traitorous blood."

"But you don't?" he pressed. "You don't give what she said any credence, do you?"

She moved to deny it, but the split second of hesitation gave her away. Before she could react, Noah was out of his chair and kneeling in front of her.

He ran his pale fingers over her arm, down to her hand. He flipped her palm over and pressed it against his. He radiated warmth, so much that it was almost uncomfortable.

"It was the first thing about you I noticed," he confessed. "Smooth as a pearl, such a wonderful color."

He looked into her shocked face.

"I think it's beautiful."

Her eyes welled with tears, and she took back her hand. He raised his face to hers, and she pulled away, stumbling out of her chair like it had been set on fire.

"And now your time is up."

She rushed out of the room, but even as she lay in bed that night, she could do nothing to still the suddenly frantic beating of her heart.

Nori swore to herself that she would tell him nothing else about her past. During their nightly meetings, she sat in silence, with her face turned towards the wall like a stubborn child. But she always came. Her feet led her there every evening of their own accord.

Noah was not dissuaded by her silence. He was always ready with a small glass of wine for himself and a steaming mug of apple cider for her. He told her quite candidly that she did not have to stay if she didn't want.

But she always did.

He did the talking. She tried to tune him out, but his voice was so charming, invoking an image of rolling green hills.

And so she listened.

He'd grown up in Cornwall, the youngest of four boys. His French mother was a drunk who died young and left him nothing but recipes for jams, which he'd tried and failed to re-create.

It was his way of trying to know her and of dealing with his anger at having never got the chance.

He made her laugh with his terrible French.

His father was a teacher who had died four years ago. His oldest brother had sold the family home, and they'd all been forced to fend for themselves.

"We never had much," he confessed sheepishly. "And me being the youngest, I usually got leftovers. But there was lots of love."

He told her how the nuns at school taught him to play the piano.

"I didn't like it at first," he said with a chuckle. "It was awfully difficult. But once I realized how happy it can make people . . . I was never good enough to be professional, of course, but I love children, so, you know, I pass the joy on."

She caught herself staring at his lips. His perfect pink lips. Nori sat on her hands to stop herself reaching out to him.

She looked away. "I think that's time."

He smirked at her. "It was time an hour ago. I was wondering when you'd notice."

She flushed. "I didn't want to interrupt."

He nodded. "So, Nori. Are you going to marry me or not?"

She bristled. "Don't joke."

"I'm not joking," he said simply.

She rose from her seat and smoothed her skirt. "No."

He nodded, unperturbed. He'd expected this.

"Maybe tomorrow, then."

Nori pressed a hand to her mouth and walked away.

The days rolled together. She'd stopped counting.

Christmas came and went, with Nori getting three new dresses from Alice, a pearl necklace from George, and a hand-made card from the girls.

Alice was busy and happy, throwing herself into decorating the nursery upstairs. She was confident she would conceive again soon. This time, it would be a boy. This time, surely, he would live.

Nori was grateful for her friend's distraction. Whatever this thing was between her and Noah, it was growing harder for her to hide.

He got her two sugarplums and something called a pasty, which was quite good.

Though she did not wish to encourage his affections, she made him a scarf from gold yarn.

She knitted constantly, to quiet her thoughts.

The two of them took long walks in the snow, with their heads bowed against the wind, saying nothing. He wrapped his arm around her waist, and she did her best not to think how warm he made her feel.

He made her feel safe. And that was a luxury she had so rarely known.

They talked about music often, and she could see his idolatry of her slowly shift into something deeper.

Against her will, she told him everything. She even told him about William. It was the only time she'd seen him truly angry, but he had reluctantly agreed not to tell anyone.

Every night, at the end of their fireside chats, he would ask her to marry him.

She would say no, he would nod, and that would be that.

He never tried to kiss her, though she could tell that he yearned to by the way he held his body very close to hers. Their hands would rest half an inch apart, their eyes would meet, and it would feel just like a caress. She felt shameless before him, full of a wild desire that she had never known, had never even contemplated.

Nori knew she had to stop this. There was no future for it, none at all.

She would not be his whore, and she could not be his wife—society wouldn't stand for it, even if the law allowed it—so what was there? What end to this was there but disaster? Had her mother's treacherous lover and William not been enough warning?

If she had the sense that God gave a goldfish, she'd tell him plainly that they could never be and that if he continued to persist, she would have him sent straight back to the countryside.

In fact, she had resolved to tell him this a great many times. But never could.

Noah had tapped into her secret, shameful need to be wanted. She was drunk on his attentions; she reveled in his love of her skin and hair like it was salve on a lifelong burn.

She had brief snippets where she could see herself through his eyes. And there was so much beauty there it brought her to tears.

All her life she'd felt like an elephant lumbering among delicate things.

But in his honest gaze, she was no longer the elephant. She was the swan.

The days drew to a close, and though they had long given up the facade of "ten minutes," she knew that eventually, he would tell her the words she lived in perpetual terror of hearing.

Because she had to tell him no. And that would break his heart and she found that she truly, truly didn't want to do that.

She *did* care for him. As much denial as she cloaked herself in just to survive, she was forced to admit it.

He was tenderhearted, honest, generous, and full of laughter. He was more mature than his years, but still brimming with idealism. He was a wonderful person. And he fit neatly inside the tumbled mess of her psyche.

It just felt like he belonged.

But Nori was quite sure she was incapable of the love he deserved. Her heart had been snatched from her chest on the side of a dark road.

As they rang in the New Year of 1965, Nori made sure that she was well out of sight. Alice had filled the house with well-dressed strangers, and Nori had no desire to be gaped at like a circus attraction.

High in the branches of a tree, she hid.

She'd hiked her black dress up and left her shoes on the ground. It wasn't ladylike, but it worked.

Everywhere in the world there were trees. She was immensely grateful to them for their constancy.

Someone called her name. She took a firm hold of a sturdy branch before looking down.

It was Noah, wearing a thick winter coat and the scarf she'd given him.

She contemplated staying right where she was.

"Come down or I'll come up after you," he shouted playfully. "And I can't climb, so I'll probably crack my skull open."

She knew he wouldn't, but she came down anyway. She moved with practiced ease, swinging down from branch to branch until she landed before him with a thud.

He smiled at her. "Nori."

And just the way he said her name made her want to run. "Noah . . ."

He held up a hand. "I have ten more minutes."

He looked at her, and she could tell from the warm light in his eyes that they had come to it: the inevitable conclusion. She knew what he would say, and she knew what she must say back to him.

The noise from inside faded away, and the only sound was the wind rustling through the trees and the obnoxiously loud beat of her heart. "Don't," she whispered, but even as she spoke she knew there was no stopping it.

"I'm in love with you." There. He had said it.

Don't. Please don't.

He gave her a soft smile. He looked sad. "I know you wish that I wasn't," he said. "I wish that I wasn't too. But I am. I'm in love with you, Nori, and it isn't going to change. I was in love with you yesterday. And I'll be in love with you tomorrow."

Don't.

"I don't expect you to say anything," he continued. "I know you think that I only love you because you're beautiful. And you are, Nori. But that's not why. I'm not a child—I don't worship you.

I see you for what you are. And I know that you're stubborn, that you have blind spots the size of mountains. I know that you want one thing one day and the very opposite the next. I know that you have no idea who you are or what you want to be. I know you think life is over for you because your brother is gone, and you're just filling the time until you die. And I know you think that I'm just a boy who is too blind to see all of that." She really couldn't breathe now. The wind picked up and she felt herself sway.

Noah took her hand, and she was too stunned to do anything about it.

"But I also know that I love the way you hum in the mornings," he went on, and though his hand was shaking his voice was not. "I love the way your curls refuse to lie down on one side some days. I love the way you think that honey is better than diamonds. I love how tender you are towards all God's creatures. I love your sharp mind and your enduring heart. I love . . . God, I love everything about you, Nori. Even the things I wish I didn't, I do. I love you more than . . . anything I ever could have dreamed of. And that's how I know it's real, what I feel for you. Because I never could have imagined anything like this. I never could have imagined you." He let go of her hand. His beautiful face was a strained mask. He kissed her, just once, and she felt a deep pulse in the very core of her being.

"Marry me," he said.

Her mouth opened and closed and no sound came out.

"If you won't have me, I'll have to go," he said quietly. "There's no point in trying not to see you. You're everything to me."

He smiled at her one last time and went back inside the house.

Nori sank to the ground and buried her face in her hands.

Go after him.

Get up. Get up.

But she could not.

The next morning, it was Alice who found her sitting by the fire in the study, staring at nothing.

"Noah's packing," she said. "Can you tell me why?"

Nori let out a small groan.

Alice sat beside her. "He told you he loves you, didn't he?"

She nodded.

Alice took her hand. "Ah, my dear. You must have known."

"But why did he have to say so?" she burst out. "Because now he has to leave and I don't *want* him to leave."

Alice stroked her hair. "But you love him too."

Nori did not deny it. "You told me he was a poor nothing," she scoffed. "That he was beneath me."

"Oh, he is. But I think he is a good man. And I think your brother would have liked him."

There was no higher praise.

Nori shut her eyes. "I can't handle this," she said bluntly. "I am incapable of it, Alice. Really. I can deal with injustice. I can deal with tragedy. I can deal with loss."

"But you can't deal with the idea that maybe it's time for you to be happy?" Alice said gently. "That terrifies you so much that you're willing to lose him?"

She bit her lip so hard that she tasted blood. "I don't know."

"Well, you had best figure it out. He's asked if I'd have my driver drop him at the train station."

"Tell me what to do," Nori begged. "Alice, you know things about love. You know about men. Tell me what I should do."

Alice sighed. "My dear, I cannot tell you what to do. It's your path to walk. I have mine already. You are welcome to live your entire life as a part of mine, if that's what you wish. But you must ask yourself, truly . . . if there's any piece of you that wishes for more."

Nori shook her head. "But what if I choose wrong?"

Alice smiled and kissed her cheek. "No matter what you choose," she whispered, "I will always love you. And you will always have a home with me."

Nori waited for him at the foot of the back staircase.

He came down, wearing his coat and clutching a small suitcase. It struck her that everything he owned in the world was inside.

He looked at her with a calm face. "Do move," he said, pleasantly enough. "I'm expected."

She swallowed the lump of air in her throat. "Please don't go."

He raised an eyebrow. "Why?"

"I don't want you to go," she said weakly. She knew what he wanted to hear, but she could not say it.

"Not good enough."

"Noah!" she cried. "I'm trying!"

"Try harder," he said simply. "I won't accept half of you."

She planted her feet and spread her arms so that he could not get around her. "Don't be so stubborn!"

"Look who's talking," he scoffed. "You have kept me at arm's length at every chance, and now you command me to stay."

"I'm asking you," she croaked. "I have no commands to give. I'm asking you not to leave me."

He put down his suitcase and crossed his arms. "Why should I stay?"

She began to gesture wildly with her hands, as if they could convey what her words could not. "The girls adore you. And there is nothing for you in Cornwall now, you said so yourself. And you . . . well, you . . ."

He sighed. "If this is all you have to say, Nori, I have a train to catch."

Gently, so gently, he pushed her aside. She turned to stare at his back, and it hit her, full force, what a familiar sight this was. The back of someone she loved.

Be brave.

She flung herself at him, wrapping her arms around his waist.

"Stay," she whispered.

She felt the tears sliding down her cheeks.

"I love you, Noah. I love you with everything that is left of my heart."

He turned to face her and cradled her face in his hands.

"Ah, my love. Now, was that so hard?"

She choked back a sob. "Don't leave. Don't ever leave me."

He kissed her. "I won't."

And the strangest thing happened then: Nori believed him.

"So are you going to marry me or not?"

She laughed as he hoisted her up high in his arms. "Maybe tomorrow."

CHAPTER EIGHTEEN

CHRYSANTHEMUM

London, England
May 1965

The dress was made. Alice had hired an army of seamstresses to craft an ivory number that paid homage to a kimono, with long bell sleeves and a plunging neck.

The venue was set—a small chapel nestled in the ruins of a castle. Charlotte was thrilled and demanded that she be the one to choose the bridesmaids' dresses, while Matilda, who was just learning to argue, insisted that the duty should go to her instead.

Alice was debating with George over which of their many country houses they should assign the newlyweds to live in. Noah would be promoted to George's private secretary, with a substantial income boost.

Nori was grateful, but in truth paid little attention to any of it. She was constantly intoxicated, nothing more than yearning sinew and aching bones. On those rare occasions she could drag herself out of Noah's arms, all she wanted to do was dream.

Her happiness was complete.

Well, almost.

There was something missing. There would always be something missing. But she knew he would have been happy to see this.

It was in these sunny days that she finally told Noah about the diaries.

For whatever reason, she had been holding on to this secret. This and one other thing—she had never spoken about the night Akira died. Nor would she. Ever.

She took his hand and led him to sit on the stone bench beneath the birch trees, with the branches fanning out over their heads like protective halos.

The last of her mother's diaries, which she had never finished, lay heavy in her lap.

Noah looked at her with his honest blue gaze. "So why have you not read it?"

She waved a hand as if to say that there were thousands of reasons. He snatched it out of the air and kissed it.

"Is it that you are afraid that your mother will talk about your father?" he asked simply. "Or that she will talk about you?"

Nori fidgeted. "I read them because I wanted to know who she was. Before me. I never wanted to know who she was after. There must be a reason I can't remember. Maybe I'm not meant to know."

"Do you think she hated you?" Noah asked, with that country bluntless that she hated and loved so very much. "Do you think she will say that she hated you?"

"I don't know."

"Well, obviously you must read it, then. Come on, I'll sit here with you."

She gave him a pained expression. She could not bring herself to tell him that it took her hours to read one line, days to read one passage, months to read one full entry. This journey through her mother's past was like a very steep climb. She had always done it carefully.

And now Noah wanted her to just read it.

He laughed at her pout. "Come, come, love. You wouldn't have told me if you didn't want to read it. You've always wanted to know, but you doubted that you could bear it. After your brother . . ."

"Please don't," she whispered through numb lips.

"I only mean that without him, you could not risk it."

"Risk what?"

He squeezed her hand. "Anything."

She looked away. "Oh, Noah."

He smiled that enchanting smile of his. "But I'm here now," he said brightly. "So you can put your past to rest, and the future is all ours."

She shook her head. "I can't read this with you here."

"Of course you can," he teased. "I'm to be your husband. You can't hide from me, Nori. You really must stop that."

He chided her as an optimist to a cynic, and she knew that there was no point in arguing with him. Besides, she did not want to disappoint him. She had grown protective of his joyful spirit, as one should always be protective of rare and delicate things.

And he was right: she was ready now to face whatever lay inside these pages.

"Fine," she conceded, ignoring the frantic pounding of her heart. "But you must turn away. I really can't do it if you stare. And I may take my time."

He beamed at her. "I'll go up in the tree," he promised. "I won't come down until you summon me."

"You can't climb trees, my love," she said warmly.

"I have been practicing. Soon I will catch up to you, and where will you hide from me then?"

He stood up and leaned down to kiss her tenderly on the mouth. "I love you," he said simply.

Her cheeks blazed; she could feel the heat from her collarbone to her forehead.

"I love you too," she whispered.

She took the diary and retreated to a small corner of the garden, sinking down into the damp grass.

And then she read.

April 13th, 1939

My Akira is a marvel.

Every day I look at him, and I look at his fool mother and his dull father, and I cannot believe we have made him.

He is going to be a prodigy, I'd lay my fortune on it. He can already read music though he is only three and he can play the piano better than I could at twice his age.

He has perfect hands. Perfect.

He plays the violin too, and I think he likes it better. But I do hope he keeps playing the piano.

I am teaching him French as well and he can remember whole sentences—this morning he recited a poem I taught him last week.

And such a handsome boy! He looks just like me, not like his father at all—thank God.

But he is so serious, terribly serious. He is shy with his smiles, and when he laughs, he covers his mouth as if he is ashamed. He is soft-spoken and thoughtful, and though he is just a child, he judges very carefully before he acts.

This he does not get from me.

I must take great care or his father will ruin him. Yasuei says that I will make him soft, that he must be molded from the cradle for his calling in life.

But I want a happy child. God knows there is precious little joy in life—I want him to have his sunny years.

I want everything for him, actually, and I have never known pain like the pain I feel when I think that I really have nothing to give him.

I will take him to the countryside this summer and dip his precious toes in the salt water of the ocean. I will feed him sweets and teach him to play Beethoven.

I will wipe the frown from between his brows and kiss his cheeks until he giggles.

And I will pray that he remembers.

I think it will be the worst thing in the world to watch him grow up. Unlike other mothers, I cannot hope for my boy, I cannot dream what he will become.

I know what he will become.

And I can find no joy in it.

May 2nd, 1939

My mother is here.

She has invited herself, of course, and told nobody that she was coming. She says she will stay for an entire month. Yasuei has taken up an assignment abroad just to avoid her, so now I am all alone.

She has brought her own servants because she says that she cannot trust mine to do anything properly, and they must have rooms as well.

I cannot see how I'm going to bear this. The only mercy is that she did not bring my father.

I don't need him looking at me like I'm a whore.

He would have beaten me within an inch of my life when I returned from Paris, but Mother didn't let him. She said that I could not have marks on me before the wedding.

Actually, that's the funny thing about Mother. She is ruthless, but she is not sadistic. She does not enjoy cruelty, she doesn't inflict pain for the sake of it like Papa does. And sometimes, when she appears most awful, she is actually protecting me from something worse.

If she can keep me safe, she will. But only if I serve the family. Or, really, only if I serve her.

July 5th, 1939

She is still here.

God help me.

I can tolerate her constant criticism of absolutely every-thing I do, from the way I run my household to the way I dress, but I cannot tolerate her stealing my son away from me.

Her passion for him is overwhelming the poor boy. I think she wants to dip him in gold and put him on display as a holy icon.

He is respectful towards her, he is a most well-mannered boy, but he looks desperate for rescuing.

She talks to him like he's a grown man, not a child at all, and she showers him with gifts as if this is the way to win love.

I can do nothing. I am unable to stand up to her, as usual.

She asks me when I will make another grandson for her, but she is not asking as a loving grandmother.

She is asking as the guardian of a dynasty. If I have a girl, I doubt she will trouble herself to come back here.

She only needs boys.

I won't tell her that I haven't slept with my husband in months. He doesn't come to my bedroom. I suppose he has mistresses. I can't be bothered to ask.

Eventually we'll need another son, but for now I'm free.

Now if only my mother would go home to Kyoto.

It's a miracle the city has not crumbled to dust in her absence.

August 1st, 1939

My mother has taken my boy.

She has taken him away, just as a falcon will pick up a shiny object and fly it back to the nest.

I can barely write for grief.

She has insisted he spend the whole of August with her in Kyoto and I am not invited. Though I am a married woman and the mother of our family's heir, apparently I am still too tainted to soil the threshold of her beloved city.

Yasuei is still not back. I write to him and tell him that he must come home at once and take command of his household. My mother is running roughshod over us all.

I dismiss all the servants, every one, and I tell them I will send for them when I want them to return.

I am left alone in this great house. I can hear my footsteps echoing as I walk.

But I cannot stand to be here, trapped within the walls of my husband's house, in a city that still doesn't feel like home.

I have to get out.

I must get out.

I will go where I always go when I cannot tolerate my life.

I will go to the music.

August 20th, 1939

I have met an American.

I have met an American at the symphony.

He touched my shoulder as I was walking out, just slightly, and he smiled at me and told me I had dropped my fan. He spoke in English, he cannot speak a word of Japanese, and he lit up when he realized that I could understand him. He says he's been very lonely with few people to talk to.

He's in the army, or the navy, or something of that sort. He has a uniform in any case. But since it is peacetime in his country, he is on leave, and he came here to paint the cherry blossoms.

He has brown skin like a coconut, unlike anything I've seen before, and eyes like amber. They're the oddest color. But they are beautiful.

My God, they are beautiful.

And he is tall, very tall, with strong arms that he says he got behind a plow. I don't know what a plow is—I think it is some kind of peasant farming device. He has the most per-fect full lips.

He is the most extraordinarily handsome man I have ever seen.

But I have been here before. I know better.

I have quashed desire, I have not dreamt of love since my husband slid a ring on my finger and a halter around my neck.

I am his chattel, his broodmare, his loyal and obedient wife, and I will be until I die.

This is what my mother would say. This is what I should say.

But I have seen the American five times now, every night this week. He is renting a horrible little room in the worst part of town, but I don't care. I throw a scarf over my head, I put on dark sunglasses, and I go into the ghetto as if I were not cousin to royalty, as if they did not used to call me "little princess."

He is a gentleman. He never tries to touch me, though I cannot miss the way his eyes graze the skin at my collarbone, as if he thinks of nothing but kissing me there.

And we talk. Amazingly, we talk about everything. We have almost nothing in common and yet we understand each other perfectly.

I have never been able to speak to anyone this way.

My boy will be home soon, and though I am so happy, I know this will bring my husband back too. For all his faults, he loves our son.

He sees me no more than he sees the furniture, but I fear that he will smell the desire on me. I am a dog in heat, surely he will know?

This is a dangerous road I am treading down.

I should go back.

But I cannot.

Oh, I cannot.

September 7th, 1939

Something is happening in Europe, everyone is talking about it. Germany is causing trouble, just as they have always done, and my husband says that it will all end badly and that he hopes Japan has the sense to stay out of yet another war. We are already at war with China, and there has been terrible loss of life on both sides. But the Emperor has declared that Japan must expand and my husband says that another Great War is looming.

But I don't care about any of this because I am in love for the first time. Really, truly in love.

I have found someone who turns my very world. And I never thought it would be an American, as Mother says they are vulgar people, but it is so.

I spend my days with my son, teaching him songs, tickling him, and watching him try not to laugh, taking him to the little antique shop I like so much.

I am heart and soul for him during the days. No one could doubt my motherhood—certainly he does not. Every evening before bed he takes my face in his hands and kisses me on my dimples. He says, "I love you, Maman," in perfect French, as solemn as if he were giving a speech.

I tuck him into bed, my little angel, and then I shut off the light and leave him to dream.

And in the nights, I am free. Free as a blackbird, invisible against the dark sky.

And then I go to him—my American. My love.

I don't feel like I am sinning. I know it sounds strange, since I am an adulteress and perhaps a whore, but this feels . . . pure. It's the purest thing I've ever known.

We make love until the early hours of the morning and then I doze in his arms until the sun rises. The light is so unwelcome that when I see it creeping through the window, I want to take hold of it and fling it back.

In these last, precious moments we whisper of our plans for a future that can never, ever be.

He says that I must get away from my husband, that he will take me back to America with him. He says that we will live on a farm in the middle of nowhere, away from the white people who would not like it and the black people who would not understand it.

He says that we will have beautiful children, and that he will not care whether they are boys or girls. He says he would love a daughter as well as a son and perhaps more, because she would be as beautiful as I am.

And I think I would do it. I think that I would give up my servants and my silks and my dangerous Kamiza inheritance. I think that I would churn butter and milk cows and count pennies if it meant that I could lie in his strong arms every night and hear him say my name.

I love him so much it is like a physical pain to tear myself out of his arms.

But I have to go back to my son.

No matter what happens, I can never leave him. I can never leave him with a father who would see him turned into a block of stone and a grandmother who would tear him apart with the fervor of her ambition.

But the walls of my grand house have never felt so suffocating before. I don't think I can breathe here anymore. I am suffocating like a fish on dry land.

I am so torn and so distraught that some days I can do nothing but cry.

I sit at the bench of my piano and I am sick with grief. I try to think how I could steal Akira away. He is my son, he belongs with me. And he would be welcome, my love has told me that he would be most welcome.

But I know this is impossible.

We would never make it out of the country. They would take Akira from me and I would never see him again.

Nothing can be done. I will have to stay here, as daughter, as wife, as mother. There's no way out for me. There never was.

Any freedom I had was always an illusion. Any movement forward was always temporary.

I am a Kamiza.

And in the end, all roads lead home.

October 16th, 1939

Akira has won his first contest. He is so proud of himself, but he will not say, and instead he says that it is all down to my teaching.

Blessed sweet child.

His father glanced at the trophy when Akira carried it in, but didn't say anything except "Good." I know my boy was wounded. But—and this is how I know that he is already ruined—he did not show it. He composed his face and went up to his room without a word.

I can't wait for the nights to see my American anymore, and often I sneak out during the days. We can't meet privately, of course, but I tell him where I will be and he is always there.

I make up some imaginary errand and I go out to the market and I feel his gaze on my neck.

I have given up trying to resist the power he has over me. I know that I have grown reckless. I come home smelling of sweat and lovemaking and cigarette smoke—and I don't smoke. Sometimes I don't come home at all until noon, and I go in through the servants' entrance and slip up to my room.

If I had a husband who loved me, he would have noticed by now. But thankfully, I do not.

My maids make excuses for me, they all love me, and my husband is not a man who inspires love.

Akira is too young to know what is happening, but he is a clever boy and I must take care.

I couldn't bear to hurt him.

He must never doubt for a moment that he is the beating of my heart.

November 22nd, 1939

Yasuei says that it's time to make another child, now that Akira is nearly four. He says that the children should be close in age so that they can be a comfort to one another. I don't know how he would know; he has only one brother and they hate each other.

I tell him that I am unwell, that I have had womanly problems lately and cannot lie with him. I am buying time.

In truth, I cannot bear to let him touch me.

And anyway, there really is something wrong with me. I am tired all the time and I have a strange heat in my bones.

Akira is happy to be turning four. He says that he wants to grow up so he can help me with all my little troubles and make it so I am never sad again.

I tell him that he is the cure to all my sorrows and I kiss his face until he shows me his rare, elusive smile.

December 3rd, 1939

This is the worst day of my life.

I have seen the doctor, and he has confirmed my very worst fear.

I am with child.

January 9th, 1940

I cling to hope. Or, more honestly, to denial.

I tell myself that the doctor was wrong. For he was not my usual doctor, but some fool who would never recognize me, clear across town. He might have been trained in a back alley for all I know. He might have been wrong.

But I have not bled since October. My breasts are full and sore. My belly is tender and I am sick with every sunrise.

I am no blushing maiden. I am a married woman with a child already.

I know what this means.

What I must decide now is what I will do about it.

I know of sinful things. It was an open secret in Paris among the artists and musicians. Everyone knew where you could go, where you could find doctors—or people claiming to be doctors—who would solve these sorts of problems. Beautiful young women were advised as to where they could go to avoid being forever shamed.

But everyone also knew that some of those girls never came back.

I can't do it.

Not because I fear for my life, but because this child is part of the man I love. And I cannot bring myself to harm any part of him.

This child will have his skin. There is no hiding it. I cannot pass it off as trueborn, as sluts have been doing since the dawn of time. And I think that I would do this if I could, as shameful as it is, if it would keep me with my son.

But that path is closed to me.

And so if I must have this child, then there is really only one option. I am three months now, and soon my belly will show, for all the world to see. My husband knows I have not shared his bed for months. My father would have me killed for this.

The choice is obvious. Unspeakable, unbearable, but obvious.

I have to go.

February 11th, 1940

My heart is ripped from me.

I have kissed Akira goodbye, and I will not see him again for years. Perhaps not ever. If he grows to manhood and does not forgive me for this betrayal, I will never see my son again.

This child sits low in my belly and I am poisoned with hatred for it. I think my hatred will kill it, and then I hope so, and then I hate myself for my own thoughts and I can do nothing but cry.

James—for I can say his name, now that I am out from under my husband's roof—James is my only comfort. He says he won't think of going back to the military now. He'd rather be marked a traitor and a coward than leave me. I tell him he could never be a coward and that I am a traitor too, so he is in fine company.

We live together at last, as if we were a poor married couple and not a pair of sinful adulterers.

I have brought us as much wealth as I could carry, and all my jewels, so we will not want for things when the baby is born.

We are renting a little cottage by the sea in the middle of nowhere, far from Tokyo. This is one of the the smallest islands in Japan, and this is the smallest village on the island. I could barely find it on a map when I was looking for a place for us to hide.

They will be looking for me.

It is better for us all if they never find me.

James is tender towards me. He pats my firm belly and tells me to be of good cheer, that this child is a blessing and that I will get my son back one day soon. He really believes this. He still thinks we can get my son and get back to America and live a happy life once things have died down.

He does not know my family.

Good thing, for if he did, he would be dead.

July 13th, 1940

I have given birth to a little girl.

It was a long and difficult labor, and I was near death by the time it was finished.

Akira was much easier. Already, she is proving difficult.

James is besotted with her. He wants to call her Norine, after his grandmother, which I think is quite terrible.

Besides, this baby is a Kamiza. Though she is only a bastard, she too will have a part to play. She too will have a destiny that is tied to mine, that is tied to all my cursed family. I know it.

She will have a proper name.

I will name her Noriko, and we will call her Nori.

September 2nd, 1940

James is not well. He is growing too thin, and he has coughing fits that cause him great pain. Sometimes he coughs up
flecks of blood, and I am terrified that he has caught some
disease in that filthy hovel he was living in.

He laughs at me and insists that he doesn't need a doctor. He has me bring him our daughter and he hoists her
high into the air and tells her she is the most beautiful little
girl who was ever born.

She cries more than Akira did, and she is difficult to feed.
She is tiny, not big and strong as he was, and her face is always red.

She has a ridiculous amount of hair that I have no idea
how I will manage.

But she does have lovely eyes. She has her father's eyes.

It's not her fault about Akira. This is what I must tell myself, this is what I will tell myself forever.

Poor little girl, it is not her fault.

I will do my best for her. Though I doubt it will be
enough.

But she has her father. He loves her, and he loves me, and
he is the best of men. I don't have the same need for this diary as I once did. I have no need to keep secrets from him.
Ours may not be a marriage in name, but it is a marriage of
souls, and I am the luckiest woman in the world to have him.

Perhaps it will all come right after all.

January 28th, 1941

It did not come right.

He is dead.

James is dead.

He stopped breathing in his sleep, without disturbing me, without waking our daughter, who sleeps in the bassinet by our bed.

He died here, far away from his home, far away from his family.

The doctor says that his lung collapsed. There was nothing anyone could have done. There is no cure for the wasting disease he suffered from. Some live, some die, and nobody knows why.

But I know why. This is the price for my sin. This is the curse on my family doing its fatal work.

I bury the love of my life quietly, with only a priest in attendance.

It is so much less than he deserves. He was not a prince, he was not heir to any dynasty, but he was a remarkable man. He was kind. He was patient. He was better than I will ever be.

And now he is dead.

It is strange. I still love him. I think I will always love him, though he is dead and no longer here to love me back.

I could go back to my son. It is a horrible thought, but I could do it. He is too young to hate me yet.

I don't know if my husband would have me, but my

mother might insist. She might be desperate to save face. She might command him, as she commands everyone, and everything might be as it was before I fell in love.

I could go back.

If it weren't for Nori.

James's daughter, our daughter, the only thing I have left of him. The last child I will ever have, the child who will always remind me of her brother, the son who is lost to me.

I look into her face and I think she looks so much like me.

But I am determined that she will be nothing like me. I fought against my destiny, I fought against my place in the world, and now I am destroyed.

This girl, this poor girl, will know better.

I will teach her to obey.

I will keep her safe.

And, if I can, I will try to love her.

This will be my penance. Spending a life in obscurity with this child. I, who have been brought so low after being born so very high.

God forgive me. God pardon me for my sin.

For I never will.

So long as I live, I will never forgive myself.

Nori pressed the diary against her heart.

It was dark in the garden now, and the crickets were chirping. She sobbed quietly, letting the tears flow freely.

She had wanted her mother to be a monster.

It was easy to hate monsters.

And hatred was easy to feel.

This, all of this, was so much harder.

Wordlessly, Noah came to sit beside her. He wrapped her up in his arms, and she allowed herself to lean into his warmth.

Neither of them spoke for a long time.

Finally, Noah broke the silence.

"Do you feel like you know her now?" he asked quietly. "Your mother?"

Nori shut her eyes. "Yes."

"And do you hate her?"

At once, she was back in the attic, asking Akira this very same thing. She clutched the fabric of Noah's shirt to pull her from the memory.

"No," she said honestly. "I don't hate her."

"Do you forgive her?" Noah asked, very softly.

Nori tried to speak, but her voice broke. All that came out was a gasping sob.

Noah was learning, for he did not ask her again.

After a few days, Nori started to return to her state of easy joy. The weather was fair, and it was impossible not to smile. She played games with Alice and the children; she spent the nights wrapped up in Noah's arms, laughing until she cried.

A great weight had been lifted from her shoulders, one she had grown so accustomed to, she'd forgotten she was carrying it.

The past was written.

The future was just starting, and for the first time in years, it looked merciful.

She wandered around the garden, basking in the sunlight and breathing in the scent of freshly bloomed honeysuckle. Noah was back in Cornwall for the week, trying to track down his brothers.

"I won't be gone long, my love," he'd promised. He'd winked at her. "And I'll bring you back that engagement ring."

"I don't need a ring, sweetheart."

"Nonsense. It was my mother's and I want you to have it. There is no other woman in the world who should. I'll be home soon."

Nori did not doubt him. The fear that had lapped at her heels for all these years was finally beaten.

It was a strange feeling, to be so wondrously free.

Bess found her sunning underneath a great oak.

"My lady," she said, in her lilting country accent, "there's a letter for you."

Nori leaned up on her elbows. Nobody wrote letters to her.

"Thank you, Bess."

Bess nodded and went back into the house. Nori could hear her shouting at Charlotte to get off the table.

Nori leaned back against the tree and inspected the letter in her lap.

It looked benign enough from the outside. There was nothing but the address and her name. No return address.

She slid her pinkie finger beneath the seal and opened it.

Immediately, she felt the blood whoosh out of her body, as surely as if someone had sliced both her wrists.

Because the letter was written in Japanese.

Her vision swam. She felt a strong urge to retch and barely choked it back.

It was a long time before she could read the letter in her shaking hands.

Lady Noriko,

Please be informed that your honored grandmother, the Lady Yuko Kamiza, is dead. Your grandfather, Kohei Kamiza, is also dead, having died in 1959.

Your lady grandmother has assigned to you all of her worldly goods, as well as those goods previously belonging to your half brother. You must return to Kyoto immediately upon receipt of this letter to collect them.

If you do not return, we will send an escort for you.

It would be better for you to come peacefully.

Once you have done what is necessary, you will be free of us. You have our word on the souls of the ancestors that no harm will come to you.

We look forward to seeing you soon, at the estate in Kyoto.

You remember.

Sincerely,

The Kamiza Estate Trust

Her grandmother was dead.

A deep grief washed over her, not because there was any love between them, but because the last person in the world who shared her blood was gone.

She crumpled up the letter.

Every part of her wanted to ignore it. She had no desire to return to Japan, the country that had been so bitterly unkind to her. She wanted to believe that if she just pretended she had never received it, that all of this would go away. She wanted to believe that she had a choice.

But she knew better. She would have to go.

In just a moment, the fear had returned, wrapping her up in its dark arms.

Ah, my dear, she heard it whisper. *Did you miss me?*

"But why do you have to go?" Alice pouted. "The wedding is in three weeks!"

"I'll be back before then," Nori assured her. She swept some clothes into her suitcase in a disorganized heap. "I'll fly there, collect my money, and come straight back."

If she hurried, she could catch the very last flight out for the day. First class was never full. She wanted it over with.

"I could give you money," Alice grumbled, "if you'd accept it."

"One trip and I will never need a penny from you again," Nori assured her. "I'll be rich beyond my imaginings. And most importantly, I will be done with my family forever."

But Alice was not convinced. "And is that the only reason you're going?"

"Of course," Nori said curtly. She tucked her hair up in a bun. It had grown out again and she could hardly manage it. "Why else?"

Alice hesitated. "You aren't hoping for some kind of . . . acceptance?"

She scoffed. "Don't be ridiculous. And in any case, the last person who could give it to me is dead. I hope for nothing but to collect my filthy blood money and be done with it."

Her friend relented. "Well, you have certainly earned it."

They shared a long embrace.

"Be careful," she said fervently. "I don't like you going into that lions' den."

Nori managed a smile that radiated a confidence she did not feel.

"But look now, Alice," she said brightly. "I have become a lion too. The very last one, as it turns out. And so now I will be safe."

June 1965

It was not until she was forced to sit still for so many hours that the panic truly set in. It was strange to hear people speaking her native tongue after all of this time. No one recognized her as Japanese, it seemed, with her tan skin and curly hair; everyone spoke to her in English.

After all of this time away, perhaps she had become a foreigner in truth. It took her longer than it should to read in Japanese, and though she could understand, she sometimes hesitated to find the right words.

Nori looked around at the wealthy businessmen and their wives, many of them happy American and European couples on holiday.

The war, it seemed, had finally been forgotten. Every country in the world had changed almost beyond recognition.

If she were a betting woman, she would lay money down that the Japan her grandmother had clung to so fiercely was finally gone.

In her travels, she had seen firsthand the culture war between the old and the new. The young people went around with long hair and short dresses above the knee, holding hands and kissing in public, while the old people gave them horrified looks. Though some had given her suspicious glances, most people had taken her money with a smile.

It seemed like that was the great equalizer after all.

She wondered what had happened to Kyoto, the city of tradition, the old capital.

She wondered if it would be any kinder to her than it had been before.

Her stomach churned, and she gulped down some seltzer water. It had been bothering her for weeks now, but that wasn't unusual. Something always hurt.

In the empty seat beside her was Akira's violin, secure in its case. She had been carrying it around with her for years, never letting it leave her side, though she never dreamed of playing it. She wouldn't soil it. Not that too. She had done quite enough.

Tucked neatly inside her purse was her mother's last diary, bound with her white ribbon. She wore her grandmother's pearls, cold and heavy against her neck. And though she had never known her father, there was a sprig of white dogwood tucked into her hat. It was the state flower of Virginia, the place he'd left to come to Japan, where she had been born and he had died.

This was what was left of the family that might have been, in a kinder world than this. This was how she kept their ghosts close to her.

Nori fell into an uneasy sleep.

She dreamed of the faceless woman calling her name, of glittering broken glass stained with innocent blood, of fire and snow and light.

When she woke up, there were tears on her face. The plane

had landed. Outside of her window, she could see the Japanese flag flying high.

And so she waited to feel it—that sweet familiarity that could only come from returning to the nest. The rush of warmth.

But she felt nothing.

When she loaded her belongings into the taxi and gave the driver the address, he gave her a startled look in the mirror.

"But that's the Kamiza estate."

She swept her hair back to reveal the shape of her face, her mother's face.

"*Hai. Shitteimasu.* Please take me there."

"It's not open to tourists," he told her, not unkindly. "If you want to see one of the old palaces, I can take you somewhere else, miss."

She met his gaze. "Sir. I know very well what it is. I have come by invitation."

He looked at her, truly looked at her for the first time. A spark of recognition lit up his face.

"You're from here?" It sounded more like a statement than a question.

"I am," she said quietly.

He smiled at her and said nothing else. That was one thing she had always loved about her people. They knew when to be quiet.

She looked out the window and watched Kyoto pass her by. It struck her that she had never seen the city before, not truly. So much of it had been kept from her.

And so she watched, with a keen fascination she had not felt in a long time.

She saw the charming cobblestone streets, the grand temples, the trees of deepest green and noble purple and scarlet red. She saw *miko* shrine maidens in their distinctive garb and children running around wearing overalls, all side by side.

She saw bright billboard lights and dimly lit candles at makeshift altars, with paper prayers hanging above them. She saw street carts and gourmet restaurants, stray dogs and horses moving past one another in the street.

And she saw the water.

She rolled down the window, and the salty smell washed over her.

Nori realized now that there was no need to wonder which side of the culture war had claimed victory in her city.

Kyoto was Kyoto.

The car pulled over to the side of the road and stopped.

Before she could lose her nerve, Nori stepped out.

The house was exactly the same. It didn't seem right. After everything that had happened, it didn't seem right that it could remain so untouched.

The fear lapped at her heels. There was only one thing to do.

She handed the driver his fee and took her few belongings from his hands.

"*Arigatou.*"

He bowed very low to her. "Have you been away long, my lady?"

My lady.

She managed a tiny smile, but she knew her eyes were sad.

"Yes. I have."

He bowed again. "Well then. *Okaerinasaimase.* Welcome home."

This was her beginning.

Nori stood in the shadow of the great house with her feet rooted to the ground.

Absolutely nothing about this place had changed. But she had. She did not look over her shoulder; there was no merciless light to hold her in place.

Be brave.

There were only ghosts here now.

The gates had all been left open. She marched up the walkway, her head held as high as a soldier's.

It was not until she raised her hand to knock on the front door that the wave of nausea hit her, so powerful that it could not be ignored. She turned to the side, doubled over, and retched.

Her eyes welled with tears, but she willed them back. She took her handkerchief out of her pocket and wiped her mouth.

Her head swam, but she forced herself to stand up straight.

As she had learned to do so long ago, she gathered every last bit of her strength around her like a cloak.

And then Nori knocked.

In an instant, the door flew open. Standing there was a plump woman in her late forties, with streaks of gray in her dark hair. Her maid's uniform had a spot of jam on the apron.

"My God," she breathed.

There was no mistaking her.

"It's good to see you, Akiko-san."

Akiko threw open her arms, and Nori fell into them. They stood that way, both shaking, for a long time.

"I'm so sorry," the maid sobbed. "I'm *so sorry*, little madam."

Nori shook her head. There was nothing Akiko could have done. In this world, there were those with power and those without.

"I don't blame you," she said simply.

Akiko drew her inside by both hands, shouting at someone to fetch the gentlemen, and refreshments.

Before Nori could blink, someone had taken her things and run them up the stairs.

Akiko guided her into a chair and knelt at her feet.

"My God!" she exclaimed again. "Let me look at you. Such a beautiful young woman you are. And if you aren't the image of your mother."

Nori inclined her head. "You're very kind."

Akiko's face was streaked with tears. "It is so good to see you. Alive and safe and well. Thank God."

Nori smiled and said nothing.

Akiko grasped her hands. "I wish I could have . . ."

"I know, Akiko-san."

"I prayed for you," she whispered. "Every night I prayed . . . and then I heard that the young master had . . ."

"Yes," Nori cut her off sharply. She couldn't hear his name. That was the one thing she really couldn't bear.

Akiko fell silent. She knew this.

"And I have a daughter now," she said, wiping at her face with her stained apron. "She's twelve. Her name is Midori."

Green.

Nori managed a small laugh. "That's lovely. I'm so happy for you."

Akiko reached up to press her palm against Nori's cheek.

"I tell her of you," she whispered. "I tell her all the time."

Nori bit her lip. After all these years, in front of Akiko she felt like a lost little girl again.

"Thank you."

There was a commotion in the other room, and Akiko shot to her feet.

"And these are your third cousins," she said rapidly, in a low voice. "They will explain everything to you. I'll be just outside."

The look on Nori's face must have betrayed her, and so instead Akiko retreated into the corner, silent but there.

Nori rose to her feet. Two gentlemen, both in dark suits, came into the sitting room and bowed.

There was an air of mockery about it that she did not like.

"Noriko-sama," the first one said. He had an *L*-shaped scar on his right hand. "It is my great pleasure to welcome you back to your ancestral city. I am Hideki. And this is Hideo."

He gestured to the man beside him, who smiled but did not speak.

"You wrote me the letter," Nori said, ignoring the pleasantries. "Didn't you?"

"Indeed I did," Hideki said smoothly. "And may I say how pleased we are that you chose to come so promptly."

Nori clenched her fists behind her back. "There was no need for your veiled threats," she said flatly. "Now, please give me whatever it is that you need me to sign. I do have to be getting back soon."

Hideki bowed his head. "I did not mean to threaten, my lady, of course. Your grandmother gave clear instructions that you were to be treated with all due respect."

"So give me what I asked for, please."

He exchanged a bemused glance with his cohort.

"We were told you were a shy, stuttering mess."

Nori raised herself to her full height. "I was. Now, the papers, if you please."

Both of them bowed simultaneously. "You must forgive us again, little princess."

She felt a cold wind blow. "Why?" she said, through numb lips.

"Your lady grandmother gave strict instructions. It was not our intention to deceive you. Please know that we take no pleasure in it."

There was a high-pitched whirring sound in her ears. The ceiling and the floor swapped places for a solid five seconds.

"What are you talking about?"

"Your grandmother will explain everything."

The faces around her began to blur together like a grotesque watercolor painting.

"My grandmother is dead," she whispered.

"Alas, no, my lady. She is upstairs, waiting for you."

Nori felt it then. The sick fear that told her she was, indeed, back where she belonged. This was her true homecoming.

Once again, she was caught in the spider's web.

AKIKO

She is horrified, as I knew she would be. I was vehemently against the plan to deceive her, but then, what I think has never made a difference.

I show her to one of the guest rooms, and I sit by her side as she collects herself. As she begins to calm down, she looks more annoyed than anything, and I smile at her defiant spirit.

She starts to ask me something, but then her mouth twists and she leans over the side of the bed and vomits into the trash can.

I fetch her a damp towel to clean herself with and frown. "Let me call a doctor."

"I'm fine. Damn airplane made me nauseous."

I take her in. Her face is flushed and her hands are shaking. Something in my gut tells me she's not fine.

"I'm calling a doctor," I declare.

She starts to protest again, but then she smiles ruefully and sighs.

When the doctor arrives, she answers his questions with a minimum of fuss. When he is finished with her, he crooks his finger at me and we retreat to the doorway.

"She'll be all right," he says, wiping at his sweaty face. "But I must advise against any undue stress. It's not wise in her condition."

I look at him blankly. "Condition?"

He frowns at me. "Well, yes. The lady is expecting."

I croak like a frog, covering my mouth with my sleeve too late. "That's quite impossible," I say firmly.

But then I remember that she is not a child anymore, but a twenty-four-year-old woman who has been away from me for over a decade. I don't know anything about her life now.

He looks at me like I'm a peasant.

"By various ways I can tell," he says pompously. "I'd estimate she's about three or four months. I'd need her blood to be certain of the progression. But one look at her told me she's with child. I would bet my house on it."

I look at the little madam, waving away another maid who is trying to get her to drink some tea. One glance at her face tells me that she doesn't know.

He follows my gaze. "Oh," he says. "Is she unmarried?"

His voice oozes condescension, and instantly, I am on the defense of the girl I could never protect.

"None of your damn business and you will mind your tongue in this house," I hiss, "or I'll have a word with my mistress about you."

He bows his head. "I meant no offense. I can tell her the news, if you like."

I don't even consider it.

"I'll take care of her. You may go. Speak nothing of this."

He goes out. I dismiss everyone else from the room and the surrounding hallway, including that vulture Hideki with his beady, soulless eyes.

I smooth her hair away from her tired face.

"Now then, my dear, let's get you into a hot bath."

I guide her to the bathroom and fill the large tub up with steaming water, just as I used to do. I strip her naked and brush her hair, as I used to do.

I note the fullness of her breasts and the ever-so-slight curve of her stomach, and I know what the doctor said is true. My eyes are drawn to a jagged scar, just above her heart. I know better than to ask how she got it.

I wash her back and agonize over what to say to her, how to break the news to this gentle creature who has already suffered so much.

"Tell me of your life," I say, and she smiles.

She talks for hours, until the water goes cold. She speaks of the inhumane with grace; she shrugs off the unbearable with a grim smile. Her voice breaks when she tells me of Akira-sama, but she doesn't cry. I think the only way she survived that loss was to carve out a piece of her heart.

He was everything to her.

When she gets to the part about her life now, I see her face light up with joy.

"And your lover, this boy . . . he is to be your husband?"

"As soon as I return to London."

I feel truly sick at what I have to tell her.

"And what if you didn't go back?"

She gives me a bewildered look. "Why wouldn't I go back?"

"Your lady grandmother—"

"Is dying," she cuts me off. "Yes, they mentioned. She has called me halfway across the world to absolve her old soul."

I bite my tongue as I have done so often before. It is not my place.

There is only one thing I have to tell her now.

"Little madam . . . have you been feeling ill?"

She shrugs.

"I've felt worse."

"Yes. But have you been . . ." *Have you been with child?* I'm an idiot.

She turns to face me, her amber eyes full of alarm. "What's wrong?"

"My dear girl . . ."

"Tell me quickly," she demands, and I am reminded that she is used to bad news and there is no point in me dragging it out.

"You are with child," I say, as gently as I can.

She blinks at me. "I am not."

"You are, my dear. Listen to your body and you will know. You haven't bled for some time, have you?"

Nori-sama raises herself out of the tub, splashing water everywhere. She heads for the door, hastily covering herself with a towel.

"You are quite mistaken. I don't want children. Ever."

Why does this not surprise me? After the life she has had, this must be her nightmare.

She sits on the bed, and I manage to coax her into a silk robe. Her eyes are blank; her hair clings in wet tendrils to her face.

I pat the sides of her cold cheeks.

"It will all come right," I promise her.

Nori-sama closes her eyes. "I can't deal with this, Akiko-san. Not now. Not when I have to face her."

She looks so very young, but she sounds so tired.

I realize that it is taking every scrap of resolve she has just to stay afloat. This is one burden too many. She will accept it later. But right now, her denial is a necessity.

And when she chooses to feel, I will be here.

"So you'll see her, then? For the money?"

She laughs, and it is full of bitterness. "No. Not for the money."

She looks up at me as if I can help her. "Will you dress me?" she asks shyly, and I think how dear she is, this girl.

This, at least, I can do. I can fix her hair and bundle her into an expensive silk kimono; I can put jewels in her ears and makeup on her face.

I can make her shine like polished silver.

"Yes, little madam. I can do that."

She sits like a doll as I brush and plait her long hair. I pull out three kimonos, and she chooses the one of dark blue with gold stars embroidered on it.

I put some blush on her cheeks, to try and cover the pallor in her skin.

In her hair, I put a simple diamond clip.

"There," I say softly. "You look lovely."

She smiles as if she does not believe me and pats my hand. "Where is Obaasama?"

"She is in bed, little madam. She is very ill indeed. The doctors don't think she will see the end of the month."

Nori-sama rises from her chair. "I see. I'll go and see her, then."

"She indicated that she would send for you."

She shrugs. "I will see her now or I will not see her at all."

"I can escort you . . ."

"That won't be necessary, Akiko-san."

And then she goes out, without looking back. I remember the girl who used to cling to my hand and hide her face in my skirt. She had a smile that begged for love.

I think that little girl is gone forever now, ruthlessly dismembered by the people who were supposed to take care of her.

Including me.

It was not difficult to find the master bedroom.

Nori walked up to the double doors with the figure of a golden dragon etched onto them, located at the very end of the hall.

You have never met a defeat that you did not rise from, she told herself. *Do not be afraid of a dying old woman. Now she is weak and you are strong.*

She pushed them open and went inside.

The first thing that struck her was the smell. The room smelled sickly sweet, like dried rose petals and peppermint oil. It made her nostrils burn, and beneath the sweetness, she could detect something else: the stench of meat gone off, of something stale. It smelled like rotting flesh.

It smelled like the slow coming of death.

The room was dark; someone had drawn the thick velvet curtains over the windows, and the only light came from a small bedside lamp. Still, even in the darkness, Nori took in the oil paintings on the walls, the vase of chrysanthemums on the mahogany desk strewn with papers, the sewing thrown casually on the afghan at the end of the bed. Two swords in sheaths with dragons painted on them hung crossed on the wall above the bed.

She took a tentative step towards the grand bed, which was draped with heavy white curtains. For one ridiculous moment she thought that this was all a joke, that the bed would be empty and she would go out to find Akiko laughing, with a suitcase full of money, and she could go back to London and her new simple, happy life.

But then she took another step forward and there was a soft rustle, and then Nori saw her: Yuko Kamiza. Her grandmother.

She was half hidden by the shadows, but Nori could tell at once that this was no joke, that she was truly living her last hours. The woman she remembered was uncommonly tall for a woman, with hair so long that it nearly brushed the floor and brilliant gray eyes that missed nothing. This was not that woman. She looked so . . . small.

Yuko had the plush comforter drawn up to her breastbone; Nori could just barely make out the dark green kimono that she was wearing beneath it. She was propped up on a mass of silk pillows, and her once glorious hair was white and brittle as chalk. But it was braided neatly and left to fall forward over her right shoulder.

Nori took another step forward, and Yuko's eyes snapped open, like a dragon alerted to an intruder in its lair.

Nori ducked her head, and before she could stop herself, she folded into a low bow. By the time she realized what she had done, it was too late. She could feel her face burning.

Slowly, she rose up to meet her grandmother's pensive gaze.

"Obaasama," she said quietly.

There. She had spoken. She could no longer pretend that this was all some fever dream, one of the countless she'd had before.

The ghost leaned forward in the bed.

"Noriko-san," she rasped, in a voice that was unfamiliar.

Nori inclined her head in acknowledgment, but said nothing.

Yuko squinted at her and beckoned her forward with a long finger. "Come here," she said. "Let me see you."

She went unwillingly, making sure to keep her shoulders squared. She stopped a little ways away from the bed, and Nori could see her grandmother's lips curl in a wry smile.

She crooked her finger again. "Closer. I'm an old woman, Granddaughter."

Nori did not acknowledge the familiarity, but she did inch closer to the bedside, and now she could look fully at her grandmother's face.

Her skin was like papier-mâché pulled over a skull, so thin that every vein was visible. But her eyes were the same and Nori felt a shiver down her spine.

Those gray eyes looked her up and down several times. And then, finally, Yuko spoke.

"You're a real beauty," she said at last. "Truly. I always knew you would be."

Nori was thunderstruck.

Yuko said this without a hint of irony, as if they had seen each other yesterday and parted on the best of terms.

As if she did not bend me over a chair and whap my bare ass with a wooden spoon for some imaginary infraction; as if she did not bleach my skin and belittle my hair; as if she did not make me feel like some terrible ogre unfit to see the light of day. As if she did not sell me as a whore and then try to have me sent away. As if she did not steal my brother's body before I . . . before I could even . . .

She bit her lip so hard that she could taste blood.

"Is that why you called me across the world?" she said bitterly. "To prove yourself right?"

The ghost smiled wryly. "No. I called you here because I'm dying."

She paused, clearly expecting Nori to say something. When she did not get a response, she laughed, dissolving into a cough as she did so. She pressed a handkerchief to her mouth, and it came away stained with black blood.

"You've changed," she said, and Nori could swear she sounded amused. "You've lost your shyness."

Nori shut her eyes for a brief moment. She knew they were still far too honest.

"I have lost many things."

"And about the exile . . . you will understand, of course. I was upset. I was understandably upset."

Nori looked at her blankly. There was nothing to say about this. There could never be any forgiveness, not in the least because Yuko hadn't even truly apologized. Nor would she. It seemed to be a theme in this family that Nori was the only person who ever had to be sorry.

She let it pass.

Yuko went somber and dabbed at her mouth with the clean side of the handkerchief. "I was very sorry," she says. "Very sorry to lose Akira-san."

Nori gritted her teeth. "Don't you dare," she whispered, feeling her rage pick up like the winds of a storm. "Don't you dare say his name."

"I loved him," Yuko protested. "He was my special boy."

"You didn't know the first thing about him. You never *saw* him, he was just a thing to you!"

"I knew him," Yuko seethed. "I knew him, you insolent girl. He was mine, after all."

Nori threw herself at the bedpost, gripping it with both shaking hands. *"HE WAS NOT YOURS!"*

Her grandmother gasped. "How dare you—"

Nori was beyond caring. For years, thinking of Akira had been treacherous. She'd avoided it with every ounce of her being. But now she allowed the barrier to come down. The flood hit her full force, and she could scarcely stand.

"His favorite color was blue. His favorite composer was Beethoven. He didn't eat anything without wasabi. He loved the heat more than the cold. His favorite orchestra was the Berlin Philharmonic. He took his coffee black. He never liked gardens until he met me. And he hated, *hated* you."

Yuko was silent before this onslaught, her lips moving aimlessly.

"You would be so cruel to a dying woman?" she gasped. "You would tell me such poisonous lies!"

Nori said nothing else because she could not speak. Her heart had lodged itself in her throat, and she was shaking with indignation.

You fool. She hasn't changed. She'll never change. The way she sees the world is set in stone.

"Well, he is dead now," Nori said coldly, and the words pierced her through. "So it doesn't matter. He is dead, and what he was and what he would've been are dead with him."

Her grandmother narrowed her eyes. "You loved him," she said, and it was clear she was realizing it for the first time. "You really did love him."

Nori did not dignify this with a response.

Yuko made a terrible wheezing sound. "I thought if I let him amuse himself with you for a while, play his music, he'd come home eventually. I thought—"

Nori cut her off. "Tell me why you summoned me here," she said sharply. "No more games. If it's to kill me, do it already."

Yuko leaned back on the pillows, her rage spent.

"I have a proposition for you."

"Yes. You wish to leave the estate to me. I suppose that's slightly more tolerable than seeing it given to the state and divided up."

Her grandmother started to speak but broke off. She

coughed, and this time, she doubled over and started shaking like a woman possessed.

Nori looked around the room for some water and then turned to the door, thinking that she would call for someone, but Yuko's hand darted out and gripped Nori's sleeve.

She stared at her grandmother in absolute shock.

"Don't," the old woman gasped pitifully. "Don't go." Nori turned back to her and waited until the coughing subsided. As soon as it had finished, she stepped back.

"You should rest," she said softly, and she hated the way her tone was tinged with sympathy.

"I have a long rest ahead of me," Yuko said bleakly. "Time enough for that. I need to prepare you."

Nori's ears pricked up. "What?"

Her grandmother looked as if she was stunned that it wasn't obvious. "You're my heir."

Nori's heart was beating wildly now. "All I have to do is sign some papers for the money."

Yuko rolled her eyes. "I'm not talking about the money, girl," she snapped. "I'm leaving you everything, don't you understand? The titles, the family businesses, the land. That means you must stay here. You must live here and live as I have lived."

"What?" Nori asked, stupid as a dairy cow. "What?"

"And you must marry. Immediately, as soon as possible— how old are you? Twenty-four, nearly twenty-five? Anyway, you must marry. You have some distant cousins who will be suitable. I will show you pictures. You can choose the one you like best." She nodded, as if pleased with her own generosity. "I never allowed your mother this freedom."

Nori looked at her in stunned silence. Her thoughts were

turning like the heavy cogs of a very old clock. Then, finally, it clicked. "Absolutely not," she said.

Yuko clucked her tongue, and it made a sticking noise. "Of course you will."

"No."

The ghost narrowed her eyes. "You were always such an obedient child."

Nori felt her temples start to pound. "I am not a child anymore. And you do not command me."

Yuko looked truly bewildered. Clearly, she had not been prepared for a fight.

"I'm offering you everything," she pointed out, jabbing her finger in Nori's direction. "More than you ever could have dared to hope for. You'll never want for anything as long as you live. You'll have everything that you need, always."

Nori reared up like a viper about to strike. "I need nothing from you. It is you who needs something from me."

"But—"

"I have my life," she snapped. "Not that you ever bothered to ask. I have a man who loves me."

She felt childish, insisting that someone loved her. But it was something her grandmother had never deemed her worthy of.

"A boy, you mean," Yuko scoffed. "I know about the music teacher. I am embarrassed for you, since it is clear you don't have the good sense to be embarrassed for yourself. I know everything, girl. Don't think you escaped these eyes of mine. Not for a moment. Everywhere you went, my eyes were on you."

Nori's knees knocked together with rage, but she held her tongue. This had gone on long enough.

"My answer is no," she said, with all the dignity she could muster. "It's done."

"I am offering you a destiny."

"I don't want it."

Yuko sighed. "Then again, it was not meant to be yours, was it? It was meant for Akira-san. And now I must go to my grave, knowing what happened to him. Knowing I found out too late to stop it."

Nori froze. The world around her ground to a screeching halt.

"What are you talking about?"

Yuko smiled, and it was full of smugness. "Oh, come now. You must have suspected."

No. She had not.

"It was an accident," Nori said, and her voice cracked. Her composure was gone, flown away in that instant. "You couldn't have stopped it. It was an act of God."

"Oh, my dear girl. Have you been paying any attention at all?"

The room went cold.

"You would never have hurt him," Nori said defiantly, standing on the one thing she was certain of. "Never."

Yuko's eyes were hard. "It was not the intention. He was meant to be in Vienna. The spies assured us—"

Nori gripped hold of the bedpost to stop herself from collapsing. "Spies?"

"Yes, spies," the old woman spit. "Don't be a fool, girl. Half your kitchen was in my employ. The yard boy too. Did you really think we'd let you run around unattended? Children in charge of the nursery?"

Nori lost the power of speech. She could only stand and watch in horror as the threads of her world unraveled.

"He was meant to be gone, safely abroad," her grandmother went on, in a voice devoid of feeling. "Don't you understand, girl? It was all a trap, from the very start. Hiromoto was our man. It took next to nothing to buy him off. Don't you think it odd that he would single you out for favor? For recognition? He was following orders. The household spies promised us Akira-san would be safely away. Hiromoto's job was to wait for the perfect moment to get you alone. Don't you see? And the driver too, of course. He owed us a fortune—more than he could ever pay. He was promised his debts would be cleared and his family would be unharmed and well kept. He was willing to die to carry out his duty. Ah, think, girl! Remember! It was no accident at all, but only made to look like one."

She leaned forward, sweating and panting with the effort. Her voice was low and weak, but Nori knew that every single word was true.

"From the first, the only person supposed to be in that car was *you*."

Nori doubled over.

It all made sense. The horrible truth grabbed hold of her heart, squeezing and squeezing until she could feel nothing but searing pain.

"You killed him," she whispered.

"Don't insult me," Yuko snapped. "I would never do something so sloppy. It was your grandfather's doing, all of it. I had no hand in it. I would've stopped it. I tried to stop it when I found out, but I was too late, and now I will go to hell with that black sin on my soul."

She pointed a bony finger at Nori's heart.

"*You* provoked him beyond all reason. He couldn't bear to

see Akira-san reach manhood still trapped underneath your bastard heel. He wanted to free him."

"He *killed* him," Nori sobbed. Her resolve was broken. Her heart was broken. Her mind was broken. "All of this. All of this for your hatred of me. And look what it has brought you. You have destroyed your own line, you have sealed your own fate. Mother, Akira. Me. You have burned it all to the ground."

"But that is why you must take your place!" her grandmother cried. "So that there can be meaning. So that all of it will not have been for nothing!"

"It was always for nothing," she gasped. The fist around her heart was squeezing so tightly that she knew she did not have long to live. The life was draining from her body.

But she didn't care.

"But it can't end here!" Yuko moaned, and her eyes filled with tears for the first time. "For the love of God, it can't be over! You must take your place. You're all that's left. Don't let it all be in vain, don't let his death be in vain. This is your chance to do some good. For the love of God! Nori!"

For the love of God.

Nori turned on her heel and ran. She ran blindly, without thinking. But she did not need to think.

There was only one place for her to go.

The attic was the same.

As she fell on all fours like a dog, Nori realized this was the only place that had ever truly felt like hers.

It was a fitting place for her to die.

And really, she was dying this time.

Whatever her limit was, whatever capacity for suffering was built into her, she had gone well past it.

She tore at her hair, watching the hated curls fall to the floor in tufts. She raked her nails along her skin and watched the flesh split open. And she sobbed and sobbed until she was vomiting up green bile. And then, when the bile was gone, she vomited nothing but air.

Through the burning haze of tears she could see her reflection in the mirror.

I hate you, she thought. *I hate you. I hate you.*

And then she was screaming.

"I *hate* you!"

You should have known.

You stupid girl.

She collapsed to the floor and felt a crack against the side of her skull. There was no air left in the room, and now her breath came slower and slower as her vision swam. She spread her arms out and stared up at the ceiling.

A feeling between pain and release enveloped her.

Release me from my promise, she begged no one.

Let me go now.

That's enough. I tried. I tried so hard.

Let me go.

There was a startling white light, brighter than any sun, and then, for the first time in her life, someone answered her.

NORI

I wake in a garden.

Someone must have carried me here. I can smell the flowers before I even open my eyes. The scent of every exotic bloom in existence fills up my entire body. I am surrounded by it.

This is not my garden.

I open my eyes and I see that it is endless; it stretches past the horizon and into nothingness. The sky is a perfect Prussian blue, and the clouds are fat and creamy, like a pastry chef crafted them by hand. The sun is gentle, bathing everything in a soft white light.

I know that this is no ordinary garden. I also know that I am meant to be here.

I rise to my feet and place a hand over my eyes to shield them from the light. The cuts on them are gone, as if they never were. I bend down slightly and pull up the hem of my kimono, which is white as alabaster and made of the most delicate silk. It is hung with tiny seed pearls and embroidered with *kiku no hana*, chrysanthemums. I pull it up to my waist and run my fingers along the soft flesh of my inner thigh. My scar is gone too.

I drop the skirt and start walking, where I don't know, but forward. I walk beneath trees with low-hanging branches heavy with ripe fruit, pomegranates and apples, bananas and limes, plums and apricots and cherries and fruits I cannot even name. There are clusters of red flowers all through the tall grass, scattered about like fallen fireworks. I bend down to pick up a blush-colored rose.

The stem has no thorns on it.

I hear something then, a soft, perfect sound. I don't even hesitate before following it. It's like a siren song. I could never resist it. I would never want to.

I don't ask myself where I am going or why I am in this place, which is obviously not meant for mortal eyes. Maybe I am dead. I press my hands against my slim belly and I keep walking. If I am dead, I cannot say that I mind. This place is . . . paradise. And nothing hurts here. All my life, I have carried a dull ache inside me, so constant that I hardly notice.

But I notice now, because it is gone.

I hear the steady murmur of a babbling brook somewhere nearby, beneath the song. It is starting to sound familiar. I find myself walking a bit faster in an attempt to catch it. *I know this song. Where?* I pick up the hem of my skirt to walk faster. The ground is warm beneath my bare feet. *Where have I heard this song?*

It is growing louder in my ears and the sound is becoming richer, washing through me and purging me of every pain I have ever felt. Now I am running. I run through a grove of trees whose branches all arch together to form a halo above my head. I run beside a clear pond with ducklings splashing about. I run until I am in a meadow with deep purple delphiniums that reach up to my waist and red poppies that seem to smile up at me. I pause, my heart thudding in my chest, my eyes roving frantically to find the source of the music. There's a tree a little ways ahead of me. I crane my neck to see better, and I can see that it is a peach tree.

Then I know.

It's Schubert's "Ave Maria." It is my first and only lullaby.

I don't run this time. I walk like a child just learning to toddle. I don't dare walk faster. I don't dare breathe. I don't dare to do anything that could tip the balance of whatever line I am walking, whatever plane of existence I am on that allows any of this to be possible. I push the tall grass aside and I stand quivering before the base of the tree.

And there, sitting on the ground with his violin resting casually at his side, is Akira.

Oniichan.

He looks exactly as he did when I last saw him. His pale skin is smooth, his dark hair is neatly combed back from his face, and he is smirking at my frozen expression. He is wearing a loose-fitting blue yukata.

Oniichan.

"Little sister," he says. "It's been a while. *Ne?*"

I am crying. The tears are sliding down my cheeks though I am not sad. I try to speak, but nothing comes out but air.

Akira.

And then I am flying into his arms. He folds me into a tight embrace, pressing his head into the top of my hair. My face is buried in his neck, and I sob helplessly, listening to his heartbeat and feeling his burning warmth. He doesn't try to shush me. He just holds me until the sobs cease, and then he pulls back, gripping my shoulders so that he can look at my tear-stained face.

"None of that," he says simply, brushing a tear from my cheek with his thumb. "You're all right now. You're just fine."

I sniffle and look into his clear gray-black eyes. "You died," I whisper.

He chuckles. "I did."

"But . . . you're here." I can feel the heat coming off his flesh. He is very much alive. "You're real."

He nods. "I am."

I have no more questions. I don't care if this is heaven or hell or purgatory. Akira is here. Here, with me. I press myself against his chest as if I could meld us together through sheer force of will.

"I'm so sorry," I say. "Oniichan, I am so sorry. It's all because of me. You died because of me."

He shakes his head. "I died because of fear and hate. Not because of you."

"It was supposed to be me," I sob. "You were supposed to live. I can't do it. I've made such a mess. I've done nothing of worth, I'm not like you. I've failed. I'm so sorry."

Akira sighs.

"*Aho*," he says at last. "All this time and you still don't understand."

I peep up to look at him through my lashes. "What?"

"Every choice I ever made was my own. I regret nothing."

"But if you'd never met me . . ."

He lifts my chin with a finger and looks into my eyes.

"Nori," he says very quietly, "I would rather have died young than lived a hundred years without knowing you."

I have no words for this. All I can think of is . . .

"Why?"

He shrugs a shoulder. "You are my sister."

"Tell me what to do, Oniichan," I plead with him. "Tell me what to choose. Please."

He tuts. "Oh, Nori. You know I can't do that. You must choose your own path."

"I can't do it," I whisper. The paths laid before me are all winding, and I cannot see where they will lead. There is no choice that will not require sacrifice; there is no way to escape pain. "What if I choose wrong?"

Akira winds his hands into my curls. "No matter what you choose," he says patiently, "just keep going forward."

"I can't do it, Akira-san. I don't want to go back. Please don't make me go back."

He tucks my palm into the crook of his arm. "That's not up to me," he says gently. "If it's not your time, you can't stay here. You'll have to go back."

"But I'm dead?" It is half a question and half a statement. But the hope in my voice is undeniable. "This is heaven."

Akira shrugs again. "You know I don't believe in heaven, Nori. This is just a garden."

"I don't care where it is," I wail. "I just want to stay with you. Please."

I wind my hands into the fabric of his yukata, as I used to do when I was a little girl and begging him for just a few more minutes, a few more seconds of his time.

"Please don't make me live in a world without you."

His eyes are brimming with warmth, and he leans forward to plant a kiss in the center of my forehead. "Oh, Nori. You're stronger than you know. You don't need me anymore."

"Don't leave me," I whisper, leaning forward so that our foreheads are touching.

Already I know that he is right when he says I cannot stay here. I can almost hear the sand slipping through the hourglass.

We don't have much more time. If there is a forever for the two of us, it does not start now.

Akira wraps his arms around me and tightens his grip, holding me close with all of his strength.

"Never," he says simply. "I will never leave you."

We don't say anything else. We don't need to. I won't waste whatever time I have left with him on words. There is nothing I can say to Akira that he does not already know, and there is nothing I can do to stop the sand from slipping away. All I can do is hold him, right here, right now.

I don't know how long it is. In any case, it will never be enough time. I shut my eyes so that I don't have to see the sky darkening and the garden falling away.

It's time to go back now.

The way Akira gives me one final squeeze, one last feather-light kiss on the top of my head, tells me that he knows it too. But I will not say goodbye.

I will see him again.

I open my eyes and look into his, hoping that they will say all of the things that I don't have time to. Somehow, I know that whatever I say now will be the last words I am granted. This is the end of my miracle. I take his hand in mine, even as some invisible force pulls me away.

"You are my sun."

He pulls my hand up to his lips and kisses it. And then he smiles at me. Even as the darkness comes up behind him to swallow everything, I can see it, the memory of his beautiful smile. But I can still hear. It is faint over the sudden ringing in my ears but it is there. I hear his response.

And you are mine.

The next day, Nori faced her grandmother again. The marks on her arms were concealed by the sweeping sleeves of her white kimono. Her hair was parted in the middle and straightened, falling to her waist. She stood straight and proud.

The fear was gone.

Yuko's face was tight and sour. "I thought you would have left by now."

"I have come to give you my answer."

Her grandmother scoffed. "Well then. Don't keep me in suspense."

Nori drew in a deep breath. "My answer is yes."

Yuko's eyes went wide. "You . . . you will do it?"

"I will."

"Praise be," her grandmother breathed. For a brief moment she seemed to come back to life. "God has spoken to you, hasn't he? He has shown you your destiny is to serve our family? You have come to see what I have always tried to show you?"

Nori folded her hands in front of her. "My reasons are my own."

I will change this family, Oniichan. I will rid it of fear and of hate, and fill it with humanity and love. I will use my power to help the powerless, as I have always been. I will restore true honor to our name.

Just as you wanted, just as you would have done in my place. I swear it.

And when my work on earth is done, I will come to you.

Please wait for me.

In the garden.

Kyoto, Japan
December 1965

The child was born in the Kamiza estate, on the fifth day of December.

God's ways were mysterious indeed, for it was perfectly healthy, with fair skin, a full head of curly, sandy-brown hair, and its mother's amber eyes. Everyone remarked on what a beautiful baby it was.

More importantly, the child was a boy.

Yuko declared it was a sign from God that the house was blessed. She was so delighted that a healthy male child had been born that she hardly cared his father was a foreign nothing and his mother was her once despised half-breed granddaughter. Her frantic need to see her house restored was the only thing keeping her alive, for by all medical accounts she should have been dead already.

"If you can have a bastard boy," she said, by way of a messenger, "you can have a trueborn son with your husband. I am pleased with you, granddaughter. Ask for any favor and it is yours."

The nurse offered her the baby once he was cleaned and swaddled, but Nori shook her head.

"Give him to Akiko-san," she said quietly.

She turned to the messenger. "And tell my grandmother I would call in my favor."

"Yes, my lady?" he asked.

"Send someone to find my mother," she said simply. "And if she is alive, bring her home."

The man nodded and scurried from the room.

Akiko bustled forward and took the little bundle from the nurse's arms.

"He is a beautiful boy. I will love him well. I will take every care, little madam. I promise."

"I know," Nori said warmly. She was still hazy from the drugs they'd given her for the pain. "I would trust no one else with him."

Akiko had been the one to ready the nursery, to make the baby clothes, to think of names. But the names she thought of were only for girls.

Akiko hesitated. "Are you sure you don't want to hold him?"

Nori turned her face away.

In truth, she couldn't stand to touch him. Her choice had made him a bastard. Her choice had made him fatherless. Her choice had made him the first son, but the one who could never inherit anything, who would forever be in the shadow of his younger brother. His half brother. The son she would have by her carefully selected future husband.

One day, this boy would be old enough to understand. He would want an explanation and she had none to give.

Noah had received nothing but a curt letter, full of lies that she loved him no longer and a plea for him to forget her. She sincerely hoped that he would not notice the tearstains on the page. She hoped that he would hate her, that his humiliation and his rage would sustain him for a time until she became nothing more than a distant memory.

He was young, barely twenty, and she told herself that he would recover from this.

She did not allow herself to think of the alternative.

Because the alternative made her a monster.

Alice had received a deeper glimpse into the truth, but they would probably never see each other again.

She had broken her promise to stay. She was a Judas to those who had loved her most.

These were just the first sacrifices she'd made in pursuit of her chosen path.

She knew there would be others.

"Take him to his room and feed him," she said, and she did her best not to sound as cold as she felt.

Akiko's eyes filled with tears. "Oh, little madam. He's your son. Don't you want to touch him?"

Nori managed a small smile. "Maybe tomorrow."

With Akiko busy looking after the baby, it was her daughter, Midori, who attended Nori through most of her recovery.

She was a pleasant girl who liked to chatter about fashion and movies. She looked at Nori with a glazed expression, her cheeks flushed with hero worship.

"You're so pretty," she gushed one day as she brushed out Nori's hair at the vanity.

Nori smiled. "So are you."

Midori shrugged. "The boys at schools don't think so."

"The boys at school are stupid."

Midori giggled. "Maybe. But I'll never get a boyfriend at this rate." She hesitated and looked away. A question was written in her downcast gaze.

Nori inclined her head. "What is it?"

The younger girl blushed. "Nothing. It's not my place. Mama says I talk too much."

"It's okay," Nori said gently. "You can ask me."

Midori shifted from foot to foot. "You . . . you had a boyfriend. A fiancé, I mean. You were going to marry him?"

Nori felt her stomach twist. She tried not to wince.

"Yes."

"And he's . . . the baby's father?"

The pain intensified. "Yes."

"But you can't be with him," Midori concluded, "because you have to marry someone respectable and have a legitimate child. That's what Mama says."

Nori pushed back her irritation. "Yes, that's right."

"But why?" Midori blurted out. "Why can't you do as you like? Once Okugatasama dies, won't you be in charge?"

Nori took a deep breath and looked at her strained face in the mirror. She had to remind herself that the dark machinations of her family dynamic were lost on this naive girl.

Just as they had once been lost on her.

"That's not possible," she said bluntly. "Firstly, I'm going to have a difficult time being accepted as it is. The right husband, with the right name, is my only chance. I can't marry where my heart lies and keep power. If I married a foreigner, we'd both be turned out in a heartbeat."

Midori scrunched up her nose. "But can't you keep a lover? If it makes you happy?"

Nori raised a dubious eyebrow. "No. I'm not a man. I can't do that. They'd name me a whore—if they haven't already—and no one would listen to me. And besides . . ." Her voice cracked. "They might hurt him."

Midori gasped. "They would do such a thing?"

Of course they would. They'd slit his throat before breakfast and go on with their day. And then, after dinner, they'd slit mine.

"Better not to risk it," Nori responded. She forced herself to smile. "Besides, my Noah would never agree to sit in the shadows and watch me marry another man, watch me have another man's children. He'd never be able to watch my inheritance skip over our son—and any man I marry would insist that it does. Otherwise there is no point marrying me at all."

She closed her eyes. "And Noah deserves better. If you only knew him, you'd know he deserves . . ."

Everything.

Midori's lower lip quivered. "That's not fair. If you have power, you shouldn't have to lose what you love. That's the whole point."

Nori dug her nails into her palm. "I wish it were like that. But I have no power if I'm not respected. And I can't be respected if I don't play by the rules. Some of them, at least."

"And the rest?" Midori asked quietly.

Nori met her gaze. "I'll make my own rules."

"But can you do that?" Midori asked doubtfully. "Will they let you do that?"

"I have to," Nori said simply. "I made a promise."

Midori looked near to tears. "But you still love him?"

Nori went very still. For a moment she was in another place.

A tiny church, with fragrant honeysuckle blossoms all around, and warm hands in hers. "I do."

Midori blinked, clearly trying to look cheerful. "But you love your family more?"

Nori could smell something else now. Fresh rosin. Lemons. And wasabi. Always too much wasabi.

"Yes," she said softly. "I love my family more."

The wheel turned in earnest then. Nori rose from her childbed a few weeks later to find that the world had not waited for her to recover.

Yuko had wasted no time in arranging banquets and parties for all of Kyoto, perhaps even all of Japan, to meet the family's mysterious new heir.

The going lie was that she was the long-lost daughter of Seiko Kamiza and Yaseui Todou, Akira's father.

Nobody believed it, but nobody cared. The friendship of the family was something everyone wanted. With the proper husband at her side, no questions would be asked.

As it turned out, it made no difference to them who wore the coronet. They were all out for themselves anyway.

Stacks of classified papers were delivered to her room, and she pored over them. The amount of money soon to be hers was truly staggering. By her calculations she could buy several islands and not run out. There were dozens of other houses, some here, some abroad. There was money tied up in several Kamiza-owned businesses, legal and otherwise. Among them was the brothel she'd once been sent to a lifetime ago.

She pulled out a red pen and crossed it off the list. Other arrangements would have to be made for the girls, but there was no question of her profiting off the desperation of poor young women and the depravity of selfish men.

Her grandmother summoned her every day now.

Though Nori dreaded the trips to the shadowy room that smelled of death, a secret part of her was fascinated by the world unfolding before her. It was more than she could have dreamed of. Like a horse with its blinders removed, she could suddenly see the world she had been born into.

She sat on a little stool close to the bed and listened. Yuko certainly had a lot to say.

"And when you speak with your advisors, you must make it clear that you have the final say. You must keep your heel on their necks. You're a woman, they won't like it, but they don't need to like it. Or you."

"But don't I want people to like me?" Nori ventured.

"No," Yuko snapped. "You can be charming, you can shine before them like a holy icon, but they don't need to like you. It's more important that they respect you."

Nori shifted in her seat. Even now, she was unsure that a girl who had been born and bred to obey could command.

"And you can't show that kind heart of yours," Yuko went on. "It won't serve you. You'll end up strangled in a ditch. There are too many who will want your place and who will resent you, for being a woman, for being born so low and rising so high."

"But you ruled," Nori said, "though you are a woman."

Ruthlessly, she thought but did not say.

Yuko smirked. Her skin was deathly white, but her eyes were blazing.

"You think I'm a monster," she said. "And I imagine to you I am. But when you are in my place, you will understand. I was a girl when I came to power, younger than you, with a bad-tempered husband, but I did not shrink quietly back and allow him to rule me. I did not submit to the countless men who tried to bend me to their will. I was smarter than all of them, and slowly, I clawed my way to their respect. I was a beautiful blossom, but I had thorns. You will learn. You will understand me better after I am dead. You are a mother now—to a child and to a dynasty. You will see what you will do to protect the things you love. You will be horrified by what you'll do. And you will do it anyway."

Nori shook her head. "I will never be like you."

"Then you will fall," Yuko said simply.

Nori stood up. "I will not fall," she said quietly. "For you are not the only example I have set before me. I do learn from you— you're right—but I knew someone who was kind but firm. Who was honest but kept his own counsel. Who was clever and wise beyond his years. Who understood that it is the future, not the past, that we must look to if we are to survive. So you see, Obaasama, quite by accident, I been molded for this new destiny of mine."

But not by you.

Yuko narrowed her eyes. "You're going to have to be strong. It takes strength to lead."

"It takes strength to survive," Nori corrected her calmly. "And if nothing else, Grandmother, you have taught me that."

Her grandmother smiled wryly. Her fire was flickering out. She leaned back against her pillows and closed her eyes.

"There can only be one ruler," she said. "If it's not you, it's someone planning to destroy you. Remember that."

Nori nodded.

"Now, leave me," her grandmother breathed. "I need to sleep. I feel a long sleep coming."

Nori bowed. "I have one last question, Obaasama."

Yuko made a wheezing noise to indicate that she was listening.

"Do you have any regrets?"

The question hung in the air for a long moment.

Her grandmother turned her face away. "Many," she said quietly. "And none."

Nori felt frustration seize her. There was a lifetime of things to say and not nearly enough time.

"I don't understand."

"You will," her grandmother said, and the way she said it, it sounded like a curse. "You will, Nori."

Nori told no one of her plans to close the brothel. No one needed to know her plans. Least of all her grandmother.

In a little while, she would be free to do as she wished. There was no need to taunt a dying woman.

There was no honor in it.

And, oddly enough, she found that she pitied Yuko Kamiza more than she hated her. When her grandmother died, her death would leave a gaping black hole in Nori's world. There would be no one to guide her on this new path. She would be alone.

It had been years since anyone had seen her mother. Though everyone had given her up for dead, Yuko had still agreed to send three search parties after her. The trail was cold, and the odds were slim, but Nori had to try.

She had no peace at all in the days anymore. Everyone needed something from her. She supposed this was what the rest of her life would look like.

Akiko was fitting her for a new gown for a state banquet. The maid hummed as she nipped off a stitch of thread.

"And we must get the jewels out of the vault to see what suits your gown. Your grandmother has made it quite clear she wants you to shine." Akiko lowered her voice. "I believe there will be a gentleman there she has made overtures to for your hand in marriage. I think she hopes he will find you pleasing."

Nori wrinkled her nose and did not comment.

"I think I have enough jewels."

Akiko chuckled. "No, madam. These are the best of all. Wait until you see them—you could drown a cat with the rubies."

"But the banquet is not for weeks."

"But you're fully booked until then," Akiko reminded her. "You don't have time to spit, little madam. Your grandmother is anxious that she transition everything to you while she still breathes. People need to know this is her will."

Nori looked sulkily at her bare feet. "Is it always going to be like this?"

Akiko patted her cheeks. "It will get easier," she promised. "And you have me to look after the child, so you needn't worry."

Nori flinched. "And is he well?"

"Very," Akiko said, flashing a bright smile. She looked at Nori's strained face. "Ah, my dear, no need for this guilt. He's very well looked after. Your lady grandmother never troubled herself to visit the nursery either. That's what servants are for."

Nori went very still. Something shifted inside of her, like a boulder that was slowly but surely starting to roll downhill.

I won't be like you.

How loudly she had proclaimed those words, but now they rang hollow and she was shamed to the depths of her soul.

"I'm afraid," she confessed weakly. "I'm afraid to even touch him."

"You fear because you love," Akiko said. "To love a child is the greatest terror there is. It's a lifetime of worrying yourself sick over every move they make. It is a torture and an immense joy all at once."

"I never wanted it," she whispered. "I always knew I'd fail."

"You have just begun, my sweet girl. And as you can see—life is full of surprises."

The days were lost to her now.

But when night came, Nori found herself alone. She moved silently through the house as if she were still a child with much to hide.

The nursery was on the far side of the west wing.

She slipped inside. The night nurse was there, fast asleep in the rocking chair.

Someone had painted the walls a deep blue, like the ocean at midnight. There were stuffed animals on the shelves and a charming mobile above the mahogany crib.

Without breathing, Nori peeked over the side.

The baby blinked up at her. His eyes were pensive, as if he could understand the significance of this moment. He balled his tiny hand into a fat little fist and offered it up to her. Then he smiled.

She tapped his fist with her index finger.

"Hello," she whispered. "I'm your mother. It's not a very good deal for you, I'm afraid."

He giggled and held out both his arms to her.

Without even thinking about it, she picked him up, wrapping him in his thick blue blanket.

"I don't know what to say to you," she said piteously.

He popped a spit bubble and settled into her arms. He was the lightest and the heaviest thing she had ever held.

"It will be different for you," she swore to him, brushing his wispy curls with her palm. "I'll make sure that it's different."

He grabbed hold of her pinkie and shook it up and down.

"And I'll tell you all about your name. Someday, I'll tell you all about everything."

He smiled, stretching out his toes, and then his amber eyes closed and he went still, save for the little chest rising and falling.

She laid him back down in his crib and left the room, knowing there was only one place for her to go.

The nights were precious to her now.

And this night, she found herself in the garden, staring up at a purple sky.

Though she wore nothing but a simple kimono, she was not cold.

She hoisted herself into the low branches of her favorite tree and looked up at the moon. Tonight, she felt large enough to snatch it from its perch and wear it around her neck like a pearl.

She tucked this feeling away in her box of happy memories. Later, when she was feeling weak, she would call on it to make her strong.

Her perch was wet—it had rained earlier. And tomorrow, or the day after, it would likely do so again. She knew that this, the *amaai*—the break between the rains—could not last for long. She did not know what kind would come, but she knew that it would. And she knew that she would survive it.

The wind rustled, and she could swear she heard a knowing laugh. Though it was the middle of a December night, her skin was fiercely warm, kissed by an unseen fire.

And it was in these rare moments that she felt it: the burning light of her Kyoto sun.

ACKNOWLEDGMENTS

Thank you to my fantastic editor, Stephanie Kelly, for making this book the very best that it could be. Thank you for being such a wonderful champion for a story that means so much to me. Your talent is matched only by your patience. You're amazing, and I could not have asked for more. To everyone at Dutton: thank you so much for all of your hard work, expertise, and faith.

My utmost gratitude to my agent, the one and only Rebecca Scherer, for being my number one advocate and fan. You made my dreams come true, and you believed in me when I doubted myself. To you and everyone at JRA: I owe you the world, and I thank you from the bottom of my heart.

To the incredibly kind, generous, and patient (not at all like the character!) Yuko-san: thank you so much for all of your insight, and for being one of my first pathways to a wider, more beautiful world.

Daddy, thank you so very much for supporting me through it all. I know it wasn't easy for you, raising a dreamer. This book is just one small part of my maze of dreams, but I hope I've done you proud. I never stop trying.

Mom and Auntie, thank you both for being the earliest believers in me. Mom, thank you for the summers you drove me hours to take writing classes at CTY with my fellow nerds, the first people who ever made me feel like I wasn't an island. Thank you for spending your Saturdays letting me read everything in the bookstore, and pretending that you didn't see me with the flashlight under the covers at night.

To all of my grandparents: thank you for teaching me the value of dignity, and the strength to be kind in an often unkind world.

Hannah, my dear, I love you and always will. Liz, thank you for standing by me in the darkness. I'll never forget. Thank you both for reading the rambling first drafts of this novel, and recognizing what could be.

Oliver, Austin, Aslan, Momo, Cleo: thank you for all of the free therapy. My sweet little Lux, I miss you.

Professor O'Har, thank you so much for indulging my rants and convincing me that I had the talent and the fortitude to do this. I repeat your words like a mantra on the bad days: I am not a failure. Full stop.

I would be remiss not to thank my amazing stepmother, Antonella. It was you who first showed me that it is love, not blood, that creates the bonds we cherish. Thank you for listening to me rant about the seedlings of these characters on the way to high school. I'm sorry I killed the guy. I have far more than fifty things to thank you for, so this will have to suffice: thank you for everything. *Ti voglio bene.*

To my darling Justin: I adore you beyond the measure of words. Thank you for keeping me steady, plied with sugary drinks, and for always believing in me. You make me feel like a swan.

Thank you to everyone who reads this book: to the lost, the found, and the somewhere-in-betweens.

And lastly, thank you to my former self: for surviving the rain.